HUSH, PUPPY

THE DOGMOTHERS - BOOK FIVE

roxanne st. claire

Hush, Puppy
THE DOGMOTHERS BOOK FIVE

ISBN Print: 978-1-952196-08-9
ISBN Ebook: 978-1-952196-07-2

COVER ART: Keri Knutson (designer)
and Dawn C. Whitty (photographer)
INTERIOR FORMATTING: Author EMS

Critical Reviews of Roxanne St. Claire Novels

"Non-stop action, sweet and sexy romance, lively characters, and a celebration of family and forgiveness."
— *Publishers Weekly*

"Plenty of heat, humor, and heart!"
— *USA Today* (Happy Ever After blog)

"Beautifully written, deeply emotional, often humorous, and always heartwarming!"
— *The Romance Dish*

"Roxanne St. Claire is the kind of author that will leave you breathless with tears, laughter, and longing as she brings two people together, whether it is their first true love or a second love to last for all time."
— *Romance Witch Reviews*

"Roxanne St. Claire writes an utterly swoon-worthy romance with a tender, sentimental HEA worth every emotional struggle her readers will endure. Grab your tissues and get ready for some ugly crying. These books rip my heart apart and then piece it back together with the hope, joy and indomitable loving force that is the Kilcannon clan."
— *Harlequin Junkies*

"As always, Ms. St. Claire's writing is perfection…I am unable to put the book down until that final pawprint the end. Oh the feels!"
— *Between My BookEndz*

Before
The Dogmothers...
there was

The Dogmothers Series

Hot Under the Collar (Book 1)

Three Dog Night (Book 2)

Dachshund Through the Snow (Book 3 – a Holiday novella)

Chasing Tail (Book 4)

Hush, Puppy (Book 5)

And many more to come!

For a complete guide to all of the characters in both The Dogfather and Dogmothers series, see the back of this book. Or visit www.roxannestclaire.com for a printable reference, book lists, buy links, and reading order of all my books. Be sure to sign up for my newsletter on my website to find out when the next book is released! And join the private Dogfather Facebook group for inside info on all the books and characters, sneak peeks, and a place to share the love of tails and tales!

www.facebook.com/groups/roxannestclairereaders/

Acknowledgments

Sincere gratitude to Speech Language Pathologist Cherylann Cohen Solow, MS.CCC-SLP, for guidance on children's speech impediments; additional thanks to private plane enthusiast Sandi Moffett Parks and the representatives from Cessna and the Foothills Regional Airport for assistance and information. Any factual errors in *Hush, Puppy* are my own.

Chapter One

J ohn Santorini stared at his laptop screen, blocking out the sounds of the lunch rush in the Greek deli that bore his last name. He'd long ago developed the skills necessary to do exacting mental work in an office adjacent to a noisy kitchen, able to ignore the orders being called into the grill, the clatter of dishes, and the constant stream of semi-clean workplace banter between the servers and his flirtatious new cook.

But John couldn't ignore nine pounds of fur and attitude using his tiny snout and a chunky paw to shake the gate of a metal crate, demanding his freedom.

"Come on, Mav." He glanced at the puppy he'd adopted two weeks earlier, looking forward to when the little Lab mix grew into a big dog who'd help fill the empty house he'd recently purchased. His brother, who owned three Lab mixes exactly like this guy, had promised that "all they do at this age is sleep" in a crate.

Well, that might have been true about Maverick's "cousins" when they were puppies, but this little troublemaker's call sign should have been Mayhem, not Maverick. "You can hold it until I get my dry-goods order in for next week, right? I got to negotiate this price down."

A high-pitched whine was all he got in return. And that, he couldn't ignore.

"All right, you win. Ten minutes in the square." He clicked out of the spreadsheet, grabbed the leash, and opened the crate, laughing as Mav shot out and lunged at his sneaker to chew on the lace. "Easy, boy. I need to wear those to get us there."

He slipped the leash around Mav's little neck, but picked him up to carry him through Santorini's kitchen, sidestepping his best server as she darted between the stainless-steel pass and the condiment station.

"I gotta run him out," he said to Karyn. "Everything okay out front?"

"Define okay, boss." She grinned at him, but the spark in her dark eyes would disappear as the day wore on. "Personally, I would define it as 'an experienced and charming hostess is starting tomorrow.'"

A hostess was *not* starting tomorrow, sadly. He couldn't fill that slot for love or money. "You need me to step in?" he asked.

"Nope. Erin and I are tag-teaming it." She blew a kiss at Mav. "Go do your business, precious."

Taking the dog out was the last thing John wanted to do now, but nature called, so he hustled through the dining room. On his way out, he counted the heads waiting for a table and wished to God his sister would come back and manage the front of the house again. But Cassie, like his twin brother and all their siblings, had moved on to other businesses and lives, leaving John the last-standing Santorini still working at the family deli.

He eased Mav to the pavement as they stepped outside, and the puppy instantly yanked the leash toward one of the many dogs under the tables of their owners seated at the recently enlarged patio dining area. Then Mav turned toward the street, knowing exactly where he wanted to go.

To the playground in Bushrod Square, of course, where he'd get showered with affection from a zillion kids who'd surely be there on a hot North Carolina summer afternoon.

The sun baked the streets, which were teeming with locals, tourists, and, always, a lot of dogs. Never more than right now, in the middle of the town's first Dog Days of Summer, a month-long event that firmly established Bitter Bark as the most dog-friendly town in the state, if not the country.

They made it to the brick-walled entrance to the square, finding shade in the hundreds of oak and maple trees. They followed the perimeter path, then cut through the grassy center, making it past the statue of Thaddeus Ambrose Bushrod and almost to the playground when John's cell phone buzzed.

Pausing at an empty bench, he checked the caller ID, drew back at the name, and let out a slow, low whistle. He certainly hadn't been expecting his potential investor to call, or he wouldn't be fifty yards from a packed playground with his dog on a leash. He'd be in his office, door closed, proposal opened, game face on.

Could this day go any further south?

Not that Tom's call was a bad thing, but the timing sucked.

He settled on the bench and lifted Mav up next to him, hoping the little guy didn't get distracted by the kids behind them. "Mr. Barnard," he said easily when he answered the call. "What a surprise."

"Good. A surprise is exactly what I wanted," the man said. "And I'll do it again when I come to inspect every aspect of your restaurant before I make my final decision about investing that outrageous sum you proposed. And I will be incognito, of course."

"Excuse me? Did you say…incognito?" John pressed the phone to his ear to block out the sounds of kids squealing so he could be sure he got that right. "Like, without a scheduled meeting?"

"Are you at a kid's birthday party or something?" Impatience tinged the question, but with millions to dole out, it was a safe bet the man wanted to be heard clearly.

"I really hadn't expected your call," John said, purposely not answering the question. Because admitting that he had a ten-week-old puppy who refused to do his midafternoon business anywhere but on one particular stretch of grass in the middle of the town square might not impress his potential investor.

"I know you didn't expect my call, Santorini, which is why I made it. I love the element of surprise. It brings out people's true character."

"I see." A few beads of sweat stung John's brow.

"Let me tell you something, my friend," Tom said, lowering his voice so he was even more difficult to hear. "Your proposal is one of the most thorough I've ever seen. I like the clear understanding of the

4

business, the compelling set of numbers, and the concept that makes sense and, I believe, could make us both rich."

"Thank you." Relieved, John let the compliments sink in while he stroked Maverick's tiny head and body curled up next to him. Barnard Investments could give John the capital and connections he needed to finally turn the Greek deli started by his grandfather into a national, franchised chain.

"As I see it," Tom continued, "there's no real competition for Mediterranean food on the franchise scene, except Zoe's Kitchen, and this feels much, oh, I don't know, *warmer*. Table service with a classic Greek menu, which is very hot right now, but no one is truly nailing that niche. You could."

Giving Mav's head an extra rub, John nodded, grateful the guy understood what he was doing with the brand. "I want to keep that family-owned feeling that Santorini's has cultivated since the first one opened in 1958, but make it accessible to everyone."

"Brilliant."

Damn right it was, John thought, smiling down at Maverick, who licked his palm furiously. And with Tom Barnard's bucks behind him? That brilliant idea was destined to happen.

"But can you duplicate that family-owned vibe?" Tom asked.

"I have, in all three locations."

"Because that's the key to a good franchise. Unique, branded, well managed, and replicable."

"We are all those—"

Maverick suddenly leaped off the bench and yanked hard on his leash, barking noisily to tell John exactly what he wanted—to get closer to that playground. And he wanted it *now*.

John tugged on the leash and sent the dog a look that could make employees fly into action and vendors offer up their best deals and financial analysts scurry to fix a spreadsheet.

His ten-week-old puppy, however, lifted a leg and dribbled on John's sneaker.

"Okay, okay," he muttered, pushing off the bench to let the puppy lead him toward the packed playground to revel in the attention he knew he would get from the kids.

"Okay? So then you're good with an incognito visit?" Tom pressed.

John slowed his step and turned away from the noise, ignoring Mav's insistent pull on the leash. "So, let me make sure I understand this. You'll come into Santorini's unannounced, but then you'll introduce yourself to me?"

"Not quite." Tom let out a hearty laugh. "It's more likely you'll never know I was there. That way, I can see the soft underbelly of your flagship store from a customer's standpoint. Where's the weak spot? Food, service, front of store, total presentation and package? Every operation has a weakness. If you have one, I'm out. If you don't…"

Then John would finally kick off the business plan he'd been refining since he got his MBA. The plan he'd had to give up to run the family restaurant when his father was diagnosed with cancer. The one that could make him a multimillionaire by forty, exactly as his father had predicted.

"No weakness," he said easily, squeezing his eyes

shut as he remembered Karyn's plea for a talented person to run the front. Okay, *one* weakness. It could be fixed with the right hire.

"I will need to be blown away," Tom said.

"You will be, I promise." And John Santorini did not make promises he couldn't keep. He'd figure out the reception issue, and soon. Before Barnard showed up...*incognito*.

"If I'm going to part with a dime, I expect a few things, Santorini," Tom told him. "Do you want to know what they are?"

"Absolutely." Just then, John realized there was no weight on the leash. He whipped around the very second that Mav managed to Houdini right out of his collar and bolt toward the playground.

Damn it. For a split second, he froze, not sure what was worse—ignoring Tom Barnard or letting Mav run headlong into a pack of kids.

"For one thing," Tom said. "I expect—"

"*Puppyyyyyyyy*!" A high-pitched shriek drowned out the rest as a three-foot figure tore past John, a blur of espresso-colored ringlets and pink sneakers and outstretched hands headed straight for Maverick.

He watched in shock as the little girl pounced toward Mav, fell to the grass, and rolled right next to him.

"Destiny!" A woman's voice cut through the chaos.

"Did you get that?" Tom asked, that impatience back in his voice.

"Of...course."

The girl lifted Mav in the air with tiny hands and let the puppy lick her face from top to bottom.

"Destiny Rose Jackson!" A woman rushed to the scene, another blur, this one with wheat-colored hair and long, tanned legs in shorts. "What do you think you're doing?"

"I f-f-found him, Mommy! Th-th-this is the one!" She hoisted Mav higher. "My p-p-p-puppy!"

Uh, no, kid. My *puppy.*

"Then I'll see you...sometime soon."

John barely heard Tom's voice as he hustled toward Maverick and the child. "That sounds great, Tom."

As he got closer, the little girl managed to stand and lift Maverick even higher. "I love you, sweet baby! You're the one for me! You can be my dog, and I'll be your des-ti-ny!"

Wait. Had she *sung* that?

"That sounds great, too," Tom said on a chuckle. "Now you're at the performing arts center?"

"Um...it's a long story, and if I had known you were going to call—"

"I told you I like to catch people off guard, son. That's what I do."

John gave a wry laugh. "Well, you did it very well today."

"Good. I'll see you when you least expect it, but it will be in the next month." With that, the call dropped just as John reached the singing girl and the woman he assumed was her mother.

"Destiny," the woman said, glancing at John. "I don't think, even in a town that calls itself the most dog-friendly in America, you can just grab a puppy and claim it." She leveled eyes the same color as the sky behind her on John, with a hint of a teasing smile just to make everything...perfect. "Can you?"

For one split, frozen, insane second, he almost said *yes.*

But that was because he was awestruck. He also felt something on his arm, a tug. No, about six of them, insistent and unrelenting.

He looked down at the little girl of about five or six trying to get his attention, taken aback again by a wholly different beauty. Her eyes were a mix of green and brown, with gold flecks and long lashes, her skin the color of coffee the minute it mixed with cream, and so much hair. It was a literal cascade of brown and black coils down to her waist.

"We c-c-came here for a p-p-puppy." She worked for every word, he could tell, and the effort twisted something in his heart.

Her mother stepped closer and put a protective hand on her shoulder. "To *adopt* a puppy," she clarified. "Not snag one in the park, Des."

"What's his name?" the little girl whispered, this time her voice little more than a breath. Her eyes held a plea like he'd never seen before. Well, he had—on Maverick. And right then, he knew the true meaning of *puppy dog eyes*.

"Maverick." He crouched down to get on her level to make sure Mav didn't need an assist, since the pup was squirming pretty hard.

"Ma-Ma-Mav…"

"You can call him Mav," he said gently to help her out. "I do, all the time."

She clutched him tighter. "He's your puppy?" Again, her voice was a whisper, giving him the sense that it helped her to communicate that way.

He nodded. "He is. And he's not even three months old, so—"

"I love him," she announced, clinging to Mav and making John laugh in spite of himself.

"Well, so does this man," the woman said with the blend of gentle and stern he'd heard from many of the young mothers in his extended family.

He looked up at her, forcing his gaze not to slide down to those cut-off shorts or smooth thighs, or even higher to the white cotton T-shirt that showed a whole different kind of curve.

"She can play with him, though." He stood slowly, easily eclipsing her as he rose to his full six feet.

"Thanks." She smiled again, her gaze shifting to the girl for a moment, then back to him. "We literally arrived in town about ten minutes ago, and she couldn't even wait to check into the B&B. She saw dogs in the park and ran right over."

"If she likes dogs, she's in the right place. Even our mayor's a dog." His gaze coasted over her face, taking in each fine, delicate feature. Speaking of unexpected surprises. "I'm John, by the way." He extended his hand. "Welcome to Bitter Bark."

"I'm Summer, and this is my daughter, Destiny."

Yep, daughter. Which usually meant...husband. *Shame*.

"Hi, Destiny," he said, holding out the leash. "You mind putting this on him? If he feels the need for speed and takes off, we could be running after him for a long time."

"'Kay." She took the leash. "Can I w-w-walk him?"

He considered that, and the fact that it might give him two more minutes to talk to a woman named... Summer. A name that somehow fit her perfectly. "Not far, but sure." He glanced at the dazzling creature next to him. "Okay with you, Mom?"

"Right here, where I can see you. But, Des, don't get attached, okay? Maverick belongs to this man."

The little girl knelt down and fumbled with the leash, her tiny fingers unable to squeeze the clip.

"Here, I got it," John said, bending over to help her. "Hold on tight, though. He's a furry ball of willful determination."

She looked at him, frowning a little. "What's will...that?"

"What you are," her mother joked. "Just don't let him go, and don't take more than twenty-five steps. Count them all."

She nodded, setting off with her little shoulders squared for the task, once again making John smile.

"Cute kid," he said.

"Thanks. She's never dull, that's for sure."

"Where are you guys from?" he asked, not wanting a single second of awkward silence.

"Florida, but we just drove over from Tennessee, where we've been visiting relatives. We heard this is a good place to adopt a dog, which is the only gift she wants for her upcoming sixth birthday."

"So you came for the Dog Days of Summer?"

She looked up at him, a slight frown pulling. "It's *that* hot here so close to the mountains?"

"No, the Dog Days of Summer is a major Bitter Bark event. Our very own dogapalooza, if you will."

"A dogapalooza?" She laughed at that, a throaty, sweet sound that made him want to make her laugh a lot just so he could hear it again. "Okay, then. We did come to the right town to adopt a dog. I assume adoptions are part of the 'palooza?"

"Every Friday, all month long, at different locations." He glanced at the little girl, who was bent over talking to Maverick, who was…listening. "You going to be in town that long?"

"Two more days?" She lifted one toned, tanned, silky-smooth shoulder. "Maybe. It does explain why the B&B rooms are at a premium and all the Airbnbs are booked."

"Oh, yeah. Bitter Bark is packed. There are contests, races, dog shows. You name it. You can—"

"Oh, Mommy!" Destiny stood frozen, her eyes wide. "He's…he's…" She pointed at Mav with dismay, who had squatted and was doing exactly what John had brought him out here to do.

Summer laughed. "Oh boy, Des. You're in deep doo-doo now."

"I got this." John pulled a plastic bag from his pocket, hustling over to scoop up the tiny mess.

"I'm s-s-sorry," the little girl said softly, once again putting a crack in his heart.

"Sorry? No reason to be," he assured her. "I couldn't go back to my business until he did his, so thanks."

"Ew." She curled her lip at the bag.

"It's part of owning a dog," he told her, walking to one of the green pet-waste stations that were tucked in the bushes all over Bushrod Square. He deposited the bag, then pumped the hand sanitizer from its dispenser. "Remember, if you get a dog, there's some responsibility. Like…" He notched his head toward the bin. "But honestly, I've been out here trying to get him to do that for a while. I'm sure you'll be a great dog owner."

"Thanks for being so kind to her," Summer said, taking her daughter's hand, adding a megawatt smile that did stupid things to his stomach. "Give Mav back to this nice man, and let's go check in."

"But…" Her lower lip slipped out just a bit. "I l-l-love him."

"Destiny, it's time to go."

"Well, he loved meeting you," John said, feeling an inexplicable need to give the little girl another minute with Mav…and get another minute with her mother. "And so did I." He couldn't help giving a quick look to Summer, getting one more electric second of eye contact before saying goodbye. "I hope you find the right dog, and if you ever want to walk Mav, we're here every afternoon around this time."

Just in case there *wasn't* a husband.

"You really *do* want to lose that puppy to her, don't you?" Summer joked, tucking both hands in the pockets of her shorts, denying him any chance to check for a ring.

"No, but…" He really *did* want to see her again.

"She gets what she wants, I'm warning you." She gave a meaningful look to her daughter. "Give him the leash, Des."

Destiny's lip inched out some more, and she all but batted her puppy-dog eyes.

"Destiny Rose," Summer said in a low, serious voice. "The leash."

She finally relinquished it and hung her head, walking away with sunken shoulders and a very dramatic sigh.

"Good job walking him, kiddo," he called to her. "You can be my wingman anytime."

Summer tipped her head with a smile. "Bullshit," she whispered so that only he could hear. "You can be mine."

He stared at her, jaw open. "How did you…"

"Maverick? Need for speed?" She gave a light laugh. "Kind of a dead giveaway." With a quick wink and a wave, she rushed to catch up with her daughter, her long hair bouncing and those cut-off shorts hitching from side to side.   ·

Holy…she knew lines from *Top Gun*, one of his favorite movies of all time? And looked like that? And made him smile since the second they said hello?

And was probably happily married to the man of her dreams. Lucky bastard.

After a minute, he turned and headed the other way with Mav, but then he couldn't help it. He had to have one more look. He glanced over his shoulder to take it, at the same instant that she did.

They held each other's gaze for a few seconds, shooting a little unexpected fire through him, then they both turned away.

Well. That was…nice. So maybe the day hadn't gone completely south, after all.

Chapter Two

S ummer and Destiny stepped out of the Bitter Bark Bed & Breakfast on their second day in town, taking a moment to get their bearings and soak up some sun before setting off for lunch. And Summer knew exactly where they were going to have that meal.

She'd been in Bitter Bark for twenty-four hours now. After having spent one entire day devoted to whatever Destiny wanted—which had included a lot of time at a playground and long walks in the square to search for a certain dog—it was now time to focus on the *other* reason she'd picked this quaint little town in the foothills of the Blue Ridge Mountains for their annual vacation.

Summer had come to find a man, and she wasn't going to leave without at least trying.

Yes, she'd been disappointed when the receptionist at the B&B told her that Hoagies & Heroes was no longer in business and that a Greek deli had replaced the local sandwich shop more than a year ago. But surely someone would know how she could find the owners of Hoagies & Heroes…and their son.

The woman at the B&B had no idea where the Shipleys had gone, but suggested she talk to the guy who'd taken over the property, and then she'd raved about the deli's food.

Well, it was a start.

As Summer stood across the street from the restaurant with crisp blue-and-white striped awnings, her gaze scanning a large patio with tables covered by bright blue umbrellas, that disappointment rose again.

No, this was definitely not Hoagies & Heroes. This place was called Santorini's, like the famous city in Greece, and supposedly it was where she'd find the best spanakopita in North Carolina.

But Summer didn't want…whatever that was. She wanted a man who should be here, working with his parents, as Travis Shipley once told her he would be.

"Well, that kind of throws the granddaddy of all monkey wrenches into things, doesn't it?" Summer squeezed the tiny hand in hers a little tighter than necessary, swallowing that all-too-familiar, unwelcome, and sour taste of *guilt*.

Because it was one thing to go traipsing after a man she'd met only on a computer screen and hadn't spoken to in two years, but it was quite another to drag her little girl on the mission.

"Do mo-mo-monkeys have granddaddies, Mommy?"

Destiny's sweet voice floated up, making Summer look down and smile into her haunting hazel eyes. "Of course they do," she said. "And how would you like to taste something called a…" She tried to think of another Greek food that would sound more appetizing to a picky soon-to-be six-year-old. "A falafel?"

Instantly, Summer knew that choice was a mistake.

Destiny's lips curled, and her eyes registered mild horror. "Sou-sou-sounds kinda aw-aw-awful."

Summer laughed at the child's natural wit, buried in the stutter Summer frequently didn't notice, especially when they were alone. "They'll have other things on the menu. Come on, let's eat." And poke around for information.

But Destiny didn't budge, looking around, her brows drawn, the fresh mountain breeze fluttering some of her waist-length corkscrew curls. "Where *is* he?"

Summer knew exactly who *he* was. The adorable puppy named after a Tom Cruise character. And his equally adorable owner, she mused, remembering the man's soft brown eyes, easy smile, and that short-cropped beard and glasses that made him look a little like a professor. A tall, hot, well-built, great-with-kids professor.

"Give it up, buttercup," Summer warned. "Not your dog." And not the man Summer had come to Bitter Bark to find.

"B-b-but he said he'd be..." She lifted their joined hands and pointed to the green grass, walking paths, and massive bronze statue of the town's founder at the center of Bitter Bark. "There."

Yes, the man named John had said that. And in another life, with a different purpose for her visit, Summer might be tempted to show up for a rendezvous with Hot Beard Guy because she was certain that was what he'd been hinting at when he told her he'd be there today.

"B-b-b-but..." Destiny huffed with frustration when she couldn't get the simple word out. "You said there are ad-ad-adoption places."

"Not on every corner, Des. But do you see that sign in front of the bookstore, just like the one we saw when we checked into our room? Can you read it?"

She shot her mother a *get real* look mastered far too early in one so young. "I can read. I can't ta-ta-ta-talk. But I can read. It says…Dog Day-Day-Days of Su-su-summer." She smiled. "That's your name, Mommy," she whispered, as she often did from the exhaustion of the speech impediment, because, like singing, lowering her voice to a mere breath helped her communicate without frustration.

"It *is* my name," she agreed. "So I think these Dog Days of Summer are *destiny*, like *your* name. I'm sure that a town that celebrates all month long with"—they walked a little closer to the sandwich sign to read the list of events that seemed to be scheduled daily—"something called the Doggie Olympics and the Lost and Hound Scavenger Hunt will have a few adoption opportunities." Hadn't that handsome dog owner mentioned that they had them on Fridays?

"What is B-B-Bark-koke?" Destiny pointed at the last word. "You drink Cokes wi-wi-with a dog?"

Summer laughed. "Oh, my guess is that contest is a play on karaoke, but with a dog involved in some way, so pronounce it *Bark-e-okie*. Can you guess what that is?" She heard the teacher in her voice, but didn't bother to hide it. Teaching came so naturally to her, with her child and others.

"It's singing," Destiny replied, getting up on her tiptoes. "And I can dooooooo that!" She belted out the words to an imaginary melody that seemed to always play in her head, loud enough to make a woman passing by do a double take. Summer was used to those kinds of looks when people saw, and then heard, her preternaturally beautiful daughter. Destiny might not be able to get a sentence out easily, but she could sing like an angel, and looked like one, too.

"You certainly can sing." Summer tugged her toward the restaurant. "So maybe, if we get you a dog, you can enter the Barkaoke contest."

Destiny chewed on her bottom lip and shook her head, silent. Not matter how glorious her voice was, and how much singing helped her overcome her stutter, she hated to perform in front of other people. A crowd meant she might have to do the one thing she hadn't been able to since she was a little over three years old—talk without a stammer.

"Come on," Summer said, easily switching the conversation to something else. "Let's get an awful falafel."

Summer passed the patio, reaching for the door, but Destiny pulled hard on her hand.

"Look, Mommy," she whispered. "There are dogs!"

There were, indeed, several pooches of various sizes and breeds, most resting in the shade of the tables or slurping water from blue and white bowls while their owners ate.

"Let's go inside and get a table," she said, tugging a reluctant Destiny into the restaurant.

"Can we sit outside?"

"We'll ask the hostess." Inside, they paused at the stand in the middle of a sizable entryway, waiting for a hostess. Summer peeked inside at the cheery deli, taking in rows of tables and booths, many of which were full even though it was past the lunch rush.

The dining area was bigger than she'd expected, and so different from the walk-up-and-order style of Hoagies & Heroes, at least as it had been described to her. Patrons were eating at a counter, but this was no sandwich shop. The vibe was a festive Greek refuge, warm and inviting, with oversized prints featuring the Mediterranean Sea and the iconic blue domes of Santorini, Greece.

She spotted a server in the middle of the restaurant, but the woman seemed swamped.

"Okay, maybe we missed someone outside." She turned and went back to the patio, looking around.

A white-haired woman at a nearby table waved at her. "You can sit anywhere, lass."

She frowned, surprised at the instruction delivered with a brogue, but before she could respond, Destiny let out a little squeal.

"Look!" Destiny pointed under the table where the woman sat, zeroing in on two dachshunds snoozing contentedly. "Weiner dogs!"

"You can come and say hello." The other woman at the table beckoned to them. "Come over, dear."

"Can I talk to those doggies?" Destiny asked Summer.

Since they were the first dogs she'd shown any interest in since she'd met Maverick, Summer nodded, guiding her to the table. There, Destiny looked from one lady to the other, no doubt not trusting her brain and mouth to work together, since they so often let her down.

As the speech therapist had taught her, Summer restrained from jumping in to help when the silence lasted a beat longer than was comfortable. But it still broke her heart every time Destiny found herself in this situation.

The two women looked on, wonderfully patient, one with a puff of snowy hair, the other with dyed, dark hair and much more makeup. Summer guessed them to both be octogenarians, though one was trying harder than the other to hide that.

"What are their names?" Destiny finally sang the question, knowing that was the only way for her to get out a whole sentence without a single stutter.

"Oh, sweet Saint Patrick, that was lovely," the older-looking woman said, adjusting her bifocals as if she needed to get a better look. "Aren't you the most delightful little lass I've ever met?"

"Pyggie and Gala," the other one said. "Not piggy, like oink-oink." She pointed at a stout brown dog who clearly owned the name. "But short for Pygmalion, like the character. And that's Galatea, but we call her Gala."

"Pyggie..." Bending over, Destiny stroked the chubby dog's head lovingly. "And Ga-ga-gala."

"She's a dog lover," Summer said, putting a hand on Destiny's head.

"Then she has a good heart," the dark-haired woman said, reaching out her hand to Summer. "I'm Agnes Santorini."

"Oh." She drew back a little as she returned the handshake. *Santorini* would explain why her companion had acted as the ad hoc hostess at a restaurant of the same name. And it might mean she'd know where the previous owners were. "This is your restaurant?"

"My grandson's, actually, but my husband and I

opened and ran the first Santorini's in Chestnut Creek, and then my son ran it, and now my grandson." She beamed with family pride, and suddenly Summer could see her Greek heritage in eyes the color of black olives, her whole being exuding strength and confidence.

"I assumed the restaurant was named after the town," Summer said.

"It is, in a way. My husband's grandfather was from Santorini, but when he came to America, he couldn't spell the last name without using the Greek alphabet, so the idiot who registered them used the name of the city where they were from. From that moment on, the Iordanoupoulus family became the Santorinis." She patted the empty chair next to her. "Would you like to join us?"

"Oh, that's okay…" But she really *did* want to.

"Please do." The other woman gestured at Destiny, who was on her knees whispering to the dogs. "The little lass seems happy here. Is she your daughter?"

The question didn't surprise Summer, since Destiny was clearly a mixed-race child who bore little resemblance to her fair, blond mother. Her handsome late husband had given his daughter her curls and sweet cocoa skin, while Summer had contributed little more than good cheekbones and an optimistic disposition. She wished Isaiah could see how Destiny grew even more beautiful every day.

"She is. This is Destiny, and I'm Summer Jackson." She brightened and nodded. "And sure, I'd love to sit with some locals."

Agnes gestured toward her companion. "This is Finola Kilcannon, but you can call her Gramma

Finnie, and everyone knows me as Yiayia, which is a Greek grandmother," she added with more of that radiant pride.

"Yiayia and Gramma Finnie?" Summer smiled as she took the empty chair next to the tiny Irish woman. "Did you hear the nice ladies' names, Des?"

She nodded, not looking up from the dogs. "I li-li-like Pyggie."

"Everyone does," Agnes—Yiayia—said, smiling down at her. "She's old and fat, like I used to be. Now I'm thin and…less old." She patted her face. "Thank you, Botox and salads sans feta."

Summer chuckled just as a server came to the table with plates, paling a little at the additions. "Oh, you have more here, ladies."

"I'm sorry," Summer said, sensing that the woman was frazzled. "We can scoot to another table and wait our turn."

"Nonsense, lass." Gramma Finnie patted her hand. "We love to chat with new people, and the orders are fast. I recommend the spanakopita." She pointed at the plate the waitress put in front of her, the aroma of fresh pastry and cooked spinach wafting up to make Summer's mouth water.

"Oh, yes, I heard this place is famous for it, so I'll have some," she said without hesitation. "Is there something a little less Greek on the menu for my daughter?"

Yiayia's Botoxed lip attempted a curl. "A little less Greek? Why would anyone want that?"

Gramma Finnie tsked noisily. "Because she can't be seven years old and wasn't raised by a yiayia. Would you like chicken in a pita wrap, lass? Plain

23

with no yogurt dressing?" she asked Destiny, who looked up and nodded, but Yiayia rolled her eyes as she lifted a fork over her salad.

"A gyro without tzatziki? Criminal."

Summer smiled at the waitress. "The plain chicken would be great, in a child's portion, please. And take your time. We just made ourselves at home."

The woman, whose badge read Karyn, nodded her gratitude. "I just wasn't the one who should get the next table. We're a little understaffed today."

"And every day," Yiayia added as the girl walked away. Then she leveled her dark eyes on Summer. "You wouldn't happen to be looking for a job in food service, would you? My grandson cannot find help, and this month-long Dog Days thing is great for business, but..." She looked at the door, where a couple stood eyeing the patio seating.

"Sit anywhere," she called, then shook her head. "I should just work the front," she mumbled. "It's not like I didn't do it for years at the original Santorini's."

"I'm a third-grade teacher and not looking for work," Summer said with a soft apology. "We're visiting from Orlando."

"Visiting from Orlando?" Yiayia gave a soft hoot. "Well, that's *exactly* what I said when I stepped into this very restaurant a year and a half ago. Never went back to Jacaranda Lakes, Florida, except to sell my condo and pack my bags. Now I live with my best friend." She pointed at Gramma Finnie and winked at Summer. "Maybe that will happen to you."

"Oh, I doubt that," Summer said.

She had no plans to stay in Bitter Bark, though she might have extended the trip if an affordable rental had been available. But all she'd really wanted to do in this town was find Travis Shipley and offer an apology that had been pressing on her heart for a long time. He deserved an explanation for why she'd disappeared and ended their unorthodox, long-distance relationship two years ago.

Her guilt over that decision was strong enough that she'd orchestrated this whole trip and packaged it as the way for Destiny to get her dog. So, once she offered that apology, she'd be leaving Bitter Bark. If she could find him, that was.

"Are you here with your husband?" Gramma Finnie asked between bites.

Summer shook her head. "Actually, I'm a widow," she said softly, checking on Destiny, who was still whispering into Pyggie's floppy ear. "But we did come here to adopt a dog, so you better hang on to yours. My little girl seems to have a fondness for other people's dogs."

"A widow?"

The women asked the question in near-perfect unison, barely waiting for Summer to finish her sentence.

"Uh, yes." She looked from one to the other.

"A widow," Yiayia said again, falling back against her wrought-iron chair with an intense look at Gramma Finnie.

"A widow," Gramma Finnie repeated, like this news was somehow too monumental to handle.

"My husband has been gone for three years."

"I'm sorry, lass." Gramma Finnie adjusted her bifocals and shifted her narrow frame in the seat, as if she sensed Summer's discomfort. "We both are widows, too, but that makes sense at our age, not yours. You can't be thirty years old."

"Twenty-nine, and he was killed in Afghanistan while serving in the Army," she explained, ready to accept their sympathy and gratitude for Isaiah's service and sacrifice.

"So are you looking for another husband?" Yiayia asked, making Summer take in a soft, surprised breath.

"Don't mind her, lass. She just can't get the hang of subtlety, but I love her anyway. My deepest sympathies on your loss."

"Oh, mine, too," Yiayia added.

"Thank you."

Then Gramma Finnie waved a bony finger. "But just so ye have fair warnin', we call ourselves the Dogmothers, and we're a couple of very successful matchmakers."

"Ahh." Summer gave an understanding nod. "The Dogmothers, huh?"

Destiny popped up, surprising all of them with how close she was. "Fairy Dogmothers?"

Gramma Finnie chortled. "If you'd like us to be, little lassie, we can be fairy Dogmothers."

"All we need is a wand," Yiayia teased with a twinkle in her eye. "And to know your wish."

"A dog," Destiny whispered. Then she leaned closer and made her expression of forced determination, the one she wore when what she wanted to say was so important, she simply couldn't risk a stutter. "And a daddy."

Summer blinked in shock, and both of the other women gasped.

"Des—"

"So you *are* in the market, lass?" Gramma Finnie clapped her hands under her chin. "How wonderful."

"Yes, daddies are our specialty," Yiayia added with way too much enthusiasm. "And we just happen to have a few single men in the family."

A warm rush of blood flooded Summer's cheeks, and she knew just how bright that blush had to be. "A dog is all we're in the market for while we're here."

But Destiny was now looking at the two women with a little of the same gleam in her eyes she'd offered their cute dogs. "D-d-do you know where we-we-we can get a dog?" She fought her way through the question, lifting the smaller of the two dogs in her arms.

"Of course," Yiayia said. "Adoption Day is at Waterford Farm on Friday, right, Finola?"

"Aye, and you'll find the right dog that day."

"And…" Yiayia lightly pressed her fingers together, tapping, thinking, and openly staring at Summer. "You might find the right—"

"Oh, for cryin' out loud, Agnes," Gramma Finnie scolded. "Sorry, lass. You'll just have to put up with Yiayia when she gets on a matchmakin' roll. We're three-for-three and lookin' for our next victim, if you get my drift."

Summer laughed off the suggestion. "So, how long has your grandson owned this restaurant?" she asked Yiayia, hoping to change the subject and remembering she hadn't come only for lunch, but also for information about the former owners.

The question made the women both draw in a slow breath, staring at each other with some kind of mix of disbelief and hope in their eyes. "Exactly who I was thinking of," Yiayia muttered. "My Yianni."

Oh dear. Summer had walked right into that one. "Yianni. He's the owner?"

"Oh, 'owner' doesn't do him justice," Yiayia gushed. "Yianni took this two-bit sandwich shop and transformed it!" She waved her hand as if it really did hold a wand and the transformation was magically happening again right that moment. "Of course, he had help from my daughter-in-law, who is a professional designer—"

"Who is now *my* daughter-in-law," Gramma Finnie added, making Summer give her head a little shake of confusion, wanting only to get back to Hoagies & Heroes.

"Together, they turned it into this." Yiayia gazed around with unabashed pride. "This past year, he's slowly refurbished it into a flagship store because he's going to franchise the brand into a chain of national Greek delis. Can you imagine? Santorini's across the country! Wouldn't that be wonderful?"

"Oh yes," Summer said, shifting forward. "And whatever happened to, uh, that little sandwich shop?"

"Who knows, who cares?"

Summer cared and tamped down her disappointment.

"They leased to Yianni with an option to buy," Yiayia added. "Which he is exercising this month."

So the Shipleys still technically owned the place? She leaned in, ready to ask another question, but Yiayia dug out the two leashes from her bag and handed them to Destiny. "Dear girl, can you take Pyggie and Gala back and forth for a very short walk around the patio?"

Destiny's eyes popped at the opportunity, and she looked at her mother for permission. "Just right here, Des," Summer said. "Until your food comes."

Unable to hide her joy at the assignment, Destiny latched the leashes to the dogs' collars and very slowly walked them about ten paces. Instantly, Yiayia scooted closer to Summer, as if seizing the opportunity to talk.

"Let me tell you something," she said. "My Yianni is very smart. Has an MBA from Duke and is a brilliant businessman. He's also getting his pilot's license and recently bought a beautiful home with a view of the mountains. He's thirty-six years old, very handsome, and you'll never meet anyone with a better heart. He's the best dancer in the family, and that's saying something. He's very special. And *very* single." She took a breath, waiting only a beat for Summer to respond. "Oh, he was also the MVP of his high school baseball team."

"I'm sure he is...special." And so desperate he needs his grannie to recite his résumé and get him a date. But she did want to talk to the owner. The question was...how badly?

"Not to hit ye over the head with a baseball bat or anything," Gramma Finnie teased. "Get it? Baseball... MVP..." She flicked an age-spotted hand. "But Agnes is quite right. He's a wonderful, accomplished man."

"I have no doubt." Summer took a casual peek into the restaurant as if to assess his work. "So if he's leasing, did the owners mind when he refurbished?"

"Of course not," Yiayia said. "They're getting their rent. Yianni would never miss a payment. He's a financial wizard, actually."

"Did the sandwich place open another location somewhere else?"

Yiayia frowned and tipped her head. "No, why?"

"Oh, I'm just curious where"—*I might find their son*—"they took all those hoagies and heroes."

Yiayia put her fork down and stared at her. "Would you rather eat lousy Italian subs instead of world-class spanakopita? If so, you're not the right one for my Yianni."

"Agnes," Gramma Finnie chided.

Yiayia dropped back again, distrust narrowing her eyes. "Maybe we should introduce her to Declan, Finola."

Gramma Finnie gave her head a shake. "She's not right for Declan."

"How do you know?"

"Because you know I already have someone picked out for Declan, who is *my* grandson, and this young lady is…" She touched the sides of her glasses and slid them up her nose. "Not the one for Declan."

Summer bit back a laugh at the comedy act she'd stumbled into. "Um, ladies, I'm super flattered that you'd like me to meet *either* of your grandsons, but I'm not—"

"Don't say you're not interested until you've met Yianni." Yiayia looked past her, eyes focusing on the door to the restaurant, behind Summer. "Which you are about to do."

She started to turn just as Destiny let out a shriek that brought every patron to a dead silence, making Summer leap up to see what was—

Oh. *He* was Yianni? That tall, dark, handsome, bearded sweetheart from the square?

Well, now. That was a whole different story.

Chapter Three

"Mavvie!" There it was again—a blur of ringlets and pink shoes. Only this time, she flew across the patio, with Pyggie and Gala trotting after her, their leashes dropped like she'd been taking them on a walk and suddenly forgot they existed.

But ringlets and pink shoes meant...

John stopped dead in his tracks, scanning the outside dining area like it was a radar screen, seeking his target. There she was. Blond hair, blue eyes, and a look of happy surprise that he bet reflected the one on his own face.

Summer.

"Wow. We meet again," she said, pushing up from a table she shared with Yiayia and Gramma Finnie— wait. How the hell did *that* happen?

"You've *met* him?" Yiayia's voice rose at least an octave with astonishment.

Destiny, in the meantime, was practically dancing around him, her arms outstretched for his dog, making him suspect that chaos reigned supreme wherever this little one was.

"Mavvie!" she called out.

With his free hand, he picked up the forgotten leashes and took Yiayia's doxies back to the table, somehow making it there before the kid tackled him to get to Mav.

"*This* is Yianni," Yiayia announced. "But apparently you already *know* that."

"Yianni for her," he said to Summer, holding that blue gaze long enough to feel the effects low in his belly. "John for you."

"And Ma-Ma-Mavvie for me?"

He looked down at Destiny, letting out an exasperated laugh. "You want to see him again?" he teased.

"Or…" Summer tipped her head. "Rip him out of your arms."

Destiny giggled a little and wiggled her grabby fingers. "C-c-can I hold him?" she asked, her clarity and determination making John's heart squeeze.

He crouched down to get to her level and maybe calm her down before a customer complained.

"I think he missed you," he said softly, making Destiny press tiny fingers to her lips as if the very idea was too much for her to bear. "He barked about you a lot."

She broke into a slow smile, finally looking at John and not his precious cargo. "Me, too," she whispered, making him chuckle.

"Okay, here you go. No leash, so be careful. He does *not* understand boundaries."

"Uh, that might make two of them," Summer warned softly.

"It's okay," John said, inching Mav closer. "I trust you, Destiny."

"I'll take c-c-care of him." She dragged out the last word, struggling so hard to make her point that he almost reached out to hug her.

Once holding Mav, she buried her face in his neck, softly singing his name. Not saying it, *singing* it. Which was pretty much the cutest thing he'd ever seen.

She stroked his head and blinked up at John. "Th-th-tha…" She couldn't get the words out.

"It's okay, Des," Summer said softly. "He knows you're grateful for letting you *borrow* the dog."

"I love this doggy! Yes, I do." She belted out the words in melody form again. "And I think he loves me, *tooooo*!" Mav let out a little whine in the highest register John had ever heard.

Everyone in hearing distance on the patio reacted with laughs and light applause, which startled Destiny, or embarrassed her. She stopped instantly.

"Hush, puppy," she whispered, petting his teeny little head and getting him to curl into a ball. "We have to sing quietly."

"You can sit right at that empty table with him. Just don't let him run off." John stood slowly, next to Summer. "Wow. She's…that's…*wow*."

"A total disruption to your business. Sorry."

"Not at all." He took a glance at a few tables. "In fact, I'm thinking she just made these customers forget about today's spotty service. Lunch is on me so you can—"

Yiayia reached out, grabbed John's arm, and yanked him down next to her. "Would you please tell us how you two met?" she demanded.

Oh boy. The grannies were clearly in their

matchmaking element. Although for once, he didn't want to run and hide. On the contrary. He settled right next to his grandmother.

"Yes, please." Gramma Finnie closed a much gentler hand around Summer's wrist, tugging her into the seat across from him.

For a moment, they just looked at each other, then both gave a quick laugh.

"I see you've all met as well," he said.

Yiayia leaned into his side. "Summer's a widow. Did you know that?"

A widow? He blinked in surprise. A widow meant she wasn't... A widow meant her husband was dead. "I'm sorry," he said after an awkward beat. "I didn't...know that."

"Then you met, but didn't talk?" Yiayia said, crossing her arms so her elbows thunked on the table. "When? Where? How?"

John laughed again, looking skyward. "How did I forget to submit my full report?"

"We met yesterday in the square," Summer supplied, also laughing. "This poor man was finishing a call, and my daughter openly tried to kidnap little Mav."

"She almost had him, too," John joked, looking at Destiny, curled into a chair, quietly talking to the puppy. "Ten more minutes and..."

"Uh-uh." Summer gave him a look. "I see you teetering on the edge of surrender there, *Yianni*."

He grinned, loving the way his name sounded on her lips. Loving everything about her lips, to be honest. "What else did they tell you about me, other than my formal Greek name?"

34

"Oh, just how awful you are, how terribly you run your business, and..." She squinted playfully at Yiayia. "That you are generally the least attractive and most unavailable bachelor in Bitter Bark. No brains and..." She pointed to her daughter. "Clearly, you're heartless."

His grandmother jabbed him with her elbow. "I like a little sarcasm in a woman, don't you?"

"I like you, Yiayia, don't I?" Turning to Summer, he angled his head in apology. "Forgive these ladies. They are on a mission, firm in their belief that I cannot manage my own social life."

"Because it's work, work, work with you," Yiayia said. "Can you blame a grandmother for wanting to intervene a little?"

"Intervene?" He choked a laugh. "You do a marital status check on every woman over twenty-five and under forty who walks in this restaurant."

"In their defense, I offered my status to them," Summer said, her eyes glinting with humor at the situation.

"Did they or did they not literally lasso you into this seat?" he asked.

She shrugged. "Depends on what you mean by 'lasso.' They did lure *someone*..." She pointed her thumb toward Destiny. "With their adorable doxies."

"We did no luring, lass."

Yiayia nodded in agreement. "This woman came up to us and said, 'Hello, my name is Summer Jackson. My daughter likes your dogs. May I sit with you?' What are we going to say? *No*?"

Summer Jackson. He filed away her full name, but managed to give her a skeptical raised brow, keeping the playful conversation going.

"Never mind how it happened," she said. "Truth is, if I had known their matchmaking attempt was with you, the owner of the world's most coveted dog, I might have written my phone number on the check."

Both the grannies gasped, and John had a hard time not pumping his fist in victory.

"Oh, sure, and it's time for us to go, Agnes." Gramma Finnie gathered up a pocketbook hurriedly and nudged Summer out of the way. "Our work here is done."

"Oh, don't go," Summer said.

"We must," Yiayia agreed. "Your spanakopita is coming soon, along with the little girl's pathetic plain chicken." She added a smile as she pushed her chair in and slid behind John, patting his shoulder. "And you, young man, will sit here and talk to her until a date is set."

It was Summer's turn to suck in a soft gasp, but John just closed his eyes and fought a smile. But his mind was already whirring. He'd learned at an early age that there were two kinds of people in the world. The ones who were just born lucky, like his younger brother, Theo. And people like John, who made their own good fortune.

That realization made him a man who seized the day on a regular basis. Which was why he wasn't about to let Summer Jackson slip through his hands again. Yesterday, he had to assume she was married, and asking her out would have been a douche move. But today, he knew she was a widow, with no rings at all on either hand.

"Whatever you say, Yiayia." He took his grandmother's hand off his shoulder, kissed her knuckles, and leveled his gaze on the woman across the table, waiting for her to finish saying goodbye to the ladies. Then he leaned forward. "So, how's Friday sound to you?"

"Friday?" Summer drew back, obviously not sure if he was joking for Yiayia, who hooted softly as she walked away with her dogs.

"Didn't you say you want to adopt a dog?"

"Yes."

"Then I'll take you and Destiny to Waterford Farm on Friday," he said, deeply pleased with the idea.

"Waterford Farm?"

"It's an elite canine rescue and training facility and the site of this week's Adoption Days event. It also happens to be owned by my stepfather. There will be eleventy-hundred dogs. And cousins. And step… people." He frowned a little. "On second thought, maybe just skip that and head right to dinner?"

She stared at him, searching his face a little, obviously not quite sure what to make of the invitation. "I'll think about it."

Think about it? He rested his chin on his knuckles, drowning in the blue that was the very color of skies that bore her name. "My grandmother's recitation of my résumé didn't work, huh?"

She laughed. "MBA from Duke *and* getting a pilot's license? Pretty impressive."

"But not enough to say yes." He stole a quick glance at the table where Destiny all but set up the service to have tea with Maverick. "I could throw in the puppy."

She dropped her head back and gave that throaty laugh, officially making it his new favorite sound.

Just then, Karyn reached the table, order in hand, pausing at the sight of him, a little exhaustion and exasperation at the edges of his best server's faint smile. "Did you want something to eat, John?"

"No, I'm good, Karyn. And this place is clearing out, so you can clock out anytime. I know it's been a crazy-long day for you. Lunch is over in fifteen minutes, and Erin can handle a straggler or two. I'll close and do the bank today."

Karyn's shoulders relaxed as she put a steaming spanakopita in front of Summer. "God bless you, boss. My feet are screaming, and my kids are home no doubt doing the same thing."

"Then definitely go." He took the plain chicken gyro from her. "Thanks for working so hard today."

She smiled at him, then at Summer. "I heard your little girl sing before," she said. "She's amazing."

"Oh, thanks. It helps her to get her thoughts out, so we're lucky it's on key most of the time."

So she sang to avoid stuttering, John mused, filing yet another piece of the puzzle that made up this intriguing mother-daughter duo.

"Well, she's beautiful. She can come in here and sing anytime. Thanks, John. I'll be in early tomorrow morning." Karyn stepped away as John put Destiny's chicken on the table.

"Honey?" Summer called to her daughter, opening her purse to pull out some hand sanitizer. "Your lunch is here."

"Can I sh-sh-share it with Mavvie?"

"You can sit here next to me and give Mav back to John."

For a second, the little girl looked like she might put up a fight, so John pushed his chair back and stood. "Let me take him for you."

She gave him up reluctantly, handing over Mav, and then holding her hands for her mother to sanitize before she sat down. John remained standing, waiting for Summer to look up so he could close the deal on Friday and let them eat.

"Please stay, nice man." Destiny whispered.

He felt his eyes widen, and Summer bit back a soft laugh. "Go ahead, say no to that. Nice man."

"Well...let me put Mav back in his crate."

Destiny gasped. "No crate!"

"He likes it there," he assured her. "It's his favorite place to think about you."

Summer slid him a look. "Slick."

Wasn't it? "I'll get some coffee and join you. Be right back." He didn't waste a minute on that errand, crating Mav and grabbing a cup of black coffee to head back to the table. The restaurant had really emptied out, with only a few tables ready to close their tabs.

By the time Summer and Destiny finished their lunch, he'd have that date for Friday, John was certain.

When he got back, Summer and her daughter were still side by side, talking and laughing as they ate.

"How's the food?" he asked, sitting across from them.

Destiny looked up. "Not aw-aw-awful."

"Whoa, that's...some faint praise."

"I mentioned falafel earlier, and all she can hear is that it rhymes with awful. She likes rhymes and makes up songs with them."

"Cool. I bet our cook could make a falafel you would sing about."

The little girl gave him a skeptical look, a hint of a

smile pulling at her mouth as if she didn't quite know what to make of him.

"While you were gone, I was telling Destiny that your restaurant name is also a beautiful place in Greece," Summer said. "Have you been to Santorini?"

"A few times," he said as he stirred some sugar into his coffee. "I got a lot of inspiration for this place from going to the restaurants there. I wanted it to be somewhat like the original location, over in Chestnut Creek, but I really went all-in for that authentic Greek feel. I loved it in Santorini. The food, the music, the people. It's amazing." He leaned a little closer. "It's where I learned to dance."

"I heard you're the best in the family." Summer smiled at his surprised look. "The Yiayia PR machine," she explained.

He rolled his eyes. "She's proud of my sirtaki, which is better known as the Zorba the Greek dance."

"You can do that?" she asked, a satisfying glint of admiration in her eyes.

"Add it to the pro column for Friday."

She laughed softly. "I will." Then she flaked some of the pastry with her fork. "If you tell me you made this, you have a date."

He grunted softly. "Wish I could. That's the handiwork of Luther 'Bash' Sebastian, our newest hire in the kitchen. But Bash is following my grandmother's recipe, which was her grandmother's and so on."

"She said she and your grandfather started the first Santorini's?" Summer asked.

"They did, in the fifties after they left New York. Then my dad ran it until he got sick, and my brother and I took over. It wasn't really my plan, but…" He shrugged, not wanting to get into the history of how he and Alex jumped in "temporarily" when Dad was diagnosed with cancer.

"Alex was the cook, and I managed the store. We did pretty well." Exploded, to be frank, under John's management, which was a blessing and a curse. He was so good at his job, he couldn't quit to start his own business. So he was going to reimagine this one. "We opened a second location, and then, last year, launched this one."

Summer glanced around. "They said you refurbished it, and it's a lot different than what it was before."

"It's a flagship store that I'm going to franchise," he said, taking a sip of coffee and wondering just how interested she was in his business plans. "If I close the financing."

"And then you'll buy the building?"

He rolled his eyes. "Wow, Yiayia really *did* tell you my life story."

"Oh, I asked."

Then she *was* interested—either in him or the business. Confident, he leaned closer to share more. "So, get this. The financing is contingent on one guy right now, and he is planning to come in here, unannounced, unidentified, and unexpected…to check out the place."

Her eyes widened. "Like a secret shopper?"

He'd been thinking of it more like one of those restaurant critics who insisted on being anonymous, but he liked "secret shopper" way better. "Exactly. Some dude could walk in here any second and decide whether or not to invest."

She gave a soft grunt. "I'm a teacher," she told him. "Third grade. And when parents come in unannounced and want to observe the class from the back of the room?" She made a face. "My stomach is in knots all that day. I imagine it's a lot worse if he's your potential investor."

A teacher. The job suited her, he decided, imagining how pretty she must look in her teacher clothes. And out of them.

"I have no idea when he's coming, which is…" He shook his head. "Yeah, a little disconcerting since, as you could tell, I'm down a hostess, who is remarkably important in keeping the front of the house running smoothly."

"Well, this place certainly *looks* good," she said, gesturing toward the matching awnings and umbrellas he'd recently added. "And the food's great. Hard to believe it was once a sandwich shop. Do you—"

A noisy laugh from a group of people walking up to the door cut off her question and stole John's attention. Damn, there had to be a half dozen of them. And there were more in a group behind them.

"'Scuse me," he said, pushing out of his chair. "Unexpected late afternoon rush."

He hustled to the door and held it to invite them in. Otherwise, they'd be greeted by an empty hostess stand.

"Hey, all. How many will there be?"

"Um…" A woman turned around, half laughing. "I think there are twenty of us. There are a few stragglers on the way."

"Twenty." He managed to keep his voice steady, mentally kicking himself for sending Karyn home.

"No problem. Give me a second to alert the staff and pull together some tables."

"We don't have to sit at one table," she said. "Just close together."

"We can find another place if it's too much," a man behind her called.

"Not at all," John said. "Give me one sec." He headed back to the kitchen to find Erin and to make sure Bash hadn't started cleaning for the day. With her, they coordinated a few tables at the far back of the restaurant, then he headed back to the hostess stand, slowing his step when he saw Summer talking to the group and...*handing out menus*?

What was she doing?

As he approached, she turned. "Are we all set, John?" she asked with a smile.

He blinked, speechless for a moment, vaguely aware that her daughter sat quietly on the reception bench, swinging her ankles. "Yeah...yeah. We have three tables ready, all next to each other."

"Well, there you go." Summer ushered the woman at the front of the group toward him. "And I meant what I said about the spanakopita," she said to one of the men as he passed. "It's an old family recipe from 1958 and the best bite you will ever have outside of the country of Greece."

"Thanks for the tip," the man said, smiling at John and looking around. "Nice place."

John managed to throw Summer a look that was a mix of gratitude, amazement, and the beginnings of a life-altering crush, and all he got in return was her sunny smile and a playful wink.

"Why'd you do that?" he asked under his breath.

"Just in case," she whispered, then mouthed, "Secret shopper."

He didn't have time to respond, forced to guide the group to the other side of the restaurant and start the service. He couldn't let Erin get swamped by this unexpected party, and Bash might need some backup at the grill.

The whole process was nonstop for almost forty-five minutes, keeping him from the only place he wanted to be right now. Finally, when the last order was up and last drink refilled, he hurried back to the patio...but the table was empty.

Muttering a curse, he spied a piece of paper covering some cash to pay for the meal.

The paper was from a kid's game book, but on the back was a note.

J—See you Friday at Waterford! xo, S & D
PS. Give Mavvie a kiss from Des.

He got the date. Mav got the kiss. A win all around.

Chapter Four

"Wow." Destiny leaned forward in her booster seat as Summer turned her Nissan Rogue through the gates of Waterford Farm and down the tree-lined drive that opened up to a stunning vista.

Wow was right.

From east to west, there was nothing but rolling foothills, precious clapboard buildings, and acres of grass covered with...dogs of every size, shape, and breed.

A massive yellow farmhouse with green shutters and tall chimneys perched on a slight rise above it all, wrapped with a porch meant for sipping and rocking.

"Daddy must be here," Destiny whispered, falling back into her seat with a thud.

Summer took a slow, deep breath, a tendril of frustration worming up her chest. She had to put an end to this daddy fantasy that had taken hold of Destiny's overactive imagination ever since they'd been in Tennessee with Isaiah's family. It wasn't healthy, realistic, or welcome.

"Sweetheart, we talked about this," Summer said

gently. "We're not in Bitter Bark to find a daddy."

"N-n-no, Mommy," she insisted. "I mean my daddy must be here. My hero daddy."

She often referred to Isaiah as her "hero daddy"— and Summer liked it so much better than "used-to-be daddy" she used when she was four.

"You think Daddy is here?" Summer asked.

"You said he's in he-he-heaven."

Summer caught the wonder in her daughter's expression through the rearview mirror. "Waterford Farm looks like heaven to you?"

"Dog heaven."

From a child's perspective, Summer could see that. She slowed to a crawl between the line of cars parked on both sides of what might have been a quarter-mile-long drive, heading toward a large homemade sign that read: *Welcome to Waterford Farm! A Hundred Acres of Happy! It's Adoption Day!*

A dark-haired teenage girl and a little boy a year or two older than Destiny, both wearing Waterford Farm T-shirts, greeted them with double-armed waves, directing them to an open parking spot not far from a huge penned-in area where at least thirty dogs frolicked. Around the pen were booths of various sizes, some serving food and drinks, some with more dogs, some with what looked like crafts or toys for sale. There had to be a hundred people, kids, and dogs roaming in the late morning sunshine.

As she parked, Summer scanned the whole area, but Destiny was digging at her safety belt, desperate to get out. "Do you think that p-p-puppy's here?" she asked. "Mavvie?"

"I do, but I also think that *many* puppies are here,"

Summer said as she pushed her door open and stepped out. "I'm sure you'll find one you love."

"But I want Mavvie."

Summer froze for a moment, then turned to get the back door.

"I know, but Maverick is taken, as I think I've mentioned about six hundred times, Des. But we're going to find a dog today, and I'm sure you'll love that one as much, if not more."

"But I-I-I dreamed about him."

Summer blew out an exasperated breath, knowing that arguing was futile. She'd have to find another dog to love, maybe one that looked like Mav.

"Welcome to Waterford!" The teenage parking girl bounded toward them, extending a flyer to them. "I'm Prudence Kilcannon, granddaughter of the owner, but please call me Pru. Are you here to take home the dog of your dreams?"

"We are," Summer confirmed, taking Destiny's hand. "Where do we find the adoption dogs?"

"Everywhere!" she exclaimed just as the younger boy came forward, alongside a huge German shepherd who was darn near as big as he was.

"Pru, is it my turn?" he asked. "Can I do the tour this time?"

Next to her, Summer felt Destiny back up, her eyes popping at the dog who looked like he could eat a bad guy or two for lunch.

"This is Jag." The little boy squared his narrow shoulders and patted the dog's head with a familiar hand. "Don't be scared of him."

"I'm n-n-not s-s-s…" She shook her head. "I want a puppy."

Pru laughed and bent over to talk to Destiny. "We have a few of those," she said. "And believe me, Christian would never let you have Jag. That's his best friend. Are you looking for your new best pal?"

Wide-eyed, Destiny nodded.

"Would you let Christian and Jag walk you to the pen so you can scope out some of our dogs?" she asked.

"Where's Mavvie?" Destiny whispered.

Pru frowned and got a little closer. "I'm sorry?"

"She's looking for a dog she met at Santorini's the other day. Maverick?" And Summer was looking for Mav's owner, but—

"John's puppy?" Pru straightened, and her eyes flashed. "Oh! You must be...*her*."

Summer lifted a questioning brow. "Her?"

She nodded, staring at Summer. "Yeah, you *are* beautiful."

Drawing back, Summer gave a soft laugh, wondering if John had described her that way. "Gee, thank you. You sure know how to welcome the customers."

"Gramma Finnie actually said you were...like an angel."

Oh, so it was one of the Dogmothers who'd said that, not John, she thought with a little pinch of disappointment. "That's so sweet. She's an angel, too." She gestured to the little boy and his guard dog. "Of course you can lead the way, young man. We'll take a look at—"

"No, no. You can't go anywhere," Pru insisted, reaching out to grab her arm. "Christian, go get Uncle John, quick. I promised Gramma and Yiayia that I'd..."

She stopped for a midsentence correction. "I know your little girl wants to see Maverick, right?"

"Mavvie!" Destiny said, squeezing her fists with excitement.

"But you can't adopt Mav, honey," Summer said, already seeing this train wreck about to happen with one stubborn child. "I think we should look at all the dogs."

A trip to that pen to see any one of the adorable dogs running around ought to do the trick.

"I just want to see him, Mommy," she whispered, getting on her tiptoes to look past the German shepherd, the boy, the girl, and any other obstacle she might have to mow down to get her way.

"And you will," Pru replied. "In one sec. Christian!" She gave him a nudge. "Quick. Go get Uncle John and Mav. And if you can't find him, ask Gramma Finnie or Yiayia."

"No, that's not…" But Summer just let the rest of the argument go. If Destiny had her heart set on that puppy, she'd have to learn the hard lesson that she couldn't have him. Maybe she just needed the dog, and his owner, to help her to understand that.

And Summer didn't hate the idea of seeing John Santorini again. Not just because he was her only link to Travis Shipley. She'd barely made any progress trying to find Travis the past few days. She'd made a few inquiries among the locals, but no one seemed to have any idea where the Shipleys had gone. So, she was just about to abandon her plan, but not until she'd asked John, who had to know where the older Shipleys were, if not their son.

And once Destiny picked her dog, it would be time

to go, no matter how much fun she had chatting with John Santorini. The fact was, she couldn't afford to stay at that B&B for their usual summer month of fun anyway, and all other rentals in town were booked.

None of this had been communicated to Destiny, though, because Summer knew her daughter had to get her dog first, then everything else would work out.

"I heard you're quite a singer," Pru said to Destiny, pulling Summer from her thoughts.

"Mavvie can s-s-sing, too."

Oh boy. She had to nip this in the bud. "Listen, Des, you really need to—"

"Mavvie!" She broke free with a shout, lunging at the light brown puppy who trotted in their direction. Not ten paces behind walked the tall, bearded, brown-eyed man who'd made her laugh and kind of wish she could stick around a little longer.

He broke into a slow smile, but his gaze wasn't on the girl-and-dog reunion taking place. It was pinned directly on Summer, sending an unexpected flight of butterflies through her.

"I'd like to do this tour, Christian," John said, putting his hand on the little boy's shoulder as if he expected the child to be disappointed. "There's more people arriving, so I know you can take them around."

"Okay, Uncle John." The little boy gave another smile to Destiny and put a proud hand on the head of his big, bad-looking dog. "Jag and I will see you later."

But Destiny was lost to anyone and anything, because Maverick was in her sights.

"Okay, then." Pru clapped her hands as she stepped away from them. "Good luck with...everything." The young girl's blue eyes twinkled playfully, like she was communicating a secret message to John. She might have been, since his sly smile grew as he shook his head and gave her a tap on the shoulder.

"Get on with your job there, Prudence. And I don't mean reporting in to your two eighty-something bosses."

Pru giggled and waved as she took off, just as Destiny dropped to the grass to rub Mav's little belly. The dog yapped playfully, but it was Destiny's high-pitched coos of delight mixed with giggles, and not a single stammer, that had Summer's attention.

"Guess we can't keep these two apart," she said.

"Why would you want to?" John asked, his voice deep and just soft enough that she wanted to get closer to hear every word.

"Because…" Summer sighed and ran a hand through her hair, suddenly a little self-conscious as she looked up at him and let the full weight of her attraction hit. "You may be in for the fight of your life for this dog."

"She's *that* persuasive?"

"She's that tenacious. So you better start showing her some of your best adoption options, stat."

His dark eyes danced at that, as if a fight didn't scare him in the least. He was quiet for a few seconds, watching the two romp in the grass, then he looked directly at Summer.

"I don't even know how to begin to thank you for what you did at the restaurant the other day, and I don't mean paying for a meal I offered to comp."

"Then you must mean jumping in where I didn't belong."

"Saving my ass, more like," he said softly, with a quick check to make sure Destiny didn't hear that.

Laughing, she shrugged. "Not a problem. First of all, there's nothing a third-grade teacher likes more than settling down a group of rowdy, hungry humans."

"And second of all?"

"All I could think was what if the secret shopper is in the group? I mean, I saw this deluge of people walking in, and you'd just said he was coming in any day, so…" She shrugged. "I decided to help."

"I really don't know how to thank you." He held her gaze long enough for all kinds of tingles to shoot down her spine, then slowly shifted his attention to Destiny, who was holding Mav up to her face and singing softly as he took occasional licks of her nose.

"Don't do it," Summer said with her own singsong warning.

He lifted his brows in question.

"Don't even *think* about doing it."

Still, he didn't say a word. Then Destiny lifted her gaze, looking right into his, her irresistible eyes matching the eyes of the sweet furbaby she held. Summer stepped between Destiny and John.

"Best not to even look."

He cracked up. "You think I'm that much of a pushover?"

"Oh, trust me," she whispered so only he could hear. "Backbones of steel have been known to bend under the impact of that child's gaze. Throw in a pretty song, the heartbreaking stammer, and a will that's an actual force of nature? You do not stand a chance."

As if on cue, Destiny cleared her throat and started to sing. "Mavvie, Mavvie, the best boy ever!" As always, she made up the tune, proving that not only could she sing, she might actually be a songwriter someday. "We will always be together!"

John leaned to the right to see around Summer just as the dog let out a soft, high-pitched whine.

"Oh boy," he whispered. "She's…"

"Winning him first," Summer said. "That'll be her technique. The dog will not leave her, then you will not only be doing something for her, but you'll be making your puppy happy. And in the end…" Summer crossed her arms. "You'll be the one looking for a new dog to adopt."

His jaw loosened a little. "I don't want another dog."

"Then I suggest you start promoting every puppy in the place to your audience of one."

He laughed, obviously smart enough to see she was right. "Okay, then. Hey, Destiny, why don't we go look at the puppies in the pen?"

She shook her head.

"We have a Pomeranian named Lulu you might really like."

"Oh, cute," Summer said, trying to help him out. "Poms are so adorable."

"And Rosie, a Chihuahua-doxie mix with ears almost as big as her heart. I don't think she's been adopted yet, but she won't last long."

"Perfect. Want to look at the doggies, Des? Meet Lulu and Rosie?"

She squeezed Maverick, making John laugh, but Summer wasn't quite as amused. The bit was cute, and she knew Des was comfortable with the puppy, but she also had no desire to see John fold. Something told her he was as noble as he was easy on the eyes.

"Maverick has an owner," Summer said, keeping all the humor out of her voice so Destiny knew she meant business. "And he's going to show you all the other dogs here today so you can pick *your* new best friend. If that doesn't work for you, then we'll pack up and head right back to Orlando today. Your choice, Destiny."

Her lower lip slipped out just a bit, just enough to make Summer's shoulders tense. Years as a single mother with a daughter who had a speech impediment, a stubborn streak, and the ability to somehow get whatever she wanted had taught Summer all kinds of coping mechanisms. She wasn't the best parent in the world—who was?—but she tried not to spoil Destiny and tried to teach her life lessons while still making that life wonderful for her.

Those years had also taught her to pick her battles, and whether Summer wanted this one or not, a battle was dead ahead.

"Destiny."

"Mo-Mo-Mo-Mommy." More lip. "I love him," she whispered in a cracked voice.

Next to her, she felt John's whole body shift, but she shot him a look before he tried to be a hero and gentleman and only made this battle harder.

"And I can see why you love him," Summer said, purposely making the decision not to crouch down to get on Destiny's level. She needed the parental advantage of height right now. "But now we're going to go all over this heavenly place and meet Rosie and Lulu and…"

"And Nutmeg," John offered.

"And Nutmeg, who sounds delicious, don't you think?"

More lip. And Summer could see that nothing sounded good to Destiny at the moment. "I l-l-l-*love* him!" Tears sprang, making Summer even more tense as she rooted for the right words, the correct parenting, the easy technique that would make Destiny comply.

Next to her, John crouched down, obviously not worried about having the advantage in this situation. "You know, Destiny, this little guy isn't going to be *little* for that long. He's a Labrador mix, and someday, pretty soon, he'll be bigger than you are."

"Like a p-p-pony," she said, optimism and a slight dare sparking her eyes.

Summer bit back a laugh because…well, Destiny.

"Don't you want a little dog you can hold on your lap?" he asked.

She stared at him. "I lo-lo-lo…" She swallowed, fighting the fight, willing her mouth to obey her brain, and, of course, tightening Summer's stomach with sympathetic frustration.

"You love him," John finished for her with a nod. "You know what? I do, too."

She blinked at him, as mesmerized by his soft dark eyes as Summer had been.

"I moved into a new house and decided it was just the right place for a dog. This dog. Now, I'm going to help you find your dog. Let's go do that now."

Summer liked that he didn't add *okay?* to that order, something few parents, but most teachers, knew well. She watched him in action, taking the time to not only appreciate his kid-management skills, but the way his gray T-shirt pulled over his shoulders, highlighting his muscles. He wore casual shorts that showed strong, long legs, with worn sneakers that suggested he lived in them. His hair curled over his neck, a little untrimmed, and made her fingers itch to see if it was as soft as it looked.

But Destiny stared right into the man's eyes, oblivious to the attractive things Summer saw, no doubt gauging just how far she could push this stranger.

"How b-b-big?" she asked softly. "How big will Mavvie b-b-b-be?"

"Really big. You know, my brother has three puppies just like this guy, except they're not puppies anymore."

"Th-th-three? Like Mav?" Her eyes popped at the incalculable joy of that.

He nodded in full agreement. "And their mommy had a sister. Like an aunt. Do you have an aunt?"

She looked up at Summer, maybe a little taken aback by this new path, but still ready to put up with anything to hold that dog.

"Aunt Raven," she whispered, referring to Isaiah's sister, with whom they'd just spent a few weeks.

"Well, this little guy is my brother's puppies' cousin." He waved a finger in the general direction of the house. "Like everybody else you'll meet today," he added on a laugh. "So he's part of my family."

Summer figured out where he was going and respected the idea. It could work. Maybe.

"But he sings," Destiny said on a breathy whisper.

"Only with you," John said. "So, why don't you bring him along while we look at other dogs, and you two can be singing buddies while you find your dog?"

"I'll hold him? And wa-wa-walk him?"

"All you want," he promised. "I bet he'll help you find the right dog, too. He's very friendly and obviously a good judge of character."

That last comment might have passed over Destiny's head, but it made Summer's heart do another unexpected flip.

After a moment, Destiny nodded.

"And we can go meet Lulu and Rosie now," Summer said on a sigh of relief.

"And Nutmeg," Destiny added, finally letting go of her death grip on Maverick.

"Take his leash." He picked up the nylon strand and handed it to her. "You'll be in charge of Mav while we look at the other dogs. He'll guide you to the right one."

"'Kay." She took the leash and started to walk, letting Maverick lead the way. "Here we go, Mavvie," she sang, loud for the first time. "On a doggy hunt tog*ether*! For*ever*!"

The dog just looked up at her, then continued to walk.

"You have kids?" Summer asked as they fell into step behind Destiny and Mav.

"Nope."

"Wow. Not bad for a rookie."

He laughed. "Thanks, but you're right...she's a force of nature."

"I think she met her match." Summer smiled up at him, wondering for just one second if she'd met hers, too.

Chapter Five

As a man who proudly answered to "Spock" when his passionate twin brother accused him of being way too logical, John Santorini had little regard for things like...magic. Or kismet. Or fortune, fate, and...destiny.

But today, in the blazing North Carolina July sun and clean mountain air, with the two most charming ladies he'd ever met making him laugh more than he had in...well, maybe ever? Yeah, he might consider changing that überlogical mind-set.

Because every time he brushed Summer Jackson's hand or laughed at something she said or shared a look of dismay and humor over something her adorable daughter did, he could have sworn he'd actually been *enchanted*.

"We've failed," Summer said on a sigh as the three of them, led by the Energizer Bunny of a child, stepped out of the cool Waterford Farm kennels into the sunshine. "Every precious animal rejected."

"Not rejected, just...second to Mav." He put a casual hand on her back to lead her down a path behind Destiny and Mav. "We're not done yet," he promised her. "There's a whole bunch more in the other training section. But those were the smallest dogs, I'm afraid."

"And they were awesome. I wanted that precious Sheltie."

"Sophie? Yeah, I thought we had a winner when Destiny saw her. Also, that French bulldog, Claude. Destiny really liked him."

"She *liked* them all," Summer agreed. "But she seems to *love* only one."

He tipped his head and took a breath, already playing with the idea. It wasn't like he couldn't easily get another dog, though he was pretty damn attached to Maverick. "You know, Summer—"

"No." She held up her hand. "I know what you're going to say."

"Well, what kind of guy would I be if I didn't offer?" he asked. "She's obviously in love and has made her choice." He could rationalize the decision, couldn't he? Looking down at the woman next to him, getting lost in the endless shades of blue in her magnificent eyes, he could probably be talked into sacrificing more than his dog. Just go ahead and throw in all his attention, his house, his car, his official *Top Gun* leather jacket— and his poor smitten heart while they were at it.

"And what kind of mother would I be if I accepted that offer?" she countered, slowing her step as they caught sight of two little pugs on one double-line leash. "Oh." Summer put her hand on John's arm. "This looks promising. Who doesn't love a pug?"

"That's Ella Mahoney," he told her, nodding toward the young woman leading the dogs. "She's my stepcousin, the youngest on the Mahoney side."

"Gosh, you weren't kidding when you said everyone's related. We met two Mahoneys in the kennel, and I lost track of the Kilcannons."

"Don't worry, I made a spreadsheet when my mom married into this clan," he joked as he added some pressure to hold her back from the pugs. "Let Ella work her pug magic here. I'm hopeful about this."

"Reverse psychology is always a good fallback with my daughter," she agreed. "And I was pushing a lot of those dogs in the kennels."

"You're desperate not to have her steal my puppy."

She laughed. "I do try to teach her not to steal. Or that she can have whatever she wants just because she's gorgeous and has a heart-twisting speech impediment."

Before he could respond, Destiny seemed to realize her mother wasn't behind her, turning and looking around, her whole body visibly relaxing when she caught sight of Summer.

"You play with the pugs, Des," Summer called. "I'll be right over on this bench."

"To answer your question," John said as they stepped away, "about what kind of mother would you be if you accepted my offer? The answer is, well, I don't know how you could be any better. You're good at this."

She let out a sigh as if the compliment touched her. "It hasn't been an easy road, single motherhood. My husband was killed when she was two, and even with my parents nearby, it's been…" She gave him one of those smiles that made him feel like he was doing a barrel roll in a plane. "Fun and crazy. And there've been a few nights where I fell into the bath with a glass of wine that I emptied and then filled with tears."

"And that just makes me admire you more," he admitted. "My grandmother told me you said your husband was military? Overseas?"

She nodded. "He was in the Army, stationed in Afghanistan."

"Oh, wow. Like Aidan Kilcannon. I'm sure you'll meet him today."

She bit her lip and nodded. "Isaiah was killed by an IED." She brushed her hair back and looked away, probably to hide the pain that was evident all over her face.

"I'm so sorry. I can't even imagine." His only experience with grief like that was losing his dad. But a spouse, and the father of your kid? Tough. "You sure do manage to keep things light and happy for her," he noted. "She's lucky to have you."

"I'm lucky to have her," she countered without a second's hesitation. "I wouldn't trade her stubborn little self for anyone or anything, no matter how difficult she might be at times, or how much extra I have to work to help her through life with her stutter."

"Has she had the speech impediment since she started talking?" he asked.

She didn't answer right away, gnawing on her lower lip for a second before answering. "It started about three years ago, not too long after Isaiah died. Of course, she was only beginning to talk in full sentences, but she hadn't had any problems."

"Do the doctors think those events are related?"

"Not at all," she said. "She was too young to be emotionally affected by losing him, especially because he'd been overseas for most of her life. Now that she's past the age where it can be just a developmental phase, we're focused more on managing it and helping her learn to cope."

"How do you do that?" he asked, watching Destiny on her knees, petting the pugs, looking up to listen to whatever Ella was saying.

"Patience, for one thing. Letting her talk for herself no matter how much I want to jump in and help. Oh, and the speech therapist and pathologist both strongly recommend a dog." She smiled. "Yes, she thinks it will be her sixth birthday present, but a dog can really help her."

"Oh." Now it all made perfect sense. "A therapy dog? Will it need to be specially trained?"

"Not necessary in this case. Just one Destiny can talk to. They bring dogs into the therapy office all the time because the kids are so comfortable that they can speak without a stutter. The more she learns to trust her brain and mouth to work together, the better."

With each piece of new information, he could feel his heart shifting in his chest. And when he glanced at Destiny, currently lifting Mav's ear to whisper something, he could have sworn he felt that heart crack. "And you're *not* going to let me give her Mav?"

She gave him a long look. "She has many lessons to learn in life, John. Not getting *everything* she wants is one of them."

He blew out a breath. "I get that."

"And a little bit of stress teaches her to use those techniques she's learning, like how to breathe between words and speak at a rate that works for her. I can't pave the road to life in gold just because she has a speech impediment that might never completely go away."

"God, you are good at this, Summer."

"Thanks. Besides being a single parent, I'm an elementary schoolteacher. I get kids."

"All right." He leaned a little closer. "I promise I will not give in and hand over my dog." Holding her gaze, he added, "And I do not make promises I don't keep."

She nodded and put a light hand on his arm. "I believe that. And trust me, I'm fighting the urge to beg you to give her the dog. It would make her so happy, but..."

"You wouldn't have to beg very hard."

"It's a balancing act," she mused, smiling at Destiny with the pugs. "Especially in the summer, which is our 'no rules' time of year."

"Really? So the rest of the year is chores and timeouts?" He asked the question on purpose, still wondering if there was a man in her life. Maybe she was still grieving her husband or just too busy with being a single mom?

"Some chores, the occasional timeout, early to bed, and very little junk food. We have a pretty tight routine from mid-August to late May. But as a teacher, summer's my free time, and I usually let her get exactly what she wants in our 'fun months'— within reason, obviously. I take her somewhere special, and we get all our good times stuffed into a ten-week vacation."

"And bringing her to Bitter Bark for a dog is your special trip?" he guessed. "Just the two of you?"

"Always the two of us," she said. "Destiny and I always spend June in Knoxville, Tennessee, where her father's family lives. We stay with his sister, and the Jacksons get the entire month to enjoy her. This year, we drove over here because..." Her voice trailed off.

"It's not far and the best place to get a dog?" he suggested when she didn't finish.

"Yeah..." She nodded, absently chewing her lip again.

"And..." Okay, he was confident she was single. But there was one more thing he *had* to know. "Any chance you'd stay for the rest of the summer?" He didn't care if she knew how much he wanted the answer to be yes. He liked her, and if there was any chance of her staying, he'd do what he could to make that happen.

"Not much of one, but not because I don't like it here. Bitter Bark is exactly the kind of place we look for every summer, but there's no room at the inn. Well, the Airbnb, to be more precise. The daily rates at the Bitter Bark B&B are too high for a month-long stay, to be honest, and everything else is booked because of the Dog Days of Summer."

"That's why you're leaving? Nowhere to stay?" he asked, the problem so logically and easily solved, it actually made him sit up a little straighter.

"Nowhere affordable," she replied. "Especially if we have a dog, which will limit our options. I decided we should get the new dog and spend this summer in sticky, miserable Orlando." She dropped her head back and grunted softly. "I do hate summers in Florida."

"Mommy!" Destiny's voice drew their attention,

making Summer spring up, more from habit, John guessed, than any real need.

"You like the pugs, baby?" she asked, heading toward her daughter.

John almost got up, too, but stayed on the bench for a second, a single thought playing at the edges of his mind...women like Summer Jackson did not come along very many times in life.

Seize the day, his late father used to say. He could still remember the first time they had that conversation, the day John realized that his craptastic eyesight and an irregular astigmatism that couldn't be fixed by laser meant he would never qualify to fly fighter jets. It was the first, and last, time those shitty eyes shed tears, except for the day Nico Santorini died.

His father might be gone, but his strong guiding hand still urged John forward, along with the echo of that conversation.

"Eyes?" Dad had snorted from behind the grill at Santorini's, up to his ears in moussaka, but never too busy to dole out advice. "Kid, you got more brains than anyone in the family. You'll have millions—plural—by the time you're forty. Mark my words. Just remember, dot your i's, cross your t's, Yianni, then take what life throws at you and hit that bastard out of the park."

From that day on, Dad's jumbled analogies had spurred him on. He used the advice to guide his decisions even when life threw him more crappy curveballs than a bad pitcher. And now life had tossed him this intriguing woman, and what he wanted was...the summer with Summer. And he intended to get it with a very simple solution to her problem.

Her voice floated over as she joined her little girl and gushed over the pugs. He pushed up then and walked over, greeting Ella.

"Have you two officially met?" he asked. "Summer, this is Ella Mahoney, my stepcousin," he said.

"Summer Jackson," she said, extending her hand. "And who are these precious pugs?"

"Priscilla and Elvis," she said after shaking Summer's hand.

"Mommy, they're a bo-bo-bo…" Destiny took a breath.

"A BOGO," Ella finished gently. "It's a twofer adoption, I'm afraid." She ran a hand through her super-short black hair, making it look even more tousled than usual. "We promised the person who brought them in that they wouldn't be separated, so…"

"Oh," Summer said on a sigh. "Two is…one too many."

"I get that," Ella said. "But there are so many dogs today. Have you found one you like?" she asked Destiny.

"I lo-lo-lo…" Destiny squeezed her eyes shut. "I love Mavvie!" she sang, loud and clear. She never stuttered when she sang, John noticed. And, of course, Mav gave a high-pitched whine and nestled closer to her.

"Wow," Ella said, laughing. "Your pup's been co-opted, John."

"Yeah, they've, uh, formed a special bond," he said.

Summer gave him a grateful smile. "We better say goodbye to Elvis and Priscilla, Des. We should see some other dogs, too."

"What about the fairy Dogmothers?" Destiny asked.

"The fairy Dogmothers?" Ella cracked up. "I bet I know who you mean." Then she took another long look at Summer. "Oh, wait. I heard about you."

Summer pushed some hair off her face and gave a self-conscious smile. "I understand the grannies are chatting about me."

"Nonstop." She looked from Summer to John, nodding as if she now understood everything. "Yes, you should definitely go see them. In fact, go in with John and make their day."

Summer laughed and shared a look with John, who shook his head. "This family is…something," he said.

"Something *wonderful*," Ella added, jabbing him in the arm. "Definitely go see them. They're probably up on the porch drinking Jameson's and ouzo and pretending their glasses are full of iced tea and water."

Laughing at that, they said goodbye to Ella and her dogs, and John led them toward the house. A few feet ahead, Destiny skipped off with Mav, the pugs forgotten.

"So, listen," he started slowly, his plan well formulated. "I might have a solution for your housing dilemma, if you're interested."

She eyed him. "I'm interested."

"My house."

"Oh, no, I couldn't—"

"I have a separate apartment," he clarified.

"Upstairs, with its own entry, two bedrooms, and it's vacant."

She stared at him for a second. "Really?"

"I bought the house a few months ago, and the former owners had outfitted the upstairs as a separate unit for their parents. I've been planning to have my stepsister's husband, Josh, who's a house renovator, do some work to make it a solid rental, so it's not exactly a model home right now..." He looked skyward. "Okay, there's really not a working kitchen. A sink, cabinets, but no appliances. Well, a stove that doesn't work. But you could use my kitchen downstairs, and the view is off the charts."

"Wow...that's...that's really awesome of you to offer."

"And hey, we take pets."

"And Mav's there."

"Which might make this little love affair even more intense." He pointed to Destiny and Mav, but saw the soft flush on her cheeks at his choice of words. "Anyway, it's something for you to consider," he added quickly.

"It might be fun," she said, slowing her step as she considered it. "How much?"

"I couldn't take any money," he said.

"Don't be silly. I wouldn't consider staying for free."

"There's really no actual kitchen, so I'm not going to charge you," he said. "Why don't you think about it? Come and see it? Talk to some of my friends and family to make sure I'm not a serial killer?"

She laughed. "Definitely that."

"Ask Yiayia. She'll vouch for me."

"That's an understatement." She lifted her brows. "And we better say hello to them soon, or they'll come and hunt me down and demand to know what we're naming our first child."

The words hit with the unexpected kick of an afterburner. "So true. Better brace yourself."

She checked out the big house, the sweeping view, and finally her gaze landed back on him. "Okay, I'm braced."

"Good," he said softly, putting a hand on her back to usher her forward. "Because I'm not sure I am."

Chapter Six

It wasn't that John's massive extended family was strange or overbearing or in any way unpleasant, but the sheer volume of people was a lot to take in. Summer could handle the constant introductions, small talk, and greetings, but Destiny tended to get very, very quiet in a crowd.

As expected, she stayed close to Summer as John guided them into the kitchen, barely making it far before they stopped to meet his mother, Katie, the warm and lovely hostess of the house. She brought over her husband, Daniel, the handsome, silver-haired owner of Waterford Farm. Throughout the conversation, Destiny answered their questions with nods, her grip tight on Mav.

Then Summer chatted with a lively vet named Molly, who had a little one in her arms and proudly announced she was mother to the delightful teen greeter, Pru. Molly, in turn, introduced Summer to her sister, Darcy, who owned the local grooming shop, and two other sisters-in-law, Chloe and Jessie, both managing babies.

While they talked, Destiny pressed to Summer's

side. A woman named Andi leaned in to whisper, "My son was very shy when we first joined this family."

Summer gave her an easy smile. "She's not really shy," she said softly. "She's just a little overwhelmed by the crowd, I think."

"We are overwhelming." A tall, dark-haired man joined them, putting a hand on Andi's back to whisper, "Wee Fee is sound asleep upstairs in the crib."

"Well done, Dad." Andi beamed a smile at him. "This is Summer Jackson. And Destiny."

He turned his attention to Summer, extending a hand. "Liam Kilcannon," he said. "Welcome to Waterford Farm."

Summer shook his hand and gave a nod to his T-shirt that said *Agility: Ability to change plans for the dog.* "Are you one of the trainers?" she asked.

"Liam isn't just 'one' of the trainers," Andi replied with unabashed pride. "My husband is the K-9 Unit leader, in charge of training law enforcement dogs."

"Oh." Summer nodded, impressed. "I think I met one earlier. Jag?"

Liam and Andi shared a look. "He's ours," Liam said. "And I assume you met his sidekick, Christian, who is ours as well."

"Did someone call me?"

Summer turned, then looked down to find the smiling face of the very same boy who'd greeted them when they'd arrived.

"Oh, hello," Summer said. "Did you get to finally lead a tour, Christian?"

"I sure did," he replied. "And they adopted Nutmeg!"

"Good job, son." Liam gave the little boy a high

five, and Summer took in the child's size, figuring him to be the same age as the many boys and girls who'd walk into her classroom in less than two months.

"Let me guess," she said. "Starting third grade in the fall?"

"Yes!" His blue eyes widened. "How'd you know?"

"I teach third grade. If there's anything I can spot, it's an eight-year-old."

"Really?" He seemed mystified, as kids often were when meeting a teacher outside of the classroom, then his gaze slipped to Destiny. "How old are you?" he asked, mystified in a whole different way.

She gripped the dog a little tighter, silent for a moment, testing Summer's ability not to answer for her. It wasn't easy.

She held up her hand, five fingers wide.

"Oh," Christian said. "Then you're starting... kindergarten?" he guessed.

"Destiny will be six later this month," Summer told him. "So it's first grade for us, and Destiny's getting a dog for her birthday."

"Not that dog," Christian said, pointing to Mav. "That's my uncle John's dog."

"I *know*." Whoa, Destiny had no problem getting her point across there.

"But maybe you can bring him to play Hide 'n' Bark," the little boy added. "It's starting in a couple minutes."

Destiny lifted her head from nuzzling Mav's neck, a question in the gaze she directed at Summer.

"Hide 'n' Bark?" Summer asked. "That sounds like fun. Would you like to play, Des? I think that's what this nice boy is asking you."

She shook her head, silent.

"She's still getting to know everyone," Summer said, breaking speech-therapy protocol and covering for her. "Maybe later."

"Oh, okay. Because Uncle Shane said we need one more dog and kid to play."

Destiny searched his face, obviously tempted. "How do you p-p-play?"

"Like hide-and-seek with dogs," he replied. "Plus, you get to learn how to train your dog not to bark."

"Hide 'n' Bark is a Waterford special," Liam explained. "It actually evolved from Manhunt, which we played a lot as kids—"

"And adults," Jessie added.

Liam laughed. "Some of you play it as adults, but Shane's reformulated the game, and it's going to be part of the big camp launch next week."

"Oh, there's a camp here?" Summer asked.

"First year we're having one," Liam said. "Tails and Trails. Three weeks, fifty kids, and dogs that they bring or borrow. It's a day camp for some, and a sleepover in our dorm for others. The kids learn everything they can about training dogs, with games, crafts, contests, hiking, campfires, you name it."

"Wow, that sounds like fun."

"There's still room for a day camper," he said, tipping his head toward Destiny. "Starts on Monday, and day campers have weekends off."

Her daughter's tiny jaw loosened just enough for Summer to know that Tails and Trails sounded like sheer paradise to Destiny. But it wasn't exactly in the plans.

"I don't know if we'll still be here Monday,"

Summer said. "But, Des, go get a taste of it by playing Hide 'n' Bark now."

"C-c-can Mavvie play?" she whispered, looking up at John.

"Sure," John said. "Especially if you stick with Christian and Jag. And don't drop his leash."

"We never lose," Christian said to her. "You can be my teammate."

Destiny clung to the puppy and looked from the dog to the boy and back again, her little decision-making wheels going round and round.

"Only if it sounds fun to you," Summer said, putting a hand on Destiny's shoulder.

"It does," she whispered.

"We all get Popsicles," Christian added, obviously knowing how to close a deal. "And dogsicles!"

"Really?" she asked, eyes wide. "Can Mavvie eat th-th-that?" she asked John. At least she knew who was in charge of "her" puppy.

"Oh, he can and he will," John assured her. "His favorite is blue raspberry."

"Me, too!" she said, her enthusiasm giving Summer a shiver of sheer delight.

"You can both have blue Popsicles," Christian said, quite serious. "Just be sure Mav gets the one for dogs. There's no sugar in it."

Very slowly, she inched the puppy away, who immediately started squirming at the first taste of freedom, which he hadn't had a lot of since Destiny came on the scene. "Want a Popsicle?" she whispered in his face, then put his snout next to her ear, nodding. "Yes," she said to Christian. "He w-w-w-wants one."

"Oh man," John muttered, getting a look from Summer. "I know, I know," he said under his breath. "But did you see that?"

She put a hand on his arm, and not just for the thrill of feeling the corded muscles and dusting of hair. She had to make her point. "Be strong, Yianni."

He blinked at the name she suspected only his grandmother used, then laughed softly, shaking his head. "I don't know…" he said.

"I can't go, Mommy?" Destiny asked, misreading the communication.

"You most certainly can, honey. Go and have fun. I'll be right here."

"There's water stations and shade," Liam assured her. "Plenty of supervision, too."

"I think it sounds great," she said, encouraging Destiny with a squeeze.

"Come and see Jag again," Christian said, practically bouncing on his heels to get out there and play. "He's the best dog in the world."

Destiny shot him a look that showed exactly what she thought of *that* statement. Then she took a deep breath and stepped away, walking with Christian, who was still talking. "Jag's a *Schutzhund*, and that means he's specially trained…"

His voice trailed off as they disappeared toward the kitchen door, with Destiny not even looking back as if second-guessing her decision.

"Don't worry," Liam said. "She's in good hands."

"I'm not worried," Summer assured him. "I'm thrilled she's having fun. Even if she is scheming to steal another person's dog."

They all talked for a few minutes, then John finally

led her to the back porch to see Gramma Finnie and Yiayia, but before they made it, another man walked in, looking freakishly like John, but without the beard and glasses.

"There you are," John said to him, jutting his chin in greeting. "Didn't think you'd ever make it."

"We held the wedding that wouldn't end last night," he said with a puff of frustration, then his gaze shifted to Summer, and he smiled. "Hello," he said. "You've got to be Summer."

"I am," she said, feeling the warmth of a blush on her cheeks.

"You're the talk of the farm," John joked. "This is Alex, my twin brother."

"Oh, Alex. That explains the strong resemblance."

"It used to be more," Alex said, rubbing his clean-shaven jaw. "But I gave up the beard to save a dog, and my fiancée liked the new look."

"Now he looks like the evil twin," John joked.

"And the one who can cook," Alex added with a playful wink.

"Alex and his fiancée, Grace, own the Overlook Glen Vineyards, just outside of town," John explained.

"Technically, Grace owns it, but I'm starting a restaurant there," Alex said. "And right now, we are up to our eyeballs in events. Last fall, Scooter Hawkings and Blue got married there, and we haven't had a weekend off since."

"Really?" She let her jaw drop, truly impressed. "Those are some big celebrity names."

"And good friends now," he said proudly. "Their endorsement shot Overlook Glen to the top of North

Carolina wineries, I'm happy to say. And my good brother here…" He put a hand on John's shoulder. "Bought out my share of the deli and is officially the only Santorini left in the family business, ready to take it soaring to new heights."

John lifted that shoulder with a shrug. "With the financing."

"From the secret shopper," Summer added, sharing a look with John.

"He show up yet?" Alex asked.

"How the hell would I know?" John muttered.

"You'll know if you get a call from the guy. Hey, listen, I can come in this week and help out if you need me in the kitchen."

"Thanks, but Bash is killing it, and the kitchen isn't my problem," John said.

"I knew you'd love that chef," Alex said.

"Not as much as the servers do," he joked. "It's the front that's my problem. And damn if Yiayia isn't determined to show up every day and make it worse by trying to make it better."

Alex gave a look that said he knew exactly what that meant. "You gotta make that hire, man."

"I can't find the right person."

"Because you're too picky. Just find someone who can greet and seat and keep order where there's chaos."

John sent Summer a sideways look. "I did have someone amazing step in the other day…"

A little shiver climbed up her spine at the look, the compliment, and the secret they shared.

"Yeah?" Alex said. "So hire that person and call it a day." He looked past John toward the kitchen. "Please, God, tell me there's coffee. Those dogs had us up at six a.m., and that wasn't wonderful at all. I told Grace to sleep in and bring them over later for the barbecue."

"Good, then Destiny will get a chance to meet Maverick's cousins," John said.

"Destiny?" Alex asked.

"My daughter," Summer told him. "She's developed an, uh, unrealistic attachment to John's puppy, and I think she believes Maverick's going to be tiny for the rest of his life."

Alex gave a soft choke. "Then stick around and see my dogs. They're about fifty pounds each. Gertie still thinks she's a lapdog, though." He patted his chest. "And still likes to wake me up by sitting right here."

As the charming chef talked and asked Summer a few questions, she had the unusual opportunity to see exactly what John would look like without his beard and glasses. Handsome, for sure. But there was something about the way John looked that appealed to her. The facial hair made him incredibly masculine, and the glasses somehow fit his personality, which was much more understated and unassuming than Alex's.

And then she realized she was staring at him and he knew it.

"It's okay," he said, giving her an easy nudge with his elbow. "We're used to it. And yes, we're identical."

"I can see that…sort of."

"We're two halves of a whole," Alex told her. "I'm the official right side, and he's the left. I like food, people, a little drama, and a lot of music. Give this guy a spreadsheet, a technical challenge, or any problem to solve, and he's happy."

"Not so fast," John quipped. "Who is the one who

always gets the DJ at Bushrod's to play the music so we can do the sirtaki?"

"True," Alex conceded. "He can dance my ass off. And as far as movies, he's *Top Gun*, and I'm *Mission: Impossible*."

"But you're both Tom Cruise fans."

"Twin," John said, giving a nudge to Alex. "Go get your coffee. We're on our way to see Yiayia."

"Outside, holding court with Gramma Finnie," Alex said, sticking his thumb toward the patio. "How long are you in town, Summer? You guys should come to the winery, and I'll make dinner. And bring your daughter, of course."

"Oh, that's so kind. I'm not sure how long we'll be around, but thank you. It sounds like a wonderful place."

"It's paradise with wine," he said with a smile that softened his features and was absolutely identical to John's. "But that just may be because I met the most amazing woman there. I do hope you'll come and have some of our Three Dog Night Pinot Noir."

"I'd love to," she said, adding a quick goodbye as John finally led her to the patio.

"Overwhelmed yet?" he whispered as they reached wide-open doors that led to a huge deck-style patio populated with even more people and dogs.

"Not yet," she said. "But then, it's time for the Dogmothers."

"Remember, they do have an agenda." He led her through the doors, leaning close to her ear to whisper, "And if you think Destiny is hard to say no to…"

"Well, if it isn't our own Summer in Bitter Bark."

Summer turned to find Agnes Santorini in a

rocking chair with the smaller of her two dachshunds on her lap. Next to her, tiny Gramma Finnie beamed from behind her bifocals.

"You made it, lass."

They both shifted their gazes to John, and their smiles just grew bigger.

"I did, and it's so nice to see you again." Summer stepped closer and reached down to give them both a hug and kiss on the cheek because it felt so natural.

"Sit, sit." Agnes gestured to the ottoman in front of her. "And where is that gorgeous girl of yours?"

"Playing a game called..." She looked up at John, who leaned against the doorjamb, watching. "Bark 'n' Seek?"

"Hide 'n' Bark," he corrected. "But close enough."

"Then she's happy," Agnes said. "Did you find a dog for her yet, lass?"

Summer made a face. "She's still got her heart set on one that's taken, but maybe after this game..." She lifted a shoulder. "I'm sure we won't leave Bitter Bark without a dog." She smiled at John. "Her own dog, not yours."

The two older women looked from John to Summer and back to John again, then at each other.

"So, it's going well, you two?"

John gave an easy laugh. "I'm going to go get us a drink, Summer. I have no doubt you can handle this better without me. Sweet tea or something stronger?"

"Tea's good, thank you."

She settled a little deeper into the low seat, putting her just below eye level with Yiayia, where she suspected the woman wanted her to be for the inquisition she sensed was about to hit her.

"So, you like my Yianni?"

Hit and hit hard.

"Agnes! For the love of Saint Patrick, put your sledgehammer away."

"Ladies." Summer leaned closer. "Let's nip this right in the bud, okay? I see where you're going, and I understand that you've been there before, and quite successfully. But I'm not planning to be here for more than another day, two at the most."

Gramma Finnie let out a deep sigh and picked up a glass with a few inches of golden liquid. "Yer drivin' me to the Jameson's, lass," she whispered before taking a drink.

"I'm sorry, I—"

"Don't be." Yiayia leaned forward and pinned her with a gaze. "I, for one, appreciate your honesty. You're a busy single mother with a very active young daughter. And you have a job down in Florida."

Gramma Finnie shot her a look. "You can be subtle, Agnes, but there's no need to put the kibosh on the whole thing."

Yiayia waved a hand and picked up a tall glass of "water." "Nonsense. We're matchmakers, not miracle workers. Let's move on. I noticed a beautiful woman chatting with Darcy a while ago. Let's find out her story and introduce her to Yianni."

Summer blinked at her, oddly bothered that the woman had given up on her so easily.

"Well, I certainly understand why..." She looked toward the door where John had disappeared. "He's a great guy."

"But not for you," Yiayia said simply. "We'll find him the right match. You just go...back to Florida.

You're not interested, you're not local, and you're not Greek."

Gramma Finnie's jaw dropped at that. "I thought she might have at least made a nice summer distraction."

"We don't do *distractions*, Finola. So, not for him. Fine. Next?"

Summer bit back a quick laugh. "Wow, you sure give up easily, Yiayia."

"Not giving up anything. Just…" She made a point of moving one way, then the other, looking past Summer. "Seeking more fertile ground."

"Agnes, I do not understand you sometimes," Gramma Finnie said, snapping at the collar of her bright pink cardigan. "There's simply no need to be nasty to this sweet girl."

"I'm not nasty," she countered. "Just on a mission, and she can't be part of it."

Well, she could be if she wanted to. "Really," Summer said on an awkward laugh. "You sure are giving up fast. I mean, is the right match for your grandson so simple that any woman off the street would qualify?"

She leveled those dark, dark eyes on Summer. "Oh, I'll find the right match. And she will be perfect and *interested.*"

Just then, Destiny came flying out to the patio, her wild curls bouncing, thick from the summer humidity. John was two steps behind her, holding his own puppy, for once.

"Mommy!" She practically fell into Summer's lap.

"Honey, what is it? Are you okay?"

"Yes!" she said breathlessly. "But please, Mommy.

Please. I'm b-b-begging you." She pressed her delicate hands together as if in prayer.

"Destiny. You are not going to take this man's dog."

"No, no." She shook her head, sending the curls bouncing around her face. "I-I-I..." She closed her eyes and rooted for the focus she'd learned in speech therapy.

"Breathe, honey," Summer whispered, putting her hand on Destiny's cheek, which was hot from the sun and damp with sweat. "Say it slowly."

"Please let me go to Tails and Trails! *Pleeeeease*!" She drew out the last word so long, it actually broke into song. And her audience reacted with laughter, claps, and a cheer from Gramma Finnie.

"The camp?" For three weeks?

"It's so fun," she exclaimed on another desperate breath. "There are so-so-so many dogs and games and Popsicles and dogs and..."

"And more dogs," John said, stepping closer and easing little Maverick to the floorboards. "So I'm sure she'd find one."

"Oh..." Summer's mind spun through all the possibilities, the reasons to say no, and...then she looked up at John.

"The offer still stands." He added a smile and, with it, a twinkle in his eyes.

"I can't..." *Take a free apartment.* "And if you're in camp..."

"She'll be havin' the time of her life," Gramma Finnie said.

And Summer would be...

Oh. Suddenly, the answer was clear and good and

right and made perfect sense. She looked up at John, held his gaze, and lifted her brows.

"I won't take the apartment for free," she said. "But you know what I can do?"

He just stared at her, looking as if he were running through a whole list of things she could do and wasn't sure what she was about to say.

"I can meet, greet, and take people to eat."

"Mommy, you made a rhyme!"

John's eyes flashed as he realized what she was offering.

"Let me tell you, Yianni..." Summer couldn't resist a quick look at Yiayia. "There is no better job training for creating order out of chaos than teaching third grade. I'll run your hostess stand." Then, she rationalized, she'd be able to find out about Travis's whereabouts in a natural, organic way. Maybe he'd even come into the restaurant, and she could have that conversation with him, and no one else would ever have to know. Plus, she wouldn't have to leave this lovely place...or this handsome man.

"Summer." He barely breathed her name, and just the way he said it sent unexpected goose bumps up her arms. "That would be..." He searched for a word as if none could possibly express his reaction.

"Easy for me," she finished for him. "I can do it while Destiny is at camp, but not on the weekends. Would that work?"

"Like a dream," he admitted, holding her gaze in a way that did nothing to make those goosebumps go away.

"And I can go to camp?" Destiny almost howled with joy.

"Yes," she answered, stroking Destiny's hair but looking up at John. "I think that would be a wonderful way to spend the rest of this summer."

"Oh, saints alive, I agree," Gramma Finnie exclaimed.

"Yay!" Destiny popped up and danced around in a circle. "I'll tell Christian!" And she shot off, once again forgetting the dog she'd clung to for the entire day.

John took a step forward and reached for Summer's hand to pull her up. "You're saving my life, you know that?"

"Actually, you're saving mine and making my little girl very happy."

"And I didn't even have to give up my dog."

"Yet," she teased.

"Come on," John said. "Let's take a walk, and I'll tell you what's involved in the job, and we can get you moved into my upstairs apartment tomorrow, if you like."

As she walked off the patio with him, she turned to say goodbye to Finnie and Yiayia, but caught their quiet exchange instead.

"I don't know what ye think ye were doin', Agnes."

Yiayia pointed at Gramma Finnie. "Do not ever question the master, Finola Kilcannon." Just then, she realized Summer had heard her, and she lowered her finger and smiled. "Just a bit of reverse psychology, dear. I'm sure you use it on your daughter all the time."

Summer sighed as she realized what had just happened. "Not quite as effectively," she admitted. "But points to the Greek grandmother on that one."

That Greek grandmother narrowed dark eyes at her. "Do *not* break his heart."

They shared a long look, making Summer wonder if she'd just made a friend…or an enemy.

Chapter Seven

John looked around the apartment that he'd spent far too little time preparing, trying to see it through Summer's eyes. The unit was clean and sparsely furnished, but it had the necessities. Except for the kitchen, which had second-rate counters, no real working appliances, and a few missing knobs on the three small cabinets. And a hole where a refrigerator belonged.

"Wanna slide it right in there?" Aidan asked, wiping some sweat from his brow after the two of them had hauled the half-sized fridge up the back stairs, across the deck, and through the sliding doors.

"Yeah. But it won't fill the space."

"She doesn't need a Sub-Zero, John," Aidan said. "She's staying for a few weeks, and you've already offered her the use of your kitchen downstairs."

John ran a finger over the cracked Formica. "Hope her standards aren't too high."

"You didn't expect a tenant until after Christmas," Aidan said. "And it's free, right?"

"Well, she's going to work at Santorini's."

"Right." Aidan jutted his chin. "Come on, help me push."

He came around next to Aidan, and the two of them slid the fridge over the linoleum floor, into the hole where a much bigger unit belonged.

"There. She won't mind that," Aidan said.

"I'll throw a bottle of wine in the fridge, and she'll never notice how lacking it is."

"And she might share that wine with you." Aidan waggled his brows suggestively. "Then everybody gets lucky."

John shot him a look.

"What?" Aidan said. "I was at that barbecue after Adoption Days last night. You two didn't take five steps away from each other, and when you did, well…"

"Well what?"

"I didn't notice it, but Beck said she caught Sunshine looking at you a lot."

"Her name's Summer, not Sunshine."

Aidan grinned. "Same difference."

He slapped a hand on his stepbrother's arm. "Thanks for the fridge, man."

"Hey, it was just sitting in the back of Slice of Heaven, unused."

"And the muscle."

"You'll pay me back," Aidan said. "Just finish the landing drills and your instruction hours, log your solo time, take the tests and checkride, and get your damn pilot's license." He pointed at John. "Then you can start haulin' dog ass around when I need backup."

"You know I will, Aidan," John said, eternally grateful for his stepbrother's offer to take him up for flight lessons. His pilot's license was so close he could taste it. Aidan had been unrelenting in the cause, ever since they'd met and John had shared his dream.

Aidan, a certified flight instructor, had planted the idea last spring, when John went up with him in the 172 Skyhawk that Waterford used to transport rescue dogs. Once John passed the written and medical tests, there would be no reason not to achieve that lifelong dream. His wretched astigmatism might have kept him from his Navy pilot fantasies, but with corrective lenses, he easily passed the vision requirement for a small private plane.

"I want to finish those hours more than I want my next breath," he added. "But I can't be away from the restaurant too much this month." Not with Tom Barnard's surprise appearance on the horizon.

"Just lemme know when you want to go back up," Aidan said, just as they both heard the sound of a car coming down the long drive.

"Hey, do me a favor and plug this fridge in, okay? I'm going to greet my...I guess you'd call her a tenant."

"In the military, we'd call her a hot target."

John snorted. "Of course you would." He headed down the wooden stairs to the driveway, his eyes on the little SUV and the hot target inside. And he couldn't quite wipe the smile off his face.

He could hear Mav barking behind the sliding glass doors that led into his first-floor living area. No doubt Destiny would insist on seeing the puppy right away. And John would have no willpower where that kid was concerned. She'd go nuts when she heard the surprise he had planned, but he had to talk to Summer first.

"Hey there," he said, walking to the driver's side of the compact SUV to open the door, knocked over once again by those blue eyes. "Welcome home, ladies."

"I hear Mavvie!" Destiny strained at her seat belt in the back seat. "Can I see him right now?"

"I hope we're not too early," Summer said. "She's been up and packed to go since six a.m."

"Not at all." He stepped aside to let her get out and opened the back door for Destiny. "Aidan and I just installed your fridge, which is small but will do the job."

"Oh, thank you," Summer said, taking a look around, her gaze on the horizon of blue and green rolling foothills and the Blue Ridge Mountains. "Holy cow, John. You weren't kidding when you said there's a view. This is incredible. Oh, hold on, Des."

Destiny was still battling her seat belt, ready to tear the thing off. Summer slid in between the car and John, bending into the back seat to release the latch, inadvertently drawing his gaze—and every other cell in his body—to the blue jean cutoffs she wore.

He stepped back, the impact too much for any human, then blinking, he took another quick look at her curvy backside, tanned legs, and the adorable navy Converse sneakers she wore. Now *that* was an incredible view.

He enjoyed it for the entire three seconds it took her to unhook the belt and burned the image in his brain, where he'd be calling it up for further examination about a thousand times.

"Wh-wh-where is he?" Destiny demanded as she exploded out of the back seat. "Did he m-m-miss me?"

"Des!" Summer chided. "Let the man breathe."

Her eyes widened. "He's calling me!" She ran off toward the house, her insane curls flying behind her.

"Destiny! You can't run into someone's house."

"I'll get him for her," he said. "And I kind of think he *is* calling her. No one else has squeezed the life out of him for a whole night."

Laughing, she came with him to the lower level walkout.

"I can't believe this place," Summer said, still looking around. "A fire pit? All this yard? And that view? And so close to town. Was that a college we drove by?"

"Yeah, the only thing between us and Bitter Bark is Vestal Valley College. These houses were built for faculty originally, and some graduate students live out here, but it's pretty quiet. I think you'll like it."

"I already love it."

He tugged at the slider slowly, making Destiny squeal at the sight of little Mav's face poking through the opening. "Here's your buddy, Des," he said, reaching down to get the dog. "You can play with him on the grass, but don't let him run away."

"Mavvie." She reached out grabby little hands, taking the puppy and pulling him to her face. "I love you," she whispered in his ear, the words squeezing John's chest exactly like she was squeezing Mav.

Summer touched his arm and added a playful warning look. "Be strong."

"I am, but..." He waited a beat until Destiny scrambled to the lawn, out of earshot, and put Maverick on the grass. "I have an idea I want to run by you."

She looked up at him, a dubious expression on her pretty face. "You will not give my daughter your dog."

"I will not," he assured her, hoping to God he could keep that promise. "She will meet plenty of dogs at camp. Lots of them are still up for adoption, and she'll no doubt find the one for her. But campers are encouraged to bring dogs that need training, too." He waited a second, letting what he was asking sink in. "Mav's a little young, but Shane said it would be fine if Destiny brought him. Mav's not helping things at the deli, and I'd probably just board him at Waterford for the next few weeks during the day anyway. So, if Destiny wants to bring him to camp..."

"And get more attached to him?"

He gave an easy shrug. "I'll take that risk, but..." He looked past Summer to where Destiny sat, giggling and talking to Maverick. "I think it would make it easier for her to slide into a big group of kids that way. Maybe take some of her discomfort away." She had to notice that Destiny stuttered less when she was holding Mav, but he didn't want to point that out.

Summer's expression softened, and her shoulders seemed to sink a tiny bit. "Wow, it would. But... wow."

"Wow...what?"

She searched his face, her eyes as warm as the sun that blared down on both of them. "That's pretty much the most thoughtful thing, ever."

"Oh, well, no." He waved off the compliment. "It's just selfish, you know."

"Really?" She laughed. "Is that what you call it?"

"No, no. I just thought it would be nice for you not to have to worry about her adjusting to a new environment. So you can really concentrate on work," he added, hoping it didn't sound quite as lame to her as it did to him. "And that dog does need some training. He's a pain to have in my office, and he is desperate for affection and gets plenty of it from her. Plus, this way I don't have to worry about him or keep him crated or in a kennel all day."

"I'll take all those excuses, John, but sorry, you gave away your true colors."

"My colors are black and white," he said simply. "I'm driven by common sense and, as my brother told you, a spreadsheet. The numbers add up, that's all."

"You're genuinely concerned about her adjusting to camp."

"Of course I am. And really, if she hates camp, you'll leave the restaurant, and I'll be..." Stupidly sad. "Right back where I am, hostess-less."

"Oh, I see," she teased. "Very logical."

"How I roll," he assured her. "Come on, I'll show you the apartment. Just, keep your expectations low."

"In case I hate it and leave you in the lurch?" she joked as they walked toward the stairs.

"Yeah, that."

She laughed softly, her smile making him think his fast-developing crush was freaking obvious. Maybe it was. Oh well, he wasn't a game player.

"Come on, Des," she called. "Let's go see our new house!"

Summer had honestly forgotten men like John Santorini even existed anymore. Well, maybe she didn't get out much. She'd tried a dating app a handful of times, but that had been a total dud, and having a little one certainly limited the scope of men who showed interest in Summer.

But she was pretty sure not one of the few she'd met since Isaiah had died would have made an offer like John had just so Destiny would be comfortable. He could cover all he wanted with explanations about common sense and his need for a hostess, but she could see right through that.

The gesture made her heart swell with appreciation for a man she already found attractive. And right now, he was...

Right behind her.

Halfway up the wooden stairs, a slow heat started deep in her belly as awareness sharpened. She knew that if she stopped suddenly, he'd walk into her, and that would be...nice.

She jogged two steps, a safe distance, then turned to call Destiny in a voice that was a little tighter in her throat than it should have been. "Let's move it, babycakes."

He chuckled. "Babycakes?"

"Oh, she answers to just about anything." She took a few more steps and glanced down at him, hoping she could hide the sudden surge of affection she felt for him with a casual statement, all nonchalance. "And, oh, by the way, the answer is yes. She can take Mav with her."

"Really?" A smile pulled as he took the steps and closed the gap between them, face-to-face now that he was only one stair below. "That's awesome. You want to tell her the good news?"

"No, I think you should. Why not have a fan for life?" She tapped his shoulder, not surprised that the muscle underneath was hard. "Actually, two."

His eyes flickered at the compliment. "Well, wait until you see your crappy kitchen. The Santorini Fan Club might be back to one five-year-old."

She laughed and spun to continue up the stairs, her feet feeling oddly as light as her heart.

Of course it was light. Her problems for the month were solved with a place to live and a camp that Destiny would talk about for the rest of the year. She could have at least three weeks with Destiny in camp, and if they really loved it here, they could stay until school started. She could have freedom, fresh air, no students, no lesson plans. And she'd give her mother the much-needed break that she deserved every summer.

She shook out the thought of her mother, a thought that always came with an extra dose of guilt. Mom had been a godsend since Destiny had been born. She'd sacrificed so many of her causes and volunteer programs, given up benefits she used to chair and community service she loved to perform, all to pick up the slack when Des was a baby and toddler.

"This is absolutely glorious," she whispered as she stepped on the ten-foot deck and leaned on the railing, still not quite able to drink in the vast and endless hills on the horizon. "I couldn't have dreamed of finding an Airbnb as nice as this."

"The view won't boil water, though, so remember, if you need a stove or oven, mine is right downstairs."

She looked over the lawn where Destiny was still running around with Mav, thinking more of him *right downstairs* than seeing how much fun her daughter was having playing outside. Close proximity all day at work and all night right here.

An unfamiliar flutter tickled her stomach, making her head a little light. He obviously liked her, and she…

Had still not asked him about the Shipleys. She didn't know what was stopping her, but something was. Maybe embarrassment that she'd somehow allowed a long-distance connection to become a one-sided romance, and then she'd ghosted the guy.

"Come on up, Des," she called. "I want you to see our new place."

"C-c-can I carry him?" She looked up, hesitant, holding Mav at the bottom step.

"I'll go help," John offered quickly, hustling toward the stairs.

Just then, a young man stepped outside to join them, the sun beaming on a mop of golden hair, highlighting bright blue eyes.

"Say hi to Aidan Kilcannon," John called over his shoulder as he went down the stairs. "You met last night at Waterford."

Aidan had been one of dozens of John's extended family, and many friends, she'd met during the crowded barbecue after the Adoption Days event had ended. But she remembered the youngest of the "Kilcannon boys," as his father, Daniel Kilcannon, had lovingly referred to them.

"Hello, Aidan. We only talked for a minute, but I did have a good long chat with your wife." She shook the hand Aidan extended. "Nice to see you again."

"Same, Summer. Yeah, Beck said she really enjoyed talking to you." He gave her hand a strong squeeze that reminded her that Beck had mentioned that Aidan had been in the Army.

"That's an Army-trained handshake," she joked as she let go.

"Yes, ma'am. I was in the 160th SOAR Airborne, US Army Night Stalker."

She inched back, not even trying to hide how impressive that was. "Whoa, Beck didn't mention those credentials. But she did say you'd been in Afghanistan, at Bagram."

He nodded with just enough of a shadow on his handsome face for her to know it had been a tough tour. "Happy to never see that place again," he said with a tight smile.

"I didn't mention this to your wife, since the mood was so festive last night, but my husband was stationed at Bagram four years ago. First Lieutenant Isaiah Jackson."

"Oh. Is he…"

"He died in action."

He barely flinched, but she saw the quick, dark flicker in his blue eyes. "Really sorry for your loss, Summer."

She swallowed and nodded. "Thank you. And thanks for your service. Beck said you're a pilot?"

"Yes. And I still fly, though not a UH-60 Black Hawk," he said on a soft laugh. "Just a four-seater Cessna that transports rescues for Waterford. Did John tell you I'm his flight instructor?"

"No, although his grandmother mentioned he's

taking flying lessons." She glanced down to the lawn where John had scooped up Mav and was walking toward the steps, talking to Destiny, patiently explaining that the dog hadn't yet learned to do stairs too well. Destiny listened, rapt.

"He's ten hours away from a solo license," Aidan said, adding yet another dimension to her temporary landlord and boss.

"You can thank Aidan for the fridge, Summer," John said as he reached the top of the stairs, right behind Destiny with Mav in his arms. "They had an extra at Beck's uncle's pizza restaurant."

"Oh, we certainly appreciate that. Did you meet Destiny last night?" she asked.

"No, but I saw her running with the big dogs. Hello, Destiny. Do you like pizza?"

She looked up at him and nodded, silent.

"We love pizza," Summer said, then kicked herself for jumping in when Destiny had hesitated like that. "And we'll thank Beck's uncle with some business, I promise."

Still holding Mav, John angled his head toward the sliding glass doors. "Come take a tour of your humble little home."

"You good, then, John?" Aidan asked. "No more appliances?"

"We're good, man, thanks." He nodded to Aidan. "And if I can squeeze in a few hours for lessons this week, I will."

Aidan tapped his forehead in a mock salute and headed off, giving Destiny's hair a quick ruffle as he passed. "Have fun in camp," he said. "Slice of Heaven is catering the pizza every Wednesday, and I'm pretty sure there's a special party planned for the day we fly out some rescue dogs. You're gonna love it so much you'll never want to leave." He looked up at Summer and flashed a smile. "You might, too."

She thanked him again, and then they followed John through the sliders, stepping into a small living area with one sofa, a chair, and a simple console for the TV.

"It's…sparse," John said. "But you should be comfortable."

"It's fabulous," she said, having seen way worse Airbnbs that cost…well, that *cost*. "The view is more than anyone could want, and the kitchen is—"

"If you say nice, then I'll know you're lying."

She laughed, noticing a few missing handles and the chipped Formica. "It's more than adequate since I'll be working at a restaurant and can get our dinner there every night."

"Oh, one thing you'll get at Santorini's is great food, I promise."

She couldn't help putting a hand on his arm just for the sheer pleasure of one more touch, hoping he didn't notice how many times she'd done that. "This is perfect, John. I'll—"

"Mommy! Mommy! Look what's in my room!" She sang the sentence, loud and clear and full of enough insistence that Summer's heart skipped as she looked at John with a little horror.

"Please tell me it's not a spider. She's deathly afraid."

"It's not a spider. It's probably the gift Gramma Finnie sent me home with last night."

"A gift?"

"Butter up the lass," he said in a dead-on brogue. "Then the mother will like you." He winked, making Summer laugh. "Those two are focused on the mission, believe me."

"Mommy!" Destiny bolted out of a doorway that Summer assumed led to the bedrooms, clutching something pink tightly to her chest, her eyes bright with excitement. "It has my n-n-name on it!" She turned around a throw pillow that had been neatly embroidered with *Beautiful words make a beautiful destiny.*

"Oh my," Summer said, as enchanted as Destiny. "Can you read that, honey?"

She turned and frowned. "Words...make...Destiny!" She held the pillow up with a little squeal. "My name."

Summer walked toward her, taking the pillow, which was just worn enough to show some age and love. And the embroidery had clearly been done by a talented hand. "It says, 'Beautiful words make a beautiful destiny.' Oh, honey, I love that."

"Gramma Finnie is a world-class embroiderer," John explained, coming closer to them. "When she was a young girl in Ireland, she worked in a pillow factory embroidering Irish proverbs, so she has literally dozens and dozens of these. I swear she makes them all the time."

"Is she your gra-gra-grandma?" Destiny asked John.

"Not exactly. She's my mother's mother-in-law." At Destiny's confused look, he laughed. "Okay, basically my grandmother. And she really likes you so, last night after you left, she asked me to go up to the attic and find this for you so you'd have something special in your new house. Do you like it?"

She squeezed it to her chest. "I love it," she whispered, using the same tone she saved for his dog.

"And John has some more exciting news for you, Des," Summer said, giving him the opening.

He flashed a quick smile to thank her for that, then leaned a little closer to Destiny. "You know that the kids who go to Tails and Trails are allowed to bring a dog to camp?"

Her eyes widened as she stared at him.

"Or they can get one assigned to them when they arrive," he added. "Would you like to take Maverick and help train him, or do you want to pick another dog?"

"Mavvie!" She leaped into the air like a ballerina, singing the word and making him draw back with a surprised laugh.

"She can get a little...exuberant," Summer explained.

"It's great. Exuberance is..." He beamed at Destiny. "We could use a little of that around here. So, Maverick is yours. Now, you might have to share for special games—"

"He's *mine*?" She gasped the words.

"No, no. Des." Summer put her hand on her shoulder. "He didn't say that."

She looked hard at Summer, her eyes communicating *yes, he did* as loud and clear as if she'd said it.

"In her defense, I did use those words," John said quickly.

"But he didn't mean Mav is *yours* yours. He meant you can go to camp with him, and when the counselors set up certain games and programs, he might be your partner. Probably for sure the first day," she added, even though she hadn't gotten that much detail from the organizers yet.

"It's like you have a special friend to go to camp with," John added, and once again his tender words touched Summer's heart.

They obviously touched Destiny's, based on the smile she gave him. "Thank you," she whispered, looking down at the dog standing next to her. "I love Mavvie."

He laughed. "I know you do, and that's why I'm trusting him with you. I know you'll keep an eye on him so he doesn't get lost around bigger, older dogs. And help him get trained not to run away when he's not on the leash. Can you do that?"

She nodded, looking hard at him, almost as if she was seeing him for the first time. Understandable, since every time she'd been around the man, the world's biggest distraction had had all her attention.

But now, her green-gold gaze searched his face, looking intently at him.

"That was really kind of John, wasn't it?" Summer asked, wondering if the scrutiny was because Destiny wasn't sure she could get her next thought out without stuttering or...she had just developed a fascination with John Santorini.

Could be both, Summer mused.

"Um, are you..." Destiny whispered the words, just intently enough for Summer's heart to skip in anticipation of what she might say next. "Are you the d-d-daddy we came here to find?"

Oh God. Blood rushed to Summer's face in the mother of all blushes as she opened her mouth to say something—anything—that would smooth over the awkward moment.

"Destiny, that's an inappropriate question," Summer finally managed.

John sort of straightened. "Maybe your mom said doggy, not daddy."

Summer seized the explanation and silently blessed him for it. "Of course I did. We came to Bitter Bark to find a doggy. And not one someone already owns," she added urgently, since this conversation could go only further south with Destiny begging to adopt Mav.

"And you got a pillow with your name on it as a bonus," John said, obviously trying to help. "And you know what I have downstairs in my apartment? Popsicles," he said, without waiting for her to ask. "The last time Christian was here, his mom brought them. Would you like one?"

She nodded slowly, still staring at him, maybe not entirely falling for the distraction.

"Then let's get one. And get you guys moved in." He ushered Destiny toward the door, waiting while she put her pillow on the sofa and picked up Mav.

"John," Summer whispered. "She gets these ideas. You know, don't take it…seriously."

He gave a smile with just a hint of disappointment. "Thanks for the warning."

Chapter Eight

"**K**nock, knock."

Summer's voice floated through the screen from John's patio, a sweet and unexpected sound barely louder than the instrumental music that played from the speakers of his laptop. He lowered the volume and the computer screen to peer into the darkness of the patio, his franchising proposal and barely touched beer instantly forgotten.

"Hey." He got up to meet her at the open sliders, the warm Carolina air carrying a whiff of her flowery scent into his home. "Everything okay up there?"

"Yes, it's fine. I'm sorry it's so late, but I just got Des to sleep. And…"

As he got closer, he caught sight of her in the soft light emanating from his living room, wearing a baggy oversize T-shirt and sleep pants, her pale hair clipped up sloppily on her head. The comfortable, natural look was as sexy as if she'd come down in something from Victoria's Secret. But his favorite part of Summer at Night was a pair of red plastic-framed glasses perched on her nose.

For reasons he'd never understand, he loved that she wore glasses.

Behind him, he heard Mav rustle from his dog bed to come and investigate.

She raised a cup with a tea bag dangling from the side. "I couldn't figure out how to heat up water for my tea, which I kind of love before bed."

"It's not easy without a stove or microwave, which I should have given you. Want me to take mine up now?"

Her shoulders dropped with a sigh as if the offer was just too much. "No, I don't want you to lug your microwave upstairs, world's most thoughtful human. But thank you. I'll just stick this in for a minute and be out of your hair."

"Sure." But he didn't want her out of his hair. On the contrary, he wanted to get his hands in hers and feel all that wheat-colored silk tumble through his fingers. "Come on in."

As he slid the door open, it scraped over the track noisily, and he made a face. "Yikes. That's loud. Could it wake her?"

"No, no, God, live your life. She sleeps like a rock most nights." She smiled up at him. "But thank you for asking."

He let her in, checking to make sure Mav hadn't slipped out. "How are you two adjusting up there?"

"Awesome," she said, following him into his house for the first time, glancing around. "This is a great place."

He took the mug and headed into the kitchen, which was open to the living area and separated by a large island with a counter, where he ate most meals when he wasn't at the restaurant.

"It works for me," he said. "There are two big bedrooms down here, but I use one as an office, and what I think was supposed to be a formal living room in the front, but I have it set up as a media room. Feel free to look around." He tapped the undercounter light in the kitchen and headed to the microwave.

She walked through the room, pausing at the wall-to-wall bookshelves jammed with his personal library. "You're a reader."

"I like books," he said, punching the buttons on the microwave. "But I ran out of space and have gone digital." He gestured to a tablet on the coffee table.

"What are you reading now?" she asked.

"Right now, I'm working, truth be told."

"So, Yiayia was right. It's work, work, work with you." She tipped her head as she imitated his grandmother, making him laugh.

"She's always right. Just ask her."

Smiling, Summer peered more closely at his books. "I see you like...airplanes." She leaned in to examine the spines. "Lots of airplanes. Whoa. Many airplanes. And...are these in alphabetical order?"

He laughed. "Guilty as charged. And not just airplanes. There are some business books up there. Textbooks, mostly, from grad school."

"I didn't get to the B's yet," she teased.

"When you do, there's a lot of baseball books, too."

"Oh, yes, that was on Yiayia's résumé. MVP in high school?"

He had to laugh at his grandmother, who had spent plenty of hours in the stands watching him play. "Yep. Played in college, too. Not MVP at Chapel Hill, though."

"What position?"

"The one that requires the most brains—catcher. And I've got the blown-out knees to prove it."

"And the shoulders," she added in a low voice that made him wonder if she'd wanted him to hear. She turned back to the books, quiet for a moment as she scanned the wall. "*Dogfights of World War II?*"

"I know. Riveting." He chuckled. "Don't even think about looking at my DVDs in the front. You'll run screaming from the building."

"Lots of flying movies?" she guessed, turning from the shelves to join him at the counter.

"Starting with the best of the best, *Top Gun.*"

"Oh yeah." She crinkled her nose. "You and my brother."

"He's a fan?"

"To put it mildly. Kenny is four years older than I am and wanted no part of his pesky little sister. But I adored him—still do, to be honest—and so I'd do anything to spend time with him. Even watch Maverick and Goose lock on bogeys three thousand times."

He laughed, getting a ridiculous kick out of her seeing "his" movie. "Three thousand?"

"And one." She turned when the microwave beeped, the soft light casting a shadow on her face. "Then he went to college and med school, and now he's a doctor at the Mayo Clinic in Jacksonville. No more *Top Gun* for us."

"Really? My oldest brother is a doctor, too. In Africa."

"Doctors Without Borders?" she guessed. "Very cool. You must be proud of him."

"I am. We all are. He's...he's..." He frowned, not exactly sure how much of Nick's strange story he should share.

"He's what?" she asked.

"Nick's my brother, but it turns out we have different biological fathers, not that it matters in the least. He's still one of my idols."

"It 'turns out' you have different fathers? You didn't know?"

"My mother didn't know."

She gave him a confused look. "Seriously?"

He rounded the counter and handed her the mug of steaming tea. "She, and we, found out only about a year ago when my sister, Cassie, did a DNA test as a Christmas gift for us." He gave a dry laugh. "The gift turned out to be quite a shocker."

"Does his biological father know?"

"He sure does. In fact, you met him last night."

She frowned, trying to follow. "Daniel Kilcannon? Wait...*what*? They're married now."

"Daniel and my mom dated briefly in college, but..." He gave a shrug. "Not that casually, apparently. Anyway, they split up amicably, and she went back home to my dad, who'd been her high school sweetheart, and the next thing she knew...she was pregnant. She and my dad got married and never had any reason to think Nico Santorini wasn't Nico Jr.'s father. We call him Nick."

"And your dad raised Nick as his."

"Of course, and he died without knowing the truth. But I don't think he'd have done anything differently. He doted on Nick. On all of us." Letting out a sad sigh, he added, "I miss him every day."

She closed one hand over the teacup and stirred the liquid with the bag, studying him. "So that's where you got your good heart?"

He eyed her with a half-smile. "And here I thought it was the shoulders you liked."

"I like both," she said, the straightforward admission giving him a kick in the gut. "But I can tell you are a genuinely caring man."

He shrugged again, suddenly more aware of his *shoulders* than he'd ever been. "I just want to do what's right for people. Trust me, it doesn't always work out in my favor."

"How so?" she asked.

He considered how to answer that, then nodded to the sofa. "Want to sit down? Or make a fire and sit outside?"

"A fire?" Her eyes flashed. "Can we?"

"Of course, come on."

He grabbed his beer in one hand and Mav in the other, then they headed outside, and in a few minutes, he had the flames dancing and lighting up the backyard. Everything was so easy and natural with her, talking quietly as they sank into Adirondack chairs he'd placed around the fire pit.

She held Mav on her lap, stroking his head, staring into the fire while John did his best not to stare at her.

"So, you were saying about your Mr. Nice Guy thing?"

He choked a soft laugh. "I don't think I used 'Mr. Nice Guy,' like that's my call sign or something."

She pointed at him. "You need one of those, if you're going to be a pilot. Anything in mind?"

"You don't get to pick your own call sign," he said. "You earn it. Like…"

"Like Iceman." She hissed the name of Maverick's nemesis in the movie, making him laugh.

"I don't think I ever met a woman who loves *Top Gun* like I do."

"I didn't say I love it," she said. "I was mostly bored out of my mind during the flying parts."

He threw a sideways look. "You were all about the…other stuff."

"Like sweaty, shirtless guys playing beach volleyball? Um, *yeah*. And the *romance*." She rolled the r and dragged out the word. "Kenny always wanted to fast-forward through the 'kissing parts.' Told me I was too young to watch. Meanwhile, the language could curl your hair."

"But all strung together in the best way." He lifted his brows and leaned closer. "Want to watch it with me? I promise not to fast-forward through the kissing parts."

Her eyes shuttered as he said the last two words, her whole body moving a centimeter closer, the space as hot as the air around the fire, and just as sparky.

"I'd like that," she whispered. "Let's drink wine and watch it in your media room some night when Destiny's asleep. We can see who knows more lines. I bet I beat you."

"You'll lose that bet."

She lifted her teacup to meet his beer bottle. "You're on, Nice Man."

He closed his eyes. "*Ice*, not nice."

She pointed to him. "Good one for you, though, isn't it?"

He dropped his head back with a grunt. "Think of something else."

"Zorba?" she suggested.

He lifted a brow. "Not bad. Beats…four-eyes."

She touched her glasses. "Wouldn't dream of it. So tell me why you wish you weren't so nice."

"Did I say that?" he asked her. "Or are you putting words in my mouth?"

"You said being nice hasn't worked in your favor, and that's a quote. Why not?"

He finally looked away from her into the firelight, feeling the warmth of the flames and the moment. It made him want to confide in her and then get her out of that chair and onto his lap.

One thing at a time. "Sometimes, when you do nice things, you get screwed."

"They say no good deed goes unpunished," she reminded him. "Give me an example?"

"Well, I had an opportunity to be part of a major franchise start-up a number of years ago. You may have heard of ChiliHeads."

"That chain of spicy-food restaurants? We just got one near where I live."

He huffed out a breath. ChiliHeads had nearly 250 locations now and was one of the fastest-growing restaurant chains in the country. "I was going to be the chief operating officer of that company."

"Really? Wow. What happened?"

"My dad got sick," he said. "Someone had to run Santorini's. Alex is a chef, and a brilliant one, but he wasn't the right person for the job of managing that place. Yiayia had already retired, my mom never was in the business, and none of my siblings had paid that much attention to the *business* of the family business. We had to step in for my dad, and then he passed three years ago and…"

"Here you still are."

"But so close to that dream again. This time, instead of a high-end concept that appeals to lovers of hot food, I'm going with something closer to home, the Greek deli."

"It's a great idea."

He nodded, pulling himself from the regret of the road not taken. Life had happened, and he made the best of it.

"What else?" she asked.

He turned to her. "What else…what?"

"When else has being a nice guy caused you great sacrifice?"

He thought about it for a moment, then smiled. "Cost me a girl once."

"A girl or *the* girl?"

Drawing back, he looked hard at her. "Why would you ask that?"

"You're what? Mid-thirties?"

"Thirty-six."

"And you're great-looking, good-hearted, funny, brilliant, and ambitious. You have a terrific family and no obvious fatal flaws, other than being too nice, if there is such a thing. My guess is there was one girl, and she broke your heart hard enough for you to stay single."

"Wow." He gave an uncomfortable laugh, not sure what to do with how good all those compliments felt or how close she was to the truth. "You got all of that out of 'cost me a girl once.'"

She sipped her tea and let her eyes smile at him over the rim. "Am I right?"

He reached for his beer bottle and took a pull. "Of course you are."

"Ahhh. Talk about her?"

"Do I have to?" He didn't spend a lot of time thinking about Paige Ashford. Not anymore. "We could go back to the great-looking, funny, and brilliant stuff. So nice to hear it from you instead of Yiayia."

She laughed. "Just give me the short version. How did being nice cost you? Because I have to say, it's kind of a disconnect, unless she was one of those girls who has a thing for bad boys."

"Bingo. In her case, a former bad boy and also her ex. I knew she'd be happier with the challenge he offered, so I...stepped aside and let her off the hook."

"How hooked was she?"

"We were engaged."

"Ohhh. Wow. That's hooked. How close to the wedding?"

He smiled at her. "You really want to know all this?"

"Of course I do. How else am I going to help you figure out your call sign?"

"Okay." He laughed, sipping the beer again. "Not that close. But we were together five years."

"Long time."

"It was. But I wanted to get the whole ChiliHeads thing underway before we got married, and then..."

She made a face. "So you broke up *and* had to give up your dream job?"

"She was part of the business, too. It was all..." He tapped the bottle in his hand. "Mingled into one really sucky time of my life, followed by years of Dad battling cancer and then losing him."

"John." Her voice was thick with sympathy. "I'm sorry about all that."

"Thanks, but it's not like you haven't endured your share of crappy curveballs life throws at you."

She held up a hand and gave a little wave, the gesture's meaning loud and clear: She didn't want to discuss her loss.

"Anyway," he said quickly. "It's all on track now. I have a great plan for the future. Once I started running Santorini's, the business really boomed. We were able to open two more locations, and I was back in the multi-restaurant game. Now, with financing, I can make Santorini's a household name, which is even cooler than ChiliHeads, because it's *my* name and my family's heart and soul. I like this plan better, to be honest."

"Which grew out of your being noble and good and worthy and family-oriented," she said, then added a smile. "Any of those sound like call signs?"

"I'm looking for, you know, something with a little sex appeal."

"Oh, you got that." The low, sweet, intimate way she said it made him draw in a slow breath to tamp down his response. Then she put a hand on his shoulder. "How does Shoulders sound for a call sign?"

"Weak."

"These aren't. Sounds like they are able to bear quite a bit of weight."

He just smiled, holding her gaze, setting his beer

on the grass, and inching a little closer. Without a word, he reached up and touched the red frames, like both of them kept finding ways to make physical contact. "Speaking of sex appeal, these are hot."

Her lips curled in a half smile. "I'm starting to think you would say that no matter how I looked."

"True." He lifted his shoulder. "I like you."

"You do?"

He reached for the glasses again, sliding them off this time. "Yep. A lot."

She inched closer, too, the space between them definitely small enough for a kiss. "I like you, too."

"Well, that's...convenient."

"And complicated," she added.

"What's complicated?" He touched her lower lip, not surprised that it was warm and silky smooth.

"Living in the same house, working at the same place."

"Sounds pretty *un*complicated to me. Unless..." He drew back. "There's someone else? Back home? Because..."

"Because you're so nice you'd stop right now if there was."

"You got 'nice' and 'decent' mixed up, sweetheart." He came closer again. "If you're a free woman who wants to kiss me, now's your chance. If you're not..."

She closed the last bit of space between them, tilting her head to press their lips together. She tasted like English tea and July mountain air and everything sweet he ever wanted.

Lifting his hand, he slid his fingers into her hair, almost moaning when the strands fell over his hand, as soft and silky as he imagined her hair would be. He added some pressure, angled his head, and let the first hot kick of pleasure shoot from his brain straight down to—

"Mommy!"

Maverick leaped off Summer's lap with a noisy bark, making them both jerk away, yanked from the kiss.

"Mommmmmyyyy!"

"Oh." She sighed the single syllable with a groan of disappointment. "So much for sleeping like a rock."

"New place. I'm sure she needs you," he said.

She slid him a look of frustration, a wry smile pulling. "Yeah, you're right. But I was just starting to think *I* need *you*."

"Same." He got up and snagged Mav, who was already wandering around the grass while Summer pushed up from her chair. When he had the dog, he walked back to Summer and stood close, just as the next cry came through the window.

"Go get her," he whispered, stealing one more kiss. "I'll bring your tea."

"Of course you will." She put her hand on his cheek, looking up into his eyes. "Nice Man."

He narrowed his eyes in warning, making her laugh as she spun around and darted up the stairs and disappeared into the darkness of the upstairs apartment.

"Come on, Mav," he whispered as he followed. "Let's go be...nice."

Summer's whole body was still vibrating from that kiss. And from the tendril of doubt that had pulled at her heart when he'd asked if she was free.

Yes, of course, she was. There was no man in her life, and she hadn't had sex since Isaiah's last leave. She was starving for the affection, her whole body aching and fiery with how much she'd wanted that kiss to go on and on and on.

And she *had* come to Bitter Bark to find a man. A different man. She told herself she'd come to apologize for the way she broke things off with Travis and to get closure on their relationship…but was that the truth?

Her mind drifted back to last week's conversation with her sister-in-law. Summer considered Raven Jackson a friend as much as the sister she didn't have, their relationship close from the day Isaiah brought her home to meet his family.

Raven knew all about how Travis had contacted Summer after Isaiah died and knew that their interaction had progressed further than Summer wanted. She knew all about the ghosting and fully supported the idea of an apology and closure. But then she'd joked that he could be "a daddy for Destiny" in that sassy, Raven-like way that Summer loved so much.

Was that what Summer had hoped, deep in her heart? That the man who'd first contacted her from Afghanistan and told her he had been Isaiah's closest friend, the man who'd then been the source of such comfort in her grief, the man who'd once said he loved her…could be a man she loved back?

She really wished Raven had never mentioned it, because the idea had been planted and Summer didn't want it to take hold. She'd come to clear the air and ease her guilt over the way she'd disappeared on him.

Still, she should tell John exactly why she'd come to Bitter Bark...at least before she made out with him some more by the fire pit.

Guilt, that old familiar nemesis, crawled up her belly and settled like a stone in her chest. Was Summer ever going to get into a situation in life that *didn't* have her writhing with the most unwelcome, uncomfortable, and unpleasant emotions a person could feel?

She felt guilty because Isaiah chose to re-up for a second tour because of how rough things were at home. She felt guilty when she started a friendship with a man who'd been her husband's closest buddy on the battlefield. She felt guilty that she'd ended that relationship without explanation. She felt guilty when she relied on her mother and guilty when Destiny asked for a daddy.

And now she felt guilty for not telling John about Travis Shipley, even though there was nothing to admit other than she'd come to Bitter Bark to find him.

What would John do? Nice Man would probably offer to help her find him...and now she wasn't sure she wanted to. Which made her feel all kinds of guilty again, damn it.

"Mommy!"

"Hey, baby." She switched on the lamp next to the twin bed, finding Destiny's tear-stained face barely above the blankets. "Did you have a bad dream?"

"Wh-wh-where am I?"

"At a house in the North Carolina mountains, sweet angel." She sat on the edge of the bed and inched the blanket down over her shoulders, then smoothed her wild corkscrews of hair. "Remember? We're spending the summer in Bitter Bark, and you…" She leaned over her and kissed her nose. "Are going to Tails and Trails camp on Monday morning."

A faint smile pulled. "Where's Mavvie?" she whispered.

"I think he's asleep, honey, like all—"

A bark echoed from right outside the sliders, and Destiny instantly shot up. "Mavvie!" she cried. "Mavvie!"

Mav barked again in response.

"Can I let him see her?" John called from the living room.

"Doubt we can keep them apart," Summer replied.

A few seconds later, John stayed behind the doorjamb and held Mav with two hands, poking his little head into the room.

"Hi, Dessie," he said in a high-pitched cartoon voice, making them laugh. "Why aren't you asleep?"

Des giggled and sat up more, reaching her hands out. "Mavvie!"

John stepped into the room, keeping Mav front and center. "Here he is," he said. "Ready to give you a nice lick on the cheek for the night."

At Summer's nod, he set the puppy on the bed next to Destiny, who immediately smothered him with love and got plenty in return. While they had their reunion, Summer looked up at John with a grateful smile.

His return look wasn't exactly…grateful. It was

intense and dark and, holy hell, sexy. All the feelings that had bubbled up down by the fire came roaring back to the surface.

"Can he s-s-s-sleep with me?"

Good question, Summer thought. Can *he* sleep with *me*?

"Um…" John lifted a shoulder. "I don't know if your mom wants that."

So, so bad. She shook off the sexy musings and turned her concentration to Destiny and the dog she held. "Honey, you can't just sleep with…" She stole a glance at him, just in time to see his brow flick in interest. "He's not yours to sleep with."

"But he could be."

Oh yes, he could. "No, he is John's dog and…"

"Why doesn't he stay for a little bit?" John suggested. "Maybe until you fall asleep. Then your mommy can bring him back to me."

"I wa-wa-want him all night."

"Sometimes he has to go outside in the middle of the night," John said without hesitation. "And I don't think you want to go all the way down those stairs and stand out in the middle of the night while he does…"

"Business," she finished with a little smile. "Ew. No."

Summer laughed softly. "Then you can cuddle with him for a little bit, honey, then when you're asleep, he goes home."

"'Kay." She snuggled down in the blankets and brought Mav with her, curling him into her side. "Night."

"Good night," Summer said, standing and turning out the light. "Love you, baby girl."

"Love you, Mommy. And g-g-good night, nice man."

John closed his eyes and tried not to laugh. "Night, Destiny."

They stepped out into the hall as Summer closed the door behind her.

"I can't change her," he said, wrapping his arms around her waist and pulling her close so he could whisper in her ear. "But I can make *you* promise to never call me that again."

Laughing, she turned her face up to his, letting their lips brush. "I make no such promises."

They walked back into the dimly lit living room, and for a moment, they just stood very still, their arms around each other again. It felt natural, holding him like this and looking into his eyes. But if she let this go one more minute without telling him exactly why she'd come to Bitter Bark, she might wake up in his arms tomorrow—covered in guilt.

"I was right," she finally said.

"Hmm?"

"It's complicated. Any time there's a kid involved, it is complicated."

He frowned slightly. "What are you saying?"

"I'm saying that maybe I need a little time and space to…adjust to all this."

He studied her face for a long time, stroking his knuckles along her jaw, silent for a good many heartbeats. "It will not surprise you in the least that I will gladly give you time, space, air, and whatever you need until you don't need them anymore. Then…" He dipped his head and gave her one more long, sweet, tender kiss that sent fireworks through

121

her body and turned her knees to water. "You'll find out just how nice I can be."

"Oh...okay." She leaned back, her eyes still closed. "I'll bring Mav down when she's asleep," she said on a sigh.

"The door will be unlocked." He added with a light kiss on her forehead, then stepped away and disappeared onto the darkened deck.

She stayed right where she was, frozen in place, until his footsteps quieted and his sliding glass door rumbled to a close.

Oh, Summer. You came to Bitter Bark to find one man and somehow found yourself falling hard for another.

Chapter Nine

"Let's do one more flyover over Waterford and then head into Foothills Regional for the last landing today." Aidan's voice came through John's headset, steady and calm.

John banked the plane into a slight turn east, leaving the mountains behind him and the foothills ahead. "There it is," he said, his gaze scanning the rolling green and blues of prime North Carolina real estate. "Dogville, USA."

He could hear Aidan's laugh through the headset. "Trust me, it wasn't a bad place to grow up."

"I can imagine." Tipping the wing slightly, he got a good look at the vast acres of green grass, woods, creeks, mud paths, and ravines. Off to one side of the property stood Liam and Andi's house, then he flew over the winding stream and through deep-green woods, to see the yellow farmhouse and massive lawns, kennels, pens, and the lake that he knew so well by foot, but really appreciated only from up here. "We'll be there in a few hours for dinner," he mused. "But it won't look anything like this."

"You don't really get the scope of the place from

down there," Aidan agreed. "From up here, you can spot a squirrel in the backwoods, man."

John banked again, soaking up the view, then took his time and circled once more, loving every minute in the air.

"We better get back to the airfield, or we'll miss Sunday Bloody Marys," Aidan said, no doubt done with the two-hour lesson and ready to get back to his wife and extended family for the day at Waterford.

"Roger that." John changed his course and headed toward Foothills Regional Airport, only fifteen minutes away at this speed.

"Just watch the center line, John," Aidan instructed as they neared the runway, not quite as loud as air traffic control communicating with another plane headed in for a landing.

"Got it," John assured him, then switched his comm to alert ATC of their landing. "November Bravo six-nine-zero to runway two-one."

"Keep the nose steady and build the back pressure," Aidan reminded him.

"November Bravo six-nine-zero cleared for runway two-one," the controller acknowledged in John's headset.

"Okay, man, you got this," Aidan said. "Smooth as silk, just like last time."

"November Bravo coming in for final approach." John held his hands loose and steady on the throttle and yoke. He took his eye off the runway for one second, scanning the instrument panel, then back to the center line, gauging the wind, noting the speed.

"Flaps?" he asked Aidan.

"What do you think?"

"Not…quite…yet. Let me get to seventy-five knots," John muttered, trying hard not to just think, but to feel, as Aidan constantly told him. Feel the wind. Feel the speed. Feel the rudder pedal under his foot and the gentle bounce in the air. Don't calculate…feel.

"Now—"

"Flaps," John finished for him, flipping the switch just as the runway rose up and filled his windshield.

Center line. Center line. He bobbed a little, corrected with ease, dropped back the speed, and… touched down like a freaking feather had dropped.

"Nice!" Aidan fist-pumped. "That's three flawless landings today."

John put a loving hand on the throttle, pushing his headset back with a contented sigh. "I can't wait to log these hours and start soloing."

"Brother, you are killing it," Aidan said. "You were born to fly."

No kidding. "Best feeling in the world," he said as he turned off runway twenty-one and taxied toward the terminal.

"One of 'em," Aidan said.

"Name anything better."

Aidan gave him a goofy smile. "Uh, her name is Beck, and she's my wife."

John rolled his eyes, easing into the airfield, where a handful of private planes waited their turn to take a Sunday morning flight.

"No scoffing, Santorini," Aidan joked. "Anyway, I saw the way you were looking at Sunshine in her hot pants yesterday when she moved in."

"Summer. And I think they just call them cutoff shorts now, but who knows?"

"I know," Aidan said, sliding off his headset, too. "And what the hell's wrong with a little…summer fling?" He grinned. "Do you see what I did there?"

John laughed. "Nothing's wrong with it. 'Cept, you know, she has a kid."

"Kids sleep."

"And then they wake up in the middle of the night."

Aidan looked hard at him. "You're doing it again."

"What?"

"The only thing you do wrong in this cockpit, and probably the only thing you do wrong in life. You know what I'm going to say."

Of course he knew. "Don't think, just feel? Or some variation of that lesson?"

Aidan shifted in his seat, unbuckling his belt. "Your brain is an amazing thing, John. No question you got a stupid-high IQ. But when it comes to women and flying, and maybe a whole lot of things, you got to let that dome take a breather once in a while and think with a different part of your anatomy."

He *was*…and that was the part that had had him tossing and turning last night.

"I don't know." John shook his head with a hundred different thoughts, and not many of them were anything he'd discuss with Aidan. Or anyone.

"What don't you know?" Aidan asked. "What part is confusing you? She's gorgeous, she's single, right?"

"Right."

"She's living above you, working for you, and looks at you with the same goo-goo eyes you make at her."

John shot him a look. "You had me until goo-goo."

"Well, I don't know what they call it. Lusty. Hungry. Mama-wants-to-get-laid eyes."

She did look a little like that last night. He had felt her whole body shiver when they kissed, and her frustration with Destiny's interruption had been palpable. "But…"

"But what?" Aidan urged.

John stroked his beard, silent for a long moment. "Look, you're different than I am, Aidan. Your whole family—and mine, for that matter—is different. I'm kind of a go-it-alone type." It was one of the reasons he couldn't wait to fly solo.

"You don't date?"

"Oh yeah. I do." Couldn't quite remember the last time, though. "But relationships have a way of…blowing up in your face."

Aidan studied him for a moment. "Who said anything about a relationship? She'll be gone in what, two months?"

"Maybe less."

"So she's the perfect woman. No strings, no threat to your *solitude*." He put enough disdain into the word to let John know what Aidan thought of that particular lifestyle. "You can be a freaking monk come September. If it feels right, and she's into you?" He did that idiotic brow waggle again. "Summer fling." He gave his leg a slap as he cracked up.

"Dumb joke." But a really, really good idea.

"Seriously, think about it." Aidan unlatched his door and held up his hand. "On second thought, don't think about it. Go with your feelings on this one, John. For once in your damn life, don't think, just feel."

He wanted to, he really did. But how would he feel

127

when it was over? Maybe he shouldn't give a damn about that.

Don't think, just feel.

And, good God, Summer would feel...*amazing*.

"Baptism by fire. Can you handle it?" Cassie Mahoney's eyes gleamed playfully as she greeted Summer at Santorini's on Monday morning. "No, wait. You survived a family barbecue at Waterford last Friday night, so you're made of strong stuff."

"Survived and remembered everyone's names," she replied, shaking the hand Cassie offered. "You're Cassie, John's sister."

"Correct."

"Married to Braden Mahoney."

"Again, right on."

"And you're Yiayia's favorite."

She lifted a brow. "Which can be a blessing and a curse, as you might have figured out by now."

Summer laughed and took the menus that Cassie held out to her. "All I know is I don't want to cross her."

Cassie flipped back a lock of shiny black hair. "Then you know enough. Although, she's really mellowed in her old age. Anyhoo, I'm here to train you because my maiden name is Santorini, and I know almost as much about this business as John and Alex."

"Sounds good." She glanced around, noticing that for eight thirty in the morning, the restaurant wasn't that busy. "I wanted to come earlier, but had to drop Destiny off at camp."

"It's cool," she said. "We're kind of slow now, but brace yourself, that's going to change at ten when the runners start coming in."

"The runners?"

"There's a Five K-9 race this morning as part of Dog Days. Otherwise, we'd be a lot more crowded, but the hordes are up and down Ambrose Avenue at the finish line, and I suspect they'll pour in here when it's over. So we have an hour or so to train you."

Summer couldn't help looking back toward the kitchen. "Is John here?"

"He has the Monday staff meetings at the Chestnut Hill locations, so he's gone all day. Didn't he mention that to you?"

"I didn't see him at all yesterday," she said, trying to keep the little bit of disappointment out of her voice.

"He went flying with Aidan all morning," Cassie said, pulling some menus and a seating chart from the top shelf of the hostess stand. "Then we had Sunday dinner at Waterford, and that went into the night because everyone chipped in to get ready for Tails and Trails." She lifted a dark brow and leaned in to whisper, "Your absence was noted by the Dogmothers."

"My..." She shook her head. "I didn't know anything about it." She sucked in a horrified breath. "Was I supposed to be there? For camp or something?"

"Something." She winked. "Sunday dinner is all day every Sunday at Waterford, all family."

"Oh. Well, I'm not..."

"But they thought you'd show. There was much disappointment with the over-eighty set, and Pru, who is eighty at heart. Didn't he invite you?"

"No," she said. "But I..." *Asked for space and time.* "But I'm here now and ready for work."

"Thank God." She put the seating chart on top of the stand. "Fair warning, Summer. Being the hostess of a restaurant like this is a deceptively difficult job. For one thing, we don't even call you a hostess. You're running the front of the house, as we say, and that's a key role in any well-managed restaurant."

"I take it you've worked the job before?"

"In my sleep, but I've backed away from this business to run my own. John asked me to come in for a few hours to get you acclimated. You can thank me by naming your next child Cassie, because I had to stand on my head and do tricks to convince Yiayia not to come in and train you."

"Oh, that would have been—"

"A nightmare. She holds the dubious honor of running the front of Santorini's Deli for more years than any other person on earth. Actually, she invented the front of Santorini's, way back when it also had an actual deli counter. Her strict guidelines of front management would be the reason my mother, Katie, never worked much in the restaurant when we were growing up. Yiayia was there to find fault with every move. If she's in the restaurant, you want to be on your game."

"Duly noted." Summer replied with a smile. "So glad you're training me, then. Not sure about the name of my next child, though."

She waved a hand. "Just kidding. Kinda. Okay, any food service experience?"

"Giving out lunches to third-graders? Feeding a picky child? Um...eating?"

She laughed. "Actually, all helpful for this job. It really is more than just tossing menus at people and putting them in their seats, which is what most people think being a hostess is and why so many restaurants have problems."

She nodded. "I never really considered that before, but I can see why."

She waved Summer past the entry area and into the restaurant. "You run the show from up here. Stand in the place where you can see the door, the line, the counter, almost every table, and the entrance to the kitchen. The first thing you learn is how many tables each server can handle. Not how many they want or not, but you have to watch their faces, their body language, and those of their customers, to know whether they can handle another table."

The server she'd met the other day came whizzing by with two plates. "I can always handle another one," Karyn said with a bright smile. "Until two o'clock in the afternoon. Then I get nasty."

"Good to know," Summer said.

"We are primarily a breakfast and lunch place," Cassie told her. "Though we serve dinner a few nights a week. It's slower, and our regular server those nights usually handles the front, too, so you'll only have day shifts." She nudged her toward the kitchen. "Come on into the kitchen and meet the crew. And eat. You have to taste everything, you know. You're expected to chat up the specials on the way to the tables, which helps us move the right inventory. Big part of the job."

Cassie guided her into a kitchen that was smaller than Summer expected, with several servers taking orders, refilling condiments on a long bar, and joking around with the line cooks.

One, in particular, seemed to be the center of attention.

"Hey, Bash, quit flirting and get over here and meet our newest hire, Summer Jackson. Summer, this is Luther Sebastian, our very own Aussie just to make sure we stay international."

"Summer? Welcome aboard." A man ducked to get his face between a stainless-steel counter and the warming lights above it, beaming a wide smile from a sharp-featured, handsome face. "Lovely to meet you."

He had just enough of a lilting accent and a twinkle in his green eyes that she instantly knew why two of the younger servers were flocking around him.

"Where are you from?" Summer asked.

"Melbourne, originally. But I've spent the past five years cooking on cruise ships in the Med, until my buddy Alex Santorini convinced me to move to small-town America and make Greek food. Grab a fork and sidle up. I was just about to share my dolmades and courgette balls." He paused and slid into a dirty grin. "You like balls?"

"Shut it, Bash." Cassie put an arm around Summer and guided her away, pretending to show her the condiment and garnish bar. "He's going to want to get in your pants," she whispered. "And obviously is wasting no time. Consider yourself warned...*off*. He will next tell you that he makes love as well as he cooks. No one has confirmed that, but I don't want you to be the first."

Summer chuckled. "Thanks for the heads-up."

"I mean, do what you want," she added. "But remember, he's merely following family recipes, and he's a player, if you like that type."

"Not particularly."

"Good. Because I promised John I'd steer you away from him."

She blinked at the statement, and Cassie's candor. "He's...worried?"

"I wouldn't say he's worried. I'd say he's..." She smiled slowly and lifted a shoulder. "Smitten? Maybe just doing that 'claiming thing' Greek men do. I don't know. I married a big Irish firefighter."

Summer searched Cassie's pretty face, processing this new information about John, which shouldn't really surprise her, not after the kisses on Saturday night.

"Obviously, he knows you're short term," Cassie added quickly, as if she felt compelled to answer unasked questions. "But he's definitely interested. Are you?"

"I'm..." *Short term.* "Yeah," she said softly. "He's a great guy."

"The best," Cassie said. "I mean, I have four amazing brothers, and they're all different and wonderful. But there's something about John that..." She blew out a breath. "Just, be straight with him. Don't hurt him, okay?"

"I don't plan on it."

"Good, 'cause if that man's heart gets broken again, I'll be next in line to kill you. After Yiayia, of course."

"Let's go, ladies." The Australian accent floated through the kitchen. "Prepare to have your mouths—and everything else—melted by today's menu."

Cassie rolled her eyes. "Come on, taste. The rush'll be here soon."

After a very double-entendre-laden tasting and a quick tour of the kitchen and pantry storage, they took a slow pass through the two large dining areas with Cassie's dry-erase seating chart to help Summer learn the table numbers.

"Just remember," Cassie said when they returned to the hostess stand. "You are the first impression and the most lasting one. If customers have to wait, anything you can say and do to distract them makes the experience more enjoyable. Your job is to keep the flow, keep them happy, and be the face of Santorini's." She tipped her head and openly assessed Summer. "Obviously not Greek, but even Yiayia's relaxed on that one."

"Not Greek, but ready to go," she promised Cassie.

"When we have a wait, take names, keep the list, be tough but kind if people push for special treatment," Cassie continued, opening a drawer and pulling out a cell phone. "The more you can talk about the family, the history, and Greece, the better. Oh! Because of the race and the crush we're going to get, I'll be outside, because there'll be a lot of dogs. Normally, we let people seat themselves out there, but today will be a little crazy. On regular days, weather permitting, we encourage customers with large dogs to eat outside on the patio. I'll handle those tables with Gretchen."

"All right. Am I supposed to call you?" she asked, glancing at the phone.

"Oh, no, this is going to ring. We frequently get to-go orders and some large reservations on this line. And John sometimes forwards his phone to this number if he's in a meeting. You need to answer it. Just say, 'Santorini's Deli, may I help you?' Don't say, '*Can* I help you?' Because if Yiayia's on the other end, she'll bark back with, 'I don't know, *can* you?'" She did a dead-on impression of the older Greek woman, making Summer laugh.

"Oh! One more thing," Cassie said. "If people ask you why we don't have a deli counter at a place called Santorini's Deli, tell them it's left over from the original—"

The door popped open, and about fifteen adults, six noisy kids, and too many dogs to count entered, and Cassie immediately addressed them.

"We're having our guests with four-legged friends on the patio this morning," she called brightly, then turned to Summer. "Good luck!"

Just as she disappeared, more people spilled in, laughing, talking, distracted, and hungry.

Moving on instinct, she slipped into first-day-of-school mode, which helped her handle the bedlam of new arrivals who all want what they want and they want it now. She counted out menus, handed them to the patrons, and welcomed them all to Santorini's as she escorted them to the tables.

It didn't take long before the restaurant was full and noisy, the line was to the door, and holy hell, the phone was ringing.

She tapped the screen and pressed it to her ear, secretly hoping to hear John's voice.

"Santorini's Deli, may I help you?"

For a moment, there was nothing but silence, then a man cleared his throat. "Uh, yeah. Santorini's. I thought I was calling John."

She frowned a little at the gruff voice and the something in the tone that had a weird demand to it. Could this be the secret shopper? She straightened a little and turned from the crowd to do her best to wow the guy.

"I'm sorry, sir, Mr. Santorini isn't in the restaurant right now, but I can get a message to him as soon as possible. Can you tell me your name and number?" She slathered on the sweetness and professionalism, so hoping to help John land his financing.

"No. Damn it, Susan, he's not there." That last bit was a whisper she had a feeling she wasn't supposed to hear.

"I can tell him you called," Summer added. "He'll be checking for messages any minute." What else could she tell him that would impress the man? "He's at one of our other locations, and I can call him there if you like?"

The man grunted a little. "Your other locations?"

Shoot! Was she not supposed to say that? Did John's investor not know there were more Santorini's Delis? He had to, but—

"Excuse me, miss? Can you tell me if my name's been called?"

She spun around and gasped a little, coming face-to-face with Agnes Santorini. "Yiayia," she whispered with a little bit of shock.

"Oh, don't let me mess up the to-go order," she said as she realized Summer was on the phone. "Things seem to be running smoothly enough."

She held up her hand and returned to the far more important call, who might be John's investor.

"Can I get your name, sir? I promise he'll call you shortly."

"Shipley," he said, mumbling the word. But it came through loud and clear to Summer.

"*Travis*?" She breathed the name.

"What the hell did you say?" he demanded.

"Oh, nothing. I'm taking names at the front." Heat curled through her, the pressure and confusion of the moment nearly buckling her knees. "Shipley, you said?"

"Yes, George Shipley. The man who owns the building you're standing in. I need to talk to John as soon as possible."

"Okay, I'll tell him. I assume he has your number?"

"Yes. Tell him to use it, please."

With that, he hung up, and she stood stone-still with the phone at her ear.

George Shipley. Travis's father. The very connection she'd wanted from the minute she walked into this restaurant. And now she was working here, making friends, and…kissing the man who owned the place.

How *would* he feel when she told him the real reason for coming to Bitter Bark had been to reconnect with Travis Shipley, a man who shared a complicated past with her? How would he feel, this man who'd already asked his sister to warn Summer away from the flirtatious cook?

Guilt flashed like white lights in her head. She had to tell him, and soon. There'd be no more kissing until he knew the truth.

And if that wasn't incentive, she didn't know what was.

"Excuse me, my table?"

She lowered the phone and turned her attention back to Yiayia. The older woman had a playful smile in her eyes, and Summer knew she was busting her chops, as her big brother, Kenny, used to say.

But it was just one more reminder that she couldn't hurt John Santorini, or there would be hell to pay.

Chapter Ten

The sun was low over the mountains by the time John got home after a long day in Chestnut Creek. The rolling purple horizon faded into a peach sunset, highlighting two silhouettes on the lawn at the bottom of the hillside driveway. No, three, if you counted Mav, who was running between a slender girl and a shapely woman, chasing what looked like a beach ball they were tossing back and forth.

For a moment, before his 4Runner tires hit the driveway and stole their attention, he slowed at the top of the hill, watching the vignette unfold in his yard. Summer kicked the ball lightly, which made Mav bark and run after it, and Destiny scooped it up in her tiny arms, raising it in victory with a giggle that floated through his open window.

But the giggle faded, her shoulders dropped, and she skulked back to Summer with something that almost seemed like sadness in her body language. Her mother, of course, put an arm around her. Was something wrong?

A little surprised at just how much that jolted him, he turned into the drive, making them both look up and wave. And another jolt hit him, this time down to his toes.

What would it be like to come home to that every night?

Wheels started cranking in his head, reasons why that would never happen, how thinking about it made no sense, and the only logical thing to do was not get attached to this woman and her child.

There he went again. Thinking instead of feeling.

Okay, so how would it *feel* to come home to that every night?

As he got closer to the lawn, Summer broke away and walked toward the drive, her long bare legs a treat to watch, her woman's body moving with a mix of elegance and sexiness, a gorgeous smile widening with each step.

It would feel *great*.

"Hey there," he called as he parked and climbed out. "I heard you killed it at Santorini's today."

Summer brushed back hair that had escaped from her ponytail. "Who said it?" she asked. "Cassie or Yiayia?"

"Bash. Your new biggest fan."

She waved her hand as if she couldn't care less about the Aussie cook, thank God. "I'm only interested in the Santorini powers that be. Cassie said it went well, and Yiayia said I didn't suck, which I believe is probably a Bminus."

"It's a solid A."

And so was she. He let his gaze coast over her, taking his time to appreciate the freckled freshness of her face, and the barely there light sheen of perspiration on her collarbones, and the way that white tank top clung to her body. "Looks like you're playing as hard as you worked."

She laughed and turned toward Destiny, who was kicking the ball and trying to get Mav to run with her to get it.

"We're attempting a game to give her some confidence."

"Confidence?" He frowned. "Did she have a problem at camp?"

"No, she loved it, all but one thing. Come on, I'll let her tell you."

He paused and gestured toward the car. "I brought a ton of stuff from the restaurant in Chestnut Creek, if you guys haven't had dinner yet. Lots of that plain chicken Destiny likes. Or have you had your last bite of Greek food?"

She beamed up at him. "Wow, that was so thoughtful. She had a snack after camp, and I figured we'd run out and get something for dinner. And yes, I'd love more Greek food, thank you."

He tried to look away, to head over to Destiny, even to greet Mav—who'd yet to notice he'd arrived—but he took one more second to soak in the sight of Summer in the late afternoon sun, her hair messy, her eyes soft with a little exhaustion and maybe happiness.

"So, do you like your new job?" he asked after a beat.

"Very much," she replied without hesitation, her gaze just as intent on him. "I missed the boss, though," she added softly, as if the admission was hard to make.

"You…" He tapped her nose just to give in to the

urge to touch even one centimeter of her skin. "Asked for time and space."

"Is that why you were gone for two whole days?"

"I had family things yesterday and staff meetings today. I'm yours tomorrow. And...tonight."

She flushed slightly at that. "Cassie said you flew with Aidan."

"I did. Two more hours and four total landings, not one of which was less than perfect, I might add. I'm eight hours closer to being able to do my solo hours, then test out for my license." He paused a moment, getting slightly closer. "Will you fly with a rookie like me when I do?"

She thought about it for a moment. "You know, I'm not the best flier, but I would with you."

"A very high compliment, thank you." He put a light hand on her shoulder. "Come on, let's go hear about camp and see if my dog remembers who loved him first."

"Good luck with that. I don't think they've been more than five feet apart all day." She walked with him across the grass. "Remember, being 'camp buddies' was your idea."

Laughing, he rounded the fire pit to go out to where Des was sitting on an exercise ball, bouncing up and down.

"So how was day one at Tails and Trails, kiddo?"

Mav reacted first, barking and running in a quick circle at the sight and sound of John, then scampering toward him. John crouched down to give the pup some love, keeping his eye on Destiny as he waited for her to answer.

She slowed her bounce a little, making her insane

curls look like they were moving in slow motion. She opened her mouth to answer, then closed it again, nodding. He'd been around her enough to know that's what she did when she didn't trust herself not to stutter.

"Make some new friends?" he asked, helping her out.

She nodded again, reminding him not to stick with yes-or-no questions.

"How did Mav do?" He turned the puppy on his back for a belly rub. "Did you have fun, little dude?" he whispered playfully to the dog.

"He s-s-sat." She slipped off the ball and took a step closer. "For a t-t-t-treat."

"Really?" John plopped on his backside and scooped the dog up. "You sat like a big dog, Maverick?" He brought the puppy up to his face. "Good boy!"

Des looked up at Summer. "Did you tell him, Mommy?" she whispered.

"No, I didn't tell him anything."

John looked from one to the other, curious. Also amazed at how much beauty God managed to pack into two so different creatures. Two different creatures who seemed just a little...not happy. "Was there a problem at camp?" he asked.

"Most of it was wonderful, right, Des?"

She nodded, hard and enthusiastic. "We played games," she said softly. "And...and...and...ate chicken fingers."

"Good stuff, yeah. What else?"

"T-t-trained dogs to sit."

"Did Shane handle that part?" he asked, aching to

make her so comfortable she could talk without a struggle. "He's the best dog trainer."

"Yeah," she said, smiling. "He's f-f-funny."

"Very," he agreed. "What else did you do?"

She glanced up at her mother again, then down to the ground. "They p-p-played s-s-soft…"

"Softball?" he suggested.

She looked up. "I couldn't play," she whispered, a little crack in her voice.

"Why not?"

She gave a pleading face to her mother, as if whatever she had to say was just too much.

Summer dropped down on the grass next to John, reaching for Destiny's hand to fold the little girl on her lap. "She had a problem," Summer said, stroking her daughter's hair but looking at John. "With the ball."

"The ball?"

Summer's eyes grew wide. "I didn't like it," she said.

"Oh. Well, you don't have to play, right? I think they do two activities at once so you can pick something else."

"You didn't tell me that, Des," Summer said. "What's the other activity?"

"Singing," she said softly. "Or crafts."

"Well, you love to sing," John said. "I've heard you. You're an amazing singer."

She looked up at him, a dark cloud in her evocative hazel eyes. "Not always," she said. "Sometimes I st-st-st…" She swallowed. "I can't."

His heart folded in half. "But with Mav?" he asked. "He sings, too."

"It's during dog nap time. Mav has to take a lot of naps because he's so small."

"Then how about crafts?" John asked. "Is that like coloring?" He was woefully out of it where kids' activities were concerned.

Destiny made a face.

Summer stroked her hair some more. "She's not really a craft girl," she said. "Never liked art projects, can't stand Play-Doh, and tried to eat her crayons."

John squished his face, making Destiny giggle. "Were they good?"

"Pink was," she said with a sly smile.

"Got your mother's wit, eh?" he teased, giving Summer's arm a slight nudge. "Okay, then that leaves softball, which would be my first choice. What's the deal? You didn't want to play that, either?"

"I did," she breathed with pure longing in her voice. "But I…I don't like the b-b-ball. It's scary."

"The ball coming at her," Summer explained. "They lined up and played catch, and even with the little kids, she has this…fear, I guess, that the ball's going to hit her."

"Oh, I know that feeling," he said, absently touching his glasses. "Even when I wore sports goggles to correct my sight, I always had that low-key expectation that the ball would hit me in the face."

"I hoped you'd understand," Summer said. "I remember you said you were a catcher. You know about stuff like this."

"Fear of being hit with the ball? So real," he assured her. "Even in softball. Even with that ball." He pointed at the exercise ball. "Though it wouldn't hurt as much."

"I had that in the back of my SUV," Summer said. "We decided to try and practice with it, to get her used to catching a ball. But…"

"It's different," he said, leaning a little closer to Destiny. "I might be able to help you. If there's one thing I know how to do, it's how to catch a ball."

"Pretty sure you know more than that," Summer said.

"Yeah. Calculus. But I know there won't be any of that at camp, thank God. I'll help you with catching the ball."

Destiny looked at him. "How?"

"Well, you build up to it. First, I'll roll the ball to you and teach you how to scoop it up. Then we'll move to a toss. Very slowly."

She stared at him, considering that.

"Or you can make bracelets," Summer said.

She curled her lip. "I'll try, John," she whispered, the sweet voice practically tearing his heart out.

"Gimme a few minutes." He pushed up. "I have to dig up some old gear from the loft in the garage and change. And get a Gatorade. Because all ballplayers drink Gatorade." He winked at Des. "You do want to be a ballplayer, right?"

She broke into a slow smile. "Yeah."

As he stood, he put a hand on Summer's shoulder. "You okay if I teach her a few tricks?"

"Of course." Her blue eyes were full of warm affection. "I was hoping you would."

He gave her shoulder a soft squeeze and headed inside to change into shorts and a T-shirt, the whole time mentally going through the sports equipment he'd been dragging around with him his whole life.

In a few minutes, he'd climbed to the garage loft and started popping open big plastic containers full of helmets, mitts, bats, balls, and catcher's masks. He abandoned one, then pushed a few boxes aside with his focus on a small container in the back.

His mother had kindly kept this in their attic at home until she moved into a condo when Dad died. All the Santorini kids had their shot at the belongings in the attic. Nick had taken nothing—probably because his life had him in all kinds of foreign places, and neither had Alex, who instead wanted all Dad's kitchen equipment. Theo and Cassie had been selective and parted with a lot of their stuff.

But John had kept all of his trophies, his sporting equipment, and even his uniforms. He lifted a small mitt, nodding with the success of finding it. It might be a little big for Destiny, but it would work. And then he found exactly what he'd been looking for—a junior-sized catcher's mask that had been his first when he took the position in Little League.

Not very many guys wanted to be the catcher. First of all, one mistake and you could blow the whole game. Not to mention it hurt like a mother to crouch back there for long innings. But his coach had told him he had to do it because a catcher also had to anticipate every single possible play and be three steps ahead of the other players. That actually appealed to John more than the possibility of hitting a home run or stealing a base.

He gathered up the gear, tossed it to the garage floor, and climbed down the ladder with a deep sense of satisfaction growing. Destiny could really use this. Sports had given this four-eyed brainiac real confidence in life, and she could use a little of that.

"Okay, you ready to catch, Des?" he called as he jogged back outside. "Oh darn. I forgot the Gatorade."

"I'll get it," Summer said. "And while you play, I'll set up dinner on your patio table, if that's okay."

"Perfect." As he passed her, he leaned in a little closer to whisper, "Have you had enough air, space, and time yet?"

She slowed her step and nibbled on her lower lip, looking so directly into his eyes that he could feel the heat of her gaze through his whole body. "Maybe."

"Good. 'Cause I want to talk to you later."

She didn't answer at first, but breathed out a slow sigh. "Yes, good. I have to talk to you, too."

"Everything okay?" Because the way she said that didn't sound quite right.

"Yeah, yeah." She sighed. "But I have to tell you something."

Oh. That didn't sound promising. "Then we'll talk."

She reached up and touched his face, a featherlight fingertip along his beard. "Thanks, John. For helping her. And for being so…"

"If you say nice…" he teased.

"Actually, I was thinking…" She just smiled and let her hand fall to his shoulder, then down to the edge of his T-shirt sleeve, grazing his bicep. "Never mind what I was thinking."

Never mind? Not when it was exactly the same thing he was thinking.

He watched her walk toward the house, not surprised when Mav followed her with his tongue out, panting.

"I get that, pupper. I really do." He picked up the

child's mitt and the small catcher's mask. "All right, now, let's play ball."

Destiny stared at the mask. "What's that?"

"A confidence builder. C'mere." He slid it over her face and adjusted the strap, careful not to snag her curls. "And this…" He handed her the mitt. "Is my lucky glove from T-ball," he said. "It'll change everything for you. Now, you stand right there, and I'll be just over here. We'll start with grounders. Slow and low, and you only have one job."

"Wh-wh-what?"

"Never, ever, not for one second, take your eye off the ball. Got it?"

She nodded, her little face so serious.

"Let's go, Des. Let's make a ballplayer out of you."

That made her smile and turn to where her mother was.

"Uh-uh," he reminded her, holding the ball up with his fingertips. "Right here. Always. When it comes close, you scoop it right up in that glove."

Kneeling down, he rolled the ball to her, hard and straight enough that it went right into that glove, which suddenly felt very lucky again.

Chapter Eleven

Summer stepped out onto her deck, holding a cup of not-yet-brewed tea, and released a mother's long, soft sigh of exhaustion. It was the exhale she always let out after a busy day, a chaotic bath hour, the reading of a favorite book, and good-night kisses. Only, tonight's kisses included one from a dog who *somehow* managed to be part of the whole process.

But now that it was over, Summer could have her tea in peace and relaxation.

Except that nothing in her felt peaceful or relaxed.

Despite having one of the most enjoyable evenings she could remember, it felt like every cell in her body vibrated with…anticipation and nerves, and a mix of dread and longing.

She wanted this "secret" off her chest, because the longer she waited to tell John about Travis Shipley, the more of a wedge it could drive between them. And right now, as she slipped deeper into her attraction, she didn't really want *anything* between them.

True, they barely knew each other, but she couldn't remember the last time she'd felt an electrical current that arced like this with a man. And it wasn't merely physical.

Watching him work with Destiny to learn how to catch ground balls, marveling at his patience and humor and, yeah, his graceful moves and those delicious shoulders, she could literally feel the pull at her heart and body.

Definitely her body. They could start there. They might end there, but they wouldn't get anywhere if she didn't tell him that she'd come to Bitter Bark to find Travis Shipley. He deserved to know that.

Holding her tea bag and cold water, she crossed the deck and leaned on the railing, looking out to the last drops of purple light in the mountains. Below her, she heard John's footsteps downstairs on his covered patio, and even just that little bit of proximity woke the butterflies in her belly.

How could she spend a whole summer this close—living and working within a few feet of him—and *not* give in to the tension that tugged at her? Every casual touch, every shared laugh or too-long eye contact had her wanting to lean in and feel the brush of his beard against her mouth. Against her...everywhere.

"You coming down, Juliet?"

He walked out to the yard, near the fire pit, gazing up at her deck. He hadn't started a fire yet, but she suspected he might as darkness fully descended over midsummer skies.

Sitting by the fire would be a good place to tell him her tale.

She glanced at the mug in her hand, suddenly wondering if she didn't want something a little stronger than Sleepytime tea. Because she sure didn't feel like…sleeping.

"Bath is done," she told him. "Book is read. Baby is tucked. But I don't think she's quite asleep yet, so I don't have Mav."

"Mav is fine where he is. And I have some of Overlook Glen's finest here, unless you prefer your tea."

She set the teacup on a glass-topped table without hesitation. "You are my hero. Coming down."

He was waiting for her at the bottom of the steps, meeting her eye to eye when she reached the second-to-last step. She could smell the lingering scent of soap and see that the ends of his hair were wet against the collar of a fresh T-shirt, curling and tempting her fingers to touch them.

Couldn't she wait to tell him her secrets? Couldn't she just taste one kiss before it all became a big confession?

"You look…troubled." He grazed the lightest finger along her jaw, the touch so pure and inviting, her whole body responded by moving just a hair closer to him.

And there was the perfect opening…just handed to her. All she had to say was, *I am troubled, John. I have to tell you something.*

"Tough bath and bedtime routine?" he asked when she didn't answer.

"No, not all. She's very happy," she said, a smile pulling. "Yogi."

"Is that the book you read?" he guessed.

"I think your call sign could be Yogi. Wasn't Yogi Berra a catcher?"

He chuckled, his finger moving to her hair, twirling a strand as he looked at her. "One of the best ever."

"Well, as coaches of scared little five-year-old girls go, you are one of the best ever. So, Yogi."

He made a face. "That's not very…hot."

She laughed, wanting to say, *Well, you are.* Instead, she put both hands on his wonderful shoulders and drew him a little closer. "Thank you for what you did out here before dinner. And during dinner, with all those tips and tricks about watching the ball. And…now. With wine and…" She slid her hands into those damp curls. "You're sweet."

And she didn't want this all to come to a crashing halt when he found out she was here for one reason…and it wasn't to adopt a dog, which they could have done anywhere.

"Sweet." He dropped his forehead against hers. "I think that might be a promotion from nice."

"Keep working," she teased, lightly dragging her nails over his neck, enjoying the tension in his muscles. "You are most definitely on your way to sexy."

"I've always been ambitious like that." He lifted her chin slightly, bringing her mouth a little closer to his. "What do I need to do to get my next upgrade?"

"You could…" She felt her eyes shutter a bit, his warm breath on her lips, the deep ache in her body making her want to press against him just for the pleasure of feeling his hard chest against her breasts. As if he read her mind, and body, he wrapped one arm around her waist and eased her closer. "Do that."

He brushed her lips with an air-soft kiss. "And that?"

"Mmm. Yeah." She added pressure to the kiss, loving the tickle of his soft beard around her lips. Splaying her hands against his head, she deepened the kiss to elicit a low, sexy groan that rumbled in his chest as his tongue met hers for the first time.

All that teasing touch did was make her ache with a sudden need.

"Much more of this, Summer," he murmured into the kiss, "and we're gonna start a whole different kind of fire."

She sighed into his mouth, taking one more taste of his lips, like licking the last drop of chocolate before the dessert spoon was taken away.

"And I'm fine with that..." He leaned back, cupping her face. "Way more than fine, frankly." He glided his thumb over her throat, making her knees nearly buckle. "I could kiss you until tomorrow. Until..." He smiled and inched her closer so she could feel every muscle and the effect she was having on him. "The end of summer, Summer."

"Mmm." She closed her eyes completely and leaned into him, the echo of all she had to tell him deafening in her head.

"But that's not what you want," he guessed. "Which I completely—"

She placed a finger over his lips. "Yes, it is," she said, looking right into his eyes. "But let's talk, okay? Make that fire and...talk." She stroked the soft whiskers again. God, it would be so good with him. So easy and fun and hot and...*damn it.* "I have to tell you something."

"Oh, that's right." He backed up a step, taking a breath for composure. "I forgot. Is it something at work?"

How to blurt out this story? It was complicated and emotional. Would he understand? Was he that nice? Or would he see her in a whole different light, like a woman who'd unfairly led a man on and then dumped him in the most unceremonious way?

"Hey, I'll take that wine now," she said.

"Come on." Holding her hand, he guided her across the grass to the fire pit, where a bottle and two plastic glasses were on a table next to one of the chairs.

He poured with a little ceremony, then offered her a glass. "What should we drink to?"

She smiled and lifted her glass. "Your promotion from nice to sweet to sexy to…"

He raised one brow, waiting.

"Understanding."

While she sipped, he studied her, a little confusion in his eyes, which softened to something sad. "You're leaving," he said, obviously misinterpreting the toast. "Quitting. Taking Des. Walking out and ending my Summer fling before it happens."

She had to laugh at *Summer fling*. "Not quitting or leaving…unless you fire me and kick me out."

Relieved, he finally took his sip, then set the glass down to work on the fire. "If you're cold before I get this going, there's a blanket on the back of that chair."

She wasn't cold, but she took the soft throw anyway, wrapping herself protectively. She watched him pile the logs with precision and a plan, admiring his grace and strength, his spare movements, the athlete's body, all topped by that keen brain.

She took another sip and waited until the fire was started, and he sat down next to her and picked up his glass to take a drink.

"So, did you get the message that George Shipley called you?" she asked.

He stopped mid-sip, fighting to swallow. "Yeah, Karyn told me when she did the bank tonight and checked in." Then he turned to her. "Is that what you're worried about? That I didn't get a message?" He searched her face for a moment. "Is that what you had to tell me?"

"No. Yes. Kind of."

"Well, I got the message. Called him back and left one in return." He put his glass on the fire pit's brick wall. "He's my landlord, at least for the moment. Did anyone tell you that? Did you say something you think you shouldn't have?"

"I know who he is," she said slowly. "In fact, I know...I know a bit about him."

He stayed very still, except for the frown that formed and the fact those shoulders she'd just admired so much tensed slightly. "You do? You know the guy who owns my building?"

"I've never met him, but I know his son, Travis."

He stared at her for a moment. "I don't," he said. "I heard they have a son. Heard he was in..." He tipped his head a little, as if a puzzle piece had dropped into place. "The military. Afghanistan, right? Did your husband know him?"

She nodded. "Yes. He was very good friends with my husband, as a matter of fact."

"Really." She could hear the tiniest bit of something in his voice. Surprise, of course. Maybe disappointment. A little distrust. "The son of the guy who owns my building?"

She nodded.

"You didn't think to mention that to me?" he asked, just enough misgiving in his voice that it knotted her stomach.

"I didn't plan on getting to know you or living here or working…" She shook her head, as disgusted with the lame excuses as he probably was. "It's why I came to Bitter Bark. To…meet him in person. I'd only talked with him on the phone and Skype before."

He shifted in his seat, the wheels of his great brain almost visibly turning as he processed all of this and no doubt formed a million new questions.

During the moment of silence, she picked up her wineglass, seeking some liquid courage, but the fine Pinot Noir suddenly tasted metallic in her mouth, and she set it right back down.

"Did he ask to meet you?" John finally asked, putting his hand on hers as if that would help to soften his question. "To tell you something about your husband? Grieve with you? Or did you just want to help him through what must be a tough thing? Survivor's guilt or…or PTSD?"

She almost smiled, because all those possibilities were so…John. Expecting the best, looking for a logical reason why she'd leave her home and come to a small town in North Carolina seeking a man she'd never actually met.

"Yes, he had survivor's guilt. In fact, it's fair to say that's how it started."

"How…what started?"

She tried to ignore the fact that he pulled his hand away as he asked the question.

"I don't exactly know what you'd call it, but I'll go with…friendship," she replied. "Travis Shipley and I

157

had a friendship. We never met in person, but it went on for quite some time."

Silent, he listened intently, making her wish he'd ask a question, but sensing that he was just waiting for all that she'd tell him.

"He first contacted me to talk about Isaiah. They were really close over there. He'd heard a lot about me and wanted to, exactly as you say, share the grief."

"But it went further than that?" he guessed.

"Yeah, it did." After a moment, she bit her lip and looked at him. "After about a year of talking regularly on the phone, over Skype, and through email, Travis said he was in love with me."

"And were you in love with him?"

She didn't answer instantly, and she could practically feel John's body tense in those few seconds of silence. "No," she said softly. "I was grieving, lost, scared, and needed a friend who really knew Isaiah. Somehow, over time, Travis took that to mean… something deeper. I think he misinterpreted my openness and vulnerability as something more."

"What happened?"

"I ended it, but not with much…grace." She sighed again, wishing she had the right words that didn't make her feel so awful. "I changed my number and took down my Skype address, and…I ghosted him. Hard. And that's why I came here."

"To pick up where you left off?"

"To apologize," she replied without hesitation. "I owe him an explanation. I owe both of us closure."

He stared into the flames, silent. Even under his beard, she could see his jaw tense.

She blew out a breath, realizing how hard her heart was pounding. "Please say something, John."

"I don't know what to say," he whispered, pushing up. "I'm going to get a glass of water. You want one?"

She looked up at him, seeing exactly what she didn't want to see in his firelit expression. Sadness. Hurt. Uncertainty. Confusion. Doubt. And, worst of all, distrust.

"I'm fine," she said. "Thanks."

He walked away and into the house, leaving her to wonder exactly what he'd say when he came back. *If* he came back.

Chapter Twelve

For once in his life, John was feeling and not thinking.

And it didn't feel great.

He stared into the sink as cold water poured from the faucet, the urge to throw some on his face much stronger than the need to drink any. What he really needed was time to think—not feel—and decide exactly what this meant, if anything.

It meant he really couldn't trust Summer completely. Why hadn't she told him this on day one? What would have changed if she had? Was she telling the truth about not being in love with Travis? About wanting only to apologize? Because this was a mighty big trip to make—with her five-year-old—just to say something she could have handled over the phone or in an email.

And did she realize Travis Shipley wasn't just a guy from Bitter Bark, but the son of a man John was trying to close a deal with? Maybe it didn't matter, but maybe it did.

He pushed the faucet handle with a little more force than necessary, shutting off the stream and all the damn feelings rushing through him.

Be freaking logical, John. First of all, it was way too soon to care this much. This was a fling, not a relationship. Not even that yet. Just an acquaintance with a woman who happened to be in town...to find another guy who used to live here. Who cared? Yeah, she might have told him sooner, but she'd told him now.

So now they could...fling.

Even the word made him feel a little sick. Was he even capable of that kind of thing? He wasn't Aidan. He wasn't Alex. He had to be true to himself. And his unexpected response to this news kind of proved he wasn't born to be cavalier about things like this.

Taking a long, slow inhale to steady himself, he skipped the water after all and headed back to the fire pit, surprisingly relieved to see her still sitting, waiting for him.

"You okay?" she asked, looking up at him.

"Sure, yeah. Fine." He settled back in his seat, questions rising. "How about you?"

She gave a wistful smile, a mix of sadness and, oh hell, pity in her eyes. Damn it. He didn't want that. "I'm suffering from my greatest affliction, I'm afraid."

He lifted a questioning brow.

"Guilt," she said. "It's my personal demon and always has been."

He eyed her. "You feel guilty for not mentioning this to me?"

"Among other things. My guilt is like baggage I can't unload. And I thought if I apologize to Travis, I'll feel...lighter."

Travis again. "Is that the only reason you want to see him?"

She looked at him, holding his gaze for a long time. "I think it's the only reason, but..."

His gut tightened. *But.*

"My sister-in-law thinks it could be more."

He gave her another questioning look. "Isaiah's sister?"

"Raven. She encouraged me to come here and talk to him. She's always thought..." Her voice trailed off, and he didn't pursue what Raven thought. He could probably figure it out all by himself. *She's always thought they belong together*, or some such thing.

He took a sip of wine and wound up his next question. "Is that why you talked to me? To find him?"

"No," she said quickly, turning to him. "Not the first time in the square. I had no idea who you were. And yes, it was why I went into Santorini's, but again, no idea you owned the place. And to be honest, trying to find Travis did make me chat with your grandmother, because she said her name, and I figured *she* was the owner. But getting to know you? As a way to get to him? Please, no."

"Then why not tell me sooner?"

She lifted a shoulder. "I guess, deep inside, I knew this..." She gestured from him to her and back again. "Might come to a screeching halt. When you kissed me the other night, I knew I had to tell you. And I knew it could cost me..."

If she didn't have feelings for the guy, why would she worry that it could affect their own budding relationship?

He didn't ask, probably because he didn't really want to know.

Instead, he picked up his wineglass and drank, then turned to her, digging deep for logic and thoughts instead of the squishy thing called emotions that were muddled up inside of him. "So tell me about all this guilt you feel."

"Yes, Dr. Freud." She chuckled softly, reached for her own wine, and sipped again. "I've always been a bit of a pleaser by nature, anxious to make my parents and brother and teachers happy and suffering a bit when I didn't. It really came to a head after Isaiah and I got married. And especially when he went on his second tour...his last one. Then I wallowed in guilt."

"Why would you feel guilty about his deployment? You can't take the blame for that."

"Oh, but..." She ran a hand through her hair, then lifted her feet to rest them on the brick wall around the fire pit, as if readying herself for a good, long story. "Isaiah and I got married young," she said. "Way too young. Both twenty-one, literally weeks out of college, where we met on our first night at an FSU dorm get-acquainted thing. He was in ROTC, and I was in elementary ed, and after that night, we never separated, never dated anyone else, never had a best friend in the dorm or a sorority or anything. It was Isaiah and Summer, like one."

He nodded, drinking his wine, filing away this information. So she was generally a one-man woman. He liked that, and it fit his own style.

"Anyway, our parents weren't thrilled with us getting married so young, but they came around and they've been great. We didn't want to wait until after he did his whole Army service, so we got married a month after graduation. He got stationed at Fort

Benning in Georgia for training and was deployed in less than a year."

He imagined her as a very young married woman, traipsing around Army bases, worrying about a husband at war. Alone. But not for too long, he surmised, since she'd had a baby at twenty-three. "So, Destiny came along quickly?"

She sighed. "Very. We spent the weekend before he shipped out in Destin, Florida." She waited a beat, lifting her brow. "She defied the odds, or at least the birth control, so we named her after the place of her conception and how it all felt at the time…Destiny."

That made him smile. "It's a perfect name for her."

"Isn't it?" she agreed. "Isaiah wasn't there when she was born, but made it back when she was six months old. He was still at Benning, but I'd spent my pregnancy and her first six months with my parents in Orlando. Adjusting to life back in Georgia with him home was…" She sighed sadly. "Hard," she finished.

"How so?"

"Honestly, we were at each other's throats constantly, in over our heads with a baby—and, oh my God, she was *not* an easy baby. Anyway, Isaiah signed up for another tour and I think it was because he wanted to get away, though he never admitted that. So from the minute he left, I felt guilty. Guilty because I was relieved. Guilty because our family wasn't picture perfect. Guilty because I thought he chose combat duty over Destiny and me. And when he was killed…"

She closed her eyes, and John couldn't stop himself from putting a hand on her arm. "It had to be the worst thing ever."

Silent, she sat still, then put her hand over his, pressing it harder against her skin. "I was…breathless. I knew he faced danger, and I knew all along he might not come back, but when it happened…when I became a widow and single mother and knew I'd never see him again and Destiny had no father? I couldn't help thinking it was somehow my fault. If I'd been a better wife, he wouldn't have chosen to re-up…" Her voice cracked, and he squeezed her arm, lost when she turned and looked at him with tears brimming.

"When he died, I was absolutely broken. Terrified. Lost. And…" She offered him a rueful smile. "Along came Travis Shipley to bring another bag of guilt for me to lug around."

He lifted his hand and tried to cover his reaction, which was some dark and unfamiliar mix of jealousy and sympathy, and completely unwelcome. He had zero right to be jealous, that was for damn sure. And sympathy? There wasn't enough for what she'd been through.

"He emailed me with condolences about a month after Isaiah died. He sent a picture that was taken after Isaiah beat him in a ping-pong tournament. And I wrote back, of course."

So far, it all sounded pretty innocent. Neither of them spoke for a few minutes, the only sound the crackle of the fire and the faintest breeze in the trees.

She dug both hands into her hair and pulled it back off her face with a soft groan. "When we started talking, we were both pretty wrecked. He had a lot of guilt, too, about Isaiah's death."

"Why?"

"He wasn't far from Isaiah, maybe ten feet away, cleaning out an area where insurgents had been, when the IED exploded. Travis frequently said how easily it could have been him. 'There but for a few inches,' he'd say. 'It could have been me as easily as him.'" Her voice faded as she got lost in a memory that John was pretty sure he didn't want to share.

"Anyway," she continued. "Travis got a tech assignment that gave him hours and hours of free time and access to a computer with an internet connection, so we were able to talk and Skype with surprising ease. He seemed like the only person who knew what I was going through. We both loved Isaiah, both missed him, and both felt weirdly responsible for his death."

Which they weren't, but John stayed silent while she took a breath and another sip of wine before she continued.

"After about a year of these calls and Skypes," she continued, "Travis told me how he felt. Like I said, the feelings weren't reciprocated. I cared for him, but not…" She shook her head. "No, not love."

Was she trying to talk herself out of it?

"But that very same week, I got a package from the Army with some personal belongings from Isaiah's locker that had been stuck in some…I don't know, warehouse. Some clothes and things, and in the package was a letter he'd written the day before he died. He loved to write physical letters," she said. "Email was easy, but I'd sent him yellow legal pads and envelopes and stamps, and he used them to write what he called 'good old-fashioned letters.' So in his stuff was one he was in the middle of writing, and he spent a good page and a half talking about Travis, how much their friendship meant to him, and what a great musician he was. Call me crazy, but I almost felt like it was Isaiah talking from the grave, telling me...he *knew* about this...this friendship and didn't appreciate where it could go."

So it could go...*there*. He filed that, too.

"And to make it all just crazy and so much worse, this was right around the time I realized that Destiny had a stutter that didn't look like it would go away."

"Oof." He choked softly. "Talk about a flood of guilt."

She smiled at him, her eyes warm. "Thank you for understanding that. I was *drowning* in that stuff."

"So you ghosted him."

"Not immediately, but soon after."

He thought about all that for a long time, his unfocused gaze on the dancing flames and burning embers. After a few minutes, he turned to her and asked the question that burned hotter than the fire.

"Summer, do you think the real reason you came here, whether you realize it or not, was to pick up where you left off? To see if there was any *there* there?"

To her credit, she didn't answer right away, and with each passing second, his gut tightened as he waited. Because if she was here to start up a romance with another guy, he wasn't interested in pursuing even a fling.

"No," she finally said. "I am determined not to be a victim of guilt. I came to unload some of mine, offer a genuine apology, and give him that letter from Isaiah because I think it would mean a lot to him and help with *his* guilt. But I didn't want to just call or email or whatever. I feel I owe it to him to do this in person because I truly hate the way I disappeared on him."

"Why didn't you break it off in a more…"

"Classier way?" she supplied when he couldn't come up with the right word. "'Cause Travis is the most persuasive man alive. I tried a few times to slow things down or not be available, but he always had a way of convincing me that we were meant to be together. So I cut him off. He didn't know my street address and had absolutely no way of finding me, and that's how I wanted it."

Great. She was here to find the most *persuasive* man alive who already announced he was in love with her.

John pushed up to stoke the fire, using a stick to jab at the logs with a little bit more force than necessary. When the flames flared, he looked over them, the golden light capturing all the mixed emotions on Summer's beautiful face.

"What made you think he was here?" he asked.

"I knew his parents lived in Bitter Bark and that he was planning to move here after he got out of the Army and work for them. He didn't want to, because he really wanted to pursue a country music career, but he said he'd come back to Bitter Bark for a few years, sock away some money, then go do his thing in music. So I came here and figured if I couldn't find him, I could find his parents, and I…"

"Found me instead."

"Well, that was just a happy by-product," she said.

He felt his shoulders tense a little. "Why didn't you tell me this the very first day, Summer? At Waterford, even?"

"Because it's personal and private and I hardly knew you. I thought I could just figure out where he was on my own, you know? Talk to people and poke around. You made it all so nice so fast, with a place to live and the camp for Destiny. And honestly, John, I haven't been here that long. I did tell you before anything...progressed."

He nodded slowly, conceding that. "So, you want me to get his number from George?" he asked. "Find out where he is?"

She blinked and stared at him. "Are you *that* good? Because that would go beyond nice and really slip right into *gallant*."

"Nothing gallant about it. You're looking for the guy, and I have his parents' phone number. You can talk to him tomorrow."

"I'd rather wait," she whispered.

"For what? That's why you came here."

This time, she took his hand and held it tight. "Yes, it was the reason. But as soon as I found out he wasn't here, I realized that I was incredibly relieved. I really haven't thought about him since..." She bit her lip and held his gaze. "Since I met you."

He finally dropped back against the seat with a thud.

"Uh-oh."

"Uh-oh what?" he asked.

"You're thinking."

"Aidan says it's my downfall, you know. You and your guilt, me and my common sense. But..."

"But what?"

Turning to her, he touched her cheek and brushed back a silky lock of hair. "I think that I should be very

169

careful with a woman who is as tender as you and as susceptible to guilt."

"Oh, I see. And I'd love to believe that's you being nice, but I know a flat-out rejection when I stare it in the face."

"I'm not rejecting you," he insisted.

She choked softly. "Punishing me?"

"Punishing you?" He shook his head, frustration growing enough to make him stand again. "Who the hell am I to do that? No, I'm not punishing you for your past or stepping away because something you did is somehow unattractive to me. Don't think that, not for one minute."

Her shoulders dropped as if he had actually put weight on them. "Then what happened between those kisses on the stairs and right this minute? Other than now you know my past?"

He stared at her for a long time before answering, reaching to pull her up to him as he studied her intently. "Truth?"

"There's nothing else tonight."

"It's me, not you." He put his hands on her shoulders to make his point. "I would love nothing more than a...Summer fling. But..." He shrugged. "That's really never been my style. I saw you and Des when I drove up to the house tonight, and I wasn't thinking about getting you in bed tonight. Okay, I wasn't thinking *just* about getting you in bed. I was imagining...things."

"What kind of things?"

"Shouldn't be too hard to guess, Summer. I'm already falling hard for you and that sweet kid. Forget Travis."

"I have a feeling you'd like to forget Travis."

She'd be right. "Take him out of the mix. You're going to pull out of here in a matter of weeks, maybe three, maybe a few more. And all the things I started to imagine would go…" He looked away, his gaze on the fire. "Up in smoke."

"Do you want me to leave now?" she asked on a soft whisper. "Before that happens?"

"God, no." He reached for her hands, taking one in each of his and pulling her a little closer. "But I don't want you to have one more person to feel guilty about, and that's what I'd be."

She searched his face, thinking, silent. "So back to time and space and…no guilt for me, no feelings for you."

"For the time being, that's probably best. But please don't leave."

She tipped her head. "You think you're going to wake up and that apartment will be empty and my number will be disconnected?"

It wouldn't be the first time for her and he instantly hated even thinking that. "No, I don't. We both know Destiny is having the time of her life, and I need you at Santorini's. That incognito investor could walk in any minute, and Cassie told me you were amazing on the job."

Her smile was sad and slow to lift her lips. "Is that the only reason?"

No. He just wanted her close. For now, that was all, and it was enough. He lifted her knuckles to his lips. "Just stay. I couldn't stand it if you left and took all the…sunshine." He dropped a kiss on her forehead, took his glass and the bottle, and headed toward the door. "I'll leave the slider unlocked. For Mav."

"You didn't have to add 'for Mav,'" she said softly. "I won't sneak in there and climb into your bed."

Yeah. He'd just made damn sure of that.

Wow. For a smart guy, he sure could be an idiot sometimes.

Chapter Thirteen

Summer sailed back to the hostess stand after seating a sweet couple from Chicago who couldn't stop talking about how much the restaurant was like their favorite one in Greece, where they frequently traveled.

For a brief moment, everything on this Friday morning rush seemed blissfully under control. At least, everything at Santorini's was. After a week of working and living in close proximity to a man she found attractive, fascinating, and unbelievably good to her daughter, not everything on the inside felt quite so under control.

But she pushed those thoughts aside when the door opened, and an older man walked in alone, paused just inside the door, and looked around very, very slowly.

"Good morning," she said brightly, pulling out a menu. "Welcome to Santorini's Deli. Would you like a table for one, or are you waiting for someone?"

He took a few steps closer, his gaze pinned on the top of the hostess stand, his eyes narrowed as he seemed to take in every detail of her chart and notepad.

"There's no wait," she said quickly, assuming he must be looking for a list. "Just the best Greek food you'll get outside of Athens." She added her most charming smile, because Grumpy refused to crack one for her.

"Full menu or just breakfast?" he asked.

"Oh, you can have anything you want. Bash, our grill master, is always willing to stretch the menu a bit. Would you rather look at something for lunch?"

"Give me both menus," he said. "And your most slammed waitress."

She frowned at the request. "Our servers are all running at about the same pace," she said. "And if you want to be sure you're not rushed, you just let her know."

"Maybe someone who hasn't been around forever. And seat me near the kitchen, please."

For a moment, her jaw loosened, and a little frisson of excitement danced up Summer's spine.

This was him! The secret shopper! She beamed her best smile at him, so pleased that she'd figured it out already.

"You can sit wherever you like, sir, just let me take you there. And you can choose any server in the restaurant, and I promise the same fantastic attention to your every need."

He shot her a skeptical look, swiping back some thin hairs on a head that wasn't bald yet, but would be in a decade. "We'll see about that."

"Oh my, have you had a bad experience in a similar restaurant?" she asked, gesturing for him to follow her. "Because we have excellent service and some of the happiest customers in town. Have you seen our Yelp reviews?"

He snorted. "Like I care what you pay people to say."

Oh boy, he was a tough nut. But Summer was undaunted, taking him to a table next to the front window in Karyn's station. "Not only do you have a view of our bustling patio dining area here, you can also have a glimpse into the kitchen, as you requested. Of course, if you'd like to meet the kitchen staff and take a tour—"

"No," he said sharply, shutting her up. "I don't want anyone to…" He caught himself as he sat down. "No special attention, please."

Sorry, Mr. Big-Time Investor, but you are about to get showered with so much special attention.

"Of course." She handed him the menu, opening it with a flourish. "Can I answer any questions? Greek food is a world all its own, you know."

He gave her a sharp look. "I'm familiar with Greek food."

"Then you'll appreciate the quality of ours. The spanakopita is—"

"Not what I'm here for," he said, glancing at the menu, then up at her. "Water? Coffee? What does one get here?"

"Whatever one wants," she said with a cheery tip of her head. "I'll get Karyn, your server, and bring you water and coffee right away, sir." She couldn't help leaning a little closer, remembering the other night at dinner when John said one of the keys to franchising was making everything "replicable."

"The kagianas are Greek eggs, as I'm sure you know. They are amazing. And not that difficult a recipe, since even I've learned to make it."

"Simple is sometimes best," he agreed, giving her a punch of pleasure to know he was thawing.

"I'll be right back."

She breezed away, then launched into the kitchen, torn between announcing the news to the staff who would serve him and running to tell John that his investor was here. His door was closed, meaning he was probably on a call, so she made a game-time decision and rallied Bash, Karyn, and the rest of them to share the news.

"I get to wait on him?" Karyn said excitedly. "Perfect. Don't give me anyone else for a while, Summer."

"You got it."

"Sell him the fetoydia," Bash said to Karyn. "The bread is perfect today."

"Mmm." Summer nodded, remembering the Greek-style French toast she'd had earlier in the week. "Great choice, but he might want lunch."

"I got it, I got it," Karyn said, smoothing her hair. "Let me serve table six first so I can concentrate on him."

"I'll get him coffee and water," Summer said with one more glance at John's door. "Oh, and do you have one of those breakfast pastry trays, Bash? We can start him with that. It's so impressive."

They all moved with choreographed speed, and a few minutes later, she was on her way back to the table, doing a double take when she saw Secret Shopper taking pictures with his phone.

This was so definitely him.

"Here you go." She set the water and poured some coffee. "Are you from around here, sir?"

He shot her another icy look. "I'm from…here and there."

She smiled. "Well, welcome to here. Can I tell you a little bit about our town? Or this wonderful restaurant?"

He eyed her suspiciously. "How much do I want to know?"

"The history, which is colorful and long, the family who started it, and the amazing man who owns it."

He lifted a brow. "Amazing?"

Okay, maybe she'd gone too far. "Well, the staff loves him, and his attention to detail brings customers back over and over. Details that you don't find anywhere else. But could." *If it was franchised.*

He lifted a packet of sugar and shook it, dismissing her with a nod.

She stepped away and headed back to the hostess stand to seat a few locals she already recognized. As she took them to their table, she spied Secret Shopper furiously tapping notes into his phone. Of *course*.

After she chatted with the new customers, she walked past, hearing him give Karyn an order for fetoydia. And kagianas. And lalagites! He wanted to try everything, just like John had said.

Bursting with the news, she darted once more into the kitchen, practically pirouetting into John's office when she saw the door was open again.

She was breathless by the time she threw herself into his office. "He's here."

John looked up from his laptop and blinked at her, as if the information was too much for his incredible brain to process. Or she was. All week, he'd looked at her that way when he thought she didn't notice. Like he was…crushing.

Welcome to the club, Nice Man.

"Who's here?"

"The secret shopper guy. Your buddy Tom. He's here, in Santorini's, right now."

"What?" He shot up. "Tom Barnard came in for breakfast?"

"He came for everything, it seems. He ordered three different meals. And he's alone."

"Oh." He came around the desk, fully focused on this news now. "Where'd you seat him? Who's his server? Does Bash know? Wait. How do you know it's him?"

"Table six, Karyn, yes, and I suspected when he walked in and looked at everything on the hostess stand like he might find a speck of dirt or a menu upside down. Which he didn't, by the way. And after I sat him, he pulled out a camera and took a picture of the table setting, and then he was furiously typing notes into his phone."

"Yeah, that could be him." John started toward the door, but Summer sidestepped and blocked him.

"Hang on for a sec," she said, putting both hands on his chest because she needed to stop him. And it felt so good. "First of all, you can't let him see you. He'll know we're on to him."

He circled her wrists with his index fingers and thumbs, using a light touch to remove her hands quickly. "I've never met him. He has no idea what I look like."

She poked his chest again, this time where his name was sewn into the Santorini's shirt he'd worn because he'd had a meeting with a vendor early that morning. "Just another John who works here?"

"Okay," he relented. "But I need to go in the kitchen."

"We have this well under control. Karyn and Bash know. They are going to serve him the greatest kagianas, fetoydia, and lalagites he's ever had."

"Pancakes, French toast, and scrambled eggs? Bash can do—"

"Stop." Once more, she used the excuse to put her hands on his chest. "He's got fresh coffee and a view of the square. I'll check on him. You need to relax."

"I'll relax in the kitchen," he said, moving his whole body away from hers, something it seemed he'd spent the better part of the past week doing, even though it was the opposite of what she wanted him to do.

"John." She crossed her arms and looked up at him. "You'll make Bash nervous. You'll make Karyn cranky. You'll make me crazy. Well, you do that anyway, but your staff are professionals. Let them do their job."

"I make *you* crazy?" he asked on a laugh.

Of course, he said it like...she made him crazy, too. "You make me crazy when you come out to the floor when I'm running the front," she said quickly. "But you're the boss, though, and that's your job."

"Fine. I'll stay here. But come back and tell me everything." He gestured for her to leave, then suddenly put a hand on her shoulder. They both had developed a habit of constantly giving in to small, casual, unimportant touches. Which felt anything but small or casual or unimportant. "Wait. Are you sure it's him and not just a guy eating alone who likes to take pictures and text?"

"Well, do you know what Tom looks like?"

"No. He's incredibly private. I've never seen so much as a picture of the guy."

"Well, I'm sure it's him. I mean, how many men come into Santorini's alone, take a picture, inspect everything, write notes, order three meals, *and* ask to be served by the busiest waitress?"

"Really? Of course. He wants to find a weakness."

"Which he won't." She took a step back. "Now let me go be your eyes and ears out there and engage him in more conversation. I want him to know how many regulars we have and how you inspire the staff and how authentic your Greek family is."

He dropped his head back and closed his eyes, something spinning in that brain of his, but she had no idea what it was.

"No? Nothing about the family? I can tell him—"

He put his fingers over her mouth, stopping her avalanche of words and worry.

"I'm sure anything you say is going to enchant him."

"Really?" She gave a clap and shimmied her shoulders in a little victory dance. "Then let me, not you, go out there and see what he's doing, eating, thinking, everything. You sit right there and work."

"As if I could."

"Do it." She gave him a nudge. "You need to be ready to take his money and franchise this business, John."

As she took a step to back out the door, he reached for her hand, a deliberate move that sent a shiver over her.

"Anything else I should do?" she asked.

"Just…" He gave her hand a squeeze. "Know how much I appreciate this. You. All of…you." He shook his head like he couldn't believe he said that. "All you're doing, I mean."

She shot him a quick smile, casual and friendly, the way she'd tried to keep every interaction they'd had since the night at the fire pit. Sadly, there'd been no more wine and fire and long talks, just some softball with Destiny and a few shared dinners. After that, she'd headed upstairs, and after Destiny's bath and book and, finally, sleep, Summer would slip Mav through his sliding glass doors. She hadn't even bothered to borrow the microwave to warm her tea.

No tea. Maybe that was the reason she was getting such rotten sleep…and hot dreams.

"I'm just doing my job," she said, waving off his compliment. "Now, let me go before someone comes in and it looks like we can't manage the front of the house."

She slipped away, dashed through the kitchen, and just as she reached the door to the dining room, she glanced back at his office. He was still standing there, watching her, his expression as bewildered as…well, as she felt.

Had they made the right decision? What…*they*? He'd made the decision after hearing her story, exactly as she'd suspected.

Pushing the thought away, a skill she'd mastered this past week, she checked the front and then took a pass through the restaurant, where Tom Barnard—she preferred thinking of him as Secret Shopper—was diving into his meals, though not before taking more pictures and writing additional notes in his phone.

He seemed content, so Summer went back to work, seating new arrivals, dropping out on the patio to check on everything there while also keeping an eye on their VIP guest. After a while, as he neared the end of his meal, she took another walk around the floor, catching his eye as she passed.

"How was everything, sir?" she asked.

He frowned, then beckoned her closer. "I have a question about your suppliers. All local, or does inventory come from around the country?"

She had no earthly idea. But maybe it was time to bring out the boss. "Our owner, John Santorini, is in the back, sir. Can I bring him out to answer your questions?"

"No!" The response was surprisingly vehement. "Please don't bother. It's not that important."

"But every question is important," she said. "Let me—"

"Please don't," he insisted. "I'd rather he not know I'm here."

"Oh, of course. You want to be...*incognito*."

He gave a very tight smile. "Sometimes, in my business, that isn't easy. But I would prefer to maintain my anonymity, if I may, Miss..." His eyes dropped to her name tag. "Summer."

She relaxed a little, so desperately wanting to help John. "I can tell you this," she said. "I haven't worked here that long, but the environment is just...perfect. Happy, solid, well run, and everyone is respected. And I've never seen so many satisfied customers or happy employees."

He nodded. "Good to know."

"Okay, I'll back off," she said with a laugh, inching away. "More coffee? Dessert?"

"I have dessert coming," he admitted with a tip of his head. "I wanted to try as much as I could."

"Totally understand. Enjoy."

She walked slowly past the kitchen on her way back to the hostess stand, tempted to run back to John and tell him every word exchanged with the man who could make his franchising dreams come true.

But she had to stop flirting with John. Had to stop the random touches and quick encounters. He'd made it clear he didn't want feelings, and she didn't need any more guilt. But it was very hard not to feel like she'd blown it, and she had no one but herself to blame.

Chapter Fourteen

How the hell long could he go on feeling this…crazy?

John stared at the empty doorway, but instead of the corner of the kitchen and the bustling activity at the pass, all he could see was…silky hair and a blinding smile. Instead of Bash's spatula scraping iron, he heard that throaty laugh that was his favorite sound on earth. Instead of a warm waft of spice-laden air from the ovens, he felt her light and frequent touch and the scent of citrus and sunshine she spread everywhere.

Citrus and sunshine? What the ever-lovin' hell was going on in his addled brain? Blood loss, of course. It had all gone to a completely different place, now taking ownership of his being as hormones and hunger drove him instead of intellect and gray matter.

Still, he didn't move, the inventory management report in front of him not nearly as interesting as sitting right here, waiting for Summer to come floating in again, all bright and brilliant, like he'd opened every window blind and let the sun pour into the room.

"Oh man," he muttered, stabbing his fingers in his hair and shoving it back hard like that could pull all the wayward and constant thoughts—no, *feelings*—he had about Summer out of his poor, malfunctioning cranium.

For the better part of the week, he'd done nothing but battle those feelings. He'd second-guessed his decision to put the brakes on their escalating relationship so many times that it was fair to say he'd thousand-guessed it. He knew letting their budding romance die on the vine was the right, safe, *nice* thing to do. He knew it like he knew the derivative of sine was cosine or that changing speed affected velocity.

Except, all he wanted to do was…change his mind and kiss her until she melted in his arms…and into his bed.

Thankfully, his cell phone vibrated him back to reality. And the name on the screen jolted him back to his senses.

George Shipley.

They'd been playing telephone tag all week, although John had been relieved to get voice mail. Talking to George reminded him of Travis Shipley, the man Summer cared enough for that she'd hung on to his memory and driven hundreds of miles to apologize or for closure or…*something.*

"Hey, George," he answered warmly. "We finally escape voice mail jail."

"John, how are you?" The older man's voice was always gruff, and today was no different. It wasn't that he was unpleasant, but he had a cold, curt speaking style.

Was his son the same way? he wondered. Surely

Summer didn't fall for someone cold and curt. For the thousandth time in five days, he wondered just what Travis Shipley was like.

Shaking off the thought, he forced himself to focus. Forget the son. The father was the one considering a sales offer that needed to be inked before John could close the financing deal with the guy sitting out in his dining room eating fetoydia and kagianas.

"So, are you ready to ink that contract I had my attorney send over?" John asked.

The silence lasted just a beat too long, and John gave the phone a look. He *wouldn't* back out. He couldn't.

"Well, we have a little issue, John."

Okay. One issue. They could tweak the closing date or payment schedule. "What is it?"

"I'm looking at another offer."

Another offer? The words shot him straight up as irritation slammed up his spine, but he kept his response steady. "I leased this property with an option to buy, George. My offer takes precedence over any others."

"Not any others. Read the fine print."

"I've memorized the fine print," he shot back. "You can't refuse my offer for another one unless the other one is twenty-five percent or more higher."

"Like I said."

John let out a whistle as he did the mental math. Twenty-five percent? "That is over and above market value for this property. My offer is more than fair."

George was dead silent, which just ticked off John even more. *Damn* it! Tom Barnard was out there no doubt falling in love with the restaurant—and possibly the hostess—and putting together his investment deal…and George freaking Shipley was going to squeeze John out of the sale?

He had to have this flagship store up and running if he had any hope of securing the financing. Was there wiggle room? Maybe not twenty-five percent, but he knew how to dress up an offer with more benefits to the seller than just price.

"What if I send a revised offer?"

"I'd need it by the close of business."

"Today?" He choked some disbelief at the game of hardball. George was brusque, but he wasn't an asshole.

"Today," George confirmed. "I need to make a decision over the weekend. And I'm warning you, it needs to match the price."

Could he go up twenty-five percent? Maybe. If he knew the financing was coming in for sure. But how could he know, other than going out there and asking Tom Barnard if he was going to cough up a few million to help franchise Santorini's? Well, hell. Why not? That was exactly what he was going to do. If Barnard said he wasn't going to offer a deal, then John wouldn't make the increased offer. If it was a go, he could afford the price.

"Fine," he said to George. "If I'm going to make a new offer, you'll have it by five o'clock today. Will you accept a verbal?"

"Yes," he said simply. "By five."

He hung up just as Summer came in again, not as breathless this time. "He paid with cash, so I didn't get his name on a credit card. But I'm sure that—"

"He left?" He stood up, blinking at her. "He can't leave. I have to talk to him. In person, and now."

"He's gone, but he asked me where the library is, so I think he's going there."

"Why would he want to go to the library?"

"He told Karyn he needed Wi-Fi or an internet hotspot to download a large file, and she suggested the library. You could follow him there. Run into him by accident? If you're sure that's what you want to do, John. He seemed really happy. Major compliments on everything on the way out. Huge tip, too."

"That's all good, but it's not a guarantee. I need to know what his decision is."

She looked a little dubious, then shrugged. "Okay. I'll ask Karyn to cover the front for me."

"You don't have to…" Then he realized what he was saying. How would he recognize the guy without her? "All right. Let's go. Fast. I have to talk to him as soon as possible. I literally have hours to make a huge decision."

"Why?" she asked, her blue eyes scanning his face with concern.

He blew out a breath. "Because George Shipley just might royally screw me out of this deal."

She paled a little at the name, then closed her eyes. "Let me talk to Karyn. I'll meet you at the back door. That's a shorter walk to the library."

On the way across Bushrod Square, John explained everything and why he had to know what Tom Barnard's decision on financing would be. Summer listened with few questions, a burn in her gut when she thought about her connection to George Shipley.

When she'd told John she'd rather wait to figure things out with Travis, she'd been telling the absolute truth. Yes, she wouldn't mind setting the record straight and apologizing for disappearing. And she would, someday.

But the truth was, once she met John, the confusion that Raven had stirred up about what she wanted with Travis had disappeared.

"I still don't think you should pounce," Summer said as they walked.

"I don't want to pounce, but I have to know, and I have to know today."

She bit her lip and lifted her hair, her neck hot in the blazing sun. "He really didn't want to have a conversation with you."

"Well, he's about to."

"What if there's another way to find out? Something a little more natural or organic?"

"If you can think of an idea, I'd be open."

"Maybe I could—" She let out a soft gasp as she looked across the grass at a man sitting on a park bench near the playground. "John." She grabbed his arm. "That's him. Right there."

He followed her gaze and squinted at the man tapping away on an open laptop. "It could be him," he said.

"Well, it's definitely the guy who just ordered three meals, gushed about the service, and left a mongo tip."

John studied the man a good hundred and fifty feet away, quiet while he thought. "If he backs out, I can't raise that offer to Shipley," he finally said. "Then I could lose my restaurant and have to start over with a new property. A bad decision could set me back a year. More."

She heard the frustration in his voice and wanted to help more than anything. "Okay. I have an idea." She stared at the man, mentally working out the logistics.

"Talk to me, Goose," John whispered, making her smile.

"If I went around that playground, all the way to the back, and came up behind him, not too obvious, I might be able to see what he's writing."

He laughed softly. "Nice try, but not only is that rude, it's probably illegal. And what are you going to find out, even if you could read the screen?"

"What do you have to lose?" she insisted. "If I can't get anything, you can pounce away and make him tell you his plans and have at him. But he's wide open, and if I could just walk past him and glance, maybe I'll find out what he's planning to do."

He searched her face for a long moment, a smile pulling his lips up. "You're really something else, you know that?"

"You just haven't figured out what yet," she replied.

"That's for damn sure." His gaze drifted over her face, a mix of admiration and amusement and maybe just a little lust in his brown eyes. "Not for lack of trying, though."

The comment gave her a thrill and amped up her desire to impress, and help, him. She reached out and put her hand on his forearm, loving the feel of muscle under warm skin and the soft dusting of hair. So much for no more random touches. "Stay here," she said. "Way over here. And give me ten minutes."

"What if he turns around and sees you?"

She flipped open her bag, pulled out a hair tie, and made a quick ponytail. Then she slipped on a pair of sunglasses. "He'll never notice me."

"If he doesn't, he's not human or male."

She grinned and gave him a poke in the shoulder, because she absolutely adored that shoulder and it deserved to be poked. "Just a walk in the park, Kazansky."

He laughed out loud at her *Top Gun* reference as she took off toward the playground, which was as noisy and crowded as it'd been the day Summer and Destiny had first stepped foot in Bitter Bark. At least twenty kids, from ages two to twelve, ran around, along with the usual number of dogs and distractions.

As she took the long way so there was no chance of Secret Shopper seeing her, Summer turned a few times to check for John's tall figure, where he still waited in the shade, still grinning from her *Top Gun* joke. Just as she disappeared into the noise and chaos of the playground, she gave him a thumbs-up, and he returned it, which, for reasons she'd never understand, made her stomach flip.

As she came around the other side of the playground, she shifted all her attention to Secret Shopper. Now that she was closer, she could see he was pounding the keyboard noisily, sitting in the shade enough so that if she were directly in line and the sun cooperated and he had a glare-resistant screen…she could likely see what he was writing when she walked behind him.

She slowed her step and planned a natural route to pass behind him. She stayed well out of his sight and prayed he didn't suddenly turn around because a kid screamed.

When she was within two feet, she could see letters on a screen. A Word document, and the top of it was bold and big. Yes! She might be able to read it. She got a little closer and stole a look across the square at John, who stared intently. Was his heart pounding like hers?

Probably. And that made her feel connected to him and determined to go slow, close, and read the big letters across the top of the page.

I WOULD NEVER MISS THIS DEAL!

She had to bite her lip to keep from gasping. He would never miss this deal? That had to be good. Pretending to stop to tie her sneaker, she crouched down and squinted hard to read the next line just to be sure he wasn't reading some marketing email.

Santorini's has everything I wanted...

The rest was in the sun's glare, but it didn't matter. That was good news. Great news. The *best* news.

She shot up and kept going, heading along the walkway toward John, picking up her pace with each step until she broke into a run.

Ten feet away, he held out his arms as if to catch her, and she jogged right into his embrace and jumped up, throwing her legs around his waist, boosted by her success and the raw excitement of sharing it with him.

"It's a yes!" she squealed, throwing her head back with the adrenaline that shot through her.

"Oh wow!" a woman nearby called.

"She said yes!" another woman in the same group yelled out.

John froze. Summer gasped. And very, very slowly, he let her back to the ground as they both turned toward the young moms setting up a picnic for their kids.

"No, no," Summer said, waving her hands as a blush exploded on her face. "It was...a different kind of yes. Not a...no, sorry."

A chorus of disappointed groans followed them as they took a few steps away, both laughing a little nervously. Then she grabbed his arm and squeezed.

"Want to know what it said?"

"You actually read his screen?"

"I did. And it said..." She cleared her throat and swiped her hand as if announcing a headline. "'I WOULD NEVER MISS THIS DEAL!' In all capital letters, John!"

"What?" He choked softly. "Are you sure?"

"Positive. Heck, if I thought I could get away with it, I'd have taken a picture."

He looked a little horrified at the thought, then put both hands on her shoulders, pulling her close to him. "Did you get anything else?"

"Yes." She beamed up at him. "You're going to love this."

"I already do," he admitted softly.

"The very next line was: 'Santorini's is everything I wanted...'"

When she paused, he added some pressure on her shoulders. "And..."

"That's all I got. I couldn't read with the glare. But, John, that's so good."

"Good? It's amazing." He hugged her again, pulling her hard into his whole body and squeezing tight like he didn't give a damn about air and space and having any between them. "I don't even know what to say to you. You spied for me!"

She giggled, inching back to look at him. "It was fun." Of course, the best part was jumping into his arms and doing the whole *Bachelor*-contestant leg wrap. "I had my shot and had to take it, Mav."

He laughed heartily, then cupped his hands on her cheeks. "You, Summer Jackson, are a brilliant, beautiful, fearless woman. And I am blown away."

She got up on her tiptoes and kissed him lightly, completely caught up in the moment and the man.

He kissed her back, a little longer, then suddenly backed away.

"Are you sure it's not a yes?" one of the women called playfully, making them laugh.

"I, uh, better go run some numbers for my new offer," John said.

"And I better…" Against her side, her purse vibrated with a call on her cell. "Answer this."

As she pulled the phone out, John draped an arm around her shoulders and started walking down the path. But she froze as she stared at the phone, and all the high dropped like she fell down a roller coaster. "It's from Waterford Farm."

With a vague but familiar sense of "mother worry," she smashed her finger on the green button to answer.

"Hello, is this Summer Jackson?" The man's voice was just low and serious enough to kick that worry up a notch.

"Yes, it is."

"First of all, everything's fine. Destiny is fine." She barely heard the words, turning back to John to hold his arm for the support she thought she might need, tapping the speaker button so he could hear.

"What happened?" she asked.

"She's been hit with a softball. Nothing serious, but I think you better come and get her."

"Let's go," John said, taking her hand and pulling her. "We can be there in fifteen minutes."

Chapter Fifteen

"He said she was hit in the shoulder." Summer pressed her hand to her own shoulder like she could somehow telepathically send comfort to her daughter, while John broke several speed limits rushing toward Waterford Farm. "I guess it could have been worse."

"I'm sure they're not using a standard six- or seven-ounce softball with those kids," he said, hoping to reassure her. "So it depends on who threw it, how close they were, how hard the toss." He reached over and put his hand over hers. "Shane said it wasn't serious. If it were, we'd be driving to the hospital."

She let out a nearly inaudible whimper at the thought. But he heard it, and it only made him hit the accelerator harder.

"But we're not," he reminded her. "I'm sure she's just bruised. And...scared." That poor kid. She'd really enjoyed playing and wanted so much to conquer her fears. "I know how she feels."

"She'll never want to play again," Summer said softly. "And she was having so much fun."

"She has a decent arm, too. And a great head on her shoulders."

"Her bruised shoulders."

"Better than a bruised head," he said, giving her hand a squeeze. "And she has a fantastic voice. Any chance we can talk her into switching playtime from softball to singing?"

She sighed noisily as a fresh set of unshed tears dampened her eyes. "John," she whispered.

"I know, I know," he said quickly. "I understand the stutter makes it hard. I was just thinking—"

"No, that's not it." She brought his hand to her lips and laid an unexpected kiss on his knuckles. "You're so sweet to care about her."

"Sweet again, huh?" He gave an easy smile and fought the urge to pull their joined hands to his mouth and kiss her hand right back. Instead, he settled for holding her hand on her lap. "She's the best kid in the world, you know?"

"Oh, I know."

"And when she struggles to say something…" He shook his head.

"Rips your heart out."

"And stomps on it," he added.

"I told you that's why she whispers and sings," Summer said. "That way, she won't stutter."

"Well, then I'm confused," he admitted. "If she can sing without a stutter, why is she staying out of the choral stuff? That would seem to be her happy place."

"Only when she sings solo," she told him. "She was in a group at school and couldn't come in on the right note or at the right time. So a chorus situation also scares her."

"I hate for her to be scared of anything," he said.

"You helped her so much with softball, John."

He winced. "Hello, square one, we're back." He leaned a little closer and squeezed her hand. "We'll think of something to help her."

"Thank you," she whispered, looking at him with so much affection he damn near missed the turnoff to Waterford.

He'd barely had the 4Runner halfway down the long drive when he caught sight of his mother, Daniel, and Liam hustling toward them. Then John noticed another person in the welcoming committee. Little Christian held his father's hand, looking up at Liam with eyes red-rimmed from tears.

Summer noticed, too. "Oh no. It must be really bad if he's that upset."

"His favorite girl? Maybe he's just worried about her."

They both got out of the car the second he turned the ignition off, and Summer rushed closer.

"Where is she?"

"She's in the vet's office," John's mother said, immediately putting her arm around Summer. "She's fine. I promise you, she's *fine*. We only called you for protocol."

"I'm so glad you did. Can I—" Before she could finish, Christian grabbed Summer's hand and demanded her attention.

"I'm sorry," he said in ragged voice. "It's my fault. I threw the ball."

"It's okay, son." Liam put a hand on his shoulder. "You didn't mean to hit her."

"But I did hit her," he said, tears welling up.

"I threw it too hard. The coaches said grounders only, but I… I wanted to show her how good my arm is."

Summer immediately dropped down to his level. "You didn't try to hit her, Christian." To her credit, it was a statement, made without doubt, and not even close to a question.

"No!" His eyes popped. "She's my friend!"

"I know," Summer said gently, her demeanor so comfortable it was easy to see why she was a fantastic third-grade teacher. "The minute she gets in the car after camp, I hear all about how much fun she has with you and Jag."

His lower lip quivered as if this news was just too much for him.

"Will you come with me to see her?" Summer asked him.

He shook his head. "She's mad at me. I just wanted you to know what happened." He looked up at Liam. "Daddy thought I should tell you myself."

"Oh dear." She rose and smiled at Liam. "Thank you. Promise him she doesn't hold a grudge. I won't let her."

"Let's go see her." John put his hand on Summer's back and walked with his mother and Daniel toward the small building that housed all the vet offices.

"It's a bruise," Daniel said. "Nothing is broken. I know I'm a vet, not a doctor, but I raised six kids. This is a tender bruise on the front of her shoulder. She's in some discomfort, and we're icing it, of course. But I didn't give her anything or take an X-ray. I thought you'd want to make that call."

"Thanks. How is she otherwise? Upset?" She glanced over her shoulder at the little boy they'd left

199

behind. "Is she really mad at Christian? She seems so crazy about him."

"She's mad at the world," Katie said. "But Ella happened to be here today, and she's stayed with her ever since it happened about forty-five minutes ago. And of course, Maverick will not leave her side."

Summer and John shared a quick look over that, then they passed the pens where the campers were lining up for lunch and trainers were taking the dogs to the kennels for water and a break.

"I hope she doesn't quit this," Summer said, taking it all in. "She's never been to camp before, and this experience has been amazing."

"She doesn't have to go home," Daniel assured her. "But I don't think she'll want to do much activity this afternoon. And it's up to her whether she wants to come back on Monday, but we'd sure love to have her."

She smiled up at him as he pulled open the door for her. "Thanks. We'll see how she feels about it."

Daniel walked Summer and John to a back room with a long, metal exam table meant for animals. Ella and Destiny sat in the two guest chairs, with Mav on Destiny's lap.

"Mommy!" She leaped out of her seat, and Mav jumped to the floor and headed straight to John.

"Let me look at you." Summer embraced Des gently, then inched her back, making a face when Destiny lowered the ice pack to reveal a purple bruise visible under the strap of her tank top. "Whoa, that's a beauty."

"She's such a trouper," Ella said, giving Destiny's hair a ruffle. "And she can sing like a bird. And so can Mav."

Destiny looked up at Ella and smiled.

"I really would love to have you join the singers on Monday, Des," Ella said. "We're working on three songs that we'll perform at the end of camp. The dogs are going to do a parade during the last number..." She leaned very close to Destiny to add in a stage whisper, "We're singing 'Who Let the Dogs Out?'"

Destiny shook her head sharply. "Mommy," she said, pulling Summer closer to whisper in her ear.

"Why don't we all wait outside?" Daniel suggested quickly. "Let Destiny talk to her mom."

"Good idea," Ella said, patting Mav who was curled in John's arms. "He's a little traumatized, too."

"Don't take Mav!" Destiny called as they started toward the door.

Summer held her hand up. "Let him go with John," she said. "They'll be right outside. I want to talk to you without a distraction."

Of course, she wanted to know exactly what happened from Destiny's perspective and probably examine the bruise. As they stepped into the hall, Daniel was called away by one of the trainers, so John waited with Ella.

"How's she doing, really?" John asked her.

"She needs to be singing," Ella said, clearly frustrated. "Her voice is ridiculous. She's really, really talented, John."

"But she stutters," he replied. "And she's afraid that she can't come in on time with the other singers." He lifted a brow. "You're in charge of the music, right?"

"Yeah, and I want her in my little camp chorus. Can you talk her into it?"

"I don't think you can talk that little girl into anything," he said. "But I did get her over the fear of throwing a ball."

"Then get her over her fear of singing with a group." She stroked Mav's little head as he cuddled into John's chest, always happy to be "home" after his long day at camp.

"I have no idea how to do that, Ella," he said. "Softball, yes. Singing, no."

"She just needs to practice the process of coming in on cue."

"So…we should sing with her?"

Her big brown eyes suddenly got huge, and her jaw dropped wide open. "Barbie!"

"Is she another camper?"

"It's the answer." She gave her hands a clap. "Barbie's karaoke machine! Darcy had one when we were little, and we used to sing up in Gramma Finnie's apartment." She pointed in the general direction of the main house where, he knew, Gramma Finnie once occupied the third floor. "If she still has that machine, I'm telling you, it could teach her how to start on cue. It might be in the attic, but it could be long gone."

"Then I'll get another karaoke machine."

"You could, but, man, there's something magical about Barbie's. It's pink, and that microphone felt so good in my hand when I would belt out 'You Are My Sunshine.' Ask Darcy. I was a beast."

He laughed. "I believe you. I guess I could go look in the attic now. I was up there a couple of days ago to get a pillow, and there is a ton of crap up there."

"I've got to go back to camp," Ella said. "I'm

helping serve lunch. But just look for a pink box about the size of a toaster. And get all the cassettes."

"Cassettes? Like…" He made a square with his hands and a face of disbelief.

"Yes. It was the nineties, dude. Make sure you find 'Sunshine.' She'd kill that. Okay. Gotta go."

"Wait." He held his hand out. "First of all, thanks for staying with her. Second, if I find this machine and she practices, would you give her a solo during the performance at the end of camp?"

Her dark brows arched up in surprise. "No one's getting solos. It just makes for crazy, fighting kids. We're trying to be extra fair."

"Well, no one else got beaned playing ball except her, and I think she deserves something for it."

"John." She angled her head, her smile highlighting her striking bone structure. "You really care about that kid."

"Well, she's living upstairs from me."

"And maybe you really care about her mother."

He barely shrugged. "Maybe I do."

She bit her lip. "The grannies are going to be so happy."

"Of course you'll tell them."

"Of course," she said airily. "I'll think about the solo. You make a compelling argument about the getting beaned. But I have to tell you…" She leaned closer to whisper, "Christian's going to have to learn that if you want a girl's attention, you don't throw things at her."

"He…oh, yeah. I can see that little crush happening."

"More than one, it seems."

"More boys have crushes on her?" For some

reason, he wasn't sure he liked that. She was just a kid, and boys were…boys.

Ella laughed. "I meant you and her mom." She gave a little wave and jogged toward the door, leaving John with Maverick.

Well, yeah. He had a crushing crush on Summer Jackson. And if some twenty-five-year-old toy karaoke machine could help her little girl, then…

"Come on, Mav," he whispered to the dog. "Let's go hunt for Barbie and 'Sunshine' and…" He gave a squeeze and put his mouth closer to Mav's ear like Destiny did. "Who *are* we, anyway?"

The dog barked.

"Yeah. Crushed. Both of us. And poor little Christian, the Dogmothers, and hell, is there *anyone* those two haven't enchanted yet?"

Getting Destiny completely calm and even laughing a little took a lot longer than Summer had expected. There were a lot of tears and confessions. She liked softball, but didn't love it. She liked Christian, but not right this moment. And she liked camp and was scared Summer would take her out of it.

Once all of that was discussed and all the reassurances were given, they came out of the little exam room, a good forty-five minutes after they'd entered. Summer was surprised to find John in the waiting room, playing ball with Mav on the leather sofa. No, maybe she wasn't surprised. Of course he'd wait, find out how Des was, and make sure they got home safely. That's who he was.

"I saved you a box lunch, Destiny," he said as the puppy ran to Destiny. "I figured you'd be hungry."

And he'd worry that she ate because, well, John. A man who could make Summer's poor heart swell with affection with one simple act.

"Thank you," Summer answered for Destiny, giving her a break on manners and responses right now. Plus, she'd already folded on the floor to get kisses from Mav.

"Gramma Finnie and Yiayia are here for camp, doing some baking and...grandmother things," he added. "They invited us to have lunch with them. Unless Destiny is anxious to get home and rest, then I'll take you back."

"I'm not going home," Des said softly, then looked up at Summer. "Do I ha-ha-have to?"

"No, but you can't do any more camp activities today. I want to rest that bruise, maybe ice it some more. Do you want to have lunch with the Dogmothers?"

"The fairy Dogmothers," she corrected with a smile. "Yes."

"They'll be thrilled." John stood and lifted a small cardboard box with a drink and bag of chips visible. "Yiayia made Greek salad, but she won't mind if you eat this hot dog instead."

"'Kay." Destiny scrambled to her feet and tried to scoop up Mav, making a face of pain at the effort.

"Don't pick him up yet," Summer warned.

"Let's see if he'll follow you," John said. "No leash. You're learning how to get him to do that, right?"

Her whole face brightened. "Watch." She took a few steps forward and reached her hand down with an official flourish, trying to snap her fingers, but failing. Then she clucked twice. "Come, Mavvie. Walk."

He didn't move, but stared at her.

"I bet he knows I don't have a treat," Destiny said, dutifully defending her beloved Mav.

"Here you go." John opened a jar on an end table, scooping out a handful of kibble to hand to her. "Try again."

She repeated everything with a serious expression, including the flip of her hand as she clucked twice and commanded Mav to walk. This time, he got up, came next to her, sniffed her hand, and she rewarded him.

"That's amazing, Des!" Summer exclaimed.

"It really is," John agreed. "I hadn't even thought about trying to train him yet. Thanks for helping me out."

Des gave him a quick look, so fast he probably missed the warning in her eyes, but Summer didn't. And her heart dropped a little because a whole week of Tails and Trails had passed, and Summer hadn't even mentioned another dog. And that had been one of the major selling points of camp. But Summer was willing to bet Destiny hadn't spent five minutes with any other dog.

As they crossed the lawns, they saw the trainers in the pen cooling off some dogs with spray hoses. Destiny stopped and pointed at a familiar German shepherd.

"There's Jag," she said, her gaze scanning the group as if she looked for Jag's owner, but Christian wasn't out in the pen. No doubt he was with the large group of kids eating at picnic tables set up under oak trees they could see in the distance. Or still suffering from a serious bout of regret and worry.

"Do you want to find Christian and talk to him, Des?" Summer asked.

She shook her head.

"Well, he wants to talk to you," John said. "He came into the vet office twice to ask if you were okay."

Once again, a cool shrug—from the shoulder that didn't hurt.

"Des," Summer said softly. "You need to forgive him."

She clucked twice at Mav, gave him a treat, and hustled along, clearly not ready to forgive anybody anything.

Yiayia was waiting on the wraparound porch as they approached, her dark hair ruffling in the afternoon breeze, her intense gaze locked on Destiny.

"How bad?" she asked.

"I'm okay," Destiny said. "I'm h-h-hungry."

"Good, I made some taramasalata, which is so good with moussaka and melitzanosalata. Unless you want some octopus and courgette balls?"

Destiny stopped dead in her tracks and stared in silent horror, and Yiayia stared right back for five solid seconds, before throwing her head back in a laugh and coming down the steps. "I'm kidding, little one. I know you have a hot dog and chips."

She put a gentle arm around Destiny, careful of her shoulder, taking the box lunch from John. "But Gramma Finnie did make homemade lemonade. Would you like some of that?"

She nodded and let the older woman lead her up to the patio, with Mav coming right along.

For a moment, Summer stayed at the bottom of the steps, watching her daughter disappear into the kitchen with Yiayia, not even turning to look back for her. For one insane, wild second...she wished she didn't have to leave the comfort of this home and family.

"I have a surprise in the car." John's whispered words startled her.

Or the comfort of this man.

"A surprise?" she asked, tamping down the thought. "Unless it's a new dog who is every bit as cute as that one..."

"There is no such creature."

Summer smiled up at him. "Then, honey, we are in for the fight of our lives when this is over." Maybe that was the reason she suddenly didn't want to leave—the inevitable tears over Mav.

And John.

"I'm not worried," he said. "He's happier with her than anyone."

"What's the surprise?"

"If I tell you, it won't be a surprise. But it's for later, when we're home, when Destiny is settled and not still shaken up by the whole day."

"It sure has been a..." She gasped. "John! What about the sales thing? Don't you have to reply today?"

"By five," he reminded her, always so calm and steady. "It's one phone call to give George my new offer."

"So you're really going to do it?"

"After what you read on Barnard's computer? I'd be crazy not to. If I have to go looking for a new property and set up the whole concept again..." He gave a grunt like the very idea killed him. "A delay like that, and I may never get another investor on board. Yes, I'm making the offer. I feel like if I wait to have Barnard's official investment deal, George Shipley's going to accept the higher bid."

She put her hand over her chest, not knowing the amounts, but still certain a lot of money was at stake. "What if I read it wrong?"

He inched back, brows drawn. "You seemed pretty sure back in the square."

"I was. I am. I mean, I read the words 'I would never miss this deal.' But could he have meant something else?"

She could have sworn he paled for a moment.

"I mean, I know you like things well-thought-out before you take a chance."

His lips lifted into a half smile. "I used to," he said softly. "Then some Summer breeze blew into Bitter Bark…" He took her chin in his thumb and index finger, his dark eyes pinned on her. "And the next thing I know, I'm offering my house, teaching kids softball, and playing spy games in the town square."

His touch was so light, but somehow she felt it right down to her toes. "A summer breeze, huh? What if I…blew it?" She winked, making him laugh. "Seriously, John, you're counting on my having read that screen right."

"I am. And if you're wrong and he wasn't Tom or you misread the screen, then…"

She cringed. "Then…what?"

"Then you…" He leaned close to whisper in her ear. "Will have to get very creative in how you make it up to me."

She drew back a bit, steadying herself from the little wave of dizziness that threatened. "Oh," she whispered. "That's a...change."

"Not really. I'm just tired of fighting the feelings."

She let out a long, soft sigh. "To quote a famous astrophysicist-turned-instructor in our favorite movie, 'This is going to be complicated.'"

He angled his head, thinking. "I can't remember the next line."

"He didn't respond. Just got up to take a shower." She put her hand over his, pressing his fingertips against her jaw, lost in his eyes. "I told you I know *Top Gun* better than you do."

For many, many heartbeats, the world seemed to disappear. There was no one but John. No dogs barking, no kids squealing, no grannies, probably, in the window watching.

There was only this kind, sweet, sexy man who worried about whether her daughter ate lunch and made Summer's whole body feel weak and warm.

She moved a fraction closer and sensed him doing the same, like an invisible thread tugged at both of them, taking them toward the inevitable—

"Lunch is served!"

They both turned toward the voice, meeting the wry smile of Agnes Santorini. "Unless you're too, uh, busy to eat."

"Never too busy for you, Yiayia," John said, taking Summer's hand and walking up the steps with her.

Chapter Sixteen

From the moment the conversation started, John had a low-grade sense that something might be wrong. George Shipley didn't seem particularly overjoyed by the verbal offer. And John could hear Mrs. Shipley's muffled voice on the other end of the line, pulling some strings and having more influence over the outcome of this deal than George let on.

Good God, he wasn't going to make him go any higher, was he? Because at that point, the numbers for the property would no longer make sense, and George knew that.

Then what? The whole stinking deal would fall through.

"You do realize I'm offering a very quick close," John added after George had hesitated once again for far too long. "You can have the money in your bank by mid-August."

George let out a long, low sigh. "I know, John, and that's good. It's just that…" He mumbled something to his wife, then said to John, "We're not completely sure we want to sell at all."

What? John pushed off the leather sofa in Daniel

Kilcannon's office, where he'd come to make the call in private. "When we signed this lease—"

"No, no, we *do* want to sell. I do, anyway."

So it was his wife? Susan? Sarah? He couldn't remember her name, but as the long pauses continued and the woman's tone, if not her words, came through, John knew that the problematic one in this couple was Mrs. Shipley.

"Why would you not sell?" he asked, not understanding the decision at all. It wasn't like they could waltz back in and reopen Hoagies & Heroes. But if the lease agreement expired, then they could sell it to the higher bidder. Which would be sleazy and unethical, but not illegal.

"Rents are going up in Bitter Bark," George said vaguely after his wife said something inaudible.

So they wanted him to commit to another year at a higher rent before selling to him? He stabbed his fingers through his hair and paced through the masculine-toned office, glancing at the Irish setter photos on the wall of each family dog dating back to the 1950s. Then he turned to the bay window and stared out at the rolling hills of velvet green all the way to the blue mountain range in the distant horizon.

But he didn't see any of the scenery. John's mind was a literal calculator, flipping through the possibilities, discarding all of them as not feasible. One dime more, and this deal would be downright stupid.

"When are you going to make a decision?" John ground out the question.

"I'm making it," George said sharply, giving John the distinct impression the man was making his point to someone else. "We'll take the offer, John." Anger, frustration, and defiance darkened the simple statement.

On the other end of the line, he heard what had to be a door slammed in anger.

Okay, so the Shipleys weren't in agreement. What mattered was he had a verbal acceptance. "I'll send over a revised contract on Monday and have my attorney open an escrow account for the down payment."

This deal was more than fair to them, and George had to know it. Still, the man merely responded with, "Okay, sounds good."

Just as he tapped his screen to end the call, he heard footsteps in the hallway.

"John? You back here?"

"In Daniel's office," he called to his brother Alex, who appeared in the doorway a few seconds later.

"I was just chatting with Summer, and she told me you had good news on Barnard," he said, stepping inside. "She wouldn't give me details, though." He nodded toward the phone in his hand. "That him?"

Once again, John tunneled his fingers through his hair and dropped onto the leather couch. "No, it was Shipley. He had a counter on the sales proposal, and I had to meet it."

Alex made a face, understandably surprised. "What the hell? The deal was always lease-to-buy. How could he even entertain another offer?"

Alex took the chair across from him, his expression no doubt a mirror of John's. He'd been John's partner from before birth, and they might have parted ways as business partners when John bought out Alex's share in Santorini's, but not as friends, confidants, and brothers.

And right now, John could use all three.

"He can if it's twenty-five percent higher than mine." He huffed out a breath and a soft curse. "I hope I didn't make a huge mistake."

Alex's dark brows drew closer. "Words I rarely hear you say, brother."

"Because I don't usually act on instinct and... emotion. And very little information." He leaned forward, dropped his elbows on his knees, and gave Alex the short version of what happened that morning with Tom Barnard.

After he finished, he could see the same doubt that was brewing low in his gut reflected in Alex's eyes. "Whoa. Seeing a guy's computer screen? That's more of a risk than you usually take."

"I know. But I ran out of time and options. Other than, you know, the option to walk away and start over somewhere else."

Alex grunted, knowing exactly what that meant. "Then...you took a chance. And sometimes you have to. I mean, this is your dream, John. It has been ever since you had to walk away from ChiliHeads. And damn, you work so hard and deserve this."

"Thanks. Don't think I'm not inspired by how you walked away to get what you wanted at Overlook Glen. You'll have a Michelin-starred restaurant there within a few years, I'm sure of it."

Alex tipped his head in gratitude. "First of all, Grace got an incredibly lucky break with that winery, and I got an even luckier break when she fell in love with me. Second, I'm not at the mercy of an investor," he said, frowning in thought. "Are you *sure* Summer read that screen right?"

"I'm trusting that she did," John replied.

"Big step for you." There was no humor in his voice or expression, because Alex knew exactly how big that step was. "I mean, you generally don't trust anything but your brain."

"She's different."

"But I never knew you to trust someone else with a business decision of that magnitude."

"She's different," he said again.

"That's twice. Third time and I'm going to start looking for open dates to book a wedding at the winery."

"A wedding?" John choked. "Man, I am not thinking about a wedding."

"Then what are you thinking about? No, wait. Better question…what are you thinking *with*?"

He narrowed his eyes, ready to argue. But then, was Alex right? "I am feeling a little…" Off-balance. Unnerved. *Crushed.* "Stressed."

"Again, not like you. You just *calculate* your way through problems."

"Yeah, and I hope to hell I didn't just *calculate* my way to a twenty-five percent loss on a business concept that doesn't have an official investor yet." He dropped back on the sofa, the sigh of the leather matching the one from his lips. "She's *so* different," he whispered, mostly because it felt good to admit that to someone he trusted as much as Alex.

"And that's three, ladies and gentlemen." Alex grinned at him. "Look, bro, I'm not going to talk you out of her. She's an awesome woman, her kid's cute as hell, and there's definitely some serious chemistry between you two. Just be careful with major business decisions, but then, other than peeking at some guy's computer, she doesn't have anything to do with your business."

Except, she kind of did, since she was once involved with the son of the guy who just squeezed a whole bunch more money out of John.

"Does she?" Alex asked, always able to read John's every thought because they were as much the same person as two humans could be.

"Nah," he said easily, pushing up. "You're right, though. I might be thinking with the wrong body part."

Alex pushed up, too. "Easy cure for that, you know. I mean, if the thoughts are going both ways, and it sure seems like they are."

Yes, it did. But…would that be another impulsive, feeling-driven decision he might regret? "But she has a…history."

Alex raised a brow. "Who doesn't?" Then he lifted a hand as if to correct himself. "Of course, she's a widow. I forgot. Maybe that makes it harder for her to get involved again?" he guessed.

"Yeah." Except her late husband hadn't entered into the picture once. It was the guy who—for all he knew—could have been in the room with George during that negotiation.

And that thought actually made him feel a little sick.

"Hey, listen," Alex said. "I wanted to see if you're planning to be here on Sunday. Grace and I are going to bring the dogs for the day, and I know you wanted Destiny to see exactly how big Mav's going to get."

"Oh, Des would love that."

Alex frowned. "Uh, the idea was to talk her out of Mav, right? Help her realize he won't be a lapdog forever?"

"Sure, but…" He didn't even want to think about the day he'd have to look that little girl in the eye and take the dog away for good. "We can be here."

"Cool." He put a hand on John's shoulder. "Don't worry, man. You got this. I've never actually seen you fail at anything, you know that?"

He looked at Alex for a long time, considering his words and how many times his twin brother had made that comment. It used to be said with the slightest bit of resentment because John frequently—always—came in first between the two of them.

"That used to bother you," he said.

"Lots of things used to bother me," Alex replied. "Then I met Grace and…what can I say? She's different." He laughed and clapped John's shoulder. "Don't say I didn't warn you."

It wasn't until they'd finished dinner on John's patio and Destiny took Mav to the grass to practice the commands she'd learned at camp that Summer remembered something John had said earlier in the day at Waterford.

"Hey, didn't you say you had a surprise for Destiny?" she asked as she picked up their plates to take them into the kitchen that had somehow become "hers" in this new and unconventional living arrangement.

He stayed still, leaning back in his chair, looking

up at her with those black-coffee eyes that always seemed to say more than his mouth did. "I do," he said. "But I don't want her to take it the wrong way."

She made a face, setting the dishes back down and dropping right back into her chair. "What could she take the wrong way? Is it something to do with Mav?"

"No." He propped his elbows on the table and leaned forward. "It's kind of a way to get her to forget softball and reconsider the singing activity."

She didn't answer right away, letting all the responses that rose up go to war before she decided which one to seize. Because her first reaction was, *Oh my God, why are you so incredibly sweet, and why can't every man who walks the earth be exactly like you?*

But she went with something that made her feel a little less vulnerable and more like the mama bear she also was. "You know why she doesn't want to do that, John."

"I do. She's worried about coming in on time with the other singers. And maybe thinking that being watched like that while she performs will make her stutter more."

Oh, what the hell? Why not state the obvious? "God, you're sweet, you know that?"

He smiled. "All the credit goes to Ella Mahoney, who happens to be in charge of the camp chorus and is still considering a solo for Destiny, but I don't want to count on that."

"A solo? Des would sooner crawl through broken glass."

"Oh, I doubt that," he said, shifting in his seat.

"You might not be as sensitive to her self-consciousness as I am," she said. "She's so comfortable with you, and Mav, of course, that she barely stutters, and after a while, you don't hear it if she does."

"I hear it," he said simply. "But Ella had an idea, and I brought it home, and it's in the car."

"Your idea is a…thing?"

"Quite the thing," he said on a laugh. "A small, outdated, very simple, battery-operated, Barbie-approved, incredibly bright pink karaoke machine… thing."

She just stared at him, keeping her mouth closed in case something really, really embarrassing popped out, like, *Why, yes, I'm in love with you.* With each passing second, she could feel herself slipping deeper and deeper, like she could actually drown in how much she liked him.

He leaned forward, looking a little pleased with himself. "Ella said she and Darcy used to play with it as kids and thought it might be up in the attic at Waterford, and sure enough, there it was. I brought it back with a few cassettes and…" He glanced at Destiny as one of her many giggles floated over to them. "I thought you might want to let her play with it to learn and practice coming in on time."

"That would be…awesome."

"Maybe perform for us or a smaller group to get her comfortable before Monday. We're having dinner Sunday at Waterford, remember? Maybe that would be a comfortable place to try it. Maybe she'd like to… What's wrong? Summer? Bad idea? God, I'm sorry."

"No, no." She croaked the word and lost the fight against the tears in her eyes. One blink, and it was all over. "You just went way past sweet," she said gruffly, barely able to talk because her throat was so thick.

It took him a second to figure out what she meant, making him laugh softly. "I thought I'd already reached sexy."

"Past that, too," she managed. "Teetering on irresistible."

He reached over the table to touch her hand. "I'm going to take that as a yes, we can let her play with it."

"Yes," she whispered. "And you can stop right there."

He lifted his brows in question.

"Because what comes after irresistible is…" *Lovable.*

"The kind of thing your brother fast-forwarded through when watching *Top Gun* with you?" he teased.

Yeah, let him think it was sex. Because sex would be easier than where her heart was going. She playfully pointed at him. "Exactly."

"Let me get the machine," he said, popping up without a second's hesitation and making her laugh.

A little while later, after dinner was cleaned up, Destiny made her way back to the table, her step slowing when she spied the candy-colored box sitting on the table and the plastic microphone next to it.

"Wh-wh-what is that?" She stayed a few feet away, both riveted and uncertain.

"It's called a karaoke machine," Summer said.

"For singing?" she asked, the light in her eyes reminding Summer of Isaiah when something had made him really, really happy.

"Exactly. It used to belong to Miss Ella and Miss Darcy, and John brought it back from Waterford Farm for you to play with."

"Really? Just for playing?"

Oh, she was a smart one. Destiny sneaked a quick peek at John, a little doubt in her eyes.

"Playing," Summer said. "Pretending. Performing. Whatever you want it to be."

Mav forgotten for a moment, she approached the table like the pink box could be the Holy Grail, or it could be hiding a snake.

"How do you p-p-play?"

John had installed new batteries and figured out how it worked while Summer had cleaned up, so he took over, picking up the microphone and holding it out. "You turn this on using this button. Then you talk into it."

She took the pink microphone, pushed the button, then stared at it.

"Say something," John urged.

She looked down at the dog. "Hi, Ma—oh!" Her amplified voice coming out of the machine's speaker surprised her. Then she giggled, and that came out loud, too. "Cool!" she practically screamed, which came out deafening.

"You don't have to be loud," he told her. "That's what's so nice about the microphone. It makes you loud even if you want to talk or sing really, really quietly." He whispered the last two words, just like Destiny did when she didn't want to stutter.

Deeper and deeper... Summer could physically feel herself falling for him.

"Hello, Mav," Destiny said again, softening her voice, but unable to hide her delight at the sound that came out of the speaker.

"And the best part is it plays music, too," he said,

choosing his words carefully, as if he sensed—correctly—that he had to take this whole thing slow. "Listen."

He pressed the play button on the old-school cassette player, and Destiny watched, fascinated by an archaic technology she most likely had never seen in her whole young life.

A melody came out, simple and familiar—at least it was to Summer.

"Now what?" she asked.

"Now you sing to that." He inched back and looked up at Summer. "Do you know the words?"

"Not really," she admitted, picking up her phone. "I can find them on the internet."

"It's okay, I know them," he said, adding a quick laugh. "My grandfather used to sing this to Yiayia, so I only know them with a Greek accent, but I know them."

Destiny stuck the microphone in his face. "Then sing them."

"Oh, I…" He shook his head. "It's for you to sing, Des."

"I want to-to-to hear you. S-s-sing."

He let out a soft grunt and took the mic. "Okay."

Was there nothing this man wouldn't do for her daughter? Summer set the phone down and looked at him, affection rising up so powerfully she had to swallow to keep it from choking her up.

He cleared his throat. He rewound the music. He hit play, took a deep breath, and looked right at Summer, for moral support, she guessed. The machine made a soft beep, and he started singing the first line of "You Are My Sunshine."

He laughed at how off-key he was, but Summer

didn't. She barely heard him over her pounding, cracking-open heart.

Destiny waved him off. "I don't like those words," she said.

John cracked up and handed her the microphone. "Take it up with the guy who wrote the song."

She glanced at the mic, waiting a beat until the next chorus started. "You are my Mavvie!" she called out, turning to the puppy. "My little Mavvie. You are the doggy made just for me."

John's jaw slipped open.

"You and me, Mavvie, will be together... It is our destiny!"

Both John and Summer broke into applause, Summer a little less stunned than John.

"How did you do that?" he asked, nothing but wonder and awe in the question. "She's five!" he said as if Summer didn't know that.

"It's her superpower," Summer said. "She's been doing it since she could first sing."

"That's insane. Good job, Des!" He gave her a high five. "Barbie's karaoke machine is all yours. Oh, and when you hear that little beep at the beginning, that's when you sing the first word, just like if you were, you know, singing with other people."

She gave him the quickest look, as if she knew exactly where he was going with that—the chorus at camp.

But he deflected by hitting rewind and starting the music again. Before they heard the beep, Destiny impulsively threw her arms around John's neck and hugged him. He laughed, inching away like the child's affection was too much for him.

"Thank you, nice man," she whispered.

"Oh…" He patted her back with an awkward touch, but Summer could see the smile on his face, the satisfaction in his eyes. "You're welcome, kiddo."

And Summer…was sunk.

Chapter Seventeen

Aidan turned to John one second after the wheels came to a stop. "Just five more hours on the logbook, and you can do the FAA checkride, take the final exam, and you, my friend, are a pilot."

"Thanks, Aidan. For everything." He gave a genuine smile to the man who was so much more than a flight instructor and stepbrother. "If you hadn't pushed, I wouldn't have done this."

"Hey, what good is having that flight instructor's license if I don't use it? Plus, you are so going to back me up on rescue runs around the state. Garrett's adoption program is booming, and we got dogs to pick up and deliver constantly."

John eyed him, a niggling problem rising up. "Any that might resemble Mav?"

"You want another...oh." He laughed. "Yeah, Mav's been stolen." Aidan lifted his brows. "How's Operation Summer Fling going, by the way?"

He chuckled at the expression. "I crashed and burned the first time," he joked.

Aidan, of course, got the *Top Gun* reference. "And

the second?" he countered, knowing the movie like John did. "Listen, take her flying once you've passed the last test. It's an aphrodisiac."

"I might," he said, toggling off the radio before shutting down the engine. Then he huffed out a breath and slid off his headset. "You think I'm ready?"

"To solo or to fling?"

Both. "To take someone up."

"Sure, the rest of our time in this plane is just for the books and the North Carolina FAA regs, man. You're ready to solo, for sure." Aidan took his headset off, too, and sharpened his gaze. "And you're also ready for anything else with her. What's stopping you?"

"I'm not sure anything is anymore," he said honestly. "I mean, other than a kid at home."

"Bring her to Uncle Aidan and Aunt Beck. We'll babysit. Hell, anyone in the family would. We all like Sunshine, and the bets are running high."

"There's betting?"

"Have you met the Kilcannons and Mahoneys? It's all friendly. No real money will exchange hands, believe me. But once those two old ladies start matchmaking, you know the wagering starts. How long it will take? Will it happen?"

"How long will *what* take?" He sure as hell hoped his ever-expanding family wasn't betting on his sex life, although he recalled some pretty damn funny verbal wages when Alex was falling hard for Grace. Funny when it was someone else's personal life they were betting on.

Aidan got a call from Beck, so his question didn't get answered. And it was forgotten by the time they finished the final check and parted ways.

Not an hour later, John climbed out of his SUV, not even aware he was whistling until a voice from the upstairs deck floated down.

"Please. If I hear that song one more time, I might cry."

He'd been whistling... "You Are My Sunshine."

Stepping back so he could see up to the deck, he grinned. "How's the practicing going?"

Summer leaned over the railing, her long hair tumbling over bare shoulders revealed by a tube-top thing that looked like it would be incredibly easy to take off. "She's napping. With the microphone in one hand and Mav in the other. How'd the flying go?"

"Flawless. Five more hours with Aidan, and I can start my solos."

She raised a victorious fist. "We need to celebrate tonight."

And he could think of so many ways to do that. "Whaddya have in mind?"

She bit her lip and leaned farther over the railing to whisper, "I feel the need. The need for..."

"Excellent choice for movie night. After dinner, when Des is asleep. I was thinking of cooking out tonight. Can the ladies of the upstairs join me?"

"We'd be honored. I already made a salad and baked some cookies."

"I have burgers and wine. And lemonade for the under-sixers."

She gave him a thumbs-up. "It's a date. We'll be down after she wakes up. I promised her we'd have a concert before dinner, though." Turning her hand, she pointed an accusatory index finger at him. "You created a monster."

He laughed. "I'm glad she likes it. How was Mav?"

"Attached." She angled her head, making a face. "Breaking up is going to be hard to do, honey."

No kidding, *honey*. "I know," he said simply. "We're going to have to put on a full-court press. Maybe we'll get lucky at Waterford tomorrow when Alex and Grace bring 'Mav in eight months.' She might change her mind."

"I think Mav could grow into a kangaroo, and she wouldn't change her mind. We've enabled this relationship, you know."

He shrugged. "We'll figure it out. There has to be a solution." Like, *Des and Summer never leave Bitter Bark.*

He knew he had to get that idea out of his head, but it lingered through the afternoon while he did a little paperwork for the restaurant, and while he showered, and was still howling for his attention when he walked through his sliding glass doors to start the barbecue and…heard something else howling.

Was that Mav?

He rushed outside and followed the sound up the steps to the upstairs deck. At the top, he just had to stop and stare. And blink. And stare some more.

In the middle of the deck, Destiny stood on the wooden coffee table that used to be in the living room. She wore a pink…thing. A cloud of netting like a tutu that went to her feet, an actual crown on her head, and glitter all over…everywhere. Next to her—also on the coffee table—Mav sat kind of still, as if the yellow dress and straw hat he wore kept him paralyzed with fear or shock or both.

Was that lipstick on him?

She was mid-song, but not any lyrics he knew, except for the "You are my Mavvie" chorus. While she sang, Destiny looked down at Mav, and when she hit a high note, she signaled him with one finger, and he lifted his head to howl with her.

"Wow," he whispered at the very moment she took a breath, making Destiny's eyes pop open. Summer, who was sitting with her back to him, whipped around, hitting the pause button on the karaoke machine. Then Mav leaped off the coffee table and came bounding over to him.

"Don't stop on my account," he said, bending down to scoop up the puppy he saw very little of lately.

"I didn't know you were there," Destiny said, a little accusation in her voice.

"I'm sorry, Des. I loved it. And you, doggo." He gave Mav a little nuzzle. "Except for the lipstick."

"I wanted him to be pretty," Destiny said.

"He is...that." And so were they, mother and daughter bathed in the late afternoon light, one more beautiful than the other. "Can I hear you sing again, Des?"

She didn't say anything, and Summer stood, taking his breath away in a sundress with skinny straps that tied into tiny bows on her shoulders, the material gauzy enough that he could almost see through the flowy skirt.

"She doesn't like to perform in front of people," Summer said in a rare display of stepping in and speaking for Destiny.

"No problem." He held up a hand. "What time do you guys want to eat?"

"You can listen." He barely would have heard

Destiny's whisper, except she said it into her pink microphone.

"I can?"

She nodded. And might as well have said, *I trust you with my life, nice man*, since John's chest felt like it would split wide open so his heart could tumble to the floor.

"Really? Okay. Thanks. I..." He put Mav down and wasn't the least bit surprised when he trotted back to Destiny, who lifted him back onto his place on the coffee table. "I won't say a word. I'll just be back here."

"Come here." Summer reached for his hand, pulling him to the chaise where she sat, operating the little Barbie box.

He smiled at her, almost used to the impact her scent and hair and voice and entire being had on him. *Almost.*

"You're going to love this," she whispered in his ear when he settled next to her.

Yeah. He maybe already did. "Can't wait."

"Okay, Des," she said. "Positions. Three, two, one..." She hit play, and Des started to sing without missing a beat. Just as on cue, Mav howled.

They listened to the new version of an old classic about a dog named Mavvie and his...destiny. One sang like a trained professional, and the other like, well, a dog.

Oh man. He did love this. This woman, this moment, this silly music and precious girl and his lipstick-covered puppy. He glanced at Summer and caught her at the very moment she looked at him, seeing that same light in her eyes he'd seen that very first day in the square when they'd looked at each other over their shoulders.

For a few glorious notes, they held each other's gaze.

Funny, John had thought nothing could beat the thrill of flying. But that feeling paled in comparison to this. Every feeling he'd ever had was forgotten right then as something new and wild and illogical and wonderful took hold.

"It is our destiny!" Destiny finished with great fanfare, making Summer laugh and clap and John just sit, speechless.

"You just figured it out, huh?" Summer whispered.

Why lie? He was gone over her. "Kind of, yeah."

She gave him a playful poke. "The whole song is about taking Mav from you, John," she said on a laugh. "The whole dang song. We're in so much trouble."

So much. "We sure are."

Summer tiptoed down the stairs, giving in to an unexpected shiver of anticipation for their movie date night. Inside John's apartment, she glanced around, and when she didn't see him, she followed the scent of popcorn down the hall to a cozy media room. When she walked through the doorway, she caught him standing in front of a large flat-screen TV, remote in hand, setting up the movie.

She paused for a moment, adjusting the glasses she liked to wear after a long day of contacts, taking a second to admire everything about the back of him.

Broad shoulders, strong muscles, a narrow waist, and a tight backside that looked particularly good in cotton sweats. He looked sexy and comfortable and like someone she could curl up against all night.

She started to say something, but caught herself, still enjoying the beautifully simple moment—a man with his remote, the lingering scent of his barbecue still on him, the dark room, the child asleep upstairs.

She'd had so few nights like this with Isaiah, she thought fleetingly. So few normal "family moments" that let her relax and rely a little on the man of the house. So few times they hadn't been fighting after Destiny was born, too few hours of something so simple and natural as a movie date night in the house. And being a single mother was hard, and lonely. Nights like this were rare.

A soft rumble came from the baby monitor, making John turn around. "Was that Mav?"

She held up the small white box. "He's snoring. They're both sound asleep."

"You travel with a monitor?"

"When I go to Raven's house, Destiny sleeps in a tiny room on the third floor. She loves it because it's like a dollhouse, but I don't like not being able to hear her at night." She set the monitor on an end table next to a bowl of popcorn, a bottle of red wine, and two glasses. "This way, we can enjoy the movie and not have to keep checking on them."

"Them." He gave a wry smile and gestured to the only seat in the room, a long, deep, leather sofa with a comfy ottoman in front of it. "They sure are a pair, those two. Destiny has replaced me as his human."

"Oh, John." She sighed as she dropped onto the

sofa. "I knew this was going to happen. We have to find another dog for her."

"Or me."

She shook her head. "Don't give up your dog for her. Mav's related to your brother's dogs. He's family. You can't do that."

"I know, and they'll be at Waterford tomorrow, in their full-sized glory. I truly believe it'll be a bit of a shock to her to see how big he's going to get. He's not going to sleep in her bed in seven months."

"He's not going to sleep in her bed in seven months because I will not allow my daughter to waltz into town and steal someone's dog with…charm."

He laughed, settling in next to her and placing the popcorn on the ottoman. "Wine?"

"Yes, please. And then I'll take Lieutenant Pete Mitchell for *days*."

He rolled his eyes as he poured her a glass. "The blonde's not bad, either, you know."

"So you're the one," Summer said in a sultry Kelly McGillis voice.

He laughed softly. "Yes, ma'am. Four G's in an inverted flyby."

"Too aggressive," she teased, doing her best to remember some random lines even if they didn't track with the movie dialogue.

"I can see it's dangerous for you." He leaned his shoulder into hers. "But if the government trusts me…maybe you could."

"It takes a lot more than just fancy flying." She cracked up. "Do we really need to watch this movie?" she asked. "Or can we just recite it to each other?"

"We have to watch. It's a first."

"A first? The first time you've watched it...this week?"

He laughed. "First time with a...date."

"Seriously?" She turned to him, mulling over this new information. "I can't believe this isn't your go-to for the girls, John. You can show off your knowledge of planes and great movie lines."

"I didn't know there are women who even like the movie, let alone quote every line."

"Women like sexy guys who fly planes," she teased.

He raised his glass in a toast. "Let's drink to our favorite character," he said.

"Maverick?"

"Actually, mine's Goose. Loyal to a fault, has his priorities straight, and is, frankly, the brains of the operation in Ghost Rider."

She considered that, nodding. "I forgot their plane was Ghost Rider. Well, I think my favorite character is Mrs. Goose."

"Carole," he supplied. At her surprised reaction, he added, "Little-known fact, but that is the name of Meg Ryan's character."

"You're hard-core, Santorini."

He clinked her glass with his. "She does have one of the best lines, though."

Summer leaned in, very close, and whispered, "Take me to bed or lose me forever."

For a moment, neither said a word, the electricity palpable as they looked into each other's eyes. But then a soft, low bass hummed, and the room lit with an orange light, and the sound of a fighter jet roaring onto the deck of an air carrier gave them both a whole different kind of chills.

As the music rose to its first crescendo, the speakers screamed front, back, overhead, and maybe one in the floor, making Summer feel like she was *in* the movie instead of watching it.

"I built this sound system primarily for this movie," he admitted. "So..." He nodded toward the tiny monitor. "Better turn it up in case we get paged."

She did, then nestled into the arm he wrapped around her as they slid from this world into one a little older than she was, but still fresh and fun and really, really loud.

But not so loud they couldn't whisper the lines to each other, sometimes right ahead of the actor, sometimes with.

And by the time the impossibly beautiful flight instructor barreled her ridiculously expensive vintage Porsche through the streets of Miramar and fell right into Pete Mitchell's arms, John and Summer had each finished a sizable glass of wine and half the popcorn. At the first kiss between Mav and Charlie, they slid a little lower into the leather, their bodies lined up and pressed together.

"Uh-oh," John whispered into her hair. "This would be where your brother would fast-forward."

She looked up at him, so close she could see the individual whiskers of his dark beard. "He'd say 'Mom doesn't want you to watch the kissing part.'"

"So, should we..."

She slid his glasses off and set them on the table. "Mom doesn't want you to see this. You might get ideas."

"I have ideas." He took hers off, too, putting them next to his before snagging the remote to hit mute. "I don't want to hear them kiss. But I do want..." He lowered his head, holding her gaze, his intent so clear it nearly curled her toes. "To see if we can keep up with their dialogue."

"They don't talk in this part."

"Exactly." He put his mouth against hers, wrapping both arms around her to intensify the kiss.

She felt her eyes close and her lips part, and everything melted into him. He tasted like red wine and salt, his tongue flicking against hers in the first few steps of a mating dance. As he deepened the kiss, he splayed his hands on her waist, holding her so securely she felt like she could free-fall into him.

He whispered her name and lifted her chin to plant sweet, sweet kisses on her throat, making a whimper slip from her lips.

She could see the flashing of the screen as the movie played, but it felt more like white lights in her head as her whole body lit up with each new place he kissed and touched. With a gentle touch, he eased her back, taking them both horizontal on the couch.

"Mmm," she moaned as his mouth dipped lower over her collarbone. "See why this should be your go-to date movie?"

His hand skimmed her side, warm and slow and so close to the intimate places she wanted him to touch. After another long kiss, he lifted his head to look at her. "Then I'd never get to see the end."

"You don't want to watch the end?"

"I know the end." He kissed her again, settling his whole long, strong body on top of hers, letting her feel every muscle and leave no doubt he did *not* want to watch the end. "What I don't know," he whispered between kisses, "is how this will end."

"It's lookin' good so far."

He let out a half laugh, half groan at the famous final line, but even with the images playing on his giant screen, *Top Gun* was forgotten. All Summer could do was move with John, return his kisses, and feel the slow burn simmer between them.

"You know, don't you?" He lifted his head to ask the question, his fingers slowly tugging at the tie that held her dress straps on her shoulders.

"I know..." She frowned at him, not following, wondering if it was yet another movie line. "That you're looking for a way into this dress."

"Or to get you out of it." He finished one strap and started on the other. "But that's not what I meant."

"Then I know...what?"

He stilled all movement between them, his hands, his hips, his legs as they moved against hers.

"How I feel about you."

She swallowed, watching his expression as the lights from the silent movie played against his profile. "I know you like me."

He gave a hint of a smile. "Yeah, Summer, I like you."

"I know you...want me." She rocked her hips a little to underscore that.

"More than I..." His voice grew gruff. "More than I can say."

"What else should I know?" she asked tentatively.

Both straps down, he put a single finger inside the edge of her puckered bodice, both of them knowing she had nothing on underneath. One inch, and he'd be on his way to...everything.

"I'm crazy about you," he admitted. "Like, a full-blown crush. Wake up thinking about you, go to sleep aching for you, spend way too many hours in between looking for you or at you."

The confession fired a new kind of heat through her, as sexy as his fingers and his kisses. Sexier.

"Same," she whispered.

He frowned, doubtful. "You think I'm nice. Sweet, I think, is the word you use the most."

"That's a euphemism," she told him, stroking his beard and looking into his eyes.

"For what?"

"For…take me to bed or lose me forever."

He didn't laugh, but stayed very still. The only muscle moving was his heart, and it was going as fast as hers. "You don't want to test out the couch?" There was enough of a glimmer in his eyes that she knew he was teasing.

"We could start here." She bowed her back a little, offering her chest. "Maybe leave some clothes in this room and a trail to the next."

"Good plan." He tugged the fabric down, his eyes and mouth following as he exposed her breasts. "Beautiful…oh God, Summer."

He pressed his mouth to her skin, searing her, tickling her, making her rock against him and dig her fingers into his back as they moved in a natural rhythm that had been building since the day they met.

Body to body, hip bone to hip bone, mouth to mouth.

He cupped her breast, circling his thumb, kissing her mouth as she pulled at his T-shirt to get to his hot, smooth skin. Bunching the material in a fist, she arched again, hissing in a breath as his hand magically moved to a whole different place, under her skirt, against her thigh.

Everything vibrated and hummed, blood coursing through her as she eased her legs apart, eager for his touch.

"Who could possibly want me that badly?" he asked.

"Um, me?"

He shook his head and pushed up. "You don't hear my phone blowing up?"

"I thought that was me blowing up."

"Oh, you will." He gave her a heated look, and he sat up and hitched his head toward the end table where she could now see the light and hear the vibration of his phone. "Just let me make sure a restaurant isn't burning down or something. Do not move, Summer Jackson."

"Just a little move." She put her hands on the button of his shorts, pressing her palms against him as she started to unzip. "This move."

He groaned. "Good move. Just..." He turned and grabbed the phone, nearly fumbling it as she unbuttoned the fly. Taking a steadying breath, he squinted at the phone, then he shook his head. "Some...restaurant review Alex wants me to see."

"Oh. Hope it's as good as...this." She lowered the zipper and touched him, letting out an appreciative moan. He was just about to toss the phone on the ottoman when he froze and blinked, pulling the phone closer to read it again. "What the hell?"

Her hand stilled. "Not a good review?"

"What the...oh no. Oh *no*."

"What is it?" All the fire in her body instantly cooled at the look on his face and the tone of his voice.

"It's...oh..." He murmured a curse, rare and rough enough for her to push up and absently pull her top up over her breasts.

"What is it, John? What kind of review could be that bad?"

"It's on a very highly regarded review blog called 'America's Best Diners and Delis' by 'Black Jack' Jennings."

"How is that so bad? Did he hate the food? The service?" She tried for a smile. "The hostess?"

"Black Jack always visits for breakfast, never lets you know he's there, and..." He turned the phone. "Orders three meals."

Oh God. Suddenly, she realized why he looked like his whole world had just crumbled. She finally tore her gaze from his face to look at the phone, seeing the bright orange headline against the black screen.

I WOULD NEVER MISS THIS MEAL.

Meal...not *Deal*.

She skimmed the first line. *Santorini's has everything I wanted...*

"He wasn't the investor." The words strangled her. "I read his screen...wrong." She looked up at him, her heart breaking so hard she could feel her chest ache. "And you..."

"Might have just made the worst business decision of my life."

Chapter Eighteen

S ummer hadn't been kidding about her issues with guilt. From the moment John got the text the night before—killing the mood at the worst possible time—to this afternoon, when she and Destiny came downstairs to go to Waterford Farm for the day with him, Summer couldn't stop apologizing.

"It's not your fault," John assured her for the tenth time after she buckled Destiny into a car seat in the back of his SUV, and he helped Mav scramble into the seat next to her. But his words were falling on deaf ears, based on the stricken look in Summer's blue eyes when she met him at the back of the car.

"I can't believe I was so certain about what I saw," she said. "Of course, there was light on the screen, and I must have seen three letters and imagined the first one. The brain works like that, you know."

"First of all, it was a killer review with nothing but raves for food, service, and atmosphere." He put both hands on her cheeks, adding gentle pressure. "Second, I'll figure it out. No regrets. No guilt. No wallowing. Should I bring the karaoke machine?"

She shook her head as if the non sequitur threw her. "Why would you?"

"In case she gets bored."

"With all those dogs?"

"Or Ella wants to hear her sing so she can be in chorus instead of softball next week."

"Oh." She bit her lip like he'd hurt her.

"What?"

"You have huge business problems, and you're worried about Destiny's camp activities, that's what. You're so..." She put her hand over his and nuzzled her cheek against his palm. "I won't say it, but Nice Man *is* your call sign."

"*Iceman*, Summer." He tapped his chest. "Nothing but a block of ice in here."

She tried to smile, but only leaned into him, resting her head on his shoulder when he wrapped his arms around her. "I am so sorry, John."

"Stop it."

She drew her head back to look up at him. "If that investor doesn't come through, are you obligated to pay the higher price on the property?"

Ethically, yes. "You're not giving up on our secret shopper, are you? He just hasn't shown up, but he will. He could be there tomorrow, the staff will wow him, and he'll fork over the cash. Problem solved. We're worrying too soon about something that hasn't happened."

"But you wouldn't have increased your offer if I hadn't been so certain that he was the investor..." She moaned. "I feel awful."

"You're wrong," he said, holding her a little tighter.

"You would have increased your offer?"

"You don't feel awful. You feel amazing." He ran his hands up and down her sides, easing her into him, remembering how soft the silky bits of her skin that he did get to touch last night felt under his fingers. "And the worst part of all this?"

She looked up, a question in her eyes.

He leaned his head down so their foreheads touched. "What *didn't* happen last night."

She smiled up at him. "Hey, we can buzz the tower another time, Pete Mitchell."

"God, I love the way you think." He lowered his face and kissed her lightly. She kissed him back, not so lightly, then sucked in a breath, froze for a second, and looked to her right…where Destiny had turned in her car seat and was staring at them through the back window.

"Whoa," he murmured, backing away. "Forgot there's an audience."

"Oh boy," she said through a stiff smile and a quick wave. "This ought to be an interesting conversation."

He started toward the driver's side door, then held up a finger as an idea occurred. "We need a deflection. Where is it?"

"Where's…oh." She laughed softly. "In our living room. Want my key?"

"There's one hidden under the planter up there," he said.

"Really?" She gave him a sultry wink. "You should use it sometime."

That made him smile as he jogged up the stairs to her apartment, snagged the karaoke machine, and returned to the car. Summer had already gotten inside when he opened his door and held the toy up for

Destiny to see, not at all certain how she might look at him after the kiss she'd witnessed.

"You can sing on the way to Waterford," he said cheerfully.

She just stared at him, her lovely expression impossible to read. Man, this one was going to drive the boys crazy when she grew up.

"Would it make you ha-ha-happy?" she asked. "Mommy said you're sad."

"And that's why I hugged you," Summer added.

Ohhh. Got it. "I'm not that sad," he said. "Just figuring out my problems."

"Because you don't have money?"

He blinked at that, and Summer whipped around. "Destiny Rose! I never said that. And it's not polite to talk about money."

"But I heard him, Mommy. When I took Mav to the grass, and you were drinking coffee."

What had he said when they sat outside and watched Destiny walk Mav this morning?

"You said you d-d-did not have money in your h-h-hand."

No, he'd said he didn't have *that kind of extra cash on hand.* "Well, it's complicated, kiddo, but I am not worried or sad."

"Then why did you need a hu-hu-hug?"

He let out a sigh and shared a look with Summer. "Because…"

"Because I like to hug John." Summer stepped in for the save. "He's my friend."

Destiny nodded slowly, and whether she was buying that was anyone's guess, but John had to believe she was far too young to think in terms of an adult relationship.

He slid behind the wheel and pulled his seat belt. "But what I really need is the Destiny Rose version of 'You Are My Mavvie.' Right now, please."

She giggled a little, unclipped the microphone, and there was music—of sorts—all the way to Waterford. Even Summer seemed to let go a little of her guilt, and they were all smiling when he pulled into the long drive and counted cars.

"Full house today," he said, waving to Ella, who had just parked near the pen.

"How's our little patient?" she called as she strolled toward John's car.

"She's a hundred percent," John assured her, opening Destiny's door to help her out of the car seat. "You can ask her yourself."

"Hey, gorgeous," Ella said, giving a high five to Destiny and laughing when Maverick bounded out behind her. "How ya feelin'?"

"Good," she whispered, holding the karaoke box tight to her chest.

"Is that what I think it is?" Ella's voice rose with excitement as she dropped to her knees in front of Destiny.

"It's my kar-kar-kar...singing box."

"Do you know that I used to play with that toy every single day when I was little?"

Destiny stared at her, shaking her head slowly while John and Summer watched.

"My cousin Darcy and I would dress up in costumes and sing our hearts out for hours with that very toy. We have a stage we made up in Gramma Finnie's apartment on a window seat. It's the best place to sing!" She put her hands on Destiny's little shoulders. "We won the Bitter Bark Elementary School Talent Show with that very karaoke box! It's so lucky."

Destiny's smile grew, mostly because everything about Ella was simply infectious.

"Will you sing for me today? Up on that stage?"

And the smile disappeared.

"I mean, you don't have to. You can sing for me tomorrow at camp," Ella said. "But I would love to hear you. Darcy and I will give it a try, too. Would you like that?"

She nodded, still silent.

"I'll go tell her." She popped up and waved, heading off toward the house.

Destiny stared after her, then looked up at Summer. "I want to sing," she said softly.

"Good," Summer said. "I'm pretty sure you'll never have a more forgiving or enthusiastic crowd."

"B-b-but I can't," she added on a sad sigh, the very tone of it hitting John somewhere deep in the gut. "I'm s-s-scared."

"Oh, Des," Summer said. "You can trust these people."

But it wasn't the people she didn't trust, John mused. It was herself. Her ability...her *dis*ability. He touched his glasses and remembered how he'd loathed them when he realized they could hold him back from baseball...from flying...hell, from girls.

Just then, Mav saw another dog and took off, startling Destiny, who bolted after him, dropping the karaoke machine. Instantly, the ancient cassette holder popped open, and the handle cracked off, making her let out a soft cry of despair.

"I got it," John said quickly. "I can fix it."

"But Mav…" Destiny pointed to the dog dashing off toward the front entrance, which led to the street.

"I'll get him," Summer said, already on her way. "You fix the box."

Destiny looked from one to the other, a little overwhelmed.

"Hey, hey, no worries, kiddo." He knelt down and picked up the plastic cassette cover and snapped it into place, giving the play button a try. "There, it still works."

"But it's broken," she whispered.

"Just the handle." He turned it over to see how bad the damage was. *Bad.* "But you can still use it."

"I d-d-don't want to," she said sullenly.

"You don't want to use it to sing, or you don't want to sing in front of the people?"

She looked over her shoulder at Summer, who'd caught Mav about fifty yards away. "I do want to sing," she said softly. "But I c-c-can't."

"Destiny," John said, "you can sing. Better than about ninety percent of the world."

"But I can't *talk*," she insisted on a breathy whisper.

For a moment, he didn't say anything, grazing his fingers over the broken plastic handle, thinking of how to phrase his thoughts so they could help her.

"You know, when I was a kid, a little bit older than you are, I found out I had to wear glasses. I couldn't see much of anything without them."

She stared at him, suddenly rapt by his confession.

"I was so unhappy," he told her. "It meant I had to wear these really goofy-looking glasses to play baseball. None of the other kids had to wear them, but

247

my dad got them for me, and pretty soon I forgot about having to wear them."

"I'm not that g-g-good at baseball," she said. "I'm sorry."

"Don't be. You're good at singing. A couple years later, I found out I couldn't do the one thing—the *only* thing—I wanted to do in the whole world, because of my eyesight."

"What?"

"Fly planes. Well, a special kind of plane that no one can fly unless they have perfect vision. I was sad again."

She didn't say a word, but something was sinking in. He had to believe that.

"That's when I learned that no matter what happens or what doesn't work or what breaks..." He held up the handle. "If you really believe in yourself, you can find a way to make your dream come true. Whether it's baseball or flying or...singing."

Only then did he realize that Summer was standing behind him, listening.

"So..." He held the toy out to Destiny. "You think about it, and if you're comfortable, you can sing. If you don't want to..."

She made a face. "Crafts." She took the plastic box, holding it from the bottom.

"And I bet I can snag some duct tape around here. I can fix that for you."

She nodded and turned, using one hand to beckon Mav, who trotted off with her.

He stood slowly, holding Summer's gaze as he rose.

"That was some life lesson," she said.

"Nah." He shrugged. "Nothing you couldn't pick up in, say, an old Rolling Stones song. You *can't* always get what you want, you know."

"But sometimes…" She put her hands on his face, rose up on her toes, and planted a kiss. "You get exactly what you need."

"Christian's taking it kind of hard." Andi Kilcannon brushed back a lock of hair and glanced at her husband, Liam.

"I'm afraid my son is suffering a bad case of puppy love," he said.

"I assume he's here today?" Summer asked, glancing around for their little boy or his big German shepherd.

"He took his little sister to see some dogs in the kennel," Andi said.

"I'll talk to Destiny," Summer promised. "She needs to forgive him."

John joined them, handing a Bloody Mary to Summer. "I have good news," he announced to the small group.

"Destiny is talking to Christian?" Summer so hoped her little girl could rise above the softball incident and let dear little Christian off the hook.

"Not at the moment. She's in Gramma Finnie's upstairs apartment with Darcy and Ella…singing."

"How'd they get her up there?"

"That's the other news," he said with a soft laugh. "Alex and Grace introduced her to Gertie, Jack, and Bitsy, and she saw…future Mav."

"Oh." Summer lifted her glass in a mock toast. "She's not a fan of large dogs, so you may get to keep yours after all."

"Maybe." He clinked her glass with his own. "And she really is singing up there."

"With…an audience?" Summer asked.

"Probably a small one, but enough that she can feel confident to sing at camp tomorrow and bypass the dreaded crafts."

Her heart just about folding in half, Summer reached for his hand. "Thank you for caring so much about her," she whispered, softly enough so that Liam and Andi, who were talking to each other, might not have heard.

He gave her a wink in acknowledgment of the compliment. "Want to go watch? I don't think she'd mind if we joined."

She glanced at Andi, not wanting to be rude and just drop the subject of Christian. "I will talk to her," she promised again. "And if you like, I'll talk to him."

"I don't think he wants you—or Destiny—to know his true feelings," Andi said, the warmth of a mother's love coming through her eyes. "But it's killing me to see him mope like this. First crush and all."

"Oh, a first crush isn't going to kill him," Liam said, putting his arm around Andi. "Pretty sure you were mine."

"In your thirties," she said, laughing as she leaned her head on his strong shoulder. "Go on and watch your little girl. But thanks, Summer. I'm sure they'll work it out. He'll have to lick his wounds anyway when you guys go back to Florida."

"Won't we all?" John whispered in her ear as he ushered her away.

"Will you?" she asked.

He just gave her a *get real* look.

"I don't know," she teased. "You'll get your dog back, and you won't have crazy women misreading computer screens and costing you God-knows-how-much."

Alone at the bottom of the stairs, he put an arm around her and drew her all the way into an embrace. "Small price to pay."

It was her turn to give him the very same look.

"Okay," he conceded on a laugh. "Not *that* small. But I'm still confident Tom Barnard will come in. We can fix the financing problems and carry on." He paused at the top of the stairs, then stepped toward a doorway that led to another enclosed set of stairs to the third floor. "Listen."

"You are my Mavvie, my little Mavvie. You are the doggy made just for me…"

The music and new lyrics that had gone way past familiar this weekend floated down, making Summer smile.

"You and me, Mavvie, will be together. It is our destiny!" Summer whispered the words she knew well by now, but Destiny's distinct and shockingly powerful voice filled the small stairwell, along with a just as powerful, high-pitched dog howl and a noisy explosion of applause and laughter.

"*What* was that?" The voice behind Summer surprised her, and she turned to come face-to-face with Cassie, John's sister.

"*That* was Destiny Rose," he said with as much pride as any…yes, as any father.

"And Maverick, the singing puppy," Summer added with the same amount of pride.

"Holy sweet pipes, Batman." Cassie practically pushed them out of her way to get up the stairs. "I have to get them to Barkaoke tonight. There's still time to sign her up."

"Whoa. *Whoa.*" John grabbed her sleeve, slowing his sister's step. "She might not want to do that, Cass."

No, she would not, and Summer could not have been more grateful to John for knowing that and putting the brakes on such a crazy plan.

"Are you kidding? Did you hear her sing? And the dog right there with her? She could win. Believe me, I'm organizing it because my client, Family First Pet Foods, is the sponsor. And there is no one planning to sing on that stage in the square tonight who comes close to her. And Mav."

John looked like he was about to say no, then he turned to Summer. "What are the chances?"

"The chances she'll sing in front of all of Bitter Bark on a stage in the town square?" She laughed lightly. "You're the math guy. What number is way less than zero?"

"Can I ask?" Cassie put her hand on Summer's arm. "I will not push. I would like to ask her."

Summer thought for a moment, then nodded. "You can ask."

Without a second's hesitation, Cassie shot up the stairs, leaving John and Summer to look at each other.

"You said you wanted her to have a little stress," he reminded her. "That her speech therapist says it's good for her."

She leaned into him, resting her head on his

shoulder, not even a little surprised he remembered that. "I'm not sure *I* could take the stress of that if she says yes."

"Well, it's a less-than-zero chance." He put an arm around her and walked her to the top of the stairs where noise, chatter, and laughter spilled from an open door that led to a little apartment. "And if she does say yes…" He kissed her on the forehead before they walked in. "We'll have something else to celebrate." Leaning down, he whispered in her ear, "This time, we'll skip the movie and go straight to the kissing parts."

An unholy thrill zipped through her as they stepped in, greeting the small crowd of all women—plus Mav—who were gathered there.

Gramma Finnie and Yiayia sat side by side on a floral-print sofa, watching Destiny on a makeshift stage on a wide bay windowsill. She held Mav in her arms, a small, homemade microphone stand in front of her.

Darcy and Ella were on the floor like the enthralled audience, the Barbie karaoke machine between them. In front of Destiny, with her hands in a prayer position, Cassie was nearly breathless with her pleas.

"Please, just hear me out."

Destiny turned to Summer and gave her the biggest smile, the kind that made her heart soar.

"Did you hear me, Mommy?"

And she didn't stutter! "I did, angel. That was just glorious."

"It was that and more," Cassie cooed. "You two, you and Mav, could win the Barkaoke contest. You'd make the show!"

Destiny just stared at her, the smile still in place, but a little hint of dread in her eyes. Because she was being asked to sing in front of people, or because she was scared she couldn't respond without a stammer?

Summer tensed and moved imperceptibly forward, ready to jump in and answer for her, but the strong, steady hand on her back added a tiny bit of pressure. He didn't even look at her, didn't say a word, but that very little bit of a reminder was exactly what she needed.

Destiny had to speak for herself. Summer shouldn't push her one way or the other, because the decision was Destiny's to make.

"Do I have to talk?" she whispered, eliciting a soft moan from Gramma Finnie.

"You know who Connor and Sadie are?" Cassie asked. "Have you met them yet?"

She nodded, although Summer wasn't entirely sure Destiny knew the names of all the relatives and their significant others.

"Well, they are our co-mayors, along with their dog, Frank, who is *the* mayor of Bitter Bark. The three of them will be the emcees, er, announcers," Cassie clarified. "And they will introduce everyone and thank them after they perform. I promise I will make sure that you don't have to do anything at all but sing."

"In front of all the p-p-p-people?"

"There will be a lot of people there," Cassie said, somehow instinctively knowing to speak slowly. "But I am pretty sure that if you sing, twenty-five or more of them will be named Kilcannon, Mahoney, or Santorini."

"Or Jackson," Summer added softly.

Destiny looked down at Mav, then lifted her gaze and looked hard at Summer, the battle in her heart evident in every perfect feature on her face. She wanted to do this. She wanted to in the worst possible way. But fear was stopping her.

"And there's a prize if you win," Cassie added, sensing she was about to close the deal.

"What is it?" Destiny asked, her eyes a little brighter.

"Well, it's a great big trophy that is…are you ready? A microphone shaped like a dog bone." She grinned at the others. "I personally designed it, and I have to say the client was thrilled."

"Not as thrilled as he was when he saw Ella in the square during the setup yesterday," Darcy stage-whispered to Ella, who elbowed her right back.

"Shut it, Darce."

"Well, he was."

But the exchange was lost on Destiny, whose eyes widened with more yearning. "A trophy?"

John had shared his selection of "hardware" with her earlier this week, and she'd been mighty impressed by the trophies.

"Oh, and dog food for life!" Cassie clapped her hands. "I totally forgot that part. The dog who sings wins a free lifetime supply of Family First dog food. You'll never have to pay for a bite of this little guy's food."

Destiny gasped as this sank in, and she shifted her gaze to John. "Yes," she whispered, so softly that Summer wasn't sure she heard.

"Yes?" About three others asked the question in unison.

"You'll do it?" Cassie practically screeched.

Destiny nodded as if she didn't trust herself to speak, and Summer took a few steps closer.

"You're sure, honey?" she asked.

"I'm sure, Mommy." She lifted Mav closer and pressed her mouth under his floppy ear to say something, then putting the puppy to her own ear, getting a swift lick. "Mavvie's sure, too."

"Hallelujah!" Cassie practically leaped in the air. "Destiny Rose, you are going to be a star! I predict your performance will go viral, and Family First will love the PR." She stopped suddenly, taking Summer's arm. "If you're okay with that. We won't use her last name or anything. I'll protect her identity."

"It's fine," Summer said, more than a little certain Des might back out at the last minute. "As long as she has every opportunity to change her mind before she goes onstage."

"Absolutely," Cassie promised, then she grabbed John's arm. "Come with me to spread the news. The show's at seven tonight, and we want everyone there. Help me rally the troops for a family adventure. And if she wins, we'll drag the entire crew to Bushrod's for drinks and dessert, courtesy of Family First!"

"One second, Cass." John turned his attention to Destiny. "What made you change your mind, kiddo?"

She lifted a shoulder, the bruised one.

"Was it the trophy?" he asked.

"It was the dog food," she said softly. "So you don't have to pay for Mavvie's food, because you don't have money in your hand."

He blinked at her, his face a reflection of the same emotions swirling through Summer. "Destiny," he said, a little wonder in his voice. "That's not…necessary."

"I want to." She snuggled the dog. "I love him."

"And I love...that you're going to sing." He swallowed visibly, then turned and left quickly, as if he didn't trust himself in that room for one more minute.

"Sweet Saint Patrick," Gramma Finnie whispered after John and Cassie were gone. "I need a hankie for all these unshed tears, lass."

Summer felt the same, walking to the window seat so she could wrap her arms around Destiny. "I'm proud of you, honey," she whispered. "Not just for singing and for being so generous, but because you're going to be such a big girl about giving up Mav."

She slipped out of Summer's embrace, popped off the little homemade stage and darn near pirouetted in front of the grannies, who reached out for their own hug.

"You were mahvehlous, dahling!" Yiayia teased in an affected accent.

"A star is born, lassie!" Gramma Finnie added.

Darcy and Ella were cheering and high-fiving, too, still on their knees as they gathered around their little protégée.

But...something was off. Something was unfinished. Why hadn't Destiny reacted to her comment about giving up Mav? Because if she was worried about John paying for dog food, then she planned to give him back. Right?

"Des," Summer said, putting a hand on her shoulder. "Did you hear what I said? About giving up Mav?"

Destiny looked up, her expression blank. And Summer could almost always read her expressions. But this one...

Something was *off*.

"You are going to give up Mav, aren't you?"

She hugged him tight and stared, silent, while the others quieted down and watched the standoff.

"You know you have to...eventually."

"No, I won't," she said softly, climbing onto the sofa to tuck herself between the two grandmothers as if they were her pillars of support. "I won't have to."

"Yes, you will have—"

"Not if he's my daddy."

Yiayia gasped, and Gramma Finnie pressed her fingers to her lips. Darcy made a little noise, and Ella just started laughing.

Yes, it was all amusing and precious and even a little thrilling for them. But Summer was the one who would have to pick up the pieces of a child's broken heart if that didn't happen. And...maybe her own.

Right then, she felt exactly like Destiny might about tonight's performance—a little overwhelmed at how deep she'd gotten herself into a situation she really wanted, but terrified it might blow up in her face.

Chapter Nineteen

Bushrod Square was hopping on Sunday evening, packed with locals, tourists, street performers, sidewalk vendors, and so many dogs. The entire Kilcannon-Mahoney-Santorini clan had packed up after dinner at Waterford Farm, piled into all their various trucks, SUVs, cars, and one refurbished dog van previously owned by the late, great Annie Kilcannon, and headed, with many dogs, to the square.

Through it all, John was utterly amazed at how calm Destiny was about her debut performance. She rode with Summer and John, holding Mav, softly whispering to him with what seemed to be zero fear.

As if she were afraid to cause any anxiety, Summer was much quieter than usual, turning from the passenger seat to smile at Des periodically, then holding John's hand with a slightly too-tight grasp as they parked and walked through the square to the stage and three sets of bleacher seats erected for Bitter Bark's first Barkaoke contest.

As the organizer, Cassie had some serious pull and had arrived early to reserve the first four rows in the middle bleachers for the family, who were gathering in groups, chatting, and laughing with excitement—and maybe some nerves on behalf of little Destiny.

As they reached the stands, a cheer went up from the family, and Destiny squared her little shoulders and gave Mav's leash a tug.

Over her head, John and Summer shared a look.

"You nervous?" he mouthed.

"Dying," she replied, just as silent.

"There she is." Cassie swooped in with a small posse made up of Pru, Darcy, Ella, and two meddlesome octogenarians not far behind. They all made a fuss over Destiny's pretty pink dress, which John and Summer had zipped back to his house to let her change into, and the blue kerchief around Mav's neck, courtesy of Friends With Dogs grooming business, owned by Darcy.

"We're going to take her backstage," Cassie announced. "Summer, you can come with us and watch from back there, or with the family in the stands. Mama's choice."

"Do you want me with you, Des? I'll go where you want me."

She swallowed, thinking. "Stay here, Mommy," she whispered.

"You're sure?"

"I want you to see like everyone."

"Oh, honey. Okay." She bent over and folded her daughter in her arms and added a kiss on the head. "Knock 'em dead, buttercup."

When they parted, Destiny looked up at John, and his heart twisted because he was certain she'd done this for him. For the dog food, and maybe to show him she could conquer a fear. And if asked right at that moment, he would have announced to the world that he loved that little girl.

Instead, he just crouched down and gave Mav some love. "Sing like the beast you are, Mavvie."

Destiny smiled. "You called him Mavvie."

"Guilty as charged." He laughed softly and met her indescribable gaze. "You are one hundred percent sure you want to do this?" he asked on a whisper. "'Cause you don't have to."

"It's my dream," she said softly. "Like you said f-f-flying was."

Oh God. He might actually shed a damn tear.

"Then don't let anything stop you, kiddo." He plucked at a ringlet, letting it bounce. "And don't lose Mav back there, okay? Leash on all the time."

"I promise." She leaned closer, gave him a quick kiss on the cheek, and was suddenly escorted off in a flurry of female laughter and chatter. And some barking.

It took him a second to stand up, swallow his emotion, and turn to Summer. Her eyes were wide, her jaw loose with a soft quiver. He didn't know what to say, so he just put his arms around her and pulled her in for a long hug.

"You can sit with us." Yiayia's voice was sharp in his ear, pulling them apart. "Finola has Jameson's in a flask. I think you could both use some."

They cracked up and took seats, with Gramma Finnie next to Summer and Yiayia next to him, each holding a dachshund. All around, John was surrounded by all the familiar faces who'd become family in the past year, like a cloud of support and encouragement that he knew Summer could feel, too.

He took them all in, from his own brother, sitting with Grace a few rows behind them, over to the next row of Kilcannons and several small babies. Then he saw Declan and Braden both talking to a tall, dark-haired man he thought he'd seen before, but didn't actually recognize.

"Who's the guy on the end talking to Braden?" John asked Yiayia. "Another firefighter?"

Yiayia didn't look. "The gorgeous one with the strong jaw, broad shoulders, and eyes the color of a kalamata olive?"

John laughed softly, as did Summer, who'd leaned in to listen to the exchange. "That would be one way of describing him," John said.

"That's Ella's future husband," Yiayia replied.

"What?" Summer and John asked the question in unison.

"Oh, you don't know that, Agnes," Gramma said, adding a tsk. "Ella cannot stand the man."

"Which means nothing," Yiayia said. "In fact, it's a sign of how perfect that match will be. Pru says they'll be perfect for 'opposites attract.'"

"Who is he?" Summer asked, eyeing the stranger. "He's really…"

John slid her a look, and she jabbed him lightly with her elbow.

"Not cute or anything," she finished.

Yiayia finally stole a look, a satisfied, smug smile on her face. "His name is Jace Demakos. His family is from Mykonos," she added with the same inflection as if she'd said, *He's been dipped in fairy dust and is worth fifty billion.*

"Oh yeah." John remembered him then. "The

Greek guy from Chicago who works for the dog food company. You think he and Ella…"

"I *know* he and Ella…but not yet. When the time is right. Now, watch. Here comes the dog mayor."

"Another one of our successes," Gramma Finnie added as Frank, the dog of many breeds who was also known as the mayor of Bitter Bark, came trotting onto the stage, followed by Connor Mahoney and his fiancée, Sadie Hartman, who were Frank's chiefs of staff—and the de facto co-mayors.

A noisy cheer went up for Frank, who stood center stage, flipping a ridiculously long tail, not stopping until Sadie set her orange cat next to him. Then the cat and dog walked over to the side of the stage and settled down for a snooze, earning another raucous cheer and hoots of "Fremi!" from the locals.

"What's Fremi?" Summer asked.

"Frank and Demi, the dog and cat. Our celebrity power couple," John explained.

"Yianni." During the applause, Yiayia leaned very close to John to whisper something only he could hear. "I'm very excited to watch my future great-granddaughter perform."

The smile that comment elicited stayed there through the first ten of a total of fifteen performances, which included more than a few locals he recognized from the restaurant and several tourists. All with dogs, all giving decent renditions of some famous songs. One lady sang "I Will Always Love You" with a bearded collie named Seamus who circled her and danced, and a married couple sang "You're Still the One" while their matching retrievers thumped their tails in a perfect rhythm.

A few of the dogs barked with the beat of the singer, and one border collie actually performed a trick, but none of them sang.

"Think she has a chance?" he asked Summer when a young rapper finished, and his Chihuahua took a "down dog" bow for him.

"I just want her to get through it."

"She'll get through it." He took her hand between both of his and squeezed. "She's made of much tougher stuff than you give her credit for."

Biting her lip, she looked up at him. "Since she could talk, she's been singing," she said softly. "This really is her dream. I know she's young, but she's got something so special. I don't want her stutter to keep her from...anything."

"Did you see that girl on the way over here? She's so ready."

Her look said she didn't agree. "I just don't want her to go out there, freeze or have some other horrible experience, then never sing again."

"That's not going to happen." He hoped.

"Who do we have next, Sadie?" Connor asked into the microphone.

"A very special guest," she replied into her own. "This young lady and her Lab puppy are—"

"Oh God," Summer squeezed his hand so hard he thought he felt bones crack.

"—visitors to Bitter Bark, but I have no doubt we're going to want them back every year!" Sadie finished.

"Ladies and gentlemen and our esteemed judging panel..." Connor nodded toward the five local business owners who sat at a table in front of the stage. "I give you Destiny Rose and Maverick, singing—get this—original lyrics to what is sure to be a big hit, 'You Are My Mavvie.'"

A whimper escaped Summer's lips as an excited hush fell over the family in the bleachers.

John tried to breathe and ignore his heart, but all that was forgotten when Des and Mav walked onstage, and the whole audience gave a collective, "Awww!"

"What about the karaoke machine?" Summer whispered on a gasp. "They can't possibly play a cassette back there."

"Never fear, lass." Gramma Finnie patted Summer's hand. "Cassie told me they have 'Sunshine' on the playlist. She'll be just fine."

Destiny picked up Mav and stepped to the microphone that Connor had lowered to her height.

She took a deep breath, closed her eyes, and belted out the opening lines. "You are my Mavvie! My little Mavvie. You are the doggy made just for me."

When she ended the next line, Mav gave a howl, and throughout all of Bushrod Square, those two voices were all you could hear. Destiny's clear soprano tone, with not so much as a quiver when she hit a high note, accompanied on certain parts by the crazy wail she'd trained Mav to do.

With each line, John could feel Summer relax. With each finished chorus, someone else cheered. And by the time she reached the flawless crescendo of her little homemade song, every person in the bleachers rose to their feet with thunderous applause.

Except John and Summer, who sat stone-still next to each other, finally exhaling.

265

They turned to each other, neither trying to hide the tears that welled up. Wordless—maybe speechless—they shared one quick, secret kiss of victory, then popped up to clap with the crowd as Des and Mav took a little bow.

"She should run off the stage," Summer said through gritted teeth. "They'll ask her a question."

But she didn't move. She stood right there, taking in the appreciation and enjoying the moment. And when the applause died down, she leaned into the microphone and said, "Thank you."

She didn't whisper. She didn't sing. And she didn't stutter.

Right at that moment, John could have been flying supersonic with the afterburners on, and he wouldn't have been any more thrilled.

The multigenerational clan that ranged in age from a few months to near ninety piled into Bitter Bark Bar—which apparently the locals called Bushrod's—and nearly filled the place, which had been fairly quiet on a Sunday evening. It wasn't quiet anymore, Summer noted, as one big genuinely happy family filled the tables.

A dozen different rearranged tables were occupied with couples, grandmothers, children, a few high chairs, and at least three dogs. At the bar, Billy, the owner, poured wine, beer, soda, water, and a few shots. Cassie put in orders of fries and onion rings for the kids and dessert for anyone who wanted it.

The emcee mayors, Connor and Sadie, moved from

table to table as if they were the hosts of the event, the two never far from each other's side, sharing laughs and affection, as Summer would expect from the recently engaged couple. And Ella headed to the jukebox with the tall, handsome Jace Demakos hot on her heels, like Mav panting after Destiny. He wasn't treated with quite the same tenderness, however, as the gorgeous young woman had turned keeping Jace at arm's length into an artform that was amusing to observe.

And, oh, *Destiny*. Gazing across the table at her daughter, Summer couldn't remember the last time she saw her daughter glow like this. Her smile lit her whole face, with a gleam of joy in her eyes and a tilt of her head that exuded a confidence she'd never shown anywhere but in the privacy of their home. And, of course, Mav was tucked tight to her chest.

"Your girl was born to perform," John whispered as he put a glass of wine in front of Summer and slid a coke to Destiny, currently smiling up at Katie and Daniel Kilcannon as they oohed and aahed over her dog-bone trophy in the middle of the table.

Summer lifted her glass in a toast. "I pronounce this the best summer she's ever had."

"It could be mine, too," John said softly, the undercurrent in his tone sending a shiver right down to Summer's toes.

"Could be?" She lifted a brow. "What's going to be the deciding factor?"

"If you…" He inched closer. "Take down your walls…" He put his lips near her ear. "And give in to what you know you want to do and…"

All around, the sounds quieted and people faded as

every sensation in Summer seemed focused on him. On them. On the flutter low in her belly and the heat in her veins. She managed a breath. "And?"

"And..."

Suddenly, a cheer went up, and several people stood. Alex yelled out, "Opa!" and Yiayia put her hand in the air and pointed to the sky.

"For Papu Nik!" she called out.

Cassie poked John in the back.

Smiling at Summer, John whispered, "And *dance*."

In a flash, he was up and gone with Cassie, headed to the dance floor as the first strains of a classical guitar filled the bar, barely loud enough to hear over chairs moving and the whole family migrating to the same place.

"What's going on?" Destiny asked Summer.

"I think there might be some Greek dancing," she said.

"Go, lassies," Gramma Finnie said, slipping into the chair John had vacated. "I'll be in charge of the dogs while you watch this glorious dance."

Summer stood and reached for Destiny's hand, both of them caught up in the energy that seemed to electrify the room.

Ella welcomed them into a circle that was forming around the perimeter of the dance floor, and there, in the middle, Cassie and John stood side by side with their arms around each other's shoulders, their faces serious as they took a few steps in perfect sync.

The strains of a classic Greek song that Summer knew only as the "Zorba song" grew louder, and the crowd simmered down, swaying in a circle around the dancers. In the middle, their steps grew more complicated and fascinating as John and Cassie tapped, kicked, swayed, and swept their legs.

The mesmerizing dance, haunting music, and buzz of excitement somehow felt both ancient and contemporary, poignant but fun. As the rhythm increased, everyone started clapping to the beat, the family calling out encouragement, including Yiayia, who shouted the loudest, and in Greek.

Summer just stared at the tall, graceful man who moved like the music flowed through his veins and suddenly looked very, very Mediterranean and...*sexy*. Next to her, Destiny was captivated, concentrating so hard on the steps that she barely clapped, her little jaw loose as the music and a first-time experience washed over her.

As the melody reached a crescendo, Alex stepped out of the audience and reached his hand toward Yiayia, who gave a formal nod and joined him next to Cassie and John, making the line a little longer but without a single step lost. Katie brought Daniel out next, then Connor, Sadie, Darcy, and Josh started another line behind them, all following—more or less—the steps that John and Cassie were doing.

Then, as if by magic, all of the people on the outside circle put their arms over each other's shoulders and started swaying and stepping, one foot forward, one back, in a simple version of the dance.

Jace stepped into the circle and danced his way down the line toward them, obviously as familiar with the steps as John. He stopped in front of Ella and reached for her, making a slight cheer go up from the crowd, and they did a two-by-two version of the dance. Then Shane and Chloe did the same.

When the song started again, there were couples and short lines, and nearly everyone was dancing. Suddenly, Cassie and John broke apart as Braden stepped into the circle to claim his wife.

John turned to Summer with an inviting look and outstretched hand. "It's easy," he said. "Just follow me."

Vaguely aware of another cheer at this new arrival to the floor, Summer took his hand, stretched her arm up and over his amazing shoulders, and laughed her way through a few mistakes until she got the hang of the deceptively simple steps.

An inexplicable elation filled her heart, a happiness that had to come from the joyful, uplifting music, the smooth power of the man next to her, and the sheer wall of love that seemed to surround the entire dance floor.

"Summer," he whispered in her ear. "Look."

He turned her slightly to see Destiny, now face-to-face with Christian, who stood in front of her with his hand outstretched.

"Oh my God," she whispered, caught off guard by the unexpected moment, part of her wanting to run and help Destiny, and part of her praying her little girl could rise above her emotions and forgive Christian.

But she knew instantly from the look on Destiny's face that she had nothing to worry about. There was no fear, and no anger, on her beautiful features. Just that longing to try something new she already knew she'd love.

Destiny smiled at something Christian said, then nodded, taking his hand and sliding next to him, arms over shoulders, to imitate what everyone else was doing. Another cheer went up, loudest of all, as

Summer looked up to meet Andi Kilcannon's gaze. The two mothers shared smiles of relief and victory.

For the rest of the song, Summer split her attention between John, who made her knees almost too weak to follow the steps, and Destiny, who giggled and danced and might just have found yet another thing she was very good at doing.

When it all ended, Summer turned to John and wrapped her arms tight around his neck.

"Yes," she whispered. "Best summer ever."

He kissed her on the lips, and all Summer could do was hold on and try not to laugh at how loud Yiayia hollered, "Opa!"

Chapter Twenty

O f all the nights Summer wanted Destiny to settle down and get to sleep, this one was turning out to be the hardest. Of course. Destiny was wired for sound and nowhere near asleep after her night of victory, dancing, two Cokes, and chocolate cake.

She jumped on her bed, holding the trophy that was a good third of her size, singing at the top of her lungs, hair still wet from the bath that had seemed to take hours, nightgown flying.

And as much as Summer wanted to run downstairs—with the baby monitor, of course—and fall into John's arms, she couldn't see the end of this particular rush.

Mav was on no such high, though, crashed at the bottom of the bed, oblivious to the jumping, singing, and squeals of joy.

"Mommy, did you hear me say thank you?" she asked for the twentieth time since they got home from Bushrod's.

"I did, baby." Summer sat on the edge of the bed, beaming up at Destiny. "It was perfect. Every minute of tonight was perfect."

She folded onto the bed, clutching the trophy to her chest. "And did you see me dance with Christian?"

"Oh yes, I did." Summer gave her daughter's hand a squeeze. "I am very proud of you for forgiving him."

"He didn't mean to hit me with that ball," she said, her face the picture of earnestness. "He just wants to be my friend."

"I'm so happy you settled that. Now how about we get all tucked in—"

"What did you think when they said my name?" she asked with that wistful joy that seemed to emanate from her soul.

"I wasn't surprised. No one was. You got a standing ovation and blew the judges away."

She smiled, tipping her head, her ringlets falling over the trophy. "I wish D-d-daddy had seen it."

An old, familiar pain gripped Summer's chest. "He did, Des. He saw every moment from heaven."

"And been there for the dancing. I love the sirtaki! Yiayia told me that's what it's called, and she's going to teach me all the steps. She said she'll do it when Tails and Trails is over. Dance camp!"

Which meant they'd be staying longer, Summer mused, surprisingly okay with that idea. No, not surprisingly. After today? After this whole time? She had no desire to run away from John until she had to.

"I want to sing again." Destiny sighed out the words. "And d-d-dance."

"You know, Cassie said she has a great video from tonight. We can watch it tomorrow all over again. So now you should—"

"Did John take a v-v-video of my s-s-s..." She

couldn't finish the word *song*, a definite sign of exhaustion.

"No. He was watching with me. Holding my hand." Summer poked Destiny's tummy. "I was so nervous, I thought I was going to throw up. But you weren't nervous at all."

She shook her head, pride in her eyes. "Did John like it?"

"Are you kidding? He's so proud of you."

"Like Daddy would have been."

Oh yes. "Daddy would have been so proud," she assured Destiny, glancing at the clock. "And he'd be proud if you climb into this bed and close your eyes."

She shook her head, cradling the trophy. "What did John say?" she asked.

That he'd wait up for Summer with tea and…more kisses. "He said you were amazing. What everyone said."

"And Mav gets food forever and ever!" She threw her arms out, and the trophy slid to the bed.

"Why don't I put this up on the dresser so it's the first thing you see tomorrow morning?" *If you ever go to sleep.* "Right here."

She centered it on the blue dresser across the room, and Destiny dropped her chin into her palms and stared at it, quiet for a moment. Surely sleep couldn't be far off.

"How about some water, hon? A trip to the bathroom? Do you need anything else before we say good night?"

"Yes."

"What is it?" Summer went back to the bed to prop on the edge. "Whatever you want to settle in."

"I want a d-d-d…" She swallowed, frustrated.

"Dog? Mav's right here."

"Daddy," she whispered.

Summer breathed out a sigh. "Destiny, I can't conjure one up."

"But that's why we came here."

"No, it isn't," she said. "We came to get you a dog."

"And a daddy." She gave a smug look. "I heard Aunt Raven say that the night before we left."

"You *what*?"

"I'm s-s-sorry, Mommy."

"It's okay." She hated that the stutter returned at anything that sounded like a reprimand. "I didn't know you were listening to that conversation."

"I just wanted w-w-water, and I came downstairs, and you and Aunt Raven were laughing."

And drinking wine. And sharing girl talk. And talking about the possibility of reigniting a romance with Travis Shipley.

"Well, I don't think you understood what you heard."

"Aunt Raven said a man in Bitter Bark could be my daddy. A man at a restaurant."

"Destiny!" Summer was sorry if the scolding tone made Destiny stutter, but she needed to learn not to eavesdrop. "You should not listen in on other people's conversations, and you should not repeat things you don't understand."

She looked down for a moment, then slipped under her covers, chastised. "I'm sorry," she whispered as Summer smoothed the comforter over her. "I just l-l-like him."

275

Her heart folded. "I like him, too, Des. He's wonderful."

That hazel gaze shifted up with a question. Maybe a demand. "Then..." She shrugged. "Marry him."

Summer laughed softly. "It's not that easy, honey. First, you have to fall in love and live in the same town and...fall in love."

"Then do that."

"It's not that easy," she said again, at a loss for how to end this. But Mav saved her by waking up, stretching, and padding his way up the bed to sleep next to Destiny.

"Here's your co-star," Summer said, happy to change the subject.

"Hi, Mavvie." Destiny kissed him on the head, then looked up at Summer. "I love Mavvie, Mommy. It was easy." She stroked the dog's little head.

"But it won't be easy when you have to say goodbye."

Destiny slowly shook her head, but Summer put a stop to wherever this was going with a good-night kiss. "Time to sleep, Destiny Rose."

"Good night, Mommy." She reached up and gave Summer a big hug. "It was the best day of my whole life."

"Definitely one of mine, too," she agreed, kissing her again before she turned out the light. "Now, sleep and dream, angel."

"'Kay. But, Mommy?"

"Yeah?"

"I love John. It wasn't so hard."

Summer felt her shoulders sink on the next sigh. "Night, honey. Night, Mav."

She closed the door behind her and stepped into the hallway, suddenly aware that she wasn't alone.

John was in the living room, which was dark but for a soft light from the kitchen and one from his phone.

"I didn't expect you up here," she said as she stepped into the room.

He held his phone up from the sofa where he sat. "I was going to show this to you and Destiny, but…"

She slowed her step, her gaze shifting to the baby monitor she'd left on the coffee table, the red light indicating it was on. *Oh.*

How much of that conversation did he hear?

He held up his phone and used it to gesture her closer. "You have to see this."

"What is it?"

"Two thousand views already, is what it is." He tapped the phone, and the familiar colors of Facebook showed up. "It's on the Family First page."

The sounds of Destiny and Mav came through the speaker.

"Look, Summer." He held the phone out, not saying a word about the monitor. "This thing could go viral, because it is ridiculously cute. She edited it so you can see Destiny get her trophy and run to you. So, you're okay with that, right? Because I could have Cassie take it down from their page."

She just watched and listened for a moment, the thrill of the night muted as she wondered exactly how much of that conversation he'd heard. "It's fine. She's gonna go nuts."

"You want to show her now?"

"After I spent an hour and twelve minutes getting her to sleep?"

"But who's counting?" He put the phone on the table and wrapped her in his arms. "Other than me, I mean."

She melted into a kiss that she felt she'd been holding back all day. Longer. The heat built fast, sending a shock of electricity down her body the moment their tongues tangled.

"You know what I'm counting?" she asked as she nuzzled into his neck. "The number of steps to my room."

"Mmm. I'd say twelve. Maybe thirteen. And is that too close to Destiny?"

"Thirteen steps is too far." She lifted her chin and let him plant kisses on her throat. "And she sleeps like the dead. Plus...I have that monitor." She looked hard at it and raised a brow in question.

"And I have everything else we need."

"Everything?"

He put his hands on her face and looked into her eyes. "It wouldn't be that hard, you know."

She blinked, then realized what he was saying. What he *heard*. "I know."

"I'm halfway there already."

Halfway in love. "Then let's..." She slid his glasses off and put them on the table, grabbed the baby monitor, and pulled him in the direction of her bedroom. "Go all the way."

"Hey, I can't see."

She laughed softly. "Then just...*feel*."

Feel. Feel. *Feel.*

For once, that was all John wanted to do, without an assist from a single rational thought.

They kissed in the hall, at the door when she locked it, and just inside the moonlit bedroom that smelled like citrus and sweetness. Each time they stopped to wrap their arms around each other and start this incredible new dance with one kiss, then another, John let his body respond and his brain go silent.

This was not the time to think about a single word of that conversation he'd heard. He'd tried to find the volume button or a way to turn the receiver off, but he'd heard anyway.

Not now. Not now. Now was a time—*the* time— to do nothing but touch and explore and skim and stroke.

Because it all felt so damn good. Summer's corn-silk-soft hair in his fingers, her woman's body arched against him, her warm, taut skin as he lifted her top and splayed his hands around her, even the cloud of comfort they dropped onto when they rolled onto the bed together.

Thinking—about what he heard, what she said, what that meant—might throw light and logic on just how far gone he was. Much further than he should be with a woman who thought falling in love would be hard.

He yanked his thoughts back to her body, her sighs, her...*her.* There was nothing logical about love, not after knowing her for such a brief time, and thinking about it would distract him from *this.*

This wasn't love...not now, not yet. This was pleasure and satisfaction and, oh, this was *Summer.*

This was the fling his body wanted, and he needed to revel in every perfect minute of it.

She whispered his name and stroked his hair and beard, moaning when he unclipped her bra and caressed her breast. Instantly, the first shock of intimacy fueled his body with blood and need and a blissfully blank brain.

"How much did you hear?" she whispered.

He stilled his hand, letting out a nearly inaudible grunt. It was one thing to fight his thoughts, but a whole different prospect to silence hers.

He answered by pressing his mouth to her body, using his tongue to further arouse her, and finding the button of her white jeans.

That did the trick.

She rocked her hips against him, letting him work the zipper down while he showered her breasts with admiration and kisses.

"John, I think..."

He lifted his head and blinked into the darkness, the first adjustment to the light helping him see the question in her eyes. "Don't think, Summer. Just feel."

She smiled. "Oh, I'm feeling."

He slid his fingers into her now open jeans and watched her eyes widen and lips part with a soft breath.

"Everything," he whispered. "Don't miss a single thing." He stroked her silky smooth skin, loving the look of ecstasy on her face.

"Oh..." She whimpered and lifted her hips, helping him slide her jeans off and send them to the floor, grasping his shoulders to push him down to kiss more of her body. Lost, he tasted everything, all the sweet sunshine and warmth of Summer.

He took his time, finding secret places and gentle curves and getting insanely turned on by her fiery response. She clutched him and dragged him back up to kiss her lips, wrapping her legs around his hips and already moving against him before he even had his khaki shorts unbuttoned and discarded.

She helped, with trembling fingers and precious little cries of desperation, until they were both undressed. With tangled limbs and long, wet kisses and easy laughs, they awkwardly tried to get under the covers without physically separating.

They did, though, long enough for him to snag the condom he'd grabbed before he'd come up here.

"You came prepared," she said between kisses on his chest when he slid back under the comforter.

"We knew where this was going." He tunneled his fingers into her hair and pulled it back to lift her face to him. "I did, anyway."

"But then you heard us on the monitor."

He gave a sly smile. "Determined to take this there, are you?"

She just lifted a brow.

"Doesn't matter." Did it? Nothing mattered. Nothing but this.

He dragged his hands down to coast them over her body again, up and down, front and back, here and, oh, *there*.

"Are you sure? Because…"

"Shhh." He kissed her quiet. "It didn't stop…this." Because nothing could, even knowing she'd come here to find another man who might very well have been able to woo her back.

Destiny's little voice saying *daddy* still echoed.

"No more talking, Sunshine."

"Sunshine?"

"That's what Aidan calls you." He leaned over her, kissing her lips. "Sunshine. Like the song. Well, like the song used to be before our little songwriter changed the words."

Her eyes flickered at the use of the word *our*, but he didn't care. He was too hard, too ready, and way too far gone over her to worry about something like that.

"Okay." She leaned up and pressed a long, eager kiss on his chest, flattening her hand over the spot. "Your heart's pounding."

"Summer." He flicked the foil packet before he tore it open. "Honey, *everything's* pounding."

That made her smile, then she helped him open the condom and slide it on. "I just want to be sure you didn't misunderstand…"

He choked a half laugh, half moan as her fingers tortured him. "*Seriously*? Now?" His brain was officially shut down, and all other systems were in high gear. "No."

"I know, I just…" She tightened her legs around his hips, drawing him closer to the center of her. "I said it wouldn't be that easy…"

"Hey…stop talking and let me…" He cupped his hands on her backside and boosted her up. *Let me love you.*

But he caught himself before he said that out loud, hissing in a breath instead as he found exactly where he needed to be. At the very instant they joined together, they both stared at each other, silent, as heat and friction and need intensified with every long, slow stroke of his body in hers.

She turned her head from side to side as pleasure overtook her, closing her eyes and biting back a noisy reaction to the perfect connection they'd found. But John never closed his eyes. This close, his vision was flawless...and so was she.

Finally, his brain was wiped clean, and all he could do was feel. The heat and the silk and the pressure and the tension and the need that took him right to the edge, where he stayed, suspended in sustained pleasure, until she caught up to him.

Then, still lost in each other's gaze, she let go in a raw, ragged, uncontrolled release, and John followed a second or two later.

As the exquisite moment passed, he lowered himself completely, wrapping Summer into him to enjoy the way her body quivered with the aftermath of making love. Too exhausted to move or talk, they stayed still and silent except for the sounds of their breathing. The soft snores of Mav came through the baby monitor she'd carried in.

The baby monitor.

And of course, everything came crashing back.

"What's wrong?" she asked, placing a tender hand on his cheek.

"Nothing."

"You tensed up."

"Aftershock," he murmured, kissing her hair. "Very high on the Richter scale, too."

Drawing back, she forced his gaze on her. "I don't even quite remember what we were saying in there."

"Summer, we just made love."

She smiled. "Yeah. We did. I liked it."

"So think about that, not anything else."

"I can't help it. I said things…"

"Shh." He brushed her hair back. "You were having a conversation with your five-year-old. I'm not going to hold you to anything you said."

He would, however, be sure to protect his heart, which, at that moment, was wretchedly vulnerable. He'd already lost one woman because he'd thought the noble thing to do was step back and wait for her to decide what she wanted—and he wasn't interested in doing that again.

Except, if she *wanted* this Travis guy to be—

"She's fallen hard for you, I think."

He smiled. "One Jackson girl down, one more to go."

She arched into him. "I'd say you got that one, too."

In bed. But would that be enough? He already knew it wouldn't. He already knew he wanted her to stay and be in his life and—

"There you go, getting tense again."

He laughed. "I didn't move a muscle."

"Your brain is moving. I can see it when it happens. Your eyes change. They narrow when you're thinking hard, then your jaw clenches."

"I have a beard. You can't see my jaw."

"I can see plenty. I can…" She ran her hand over his arm and nestled it around his neck. "I can feel what you feel."

He stared at her for a long time, imagining how she'd react if he told her how he truly felt about her. Would it scare her or bring her closer?

Now might be the time to take that chance. Why not just tell her and get this out in the open?

"If you can feel what I feel, then you'd know that I—"

They both jumped when Maverick barked, the sound deep and loud through the monitor.

"Oh." Summer sat up. "When he barks, it usually means Destiny's asleep. That's when I go get him and bring him down. Should I..."

"Hush, puppy." Destiny's tiny voice came through the speaker, silencing Summer. "Mommy will take you away."

"You *think* she's asleep," John joked. "But she's so on to you."

Summer fell back onto the pillow. "She's awake."

"Should I go? Will she want to come in here?"

"Not usually. But I might have to go—"

Mav barked again.

"Should I get him?" John asked.

"Wait...she was really tired. She won't come in here, though. I'll have to—"

"Hush, little puppy, don't you cry..." Destiny's singing echoed, making them both smile.

"I sing this one to her," Summer said. "But no guarantee you'll get the real lyrics."

"We are never gonna say bye-bye," she crooned.

They both laughed softly.

"She really should be a songwriter or a poet," John said.

"We're gonna live together soon..." The next line was muffled by Summer moving and getting out of bed.

"Are you going to her?" John asked, missing her warmth already.

"I want to turn this down."

"Why? It's adorable. And you can hear if she needs anything."

Her finger hovered over volume button. "When Mommy marries John!" She finished with typical Destiny high-note drama.

For a second, they were silent, and Summer was just far enough away in a dark room that he couldn't quite make out her expression, but he heard the sigh she let out.

"She's just a kid, Summer," he said. "Don't go having some kind of guilt trip over it or me."

She lowered the volume, but left the monitor on, coming back to bed with slow, tentative moves.

"So, you can feel what I feel, too," she whispered. "You know that hearing her say that makes me feel guilty."

"Of course it does. You think you're going to disappoint her." Or me.

She searched his face, melting into him with a soft moan. "So much for a sweet post-lovemaking conversation."

"Hush, puppy," he teased, caressing her back with long, steady strokes. "It was very sweet. She's a little kid on a summer vacation with a new furry friend, and I am, God help me for saying this, a nice man who's spending a lot of time with her single mom. What do you expect her to think? It doesn't mean anything."

But even as he said the words, he knew it meant something. Hell, it meant everything.

Summer, and Destiny, meant way too much to him. This made no sense to a man who lived as logically as he did.

"You're right," Summer said, cuddling closer. "Please stay with me tonight."

As if there was any chance he'd say no to that. "I'll leave when Mav barks for the six a.m. visit to the grass."

She let out a little whimper of satisfaction. "You weren't kidding about nice, you know. That was… beyond nice. That was…" She bit her lip. "The first time in a long time for me."

"Second time'll be even nicer."

She looked up at him, just enough moonlight through the blinds for him to see the desire in her eyes. "Looking forward to it."

"Me, too." He kissed her, closing his eyes and still hearing the echo of Destiny's song in his head.

When Mommy marries John.

It was his last thought before he fell asleep and still there when he woke in the middle of the night and made love to her again.

Chapter Twenty-One

Taking her first weekday off since she'd started working at Santorini's nearly three weeks earlier, Summer planned a nice long afternoon in Bitter Bark. After she and John dropped Destiny off, Summer had slipped away on foot to run a few errands in town. She'd gotten a pedicure, and was now crossing Bushrod Square, soaking up the sunshine and peace of the park. She let out a sigh at the thought of leaving this precious town tucked in the foothills, full of dogs and family and...John. Everything gave her a bittersweet sense of longing lately, although she wasn't exactly sure what she was longing for.

More time here? Maybe.

She was far too aware that Tails and Trails was over this weekend, and she and Destiny would have no real reason to stay in Bitter Bark. John hadn't hired a full-time hostess yet, but Summer couldn't do the job if Destiny wasn't in camp during the day. Staying an extra day or a few more weeks would make leaving only that much harder.

The past few weeks had been filled with laughter,

good food, evenings in the yard with Des, late nights by the fire pit, and then hours and hours of making love until the sun came up. There'd been meals at Waterford Farm and a wonderful couples-only dinner at Overlook Glen Vineyards. That night, Summer had a chance to really get to know John's brother, sister, and his stepfamily, and all the significant others while Pru, along with Daniel and Katie, babysat all the little ones.

Destiny had even spent that night at a Waterford Farm sleepover with Mav, giving Summer and John complete privacy and intimacy at home.

She'd had a chance to hang out at the small regional airport with Destiny, watching John's plane take off and land, and celebrate that he was now one hour from being able to legally fly solo.

She was still reliving some of the memories they'd made this month when her phone rang, and John's name appeared on the screen. She stopped to sit on a park bench and answered with a smile.

"If you tell me Secret Shopper came in today when I'm not there, I'll be crushed."

He laughed at the greeting. "No one who could possibly qualify is here, and I have Karyn on the lookout. She's really grateful for the extra hours, by the way, so I'm glad you offered her yours today."

"No problem. I had to find some window of opportunity to do some birthday shopping for Destiny while she's not with me. Now, I'm on my way to the toy store on Ambrose Avenue."

"You're not going to find what she wants in a toy store, Summer."

"They have stuffed dogs."

He snorted. "Not ones that sing and follow her around like she hung the moon."

"John, you can't do this. I have to teach her a tough life lesson: You can't claim other people's pets or belongings as your own."

"What if I give him to her?"

"Nobody's that nice. Even you."

"You know I would. And anything else she—or you—wants."

Her heart folded over with affection and that same longing she'd just felt looking around this precious town square. Maybe she wasn't longing for more time in town, just more time with John. A lot more.

"What I want is for the secret shopper to show up and give you all his money." She gnawed on her lip, still worried that her mistake had cost him a small fortune because of the increased price for the property. "No word from George, either?"

"He's dragging his feet on the contract I sent, which is fine. The longer he waits, the better chance I have of closing the financing. I'm not tense."

"I can tell," she said.

"How could I be? Sleep-deprived, maybe," he said with a sexy intonation. "But not tense."

An easy laugh bubbled up. She knew exactly what he meant and already looked forward to their hours alone tonight. Sleep was overrated. Making love and whispering into the wee hours was...*everything*.

"Listen, I need to ask you a favor," he said. "Can you swing by Gramma Finnie's and Yiayia's place while you're out and about? Yiayia said they have something they want to give you."

"Sure." She'd been to the gingerbread-cute

Victorian on Dogwood Lane in the past few weeks and knew it was within walking distance from where she stood. The town, it seemed, was already becoming familiar. "Something for me?"

"I actually think it's something for Destiny. They didn't give details, but you've been summoned. I hope you don't mind."

"Not at all. Are you still going to fly today?"

"Aidan said he's running an errand in town, then he's going to meet me at the airfield. Oh, I have a vendor calling," he said softly. "I'll call you later."

She sat there for a moment, the echo of his deep voice still in her head, the feelings she had for him welling up. It was going to be so damn hard to leave. Impossible, in fact.

She pushed up and headed to the tiny side street with a row of beautifully restored Victorians, easily spotting the pink and blue one where Yiayia and Gramma Finnie lived. In the front garden, two flags hung on small metal posts, one representing Ireland, one for Greece. Oh, and there was a new one that had dachshund silhouettes and the words *Follow the pawprints!*

Smiling at that, Summer tapped on the front door, surprised when Cassie opened it, and she noticed Pru playing with one of the dogs in the living room. As she walked in, she spied Katie Kilcannon in the hall, headed toward the kitchen, and suddenly wondered if this summons wasn't actually an...intervention.

She could hear it now. *Don't leave, lassie.*

"Can you even believe it?" Cassie exclaimed, holding out her phone. "One million clicks on our girl."

Summer laughed. "I hardly ever look at social media lately," she admitted. "But I'm pretty sure about five hundred thousand of those clicks are Destiny watching her own performance over and over and over again on my phone."

Cassie ushered her in, stepping aside so one of the dogs could come and sniff her, then gestured her toward the kitchen. "Come on in. The gang's all here."

She lifted her brows. "John said Yiayia wanted to give me something for Destiny."

"A plan," she whispered conspiratorially. "But act surprised."

"Hi, Summer." Pru stood up, rocking Gala in her arms like she was holding a baby. "I'm good with kids," she said with a grin.

"And dogs," Summer said, giving Gala's nose a tap as she passed by, still uncertain what she was walking into, other than the kitchen.

In there, Yiayia was at a large center island, rolling dough, while Gramma Finnie sat with Katie, John's mother, at the kitchen table, coffee mugs in front of them. As they all greeted her, Cassie offered iced tea and coaxed Summer to barstools at the counter, where they could watch Yiayia work and chat with everyone.

Sun poured through the mullions of a large window as the women chattered about Destiny's success, with Cassie cooing over how happy her client was with the flurry of attention for the Family First Pet Foods brand.

"There'll be no separatin' her from wee Mavvie now," Gramma Finnie said.

"Oh please." Summer looked skyward. "John is this close to giving that dog to my daughter."

"Of course he is," Cassie said, leaning around Summer to grin at her mother. "He always was the nice one."

"He is kind." Katie stood and came closer to put her hands on Summer's shoulders. "And as a mother, I completely understand your dilemma. My husband, Daniel, tells me that he and his late wife's favorite expression was—"

"You're only as happy as your least-happy child," Pru chimed in. "Grannie Annie's saying is kind of the Kilcannon motto. My mother says it all the time."

Summer smiled. "Well, having an only child really puts that in perspective. I'm only as happy as Destiny is."

"And is she happy?" Yiayia asked, looking up from phyllo dough so thin Summer could see the veins in the countertop through it.

"She's never been this happy," Summer said, hearing the bittersweet note in her voice.

Yiayia's sharp gaze moved to Gramma Finnie, who adjusted her bifocals and peered at Katie, who tipped her head and slid a look at Cassie, who smiled at Pru.

"Okay, then," Summer said on a laugh. "Who's going to let me in on the secret?"

They all started talking at once, until Yiayia banged her wooden rolling pin. "Remember that Finola was going to go first."

Summer turned to Gramma Finnie, who was pushing out of her chair. "I was, wasn't I?"

"First for…what?" Summer asked.

"Just first." Gramma Finnie glanced around. "Oh, it's in the dining room." She walked back into the hall, then reappeared a moment later with a large pillow in her arms. A dog-bone-shaped pillow, embroidered with, *Destiny Rose and Mavvie, First Place in Barkaoke, Bitter Bark, North Carolina.*

"For the wee one's birthday."

"Oh wow!" Summer took the pillow in her arms, just about the size of Mav. "This will look so beautiful in her room. How lovely, Gramma Finnie. Thank you." She perched the pillow on the counter, still smiling. "That was so thoughtful."

And it was...*first*. What were they planning next?

"Now, about her birthday," Katie said, slipping onto the stool next to Summer. "It's Sunday, right?"

"Yes."

"We'd like to celebrate it with the whole family at our Sunday dinner, if that's all right with you," Katie said.

"We do great Sunday birthday parties at Waterford," Pru added. "Cake, presents, whatever she wants."

"Of course." Summer couldn't see any reason to leave before Sunday, so agreeing to that was a no-brainer. "I'm sure she'd love that."

"And then the following week," Yiayia added, "since camp will be over, Finola and I would love to have her spend time with us while you're working at Santorini's since..." She lifted a brow. "The place has never run quite as smoothly as it does with you at the hostess helm."

"Oh, thank you, but..." Was that true? She wasn't sure, but she also knew better than to argue with this woman.

"We'll run our own little camp," Yiayia said. "Life skills. Important ones, like how to make a world-class baklava, and some gardening, and dancing, and plenty of singing."

"I'll teach the lass some cross-stitch and embroidery," Gramma Finnie added.

"Well, if we stay for a while, that would be wonderful. She loves you both so much and—"

"But it can't be all sewing and baking," Pru added, leaning into the circle. "I'm the best babysitter in the world, as many will tell you, and I thought it would be fun for her to do some internships. She could spend a few days at my mom's vet office and maybe watch Darcy do the grooming or help sell treats at Ella's Bone Appetit store. She'd love that."

"She would," Summer agreed on a soft laugh. "I see you've all given this a great deal of thought."

"And Family First kind of wants her to do a commercial," Cassie added very quickly. "They'd shoot it here in September."

Summer's jaw dropped as she looked at one overly enthused face after another. "Is that where all this has been leading? A commercial?"

"Oh, no, lass." Gramma Finnie put a knotted hand on Summer's arm. "We just think that... We know how happy you are, and...it just seems as though..."

"You can't leave," Yiayia said, a little impatient with her friend.

Summer blinked at her.

"I mean, you *can*," Yiayia added. "But...John is so happy."

"He really is," Katie chimed in. "And as his mother, well..."

"You're only as happy as your least-happy child," Summer said, still laughing softly and shaking her head. "I gotta say, you guys are good."

"Normally, it's just us," Yiayia said, nodding at Gramma Finnie.

"Hey." Pru poked her.

"And Pru. She's a Dogmother-in-training." Yiayia stepped away, returning to her dough. "But this is a tricky case, and you could slip away at any moment."

"She's kidding, of course," Cassie said.

"Really?" Summer picked up her tea. "Everyone sounds pretty serious about my love life, to me."

A few of them gave nervous laughs, but Cassie turned Summer so they were facing each other. "Obviously, the big thing is the commercial. I came over here to tell them about it and ask how I should approach John to ask you, and then, wham..." She gestured toward the others. "They started thinking about Destiny and her birthday and you leaving and you not leaving and...John and you and..."

Summer gave her a tight smile. "The commercial sounds amazing. Of course, I need to get details of what's involved."

"A whole lot of money," Cassie said.

"Really?"

"For a commercial? Yes, a *lot* of money." She leaned in and whispered an amount, and Summer almost fell off the stool.

"Whoa."

"Yeah, commercials pay well, especially talent that can sing."

That much money would be a phenomenal nest egg for Destiny. "We'd have to come back, since school will be in session in September," she said.

"Unless you don't leave at all, lass," Gramma Finnie whispered, dropping the expected bomb with her usual sweet brogue.

Then Summer turned to Yiayia, who rolled her dough, eyes down. After a moment, she set the rolling pin aside and leveled the full power of her gaze on Summer. This could be anything, Summer thought. Reverse psychology. A dire warning. An order that couldn't be ignored.

"You'll never find a finer man," Yiayia said simply.

"I know that," Summer whispered. "It's just all so fast."

"So, stay for the rest of the summer," Cassie said. "See what happens."

"I'll…" Summers phone vibrated with a text, giving her an excuse not to respond. "Oh, it's John," she said as she tapped his message.

He's here! He's here! Get over here now!!

"Oh! The secret shopper's at the restaurant!"

"Really?" Katie pressed her hands together. "Thank God."

"I walked here, though. He could be gone by the time I get to Santorini's."

"I'll drive you," Cassie said. "I know John wants you to be there. I want to see the guy, too."

Cassie pulled her to the kitchen door, but Summer stopped and turned back to the others. "Can I take the pillow?"

"We'll have it all wrapped up on Sunday," Gramma Finnie said, clutching her kelly green cardigan with excitement. "Now, off you go, lass!"

In a few minutes, she and Cassie were zooming around the square, headed for Santorini's.

"I hope they—we—weren't too much," Cassie said, her dark eyes glinting with humor. "It's kind of easy to get swept up in the Dogmothers' fun."

"It's fine," she said, tapping an *on my way* text to John. "They're sweet, and they mean well."

"Oh, they mean business. Matchmaking business." Cassie put a hand on Summer's arm. "Listen, I'm his sister. One of his many fans, possibly the biggest. John's the best."

"I know. He's awesome."

"And he's falling so hard for you," Cassie added. "I mean, not that I want to make you feel pressured or anything, but—"

"I'm falling, too," she admitted on a whisper. "I can't imagine anything that would change that."

"Yay!" Cassie whipped into a handicapped spot in front of the restaurant. "You run in, and I'll find a parking spot in the back. Go, be a hostess if he needs you."

"Okay." She blew Cassie a spontaneous kiss and stepped onto the sidewalk, a little dizzy from the excitement of that crew and all the…love.

She took a moment to collect herself, letting the sunshine pour over her as she let her heart settle a bit.

This family. This town. This man and his world. It was all so magical, and Destiny was so happy and—

The front door popped open, and John came out, so tall and handsome and welcoming. They closed the space between each other in a few steps, falling into an easy embrace.

"Are you sure it's him?"

"Oh, absolutely. He came in and asked Karyn if I was here, and when she offered to get me, he said he didn't want anyone to know he was here, and he'd like to eat first. Of course, she came right back to get me and point him out."

"Oh, let's walk by him and see if he's having a good meal."

"You can. Go charm him. Work your hostess magic. Just tell him you were on a break and chat him up."

"Without reading his laptop or phone," she joked as he walked her in.

"Do whatever you want." He gave her a quick kiss, then inched back. "It's happening, Summer. Everything's happening."

Her heart tripped around as she looked up at him. "Yes, it is."

He kissed her again, holding her face. "I've never been happier."

"I feel the same way," she whispered breathlessly. With one more kiss, she stepped away and looked into the dining area.

"Oh, he's that tall, clean-cut guy at table seven. Young dude for this job, unless Tom Barnard sent a ringer."

She shifted her gaze and blinked, not sure if it was the sunlight or what, but...she saw the angles of his face, the piercing blue of his eyes, and the shocked smile that broke across his face when he saw her.

"Summer? Is that you?" His voice traveled across the restaurant as he stood up.

Once again, she was a little dizzy, but for a whole different reason.

"You know him?" John's voice sounded strangled, but that was probably her pulse thumping in her head.

"I can't believe you're here." The man closed the space between them, almost running to her, extending his arms. "Come here, gorgeous. God, I've missed you."

Strong arms wrapped her so tight she could barely breathe, but she managed to inch back and look up into eyes she knew so well despite never having seen them in person.

"Travis." Oh God. *Travis*.

Chapter Twenty-Two

S o...not Tom Barnard. Not by a long shot.

John stared at the man who had somehow become mythical in his head, cursing the fact that the son of a bitch was kind of...godlike. He'd seen the tall, tanned, golden-haired man only through the lenses of his own expectations about Tom Barnard, whom he'd pictured as someone closer to fifty and maybe balding. But seeing him as Travis Shipley, a man who said he loved Summer and had made enough of an impression that she traveled here, two years later, to find him?

Yeah, that threw John completely off-balance.

Why couldn't the guy be a little scruffy, maybe act like a loser who didn't have his act together? Why couldn't he look like the musician he supposedly was? Why couldn't he...not be here, looking down at Summer like she was the answer to his every prayer?

But he was, standing as tall as John, maybe a half inch taller, with a commanding presence that surely turned the head of every person he passed. He obviously spent an enormous amount of time at the gym and had just enough ink peeking from the sleeve of a casual, tight-fitting T-shirt to have an air of badass about him. But his hair was military-short, and he'd shaved his square jaw within the last few hours. Face it, he was the kind of guy his sister and her friends would probably call a smokefest or a dime or *eye candy*.

To John, he was nothing but an...interloper.

"You're here..." Summer's words were soft and laden with disbelief.

"This is Hoagies & Heroes," he said, as if she didn't know. As if it was *still* Hoagies & Heroes. "So it makes a lot more sense for me to be here than you."

"I, um, work here," she whispered, finally glancing at John. "Do you know John Santorini?"

"Oh, the very man I want to see." He extended a large hand and offered a strong and serious handshake. "Travis Shipley," he said. "I believe you know my father."

"I do." So that's why he was here? On building business?

Before John could ask, the other man's gaze shifted right back to Summer as if it had a will of its own. "I can't believe you're here. I mean, you *work* here? I knew you were in Bitter Bark, but I expected to have to track you down."

"You did? You knew I was here?" she asked. "How?"

"The video with your daughter singing." He slid into a wide, easy grin. "Damn, she's somethin', Summer. I can see Isaiah all over her."

Summer let out a sigh on a soft laugh. "Yeah. She's a lot like him."

"Much prettier and I hope not as stubborn," he joked.

"Plenty stubborn, but how did you see the video?"

"It came up on Facebook on a Bitter Bark Chamber of Commerce page that I still get in my timeline," he explained. "I'll tell you all about it, but…" He gestured to John. "I'm afraid John and I have some business to discuss first."

"We do?" John said.

"I'm here representing my father," he said. "Do you have an office where we can talk privately?"

"Of course. In the back."

Travis nodded, then picked up his phone from the table with another long look at Summer. "I can't believe it was so easy to find you," he said. "Please don't go anywhere. I'll just be a couple minutes."

"Of course I'll be here, Travis." She gave him a smile that looked a little bewildered, a little terrified, and a little…happy.

John stepped away just as he heard Travis add, "I'll hold you to that, Sunshine."

As he walked, John clenched his fists, then spread his fingers wide, tension and jealousy and resentment rocking him.

Sunshine? She wasn't *his* damn sunshine.

No, no. Relax, he told himself, glancing back to make sure Travis was following him. John was the man who'd woken up in Summer's bed and arms for the tenth, twelfth, maybe fourteenth consecutive day, not Travis. John was the man who shared bodies, hearts, and laughs with her. She was *his* sunshine, not this…trespasser's.

"Holy crap, this place is different," Travis said with a low whistle as they stepped into the kitchen. "Did you kick out the storage room and add all that dining space?"

"Yes," John said simply, not bothering to stop and introduce their guest to any of the servers or cooks in the kitchen.

"And the whole Greek thing? Great idea. It should work."

John shot him a look as they reached his office. "It *does* work. It's a Greek restaurant. We serve Greek food. It's a theme."

Travis pursed his lips and lifted his brow like...he knew something John didn't.

Inside the office, John closed the door and gestured toward the guest chair. "Would you like coffee or water?" he asked.

"No, no, I'm not going to be here that long. I just have to deliver some news, and I'll start with don't shoot the messenger."

John dropped into his chair, making every effort to keep his face completely expressionless. "I don't shoot anyone," he said. "What's the news?"

Travis folded his hands and leaned forward. "Listen, I have fought this deal from the moment I heard about it, but then...." He slid a look in the general direction of the dining room, where Summer waited.

"What deal?" John asked.

"Coming back to Bitter Bark and reopening Hoagies & Heroes."

John stared at him, a frown pulling. "Where?"

"Here." He pointed to the ground. "Where it was. Where it belongs."

"*What?*"

"I know, I know." He sat back and held up his hands like he could stave off whatever fight he expected. "I'm sure it'll be an inconvenience for you to move, but we'll give you time to find another property, and my father's prepared to shave off some rent."

"I'm not going to find another property." Irritation scraped at his chest as he said the words. "I've been renting with an option to buy and made a great offer." A ridiculous offer, but...

"We're under no obligation to take it."

"We?"

"It sounds weird to say it. I didn't ever expect to be a restaurant owner, but..." He blew out a breath. "I always knew this day would come."

John narrowed his eyes, trying to get a read on this man, but definitely not able to succeed. "You don't sound too excited about it."

He gave a soft laugh. "With all due respect to your chosen profession, my friend, it's not what I wanted to do with my life."

"Then why would you?"

Shifting in his chair, he looked down, and a little of his confidence seemed to slip.

"Because I need to do something, and after one solid year in Nashville, I'm pretty sure it isn't hitting the big time in country music. So it appears I'm going to run this sandwich shop in Bitter Bark, North Carolina."

Sparks exploded behind John's eyes. "First of all, the sandwich shop doesn't exist anymore. It's a Greek deli, one of three, part of a future franchise, and in my family for more than sixty years. Second, I have a contract with your father that states he will honor my offer to purchase this building unless he gets one that is twenty-five percent higher, and I met the one he got."

"Yeah, about that." He ran his hand through his short hair, discomfort turning the corners of his mouth down. "There is no other offer."

"Excuse me?"

"My dad just made that up because he thought you'd back out and end the lease amicably without, you know, legal wrangling."

Holy *hell*. John lifted a brow. "I took your father to be more ethical than that."

"He is ethical," Travis said quickly. "But he's backed into a corner right now by my mother, who is a force that no one really knows how to contain. It's her money that bought the building in the first place, so she kind of has control. She wants me here and…"

"You do whatever Mommy wants?" The words slipped out before he could stop them.

"When she has six months to live."

"Oh. That's a shame," John murmured under his breath, wanting to kick himself. Hard. "I've been there," he said, swallowing against his shame. "I'm sorry."

"Thanks. And I'm sorry I have to blow in here like a Grade A dick and overturn your business plan. But we have the right to turn down your offer and terminate your lease."

John sat a little straighter in his chair as another lightning bolt of fury shot through him, his brain whirring through the fine print on that contract. *Did* they have the legal right? His fingers already itched to call his attorney.

"Look, we won't use the name, I swear," Travis

continued. "We'll go back to Hoagies & Heroes. In fact, I'm going to play up the 'hero' thing with my military background. So I'll probably repaint everything red, white, and blue. We won't infringe on anything you've built here, and I'm sure you can scout out another location."

John shook his head as if that could make his brain function again. He needed to find the contract. Needed to talk to George. Needed to stop this man from blowing into his world and taking *everything*. "I have to call my attorney," he said simply, but way deep inside, he already knew that would be a costly, and possibly unsuccessful, endeavor.

George and Susan Shipley had said they wanted to retire. Moved away to the other side of the state. In fact, it had been John who'd pushed for a lease instead of an outright purchase because he wasn't entirely sold on Bitter Bark back then. What changed?

"Really hoped we could avoid that, but okay. You do that." Travis glanced at the door, obviously eager to get back to the other way he planned to ruin John's life. Then he slapped his hands on his jean-clad thighs and leaned forward, his smile tight. "I'm really sorry this didn't go as you planned."

John had no idea how to respond to that, his usually sharp brain dulled by unfamiliar sensations like loathing and disgust and rage and resentment.

"And if you don't mind, one more favor?" Clearly, no such emotional whirlwind was at work on Travis Shipley.

"You want my car, house, and dog, too?"

He laughed easily, pointing at John. "Good to keep your sense of humor, my man."

I am not your flipping man.

"But what I'd like to do is borrow one of your employees for a while." He tipped his head toward the door. "Summer and I go way back. Her husband was my buddy overseas, and we…"

Had a thing over Skype.

John waited for him to finish, curious just how much of their past he'd reveal.

"Anyway, I can't believe she's here." He shook his head. "I mean, seeing her on that video was what put me over the edge and made me decide my mom must be right. I really fought the Hoagies & Heroes idea hard, since it felt a little—no, a *lot*—like giving up. But when I saw her here? Well, that changed everything. I had to come back."

A band tightened around John's chest. "I see." But he didn't. Not at all.

"I mean, it's not just fate or a coincidence. No, she's here for me," he said, almost as much to himself as John. "Two years later, and she hasn't given up hope. How can I?"

Except she'd come to apologize and get closure and rid herself of guilt. It sure didn't sound to John like Travis was breathless for an apology.

"When I saw her daughter on that video…" Travis laughed softly. "Even her name is like…this is meant to be. Have you met her little girl, Destiny?"

Was John really expected to sit here and not explode? Not dive over the desk and throttle this bastard who didn't have the right to say Destiny's name, let alone act like he *knew* anything about that child?

"I know Summer's daughter," John said through gritted teeth.

"I wouldn't have known the kid was hers because she didn't use her last name, but then, in the video, when she gets this dog-bone trophy—she won a singing contest, did you hear that?"

Holy *crap*. "I heard."

"Then I see Summer, right there on the video. Just the way I remember her."

Because you never saw her in person.

"And I just knew I had to come here. Had to take back the business and reconnect with that girl because…" He gave a self-deprecating smile that only made him look a little more like a movie star. "She's giving me another chance, and I'm not even sure I'm worthy of it."

John stared at him, speechless, waiting for something to start working upstairs. But feelings had taken over. Feelings that strangled and nauseated and made his nostrils flare with each breath and his fists clench like they needed to punch the wall. All of it sickening and unfamiliar and so freaking powerful, he forced himself to a stand.

Travis stood, too, and extended his hand. "Sorry to be the bearer of bad news on your shop here, but I hope there are no hard feelings."

John almost laughed. Hard feelings? These went way past hard. "Appreciate that," he mumbled, shaking the hand Travis offered. As he did, he noticed a tattoo along his forearm and…a scar at the most tender place on his wrist.

One more feeling reared up. Pity. His stomach roiled at the thought of the blade that must have caused that…and just how bad things had had to be to get to that point.

Good God. Maybe Travis Shipley needed this place more than John did.

"I'll warn you, I'm not going to give up easily," John said quietly. "Not anything." *Not the restaurant and not Summer Jackson.*

"We'll work it out," Travis replied with a shocking amount of confidence. "And now, I'm going to pick up where I left off with that woman."

John swallowed hard. "Oh? Where was that?"

"We were this close to the whole enchilada, man." Travis held up his finger and thumb, almost touching. "This close to something amazing and…forever. And I screwed up. But she wouldn't be here if she didn't want to forgive me. I believe that right down to my soul."

"Well, then, you better get your soul out there and talk to her."

Travis is the most persuasive man alive. He pushed the memory of Summer's words out of his head, coming around the desk to open the door to get some air into the office and let this…this *problem* out.

"Hey." Travis put a friendly hand on John's shoulder. "Do not worry. I'm not going to steal your employees. If you find another place to set up shop, she can work for you." He grinned. "Unless she wants to make heroes and hoagies with me."

A soft tap on the door kept John from answering. And possibly winding up to clock the guy.

"John, I need to talk to you." At the sound of Summer's voice, he reached for the door, whipping it open and suddenly feeling very much like Destiny when she got her hands on Mav. He just wanted to wrap his arms around this woman and pronounce her *mine!*

"What is it, Summer?" he asked instead, unnaturally calm.

She handed him a white business card and looked into his eyes with a million unspoken words in hers. "Tom Barnard is out front. He wants to talk to you."

Tom Barnard? His throat closed, his stomach clenched, and every nerve in his body stung.

Oh hell. Was this *feeling*? Well, he'd take logic over this any day, because this sucked. Everything sucked. And not for one second did he want to talk to Barnard. He had no store. He had no franchise. He had no plan.

And if this bastard Travis got his way, he'd have no Summer.

He took the card. "Tell him I had to go out."

As her jaw dropped, he brushed by her and slipped out the back kitchen door, barely able to breathe at the raw deal life had just handed him.

Chapter Twenty-Three

S ummer had never seen John so…thrown. So pale and tense and quiet. And then he walked out on Tom Barnard? How *could* he?

Travis, of course. Travis, who stood there, looking big and handsome and confident. She couldn't imagine John being threatened by anyone, but John knew her history with Travis. And he knew she'd come here for the sole purpose of having this encounter. But John also knew how she felt about him. Didn't he?

Travis leaned close to whisper in her ear. "He said you can take the rest of the day off to hang out with me."

She inched back. "He did?"

"After I buttered him up." He winked.

"So, did you work out your business with him?" God willing, Travis came to accept the offer for his father. And with Secret Shopper out there looking pretty damn happy and interested in talking, John's troubles were over.

But he sure hadn't looked like a man with no troubles.

"The business?" He shrugged and looked toward the door. "He'll get over it."

"Get over *what*?"

He answered with a quick shake of his head. "Not important. All that matters is that you're here. Right here in front of me." He reached out both hands and set them lightly on her shoulders. "Why are you working at a Greek deli and not teaching?"

She very easily stepped out of his touch, determined to keep things casual. "It's a summer job. Destiny's in camp here, and…"

"You came here to find me, didn't you?"

She slipped her lower lip under her teeth, biting lightly, not at all sure how to answer that. "Originally, yes."

"I knew it." He fisted both hands in a little victory pump. "When I saw you on that viral video, I just knew it. The universe had spoken." He reached for her hand. "Come with me, Summer. I really want to talk to you."

She searched his face, taking in the lines and angles and differences in him in person versus on a computer screen. He was a good-looking guy with strong bones and straight teeth and robin's-egg blue eyes. But there were dark circles under those eyes and a spark that seemed to be missing. A few more lines that she didn't remember and a sadness pressed on his broad shoulders.

"I have a lot to tell you, too," she finally said.

"Not here." He took her hand and urged her to the door John had just used. "Somewhere private."

But she couldn't go out that way. She couldn't leave Secret Shopper hanging, even if John had.

"In the dining room," she said. "I have to finish up with a customer."

"Sure." He walked next to her through the kitchen, where she tried to avoid Bash's openly surprised gaze at the sight of Summer holding this stranger's hand. They'd all gotten used to John and Summer together, as a couple.

Summer had gotten used to it, too, and the feel of another man's hand in hers was uncomfortable. As soon as she could, Summer tugged her hand free. "Wait at the hostess stand, Travis. I'll be right back." She went directly to the table where the older man was just closing out his check.

"Mr. Barnard," she said as she approached. "Mr. Santorini was called away for an emergency. I know he'll call you the minute he can. Are you in town long?"

"No," he said simply. "Did you tell him my name?"

"I didn't get a chance," she said quickly.

He flinched with disapproval. "He should be at his place of business at all times."

"Like I said, he had an emergency." She couldn't help adding, "And to be fair, he didn't know you were coming today, sir."

He tipped his head, conceding her point. "Fine. Thank you, miss."

"Is there anything else you need?"

"No, I..." He took a breath and reconsidered the question, nodding. "Yes. I'd like to ask you, an employee, a question. May I?"

"Of course."

"The family that's associated with the business..."

"The Santorinis."

"Yes. Do you know them?"

"I do," she said. "And all their extended relations here in town."

"Are they good people?"

She sighed and smiled. "The best."

"How so? Be more specific."

She considered that for a moment. "Well, they love with everything they have. They care about people and the community, and I'd trust any of them with my own child. In fact, I do," she added on a laugh. "And John Santorini is no different, sir. He'd do anything for anyone and runs this business with heart and intelligence. I can't imagine a better person to invest in professionally. Or," she added a wistful smile. "Personally."

He drew back a little, probably getting more than he bargained for from the hostess. "I'll keep that in mind. All of that is very important to me."

"To me, too," she added, surprised at how much she meant it.

With a quick goodbye and another promise that John would call, she headed back to the hostess stand, where Travis waited, perusing a menu.

On the way, she took a deep breath and tried to get her head on straight for this conversation. It was time to clear the air...and get back to John. Really, that was all that mattered to her now.

"Across the street?" he asked as she reached him. "It's been a long time since I took a walk in Bushrod Square."

"Sure." It felt weird to go in the middle of the day without Mav—and without John—but she headed to the door. He took her hand again, holding it tight as they stepped out onto the sidewalk, and he looked from side to side. "Half of me is happy to be home, but the other half wants to throw up. I hated a lot of things about this town."

Who could hate anything about Bitter Bark? "I think it's charming."

He slowed his step and smiled at her. "I think *you're* charming."

"Travis, I—"

He lifted their joined hands and pressed his knuckles against her lips. "Me first. I get to go first. Come on." He crossed in the middle of the street, taking her to the entrance of Bushrod Square, where he stopped, turned, and looked at Santorini's.

"I gotta say, he's done a good job with this place. So much nicer than what it used to be."

Summer breathed a sigh of relief. At least half of the reason Travis was here had to do with his father's business with John. "It's a great restaurant, and he has amazing plans for a franchise. I hope you came to accept his offer."

He shot her a look she didn't quite understand and brought her around the brick wall into the square, walking toward the first bench under a tree. "I'm definitely accepting an offer," he said, the vague statement giving her hope that they really had worked out the sale of the building.

"So you came to Bitter Bark to find me," he said as they sat down. "I can't tell you how good that feels."

"I owe you an apology," she said, burning with the need to get the words out and end this conversation as politely and as quickly as possible.

"Shhh. Summer Jackson." He took one of her

hands and captured it between his. "I waited too long for this moment to start with an apology."

But it was all she wanted to say. Taking a breath, she eased her hand out of his again, determined not to engage in anything physical that could lead him on. "It's why I came, Travis. For the sole reason to look you in the eye and tell you that I was wrong to disappear like that, and I'm sorry I didn't give you a better explanation. Instead, you got no explanation."

His eyes flickered, then he frowned. "Excuse me?"

"When I ghosted you. It was such a small, cowardly thing to do."

He stared at her, then shook his head. "*I* ghosted *you*, Summer."

For a long moment, she didn't speak, trying to make sense of that admission. "After you said you loved me," she reminded him. "We talked a time or two, then I disconnected that phone number, took down my Skype account, and deleted the email account. I closed up all social media under my name and..." She tried to make sense of his bewildered expression, but couldn't. "Didn't you try to reach me and fail?"

"I shut down all contact at the same time," he said. "I had the Army issue me a different email by telling them mine was compromised. I took down my personal Skype account. I blocked your name and number from everything."

She leaned back on the bench, stunned. "Why?"

"Well, why did you? Fear? Guilt? An abundance of caution?"

She pressed her hands together and touched her fingers to her lips, gathering her thoughts. "Yes," she answered. "But I thought I owed you an apology, which is why I came here."

"And I saw you on that video and knew you hadn't gotten over me yet."

"Gotten over...no. No, Travis. I may not have been clear back then, or forceful when I told you I didn't feel the same. But I didn't, Travis. I didn't then and I don't now."

"Summer, listen to me." He captured her hand and inched closer, his powers of persuasion on full display. Along with a shocking scar on his wrist. "I've dreamed of this second chance for years. I didn't think I was worthy of it because the Army really screwed up my head and confidence. I went to Nashville and tried that, but I realized I didn't want to *do* life without you."

She barely breathed, the words slicing her chest, her gaze falling to that scar. *Please, God, tell me I didn't cause him to do that.*

"When I found out you were here, I believed you must feel the same way. I figured since I'd disappeared, coming here was the only way you could find me. And what a statement it is about how much you care."

"I do care, Travis," she said, as gently as possible. "But not in the way you...want."

He stared at her. "That's why I swallowed my pride and told my parents I'd take the restaurant."

She frowned, trying to process that. "Take the restaurant? What are you talking about?"

He jutted his chin in the general direction of Santorini's. "They want me to reopen Hoagies & Heroes and run it. They're actually offering to finance the business and set me up."

"Not...there." She pointed directly to the restaurant so there could be no doubt. "Surely you don't mean—"

"Shh. I just discussed enough business. And yes, there. And no, I didn't think I wanted to do that with my life, but then I saw you, Summer." He grabbed her hand again. "You. Here. Waiting for me."

Oh God. Her coming to Bitter Bark had made things worse for John. "I haven't been waiting for you," she said, as slowly and clearly as she would if trying to calm her daughter.

"Working at my restaurant?"

A bolt of resentment ricocheted through her. "It's not your restaurant."

"Semantics, really. Come on, Summer. You're here, hundreds of miles from home, working in the only place you could possibly expect to find me, and I know why."

"Travis, no. I've been riddled with guilt over disappearing after you confessed how you felt. I needed to apologize. You were an amazing friend when I needed one, but that's all." She patted his hand, as friendly as possible. "Please accept my apology."

"If you accept mine." He gave her a sly smile. "Over dinner."

She shook her head. "I'm seeing someone."

He grunted like she'd hit him. "Is it serious?"

"Yes," she said without hesitation. "I'm still figuring things out, but it's not a casual relationship."

He frowned and took a breath like he was gearing up for his next onslaught of persuasion. She stopped it with her own question. "Are you seriously going to put Santorini's out of business?"

Another grunt, this one louder. "I'm doing what

someone I care about really wants me to do. I'm getting my act together, Summer."

"What about your music?"

He snorted. "What music? A year in Nashville, and all I did was learn how to tend bar. I left four months ago to stay with my parents down in Wilmington after I found out my mom..." He shook his head. "Listen, what matters is that I'm coming here permanently and starting a business. What will it take to convince you to stay at least for a while, until we can pick up where we left off?" He squeezed her hand. "We were so close, Summer."

Oh God. He couldn't move here and take John's restaurant. He couldn't. Especially if part of his decision was based on Summer being here. She tamped down another choking wave of guilt that threatened and tried to think straight. "Can't you open somewhere else in town or near your parents?"

"We already own the building," he said. "He's a smart guy. He'll find another place for his restaurant."

"Travis. That's so unfair."

He inched back, his whole body stiffening. "You want to know what's unfair, Summer? That I am thirty-five years old, and I have to quit the one thing in the whole world that matters to me. That my mother is dying of ovarian cancer and won't ever see me get married and have a kid. You want to know what else is unfair? The shit I saw in Afghanistan, including your husband being blown to bits when it *should have been me*."

She flinched, a mix of revulsion at the graphic description and a flash of sympathy for the survivor's guilt that had always plagued him.

"And you know what else? That I have crap for talent."

"That's not true."

"No one's ever believed in me, Summer."

In her mind's eye, she could see Isaiah's distinctive handwriting, two pages on how incredibly skilled Travis Shipley was on guitar and how he sounded like a younger, and better, Blake Shelton. "Isaiah believed in you."

He stared straight ahead.

"He did, and I can prove it." She grabbed his arm this time. "If I can, will you reconsider?"

"Reconsider what?"

"Doing something you already know you don't want to do. Please."

He turned back, scanning her face. "How can you prove it?"

"I have a letter from Isaiah about you." She stood. "It's at my apartment. I brought it with me to give to you." She looked around, remembering that she'd driven to town with John. "But I can't get it right now."

"I'm parked right over there."

She remembered that John left a key hidden by the door, since hers were in her bag in Cassie's car. But should she take off with Travis?

"Summer, I can still read your every thought," he said.

"Really? What am I thinking?"

"That you shouldn't take a drive with me." He shook his head and stood. "Just give me the address, and I'll meet you there."

"I don't have my car today. I came in with my, uh…"

"Boyfriend?" he suggested.

She nodded.

That made him let out a sigh, and gave her hope that he was done with his campaign to win her. "Come on, I'll drive us both." He gestured for her to get up. "I could use a little Isaiah today, and maybe you can talk me out of opening a sandwich shop."

Maybe she could. She had to. "Then I have just what you need."

As they walked away, he draped a light arm over her shoulders. "You seriously ghosted me?"

"Apparently, we both knew what was right."

"At the time," he added.

"And now."

"Aw, Summer. You were always a good friend," he said.

"But I'm afraid that's all I can be, Travis."

He looked down at her and gave a tight smile. "I hear you. I don't like it, but I hear you loud and clear."

She smiled back up at him and put a friendly arm around his waist. "Can you let go of this? Of me? Of whatever you've been holding on to?"

"I'll try." He added a light kiss on her head, and she turned to glance over her shoulder at Santorini's, just in time to see Karyn, who was serving a table on the patio, staring at her.

She slipped out of Travis's arm, making some space between them, another punch of guilt hitting her.

She'd explain to Karyn later, when she was back with John. Where she belonged.

Chapter Twenty-Four

John drove straight to Foothills Regional Airport, doing his best to simmer down on the way. He needed to fly. To be up in that Cessna with Aidan for their last lesson. He needed to be at cloud level, thinking only about the plane and the wind and wiping away every thought of Travis Shipley.

Wiping away every *feeling*.

If Summer wanted that guy, who was he to try and stop her? He wanted her to be happy. And if George Shipley was going to screw him out of his restaurant, then he'd rise up from those ashes and find a new location. It wouldn't be the first time John had stepped aside when a woman wanted to take a different path, and it wouldn't be the first time life blew up his business plan. He'd take that curveball and hit it hard, seizing the day and soaring above the clouds. All the mess of mixed metaphors his dad preached still drove him on.

All that mattered now was getting to those clouds and forgetting everything else.

He hung on to that thought while he checked in at the airport management office to log his flight plan and sign out Waterford Farm's Cessna, which Aidan had given him clearance to do. After a brief conversation with the desk manager he knew well by now, he scanned the radar, happy that the weather was perfect, and headed to the plane.

Aidan wasn't expected for another half hour, so John dove into the preflight check. The simple, straightforward, and logical process of making sure every nut, bolt, screw, hinge, flap, gauge, and pump were in perfect working order was exactly what his soul needed right now.

He stood next to the plane, rolling up his sleeves, a sudden clarity in his head after an hour of fog. All he could see was…Summer.

Wait a second. Wait a damn second.

He *needed* to talk to her. Walking out on her—and Tom Barnard—had not only been senseless, it had been mean. And thoughtless. And not like him at all.

Before starting the electrical check, he pulled out his cell, touched her contact, and…got voice mail.

Stuffing the phone back in his pocket, he moved to the master switch, checking fuel gauges and the pump, then started to physically examine every bolt and screw in the flap. He shook the hinges of the aileron, peeked into the engines for signs of nesting birds, and tested every piece of metal on one side of the plane before heading to the other to start all over again.

Maybe she was still at Santorini's.

Pausing in his process, he called the main number, and Karyn answered with a cheery, "May I help you?"

"Hey, it's John. Is Summer around?"

He heard her sigh softly. "No, she's not here."

"Any idea where she went?"

"Mmm. I saw her head over to the square."

"Alone?" He hated that there was hope in his voice.

"No." There was nothing but distaste in hers. "She was with that guy you had in your office. Who is he, John?"

The enemy. "His father owns the building," he said.

"Oh? Why was he draped all over her and..." Her voice drifted off. "Sorry. I just cannot abide a cheater."

His gut tightened. "No one's cheating," he said, knowing right down to his bones that Summer wouldn't do that to him. Not without letting him down easy first.

"Mmm. Whatever."

"Look, he's a friend of her late husband. They go way back. Just have her call me if you see her. And fast, I'm flying soon, so I won't be able to talk."

"Okay. Oh, her purse is here, if that means anything."

"She left without it?" he asked. Why would she do that?

"Cassie came in looking for the secret shopper guy, who is long gone, by the way. She said Summer left her bag in the car, so I put it in your office."

Where could she go without her bag? Which always had her phone in it? "Okay, thanks."

Accepting this minor setback, he put his head back in the preflight game. He finished the mechanical and moved on to chemical, testing each of the fuel tanks for air and water. Then he worked his way to the brake fluid and checked the spark plugs before climbing into the cockpit.

Just as he did, Aidan called.

"Do not kill me," he said before John could even say hello.

And for the, what, fiftieth time that day, disappointment slammed John's gut. "You can't make it."

"I'm still in town. I had to take Beck..." His voice faded out. "To the doctor."

"Everything okay?" he asked.

Aidan just laughed. "More than okay. Let's just say we are going to be making a happy announcement at Sunday dinner, so be there."

He inched back, connecting the dots. "Seriously? That's amazing."

"It's also secret until Sunday, but I am terrible at keeping secrets."

"It's safe with me. Congrats, man."

"Thanks, John. I'm sorry about bugging out on you. I didn't think the doctor would take that long, and then they had to do some tests and..." He sighed. "I swear to God, you haven't lived until you've heard your own kid's heartbeat."

The way he said it raised the hairs on the back of John's neck. "Spoken like a true father," he said with a laugh to cover the punch of emotions the words gave him.

"Thanks. We'll go up Sunday morning," Aidan promised. "We'll do the final hours and sign all the papers for you to start solo. I'm really sorry."

"Don't be. Everything sucks today. Except your news. And...hey, I'm getting another call."

"Oh, yeah. So am I. Talk to you later."

He tapped out of Aidan's call and frowned at the number coming in. Shane? He didn't call that often. "What's up, Shane?"

"Where the hell is Summer?" his stepbrother demanded, his voice tight.

"I don't know. Is something wrong with Destiny?" Even as he said the words, he already knew that was the only reason Shane would call him looking for Summer.

"She's gone."

"*What*?"

"We were in the middle of Hide 'n' Bark, and somehow Mav must have run away, and she went after him without telling the counselor."

"And no one saw her leave?"

"No. She wasn't in her assigned hiding place when they went to get her, and we cannot find her anywhere. Or Mav."

He squeezed his eyes shut, picturing Waterford. "Where was she?"

"Way up by the northern border of the property, near the Wallaces' ranch."

He didn't know Waterford that well, not on foot anyway, but he thought he remembered the landscape from flying over. Some open fields, some very rough terrain, lots of dark, scary woods. "How did she get that far?" he asked, tamping down the most unfamiliar sense of helplessness.

"They took the kids on four-wheelers. We have a dozen people, more, out there looking, but I have to reach Summer and let her know. Do you have any idea where she is? She's not answering her phone."

Because it's in her bag at Santorini's, and she was...somewhere *draped* under Travis Shipley, *the most persuasive man alive.*

A whole new wave of unwanted emotions roiled

through him, but he forced himself to think of the layout of the Waterford land. He could only visualize that area the way he'd seen it last—from the cockpit of this plane, where he could…spot a squirrel in the backwoods, as Aidan liked to say. "That's not an easy area to search on foot," he said.

"We're doing our best. She's only been gone a few minutes, and I need to find her mother." He ground out the last words. "Help me."

Right now, finding Destiny was way more important than finding Summer. He glanced at the yoke, the throttle, and then the empty seat next to the one he'd been about to climb into. He could be over Waterford in fifteen minutes or less.

"I'm going to help search," he said, making the decision before his brain could talk him out of it.

"Then get here when you can."

"I'll be overhead in fifteen minutes." He was already hoisting himself into the plane.

"What? Where are you?"

"Standing next to the Waterford Cessna."

"Damn good luck, then. Get up there and start looking, John. We'll put out a full-court press to make sure Summer knows what's going on. Meanwhile, we've already called in search and rescue, and all three Mahoneys are on duty right now."

"Good, but listen, I'm alone," he said. "I'm not cleared for solo."

Shane was dead quiet. He had to know that flying solo before John had FAA clearance could jeopardize his chances of ever getting a pilot's license. *Ever.*

Like, why the hell not just give up every damn dream in one day?

Because Destiny was lost.

"But I'll be there soon."

Shane blew out a low whistle. "Are you sure?"

Was he kidding? He loved that kid almost as much as he loved her… "Yeah, I'm sure."

He didn't wait for an answer, smashing the end button on the screen as he climbed into the pilot's seat. He turned the key, and as the prop started spinning, he finally gave in to a single, unavoidable thought.

Aidan said he was ready. But technically, legally? Well, the FAA might not agree. He could very well lose his pilot's license, just like he could lose the restaurant, the franchise, and the woman he loved.

But he would die before he let anything happen to Destiny, so the decision was a no-brainer, even for a man who was driven by his big old brain.

Right now, he could take off, already cleared. ATC wouldn't even ask if Aidan was here, since they'd flown so many times in and out of this airport. It was a risk, but he didn't think about it for even five more seconds.

A few minutes later, he was cleared for takeoff, his course set for Waterford Farm.

In the brief time it took to drive to John's house, Summer relaxed. With very little effort, she and Travis talked, easily sliding back into a rhythm of friendship that had almost always been there from the very first time they'd communicated.

When he pulled up to the house and rumbled his

small truck down the drive to the back of the property, Travis let out a low, long whistle as he took in the view. "Nice digs."

"I was really lucky to get the place. It's John's house, but Destiny and I are living in a separate apartment upstairs."

"John, huh? Who drove you to town and gave you a job and..." He narrowed his eyes. "That's your man?"

"He's my man," she confirmed, a secret shiver of satisfaction slipping up her spine.

He snorted. "Then he must think I'm an idiot for asking if he's met Destiny."

"He adores her."

"Oh, man." He threw her a look. "I guess I don't have a snowball's chance against tall, dark, and bearded?"

"I'm afraid not." She smiled and unlatched her seat belt, climbing out and meeting him at the front of the truck. He had that sadness around his eyes again, but she refused to feel guilty for being honest. The worst thing she could do now was give him any hope.

"Travis," she said, putting a hand on his forearm. "I never, ever meant to lead you on when we talked after Isaiah was killed. I leaned on you, quite hard, and I never meant to give you the impression I wanted more than a friend."

"It's fine, Summer. I'm sorry for seeing you on that video and assuming you came here for a different reason." He lifted a shoulder and turned, taking in the view. "I'd love to see that letter."

"I'll be right back. Wait here."

He nodded, walking toward one of the Adirondack

chairs while Summer jogged up the stairs, feeling an incredible lightness around her heart. She had one less thing to feel guilty about, and for that reason alone, she was glad she came to Bitter Bark.

But now she had to somehow persuade Travis not to take John's business.

She let herself in, found the letter, and headed back down, where he sat, still, staring out at the view.

"Here you go." She handed him the folded yellow pages. "This was in a package of his belongings that was lost in military shipment and showed up a long time after he died. To be honest, this letter was one of the reasons I broke off our friendship. Guilt kind of consumed me, considering how much he loved and trusted you."

He flinched at the words. "I know he did and..." With a sigh, he ran a finger along the edge of the legal paper. "I think I remember when he wrote this. It was two nights before he died. He went on and on about how much he loved writing you old-fashioned letters."

"And I loved getting them. Read it, Travis. How about I get us some iced tea?"

"That'd be great."

She went back upstairs, thinking about the letter, the words nearly memorized she'd read it so many times. The second and third pages were tributes to Sergeant Travis Shipley, his talents for songwriting, his heart of gold, his nice family from North Carolina.

In the last paragraph, Isaiah had written, *Travis Shipley is going to be a big name in country music someday. I sure hope he never gives up his dreams.*

Would that be enough for Travis to reconsider

ruining John's dreams and continue pursuing his own? Holding two glasses of iced tea, she headed back down to find out. But when she reached the fire pit, she saw one of the pages rolled into a crumpled ball on the cold logs and ashes, while Travis sat back with tears streaming down his face.

"Travis!" She dropped down next to him, setting the glasses on the table to put her hands on his arm. "He wouldn't have wanted you to cry over that."

He turned away. "I can't do this, Summer."

"Do what?"

"Live a freaking *lie*."

"What…lie?"

He pushed up with a grunt, letting the rest of the letter flutter from his hand to the ground. He didn't talk right away, so Summer took the crinkled ball of paper and smoothed it out, noticing it was the last page of Isaiah's tribute to Travis. She slowly picked up the other pages, giving Travis time to say whatever he needed to say.

"Have you ever carried around something for years that weighed you down so hard you couldn't stand the strain of carrying it anymore?" he finally asked. "Of trying to forget or ignore it? Of hating that it's always, always in the back of your mind, ready to swallow you whole?"

She looked up at him. "Sometimes I felt that about the way I disappeared on you."

He snorted. "This is way bigger and badder, sister."

She stood slowly, frowning, watching him pace around the fire pit, his hands visibly shaking. "What is?"

"The *truth*." He dropped his head back and stabbed

his fingers into his short hair. "You deserve to know the truth about what happened to your husband."

She stared at him, putting her hand on the back of the Adirondack chair for support because her legs suddenly felt wobbly. "What happened to Isaiah?"

Crossing his arms, he bent over a little, like his stomach hurt, his face crushed into a look of ravaged pain. "He died saving me." He practically whispered the words.

"Excuse me?"

He swallowed and squeezed his eyes shut. "He died to save my life."

She stared at him, processing this news. "That wasn't in any of the reports about what happened," she said softly.

"Because no one on this earth knows it *but me*. And I never *told* anyone."

Her arms felt numb and her head light as the possibility that this was true settled on her heart. "What happened?"

"A split-second decision made by a genuine hero," he said. "It happened so fast, and he didn't think, he just acted. We were on a patrol and climbed out of the Humvee, and just as my foot was about to hit the ground, he must have seen something. I don't know what. He threw himself at me, shoving me out of the way, and…" His voice cracked. "The IED went off and killed him."

"Why didn't you tell anyone?"

"I don't know. I was…ashamed. I felt like a coward for having to be saved, and he was a hero. No one saw. The others were inside the Humvee, and no one saw. But I knew."

"He deserved to be recognized for that," she whispered. "He deserved to be remembered and honored."

"I know. And I live with that every damn day of my life."

Slowly, not trusting her legs, she let herself sit down in the chair, dropping the papers on the table.

"Isaiah," she whispered, clutching the armrests as if she could reach out and squeeze the arms of her late husband. "You really are Destiny's hero daddy."

Travis sobbed silently.

After a minute, he came around the fire pit and sat down next to her.

"That's why I first contacted you," he admitted in a ragged whisper. "I wanted you to know. I felt you deserved to know. But I kept chickening out, and the more we talked...the harder I fell for you. And then I convinced myself that Isaiah died so that you and I could be together."

She gasped softly.

"I know, stupid, right? But it's how I rationalized it. And then, after I told you I loved you, I started dreaming about him every night. Every single night. Really, really..." He dragged his hands over his hair. "Bad dreams. Then I decided that cutting you out of my life was the only way I could handle the guilt."

She'd decided the same thing at the same time.

"Oh, Travis. I'm just...I don't know what to say." Her head pounded with what-ifs and new doubts and the pain of reliving Isaiah's death all over again. "You said you had survivor's guilt."

"It was so much worse than that." He held out his wrists and showed her the scars from what must have been an attempted suicide. "Drugs, booze, nothing can numb the guilt. Nothing."

She took a deep breath and tried to relate, but this made her guilt look like that of a student getting caught cheating on a test. Nothing compared to what he was carrying around.

But what Isaiah had done had been his choice. And so like him.

"So it's pretty funny that you came here to apologize to me," he said. "Because if I don't apologize to you…" He tapped the scar on his left wrist. "I may finally succeed in this."

"Oh, Travis." Tears welled, making him blur. "You need to forgive yourself."

He looked at her, doubt darkening his eyes. "I took him from you."

"He made the decision, not you." She finally let go of the breath she was holding. "Of course he did," she whispered. "Because he was amazing like that."

Travis dropped his head into his hands. "I should have let him get the honor he was due."

"That would have been nice. But it wouldn't have brought him back."

"The world should know."

True. "His family should, and I'll tell the people who matter. His parents, his sister. And his daughter." She pressed her hand against her chest, thinking of the day when Destiny would be old enough to learn her father sacrificed his life for someone else's. "I'll tell them all. And you really need to tell someone in the Army."

"I know. I will. I can contact our commander and tell him everything."

After a moment, she reached out and touched his shoulder. "Travis, if you do that, now that you've told me? You can finally let go of the guilt, forgive yourself, and move on."

He shook his head, wiping a tear. "Summer, he loved you so much," he whispered. "He never talked about anything else. Just Summer and Des. His girls. He felt really bad about how you guys fought before he left. I never told you that, either. He blamed himself."

"I felt bad about it, too." She gave a soft laugh. "Guilt is an ugly thing, Travis. As long as it's got you, you won't be free."

"It's got me good," he said, looking down at his wrists again.

"How do you think Isaiah would feel if you took your life after he gave up his for you?"

His eyes shuttered. "He'd be pissed."

"Don't let him down, Travis. Not like that and not with music. Don't let his death be in vain. Forgive yourself, follow those dreams, and…"

"Let your boyfriend keep his business," he added on a dry laugh.

"Yeah. Please."

"I can only—"

A loud, long honk of a horn ripped both of their attention, making Summer jump as a car came screaming down the driveway toward them.

"Summer!" Cassie hollered from the driver's side window. "I found you!"

Her heart leaping into her throat, Summer ran toward the car. "What's wrong?"

"Get in and come with me. We've been trying to track you down for forty-five minutes."

"Destiny?" she asked, the name strangled in her throat.

"Yes."

"Is she okay?" Summer pressed her hands over her mouth, vaguely aware that Travis had come closer, but hung back a few yards.

"Just get in. I'll take you to Waterford Farm."

She whipped around to Travis as fear gripped her. "I have to go."

"Go. Go." He nudged her toward the car. "And thank you, Summer. Thank you."

She started toward the passenger door and stopped, turning to him. "Don't let Isaiah's death be in vain," she repeated. "Do good. Use your life to make the lives of others better. With music, with…whatever you can. Please."

He nodded.

"And let go of the guilt!" She yanked the door open and dove into the passenger seat next to Cassie. "Just tell me she's okay."

Cassie blew out a breath. "She's missing, so I can't say anything's okay yet."

Chapter Twenty-five

As John's plane approached the outskirts of Bitter Bark, landmarks became visible from his vantage point of ten thousand feet. He flew straight and steady, in perfect conditions with almost no wind, piloting on instinct. On feeling, thank God. Although much of what he was feeling was… fear.

What if something happened to Destiny?

He pushed the thought out of his head as he saw the hills that surrounded his own property, then the distinctive dome in the middle of Vestal Valley College. He'd flown this pattern dozens of times with Aidan next to him, growing more confident in his piloting skills, certain that he'd done the right thing, even if it cost him a pilot's license.

He inched to the side and peered down at the giant square mile of emerald in the center of Bitter Bark. From here, he could make out trees and people and the bronze statue of Thaddeus Ambrose Bushrod in the center across from the bitter bark tree that, according to more than one person, was really a hickory.

He could see the playground and walkways and bleachers that were still in place for the next Dog Days of Summer event.

Destiny's tiny face and giant voice flashed in his head, her sweet little *thank you* without a stutter, her exuberance when she ran to collect her well-deserved trophy. Something clutched at his chest, squeezing the breath out of him.

Something? Something like...what *was* he feeling? Protective? Hopeful? An ache to make sure that kid had everything she wanted and needed? Something. Something that made him break the rules, risk his dream, and take off, determined to help find her.

He checked his gauges and crossed high above the winding residential streets and heavily wooded areas east of Bitter Bark, steadily and speedily making his way toward Waterford. In just a few moments, he spotted the road that formed most of the perimeter around the land and the arteries of dirt roads dotted with woods and ponds and fields.

She could be anywhere. Lost, running after Mav...*hurt*.

He swallowed hard and banked left, a wide curve taking him over Liam and Andi's house way out on a hill, then closer in toward the big lake, then over the house and kennels. From here, he could see people spread out, the dogs in the pen, a few dozen cars and two fire and rescue trucks in the drive. Of course, the Mahoneys would be out in full rescuer force, thank God. And all of the Kilcannons would come together as they did, a force of nature to bend God's will to theirs.

He'd take it. He'd take all the help and more to

find this child and spare her, and Summer, one moment of unhappiness.

Summer.

He squeezed his eyes shut, aware that sweat was building up under his headset, wishing like hell he could talk to her. Had they found her? Where had she gone with...

Nope. Not going there.

Instead, he flew to the northwest quadrant of Waterford, then started a slow and easy descent, still well above the tree line, but willing to go lower if he had to in order to be able to spot her.

He pictured her climbing out of his car this morning with Mav. He'd stayed in the drive, talking to Garrett, who had donned his "doggone hat" for the kids because he was taking a rescue to a new owner today.

What was Destiny wearing this morning? He dug into his memory bank, picturing her walking hand in hand with Summer to the camp check-in, but truth be told, his gaze had been on Summer's jeans skirt and long legs and not Destiny's....pink. Yes, pink. She'd worn a bright pink T-shirt, with a picture of a horse that had long curly hair and ridiculous eyelashes, with shorts and those sparkly sneakers she loved so much.

He leaned over again, taking the aircraft down carefully another thousand feet, flying over the irregularly shaped property. The perimeter road, which he could have sworn didn't actually have a name, was paved here, but it snaked in and out of the hills and around some thickets of trees.

He could spot searchers from here, some in plain clothes, some from Bitter Bark FD in yellow and green vests, which gave him a great boost of confidence. But it also meant they hadn't found her yet.

He banked again, away from where they were searching, past a thick forested area that could easily hide a lost child.

He swallowed some bile that rose up at the thought of Destiny lost in the woods, terrified and alone. Maybe with Mav. Or maybe she'd lost him, which would devastate her. He gripped the yoke tighter and got a little closer to the tree line, holding the plane steady and praying no sudden crosswind blew him around.

He was good enough to get up, around, and land, but his skills were limited, and he sure as hell didn't want to make things worse for the rescuers by crashing this damn plane.

"Come on, Des. Where are you, kiddo?"

He passed the forested area and followed the creek around a hill, then reached the perimeter road again. The pavement was wider here and straighter, with very few trees, just barbed wire fencing along the neighbor's property to keep the cows and horses enclosed.

He followed the road for about a little more than a mile away from Waterford, something in his gut telling him to watch that fencing. He saw some cows grazing and a field of wildflowers, then…pink.

Something pink caught on a barbed wire fence, blowing in the breeze like a flag.

His heart hammering, he banked hard again, letting his wing dip low enough to give him a clear look at whatever it was. A pink T-shirt? It could be. It could also be some kind of property flag, but it *could* be a pink T-shirt.

And if it was…where was the little girl who was supposed to be in it?

He didn't know, but he had to find out. He checked his cell phone, not surprised he had no signal. So he had no choice.

He did one more smooth turn and brought the plane way back to the wide, treeless section of road to give himself enough room to land safely. Descending slowly, he kept his eyes on the center line.

Don't think, John. Just feel. Check the air speed indicator. Check the altimeter. Feel the balance, feel the wind. Feel the timing for the flaps.

Not quite yet… He could hear Aidan's voice.

"Seventy knots," he whispered, watching the gauge drop. He felt the rudder pedal and a bounce in the wind, getting ready, vaguely aware that he was going to pass that pink flag if he didn't get this puppy on the ground.

"Here we go."

He flipped the flap switch as the road rose up to fill his windshield, not really that much different than a runway, just a hell of a lot more dangerous. The wheels touched, bounced, then cruised forward, right past the pink flag.

He'd never used the brakes in this plane except for a quick tap to test them. And to park. But there was no easy taxi today, not when Destiny was lost and might just have been found. He heard the brakes scream as he slammed the pedal, cringing and ready to pay Aidan for new pads if he had to.

But they worked, and when he was completely

stopped, he shut down the engine, flipped off his headset and seat belt, and climbed out, his phone in hand.

While running toward the pink fabric, he tapped the number of the last call he'd gotten, and Shane answered on the first ring.

"We still don't have her," Shane said, the noise of an ATV motor nearly blocking out his voice.

"I'm up on the perimeter road, due north of the house, at the next property."

"You flew up to the Wallaces' ranch?"

"And landed."

"He landed," Shane said.

"He *what*?" That was Aidan, who must have driven straight to Waterford when he heard about Destiny. "Why the hell would he do that? How?"

Oh boy. He'd never heard Aidan raise his voice. But now? He was screaming louder than that ATV engine. Yeah, John's ass was cooked, but the closer he ran to that pink material, the more he didn't care.

"The question is why," he said as he reached the pink material embedded in the barbed wire. The fabric was torn, ripped almost in half, and most of it was missing. But what was left was the remnants of a child's T-shirt with a girly horse on the front, the long-lashed eyes staring out like they were mocking him.

What tore Destiny's shirt? He almost cried out in anguish, but then looked down to notice a break in the fence…big enough for a puppy to fit through.

Had she tried to climb over it to go after Mav? And ripped her shirt when it got caught?

"Why?" Aidan repeated.

"Because I just found her T-shirt."

"Give us a location!"

He did his best to tell them where he was, but as he did, he braced his booted foot in a square of the fence and managed to reach a wooden post for leverage. The fence was meant to keep animals in, but could it keep humans out?

Not one this determined.

He stood, got one leg over the barbed top, then the other, jumping down to land on his feet.

"I'm on the Wallaces' property," he announced. "Get people up here! We need to find her. Look for the pink T-shirt caught on the fence. And the plane parked on the road. Can't miss that."

He looked around, getting stared at by a few cows, trying to guess which way Mav would run. But it was a fairly open field, and he could have gone anywhere.

"Destiny!" He screamed at the top of his lungs and started forward, running and scanning the grass and trees for anyone, anything. "Maverick!"

A cow mooed, and in the distance, he heard a siren. But no little girl calling for help. No dog barking.

He cried out her name again, going toward a grouping of trees that provided shade to the cows, about a hundred yards in the distance.

"Destiny!" He stretched out the last syllable, as loud as he could make it, and when he stopped, he heard the faintest sound of…singing.

That was her! He could hear the song that had become embedded in his brain, "You Are My Mavvie."

"Destiny! Where are you?" He stayed still for a moment, forcing himself to figure out which direction the sound was coming from. Way beyond the trees, on the other side of a hill. He ran toward the crest, stopping once to make sure he could still hear her, then she stopped.

"Destiny?" he called again.

"I'm here!" The voice rose up from the other side of the hill, filling him with the most inexplicable joy. "With Mavvie! Help us, John!"

He shot over the top of the hill, almost stumbling when he spotted her way down the other side, by a pond, rocking Mav in her arms like a baby, two curious cows watching the whole scene.

"Destiny!" He practically flew down to her.

Tears rolled down her face as she squeezed Mav, who seemed to be wrapped...in pink.

"He's h-h-h-hurt, John," she cried. "He got cut and ran so f-f-far, and I g-g-got him and—"

He reached her and scooped them both into his arms, unashamed of his own tears of raw relief.

"Are you okay?" he asked. "Are you hurt, Des? Are you okay?"

He felt her nod and try to say yes, which just broke his heart even more as he eased her back to assess her injuries.

She was fine, a few scrapes on her arms, still dressed in a thin white undershirt and her shorts. Mav was indeed cut and bleeding, but she'd washed the wound and wrapped him in what was left of her T-shirt.

"I'm s-s-sorry I ran away," she said softly.

"I'm just so happy you're all right," he said, giving her another hug. "You shouldn't have left the camp."

"I know, but Mavvie got away, and I ran to get him, and he k-k-kept going, and I was s-s-s-scared to stop because I thought I'd l-l-lose him, and..." The

345

rest was just a sob and tears and her own over-whelming relief.

"Come on," he said, scooping her into his arms. "You hold Mav. And I'll get you out of here."

She sobbed again, but he cradled her in his arms, marching back up the hill, hearing the sirens and rumble of ATV engines before he reached the top. When he did, he could see rescuers cutting through the barbed wire and rolling it back.

Behind them, a half dozen of the Waterford ATVs rumbled up, all full of family members ready to help.

He scanned every face, looking for one. Please God. Please let her be…

Summer.

"Your mommy's here," he whispered to the weeping child.

"Mommy," she moaned the name with a mix of longing and joy. "I l-l-l-love her."

John gave her a squeeze. "That makes two of us, kiddo."

Holding Destiny tight, he strode across the field as a dozen or more people spilled through the now split barbed wire fence and rushed toward him. But his gaze stayed on only one. The one with tears streaming and hair blowing as she ran full force to them.

"Des! John!" Summer reached them before anyone else, throwing her arms around Destiny and John. "Oh, thank God. Thank God." She drew back and looked from Destiny to him and back to Destiny. "Are you okay?"

"She's fine." He set her gently on the ground, easing Mav from her grip. "Mav needs to see a vet, but Destiny is fine."

As Summer and Destiny hugged, John backed up and turned to the onslaught of Kilcannons and Mahoneys, three of them in full fire rescue gear, his gaze finally landing on Aidan, who wore a very distinct look of disbelief.

The questions poured out from everyone, and he did his best to answer, his attention split between the family and Summer, who was on the ground holding Destiny with the same love her little girl had been holding Mav.

Daniel had already swooped in to look at Mav, along with Molly, also a vet, both of them gingerly removing the tourniquet Destiny had fashioned from her shirt.

As the whole group surrounded Destiny, she tried to tell her story, stopping to catch her breath and occasionally whispering the tale.

John picked up most of it, surmising the rest before stepping to the side to take a bottle of water offered by Connor Mahoney.

"Good job, man," he said. "If you ever get sick of running restaurants, we could use you at the department."

Sick of it? He might not have a restaurant to franchise after walking out on Tom Barnard and losing the business game to…

Hey, where was that guy, anyway? Travis Shipley? Hadn't she been with him?

"You are one ballsy pilot." Aidan's voice from behind him was low…and not happy.

John turned and met the blue eyes of his friend and stepbrother, but he looked more like a very pissed-off instructor. "I know, sorry. I had to do what I could to find Destiny. No doubt when this gets out, I'll get removed from FAA consideration."

His eyes narrowed. "They think I was with you."

"I logged you in before I knew you weren't coming," he said. "Then I got the call. I'm sorry, Aidan. I had to make a choice and…" He shrugged. "There was no choice."

Aidan swallowed. "I guess someday I'll understand that."

"Someday soon." He lifted a meaningful eyebrow to remind Aidan of the secret he'd let slip out earlier.

"Then let's get back in that plane right this minute before someone from the local paper shows up. I can take off from here and get us back to Foothills Regional with no one the wiser."

"You can?" That was not exactly a sizable runway for takeoff.

Aidan's eyes shuttered closed. "Of course I can. But we have to get out of here, fast. And thank God half the fire department is family."

Aidan gestured for him to move, but John turned to see Summer in a deep conversation with Declan Mahoney, the fire department captain, as one of the EMTs carefully walked Destiny away from the group toward the ambulance.

She was too busy now to talk to him. So he hustled off with Aidan, slipping through the open barbed wire and jogging back to the plane.

As they climbed in, Aidan fired off a few questions, with no small amount of admiration for John's piloting skills buried in the subtext.

"I couldn't have done it in a field," John said. "But when I—"

A bang on the side of the door made him whip around to see Summer standing outside the plane.

"Make it *fast*, Mav, then let's do some of that pilot shit."

John laughed at the *Top Gun* reference as he unlatched the door and opened it, looking down at Summer's tear-streaked face. "Is she okay?"

"She's shaken up, a little scratched, but perfect."

"Good. I—"

"John." She got up on her tiptoes and wrapped her hands around his neck, pulling his face close to hers. "I love you."

"Oh." He barely breathed the word, stopped short from responding when her lips crushed his for two perfect seconds.

Then she pulled back, stepped away, and put both hands on her lips, blowing him another kiss. "Fly safe."

He just looked at her, knowing there wasn't enough time to say everything he wanted to. So he just nodded, closed the door, and watched her back far away from the road without taking her eyes from his.

As Aidan started the prop and fired up the engines, he slid a look to John. "Sunshine loves you."

"Yeah," he said with what had to be a stupid grin. "Looks like she does."

"So it was worth risking your pilot's license?"

"What do you think?"

Aidan just laughed as he rolled down the perimeter road and took the Cessna up into the clouds like the pro he was.

Chapter Twenty-six

"**H**appy birthday to me! I am happy to be…six years old todaaaay…happy birthday hooray!" Destiny's voice floated through the baby monitor on the dresser, filling Summer's bedroom. From his crate next to Destiny's bed, where he had to sleep due to his bandages, Mav barked his approval.

Laughing softly, John folded his arms tighter around Summer, curling her body closer into his as they spooned deeper under the covers. "She can't even do the lyrics of 'Happy Birthday' as they're written?"

"Nothing is sacred," Summer mused.

His lips pressed against her bare shoulder. "This is sacred." He punctuated that by sliding his hand up her belly and over her breasts, his fingers searing her skin and making her wish Destiny hadn't woken up early on her birthday.

She moaned softly and turned in his arms, lining up their bodies the way it always felt like they were meant to be. She held his gaze, lost in the depths of his dark eyes, which looked sleepy and gorgeous without his glasses.

"Big day today," he said.

"Her birthday party at Waterford Farm?"

"George Shipley is calling me in less than half an hour with his final decision."

She let out a low, long breath. "I haven't talked to Travis since I left him to go find Destiny," she said. "He's a wild card, John. I don't know what he'll do or ask his father to do."

John rubbed a comforting hand on her back. "If it doesn't go our way, you have to know that I don't blame you. No guilt, promise?"

"I promise." She kissed him lightly on the lips. "That conversation with Travis was cathartic for me, too. Helping him see how crippling guilt is allowed me to see the same thing. So, if George backs out, I won't take the blame. And if he sells you the property?"

"You get all the credit."

"I don't want credit," she whispered, sliding a leg over his and taking a shuddering breath when she felt his whole body react. "I want...you."

He let out a soft groan of satisfaction and moved against her, sending chills over her whole body despite the fact that they'd already made love before dawn. "I want you," he murmured into a kiss, "not to leave."

"I already told you I'm going to let Destiny go to Dogmother camp for another three weeks."

He eased back. "Yeah, I know." He cupped her breast, thumbing the nipple lightly, adding more kisses to the crook of her neck. "But what about after that?"

She arched into him, her body automatically

responding, as it did with him night after night and most mornings. "Well, I have this thing called a job and a life in Florida." Neither of which held much of an appeal anymore.

Every day in Bitter Bark with John only made her want...more days in Bitter Bark with John.

"You could have a job and a life here," he said as if he could read her mind. "And a house with a view and a man who..." He grew very still.

"A man who makes me..." She rocked against him. "Crazy."

He chuckled. "That beats guilty."

"It beats everything," she admitted, coasting her hands over the muscles in his back, loving the hard strength of him as he kissed her for a few minutes.

"I still can't believe you risked your pilot's license for me," she whispered.

"I risked it for Destiny," he said. "So, for you by association."

"But you skirted the law."

"Aidan covered for me, and after I get that call with George, we're going back up for my last official hours." He grinned. "Does that mean my call sign can be something like...Law Breaker? Wildcat? Oh, oh, I got it." He lifted his brows. "*Reckless.*"

She snorted a laugh. "We could go simple with Bad-Ass."

"I like it."

"Seriously, John. That was an amazing move, but a potentially huge sacrifice."

He shrugged. "I didn't give it too much thought."

"Words no one ever expected to hear from you."

"Well, you know how you've let go of your guilt

issues? I'm learning to let go of my need to overthink everything and sometimes just go with what I'm feeling."

She studied his face for a long time, drinking in the long lashes, the gold specks in his eyes, and the few creases from years of easy laughter. "What are you feeling right now?" she whispered.

"Oh, let's see. Happy doesn't quite capture it, but elated feels a little, I don't know."

"Not manly enough for Bad-Ass Santorini," she teased, giving his muscled arm a squeeze. "How about content?"

"I sailed past content about an hour ago when you…" He looked down where their bodies were pressed together. "That was amazing, by the way."

She laughed. "You still haven't answered my question. What are you feeling right this very minute?"

He looked into her eyes for a long, long time. "There's a word for it. A simple four-letter word."

Her heart kicked up. "Yeah?"

"And that's how I feel, Summer Jackson." He placed his hand on her cheek. "The deepest, wildest, most indescribable feeling in the world. Love."

She sucked in a soft breath.

"I love you," he said. "And I know you already said it, but you were high on adrenaline and relief, so I'm not holding you to it."

"Hold me to it," she whispered. "I love you, too."

His eyes closed for a second, as if he just had to let the moment sink in. "Oh, that's good to know."

"You didn't believe me when I said it by the plane?"

"I didn't know what to believe, but I wanted to."

"Believe it," she said, tightening her grip on his whole body. "Because it's true. I love you."

"Summer." He grazed her cheek. "I never want you to leave."

The words floated over her, warming her with possibilities and hope and a great big delicious future as his—

"There's my call." He jerked away, silencing her thoughts.

"I didn't hear the phone."

"It's vibrating on the dresser." He rolled over her, dropping a kiss on her forehead on the way. "Wish me luck."

She bit her lip and nodded, but the only thing she wished was that Travis Shipley persuaded his father to drop the plan to reopen Hoagies & Heroes and let John buy the property.

"George, good morning," John said, answering the phone with one hand as he yanked on his boxers with the other. "How's your Sunday?" He sat on the edge of the bed, taking her hand in his and tapping the screen to put George on speaker.

"Good, fine. I just want to..." He hesitated for a moment, then cleared his throat. "I don't actually know what happened when my son visited last week, but it's changed everything."

Everything? Summer sat up a little, squeezing John's hand.

"How so?" John asked.

"Travis has decided he's not quite finished pursuing music, it seems."

Summer bit back a squeal of joy.

"Is that so?" John was way cooler, thank God.

"Boy has his dreams, you know?"

"Oh, I know," he replied. "And you're a good father to help him pursue them."

He snorted. "I got my hands full with my wife."

"I understand she's sick," he said. "I'm sorry to hear that."

"Thank you. It is…what it is." He let out a sigh. "And I had no right to corner you into a higher price, John. Let's go with your original offer. I'm going to sign those email documents right now and send them right over to you. We can close in ten days."

Summer dropped back on the pillow, sighing with relief.

"That's awesome, George. I really appreciate it."

"Hey, thank Travis. He was the one who came back here, went into his mother's room, shut the door, and didn't come out for two hours. When he did, she'd changed her mind about everything. And I do what my wife wants, if you must know the truth."

John and Summer shared a look, and she nodded, imagining that Travis took his story back to his mother and convinced her that the life she wanted for him wasn't what he wanted.

Because of Isaiah's letter? Maybe. The pages of the letter that talked about Travis had been missing when she got home that day, so she hoped he'd shared Isaiah's words with his dying mother.

"Oh, one more thing," John said as they were signing off. "We happen to have close family ties to country singer Scooter Hawkings. Do you know of him?"

Summer sat up, a little surprised at the question.

George responded with a snort. "Only because Travis played his music nonstop when he was here. Said he married that pretty singer, Blue, not long ago."

"He married her at my soon-to-be sister-in-law's winery, and my brother was the chef at the wedding."

George let out a whistle. "Big-time celebrities."

Seriously big-time.

"Actually, Scooter and my brother are good friends now, and I'm sure Alex would ask Scooter to meet with your son when he's settled back in Nashville. Could be a good industry contact for Travis."

Summer felt her jaw loosen. He'd do that for Travis? A man who had waltzed into Santorini's and threatened to take it and her from him?

George was gushing. "That's just...wow. Thank you. Susan! Honey, wait till you hear this..."

As John tried to say goodbye, Summer sat up and wrapped her arms around him, kissing his shoulder first. Laughing, he finally managed to sign off as professionally as possible before tossing the phone and turning his full attention to her kisses.

"You..." Summer said, smacking him with her lips on every surface she could find. "Are..." Cheek. Neck. Shoulder. Bicep. Mouth. Mouth again, making him laugh.

"I am what?" He pushed her back down on the bed, bracing himself over her. "Go ahead. Just say it. I can take it. I can take anything."

"Nice." She grinned at him. "And I love you, Nice Man."

"I can't fight it. That's my freaking call sign, isn't it?"

"Yep." She continued her kisses, whispering his new name, loving him with everything she had and then some.

Destiny's loud shriek of laughter made John turn and look out over the grass of Waterford Farm where she and Christian were playing tag with at least four dogs and poor Wee Fee, who toddled between them, trying to get in on the fun.

The Sunday meal was finished, and the sun had started to drop low behind the hills around Waterford Farm, adding a golden glow to the porch where he sat with Summer, Mav curled between them, chatting with the grannies.

"Our little singin' birthday lass is no worse for the wear, I'd say," Gramma Finnie mused as she rocked and watched the children play.

Yiayia leaned forward in her rocker and put a hand on Summer's arm. "And how's the little pupper doing?"

John lightly stroked Mav's bandage, covering a laceration. "He's in the best possible vet hands and will be fully healed in no time," he said.

"And my daughter has learned her lesson about leashes and listening to the counselor's rules."

Just then, John's mother stepped out on the patio, her husband, Daniel, right behind her.

"We bear some responsibility," Daniel said as they sat side by side on the sofa, facing John and Summer. Daniel's old setter, Rusty, trotted out, followed by the much-younger retriever, Goldie, the two of them as attached to each other as Daniel and Katie Kilcannon.

"I don't blame Waterford Farm," Summer said. "I know my daughter all too well. She can be willful and wily."

"And Mav ran away," John added, gently flipping the puppy's ear. "So he's the one who should be held accountable."

"Well, it was a bad situation," Daniel said. "Thank God you saw her T-shirt from the air, John, but it should never have happened. We'll be looking into additional security around the areas where the kids are camping for next year."

"Shane and the counselors walked me through exactly what happened," Summer said. "No one did anything wrong except Destiny, who should have known better. She even admitted that she thought if she told the counselors, they wouldn't let her run after Mav, so she took it upon herself to do so. And she has learned a lesson, I hope."

Daniel nodded, clearly appreciating her attitude. "You'll have to come back and give Tails and Trails another chance next year," he said. "We sure hope you do."

"Better yet," Yiayia said with a raised brow, "don't leave at all."

John fought a smile—and the urge to sneak his grandmother a high five because, well, he couldn't have said it better.

Summer gave a soft laugh. "Believe me, I'm tempted. But I do have this thing called a...job."

"Third-grade teacher, right?" his mother asked. "Andi just told me she got a notification from Christian's school that he's starting the year with a substitute because his teacher decided to take a job up in Holly Hills."

"Oh, there's an opening, then, lass," Gramma Finnie said excitedly. "You should fill it."

"Okay, okay," John said, holding out his hand. "We do not need to do a full-court press to try and convince this woman to move her entire life from Florida to Bitter Bark."

Yiayia leaned close to him. "Good one, John. I know she responds well to reverse psychology. I've used it on her myself."

They all laughed, but the attention shifted to the drive as a car pulled up, and Daniel stood, frowning. "Who's this?" he asked.

"Someone who can't read the closed sign at the gate." John's mother stood, too, and gestured toward Gramma Finnie and Yiayia. "I think it's time to get that birthday cake ready for Destiny and gather everyone in the family room."

"I'll help you, lass." Gramma Finnie pushed her old bones up with a grunt. "I have a wee gift for the child."

As they departed, John watched Daniel continue to frown at whoever was pulling into the drive. "Not a parent from camp. Not a boarder. Who is that guy? He's wearing a sports jacket and tie?"

John looked down when Mav stirred, but Summer turned around to follow Daniel's gaze and took in a noisy breath.

"What?" John asked.

She pressed her hand to her chest, her eyes wide. "It's Secret Shopper."

"Tom Barnard?" He shot up, whipping around to

see the unfamiliar man climbing out of a black Mercedes. "He's here?"

"You know this guy?" Daniel asked.

"He's my potential investor," John replied, looking not at the new arrival but right at Summer, whose eyes glinted with optimism.

"He wouldn't come here to turn you down," she whispered.

"I know." A slow smile pulled. "Let's go talk to him."

"You want me to go with you?" she asked.

He took her hand and gave her a gentle pull. "Everywhere, always," he whispered. Then he turned to Daniel. "Can you keep an eye on Mav?"

"Of course, son."

Hand in hand, Summer and John jogged down the porch steps to the long driveway, walking slowly to meet Tom Barnard halfway.

"Hello, Tom," John said as he extended his hand. "I left a message yesterday, but when I didn't hear from you…"

"I told you I like surprises." He shook John's hand and then smiled in greeting to Summer. "Hello, again. I stopped in at the restaurant."

"Oh, we're on a skeleton crew on Sunday afternoons since it's so slow," John said.

"They weren't slow, but your skeleton crew was doing a great job. A nice woman named Karyn told me where to find you." He looked around. "Dogs, huh?"

"My stepfather's home and business. Would you like to come up, meet the family?" John gestured toward the house. "We're about to celebrate a birthday so you're just in time for cake."

Tom shook his head. "I don't mean to intrude, and this young lady right here told me all I need to know about the family." He reached into his jacket pocket and pulled out a folded paper. "This is a preliminary contract for a healthy investment and a reasonable percentage of equity in what I think is going to be a booming franchise business."

John felt his jaw loosen as he took the paper. "Thank you, sir." He let out a surprised laugh. "We haven't even had a meeting."

Tom waved that off. "I've done my homework on you, Santorini. You have a strong reputation, and I know a good idea when I see it. Next week, we can sit down and hammer out details. But this investment opportunity is money in the bank, and I wanted to get in on the ground floor." He angled his head. "I don't like to spend too much time dallying about thinking, you know? I go on my gut, and when I see a great thing, I go for it. That's my philosophy."

John felt a smile pull. "It's a good one, sir. And it's mine as well."

"Good to hear." He reached to shake John's hand again. "When you see something and know it's right, you have to dot your i's and cross your t's and swing that bat, if you get my general drift."

John laughed again, transported back to his childhood and his father and his mixed metaphors of advice that lingered to this day.

"Tom, I'm going to like working with you."

"Looking forward to it." He added a pat on John's shoulder, then turned to Summer. "You belong to him?"

She laughed. "Well, I..."

"Oh, I know," he said. "You young ladies don't belong to anyone. I've got a feisty daughter who tells me that all the time. But are you..." He tipped his head from one to the other, a question in his eyes.

"We're still working that out," John said quickly when a blush deepened Summer's cheeks.

Tom flashed him a look. "Didn't you just say that when you see a great thing, you go for it? That's your philosophy?"

"Well, yes, I did and..."

Tom lifted his brows and pointed to Summer. "Here's a great thing, son. Her whole face lit up when she talked about you. I will call you next week." With that, he pivoted, headed back to his car, and left them holding a piece of paper that was going to change his life.

Except...it wasn't the change he wanted most.

"John!" She grabbed him by the shoulders. "You did it! You got the investment!"

"With a little help from my hostess."

She lifted a shoulder. "Hey, teamwork, baby."

"Summer." He took her hands and drew her closer. "Don't leave."

She blinked. "I won't. There's cake and—"

"Don't leave me. Don't leave Bitter Bark. Don't leave the future you know we can have together."

She stared at him, her mouth in a little O. "We've known each other for less than a month."

"Then we'll get to know each other even better..." He wrapped his arms around her. "Here, together, as a family."

"Mommy!" Destiny came tearing at them, ringlets flying. "It's time for cake and candles and presents!"

She sang the words in a Destiny-like melody that had them both laughing. "Let's go."

She tugged on both of them, getting between them to take their hands and drag them toward the house.

They shared a look, the request he'd just made hanging in the air between them, but both stayed silent as they walked to the house.

The whole family gathered around the dining room table, far too big a group to eat there as one anymore, but it was the traditional place for forming a circle and singing "Happy Birthday" over cake and candles, something that happened at least once a month, if not more often, with this many people.

Chaos reigned, of course, with a hum of excitement and happiness in the air, made extra special considering what they'd all gone through recently for this little girl. Cassie guided Destiny to the head of the table, whispering something that made Destiny giggle.

Summer followed, turning to John to get him to come with her.

"I'll be right back," he said. "I have to get her gift."

"You got her a gift?"

"Of course." He stepped outside, chatting with a few rowdy relatives and sidestepping some dogs to get to where Daniel stood holding Mav.

"I'll take him now, thanks." John reached for the dog and gingerly held him in his arms. "Come on, Mavvie," he whispered into the tiny ball of fur. "Yeah, I called you Mavvie. You should hear what they call me."

Mav snuggled against his chest. The pain meds had mellowed him, making him pliable and easy to carry.

But not so easy to give away.

As he returned to the dining room, nearly everyone had gathered. Pru was informing Destiny about exactly what to expect and how they would sing and when she should blow out the candles.

"Easy, General Pru," Shane called out. "She's probably been to a birthday party before."

"But not a Kilcannon-Mahoney-Santorini birthday party," Pru fired back. "Ours are special."

"They are," Destiny agreed, her magical eyes dancing as she took in the cake and all the people. She turned and looked up over her shoulder at Summer. "This is fun, isn't it, Mommy?" she whispered.

"It sure is, Des."

Pru raised her hands and called for silence, which only made her aunts, uncles, and cousins a little noisier, but finally she got them all singing "Happy Birthday" to Destiny. As they ended on a high note, Mav managed to let out a soft whine, but the noise was too much for anyone but John to hear.

After Destiny blew out her six candles and everyone clapped, John made his way to stand next to the birthday girl and her mother.

"Mavvie!" Destiny jumped out of her seat, then caught herself, looking up at John. "Can I hold him?" She'd been extra careful and even a little tentative with him since the incident at camp.

"You can hold him forever," he said softly, vaguely aware that a hush had fallen over the room. "Destiny Rose, I present you with Maverick Santorini, your sixth-birthday present. From me to you."

She blinked at him. "He's m-m-mine?"

"He's yours, kiddo," he said with a thick throat. "I've never known two creatures who belong together more."

Her smile was slow, then blinding as she reached up and wrapped her arms around him, and the whole room let out a boisterous cheer of approval.

"Mavvie!" She gathered him in her arms and rocked him. "Happy birthday to us!"

John straightened and met Summer's teary gaze. "You broke your promise."

"Every once in a while, a promise has to be broken." He looked down at Destiny and Mav, then into Summer's eyes. "But I can make you one that will last a lifetime."

She leaned into him and wrapped her arms around his waist, lifting her mouth to whisper, "You know as well as I do that dog, that child, and this woman are not going anywhere."

"Good." He gave her a light kiss. "Because just like Mav and Destiny, we belong together."

As he pulled her closer for a celebratory hug, he looked across the room and caught Gramma Finnie and Yiayia giving each other a not-so-secret high five.

Epilogue

"We have good news and bad news." Cassie and Summer sat down on the bleachers, flanking John. All around, the family had gathered once again, this time to watch a commercial being filmed in the middle of Bushrod Square.

John didn't really want to hear any bad news, not today. Not when autumn was painting Bitter Bark in a new color, and his Summer fling had officially entered its next season.

"Everything okay back there in the star's dressing room?"

"It's a dressing…awning," Summer said. "And we have come to inform you of the news."

"Good first," he said, automatically reaching for Summer's hand because he loved to be touching her at all times.

"Destiny knows every line to the new version of her song," Summer said.

"And, good God, that kid should be in Juilliard, not first grade," Cassie added.

"Tell me something I don't know, Cass," John said, shooting a proud smile to Summer.

"The bad news, then." Summer bit her lip. "Mav's been cut."

"He's hurt?" He nearly jumped off the bleacher.

"No, no. Cut from the script," she explained. "The director nixed him and picked another dog from that crew the producers brought as backup."

"What?" John felt a scowl form. "None of them can sing with her."

"They're going to do some very fancy editing and use Mav's voice, but this is for a special puppy blend of food, and Mav's a little bit bigger than they want for the part."

"He's aged out of fame and fortune," Cassie said on a dramatic sigh.

"That's fine, but what about Destiny?" John asked, already worried about this stressing her out. "She won't want to sing with a dog she doesn't know."

Cassie lifted a brow. "Tell that to Lexie Lu, the snow-white toy Pomeranian who already has four commercial credits, an amazing owner-trainer, and looks like she was born two weeks ago even though she's one and a half."

"Destiny's good with her?" John asked.

Summer shared a look with Cassie. "Good?"

"The owner already looks a little worried she may not get her dog back," Cassie added.

John laughed. "She may not. Where's Mav? Should I spring him from the casting couch?"

"Yeah. Come with us." Cassie waved them around the stage, currently loaded with lights, cameras, microphones, and about six dozen more people than

John imagined was necessary to shoot a thirty-second commercial.

Holding hands, Summer and John followed Cassie to a temporarily fenced-in area where a number of dogs romped and slept, each being watched by a handler. Professional TV dogs, then. Only one roamed freely and came straight toward them.

"Hey, Mavvie." John crouched down and stuck his face close to the fencing. "I'm afraid you're a face on the cutting room floor."

He licked John's nose.

"I'll go spring him," Cassie said, walking to the gate to talk to a production person with a clipboard.

"Mommy!"

John turned to see Destiny under a large open-air tent, sitting in a tall chair with one person working on her hair and another in front of her with a palette of makeup. On her lap was a literal ball of white fur, watched carefully by a woman in khakis a few feet away.

"She's having the time of her life," Summer said. "This whole stardom thing comes a little too naturally to her."

He smiled and waved at the child who'd taken up residence, right next to her mother, in his heart and home. "She's got makeup on," he said, frowning as he realized that. "She doesn't need makeup. She's six."

Summer laughed. "It's just to accent her gorgeous bone structure."

"She's naturally beautiful." He stared at her for another long minute. "And talented. And smart. And, oh my God, she's stubborn."

"She's going to be a handful as a teenager." It almost sounded like Summer was warning him.

"I hate to have to kill sixteen-year-old boys, but…"

Summer laughed. "I love when you go bad-ass, Nice Man."

"Liam already told me he'd lend me Fiona's chastity belt and two guard dogs when she starts high school."

"Really?"

"You think I'm kidding?"

"I think you're…" Summer let out a soft, surprised laugh. "Planning a future."

He shifted his gaze from Destiny to her mother, looking right into those sky-blue eyes. "And how would you feel about that?"

"I moved here from Orlando and took a job at Bitter Bark Elementary, didn't I?"

"You sure did."

"And I'm helping you and Josh design a two-story, single-family home out of the one we're sharing, aren't I?"

"Yes, you are."

"Well, then…" She lifted a shoulder. "Plan that future, darling, but leave out the chastity belts and guard dogs. By the time she's that old, Christian and Jag will be her personal bodyguards."

A wholly wonderful sensation filled him, one he was getting so very used to, but never took for granted. That had to be the final cue he'd wanted and needed to hear. He'd been waiting for weeks for the right moment. Today? In the square? He'd kind of hoped to take her flying, but…he didn't really want to wait another day, did he?

He'd just have to see Yiayia first.

He turned at the sound of a familiar bark, crouching down to give Mav some love as he bounded forward…and blew right past him.

"Hey!" Cassie got jerked at the other end of his leash.

"Sorry." John took it from her, using his strength to stop forty-pound Mav from crashing hair and makeup to get to his girl.

"Mavvie!" Destiny waved from her beauty throne, but that just made Mav bark again, then let out a low growl at the fluffball on her lap.

"Don't be jealous, Mavvie," she called. "I love you best of all!"

Summer darted over to talk to Destiny, but John stayed back, keeping Mav from causing any chaos. After a moment, she came back, slipping an arm around him.

"They're taking her back for another rehearsal. It could be awhile."

"You want to stay with her?"

"I think Cassie's got it. I'm kind of turning into a stage mother, and I don't like it."

"Want to take a walk with Mav and me?"

She brightened. "Sure." With another quick goodbye to Destiny, they started off, but John steered them back to the bleachers first. "Hold Mav for me, okay? I want to tell Yiayia something."

Summer gave him a quizzical look. "And I can't come?"

"No. It's a secret." He winked at her and headed over to where Gramma Finnie and Yiayia were side by side, surrounded by Kilcannons, Mahoneys, and Santorinis.

Sliding up next to his grandmother, he whispered in her ear, "You got it?"

She drew back, her dark eyes widening. "Of course. I told you I would. Now?"

"Now."

"Now?" Gramma Finnie asked, her little voice rising with excitement.

"Now," he confirmed.

"Now?" Alex, sitting behind them, stuck his head into the mix.

"Now."

"Right now?" Aidan, holding Beck's hand, stepped closer to join them.

"Oh, for crying out loud, can I just do this without the entire family watching?"

Laughing, Yiayia dipped her hand into an oversize bag and surreptitiously slipped a small box into John's waiting palm.

"Is it now?" His mother appeared from nowhere, with Daniel right behind.

John just laughed and looked from one to the other.

"What's going on over here?" Declan Mahoney slid over from where he sat on the bleachers, a navy ball cap pulled low over his sunglasses.

"You just watch and learn, lad." Gramma Finnie patted his leg. "Because I have a plan for you."

John laughed and looked into the blue eyes of the fire captain. "A word of advice, Dec?"

"I don't need any advice," he said, making a few of the others laugh.

"Trust the process," John replied anyway. "These ladies know what they're doing."

Declan looked skyward as John dropped the box into his pocket and managed to escape as the level of family excitement rose.

"What was that all about?" Summer asked, standing to the side of the stage with Mav.

"My family's nuts." He put an arm around her, taking the leash. "Let's go to the playground."

She inched back. "You want to swing?"

"I want to be on the very spot where I first met you."

"Aww." She tucked her arm around his waist and nestled closer. "That's so sweet."

"That's me. Nice and sweet and…"

She shimmied against him. "Hot and sexy."

The playground, along with all of Bushrod Square, was empty and eerily quiet, but that was because the Family First Pet Foods commercial had asked the town to let them have exclusive use of the entire square.

Happy for the privacy, John walked her closer.

"Here," he said. "This bench."

"I remember this bench," she said, running a finger over the wood before sitting down.

"I was sitting on it talking to Tom Barnard on the phone when a wild five-year-old and her gorgeous mother walked into my life."

Mav pulled a little, like he had that day, toward the playground, but he instinctively seemed to know he wouldn't get the love there today. He lay down under the bench while they sat.

John's heart ratcheted up a beat as he realized the magnitude of the moment.

But Summer was relaxed, stretching out her legs and letting her head fall back to get sun on her face. "I'm so glad I came to Bitter Bark," she said softly. "I never want to leave."

"I never want you to leave."

She lifted her head and looked at him. "This is it, isn't it?"

"Yes, it is."

"This is love." She put her hand on his face. "This is forever. I can't believe how certain I am of loving you, John."

"You are." It wasn't a question. "I am, too. I don't think about it, I just feel it."

She smiled. "And I haven't had one moment of guilt."

He took a deep breath, stood up, and took her hand, pulling her toward him.

"What is it?" she asked.

He swallowed and inched back, ready to get down on one knee but feeling the need to draw the moment out. "If I may quote a great song not written by Destiny Rose...you take my breath away."

She smiled up at him. "The anthem of the kissing part."

"And I want to ask you a question. But, I guess it's done like this." Slowly, he lowered himself to one knee, getting a deep and joyous gasp in response. "Summer Jackson, you are the brightest light that's ever come into my life. You are everything warm and wonderful. I had no idea I could love you, and Destiny, the way that I do."

She bit her lip, her eyes filling as she looked down at him.

He pulled out the ring box and flipped it open, not surprised his hands trembled. "Will you marry me?"

"Oh." She breathed the word, glancing at the ring, but looking right back into his eyes as she pulled him up, her fingers, also trembling, pressed to her lips. "Oh, John, I love you so much. I would be honored to marry you. Yes, yes, yes!"

He slid the ring on her finger and kissed her again, just as Mav jumped up and started barking.

"Mommy!"

"Destiny!" They turned to see her running toward them, ringlets flying.

"What is she doing?" Summer asked.

"Look behind her." There, Cassie—and half the clan—stood in a group, watching everything. "Word travels fast in this family. And they probably knew she'd want to be in on this."

As Destiny reached them with her arms outstretched, John reached down and lifted her up.

"Is it true?" she squealed. "Will you be my daddy?"

"Only if you'll be my daughter."

"Yes! You are my daddy, my favorite daddy!" she sang in her signature melody.

Laughing, she threw her arms around his neck, and John looked through her hair to see the tears flowing down Summer's cheeks.

Mav barked and ran in circles, while across the square, one great big Greek and Irish clan clapped and stretched out their arms to welcome two more members.

Leaning around the squirming child, John pulled Summer in for a kiss, his arms and heart full of the two most beautiful ladies in the world.

The Dogmothers matchmaking work isn't close to done! Watch my newsletter or reader group for updates on Declan Mahoney's love story…book six in The Dogmothers series.

Want to know the minute it's available?
Sign up for the newsletter.

www.roxannestclaire.com/newsletter-2/

Or get daily updates, sneak peeks, and insider information at the Dogfather Reader Facebook Group!

www.facebook.com/groups/roxannestclairereaders/

The Dogmothers is a spinoff series of
The Dogfather

Join the private Dogfather Reader Facebook Group!

www.facebook.com/groups/roxannestclairereaders/

When you join, you'll find inside info on all the books and characters, sneak peeks, and a place to share the love of tails and tales!

The Dogmothers Series

Available Now

HOT UNDER THE COLLAR (Book 1)

THREE DOG NIGHT (Book 2)

DACHSHUND THROUGH THE SNOW (Book 3)

(A Holiday Novella)

CHASING TAIL (Book 4)

And many more to come!

For a complete list, buy links, and reading order of all my books, visit www.roxannestclaire.com. Be sure to sign up for my newsletter to find out when the next book is released!

A Dogfather/Dogmothers Family Reference Guide

THE KILCANNON FAMILY

Daniel Kilcannon aka *The Dogfather*
Son of Finola (Gramma Finnie) and Seamus
Kilcannon. Married to Annie Harper for 36 years until
her death. Veterinarian, father, and grandfather.
Widowed at opening of series. Married to Katie
Santorini (*Old Dog New Tricks*) with dogs Rusty and
Goldie.

The Kilcannons (from oldest to youngest):

• **Liam** Kilcannon and Andi Rivers (*Leader of the
Pack*) with Christian and Fiona and dog, Jag

• **Shane** Kilcannon and Chloe Somerset (*New Leash
on Life*) with daughter Annabelle and dogs, Daisy and
Ruby

• **Garrett** Kilcannon and Jessie Curtis
(*Sit...Stay...Beg*) with son Patrick and dog, Lola

• **Molly** Kilcannon and Trace Bancroft (*Bad to the
Bone*) with daughter Pru and son Danny and dog,
Meatball

• **Aidan** Kilcannon and Beck Spencer (*Ruff Around
the Edges*) with dog, Ruff

• **Darcy** Kilcannon and Josh Ranier (*Double Dog
Dare*) with dogs, Kookie and Stella

THE MAHONEY FAMILY

Colleen Mahoney

Daughter of Finola (Gramma Finnie) and Seamus Kilcannon and younger sister of Daniel. Married to Joe Mahoney for a little over 10 years until his death. Owner of Bone Appetit (canine treat bakery) and mother.

The Mahoneys (from oldest to youngest):

- **Declan** Mahoney and…

- **Connor** Mahoney and Sadie Hartman (*Chasing Tail*) with dog, Frank, and cat, Demi

- **Braden** Mahoney and **Cassie** Santorini (*Hot Under the Collar*) with dogs, Jelly Bean and Jasmine

- **Ella** Mahoney and…

THE SANTORINI FAMILY

Katie Rogers Santorini

Dated **Daniel** Kilcannon in college and introduced him to Annie. Married to Nico Santorini for forty years until his death two years after Annie's. Interior Designer and mother. Recently married to **Daniel** Kilcannon (*Old Dogs New Tricks*).

The Santorinis

- **Nick** Santorini and…

- **John** Santorini (identical twin to Alex) and Summer Jackson (*Hush, Puppy*) with daughter Destiny and dog, Maverick

- **Alex** Santorini (identical twin to John) and Grace Donovan with dogs, Bitsy, Gertie and Jack

• **Theo** Santorini and…

• **Cassie** Santorini and **Braden** Mahoney (*Hot Under the Collar*) with dogs, Jelly Bean and Jasmine

Katie's mother-in-law from her first marriage, **Agnes "Yiayia" Santorini,** now lives in Bitter Bark with **Gramma Finnie** and their dachshunds, Pygmalion (Pyggie) and Galatea (Gala). These two women are known as "The Dogmothers."

About The Author

Published since 2003, Roxanne St. Claire is a *New York Times* and *USA Today* bestselling author of more than fifty romance and suspense novels. She has written several popular series, including The Dogfather, The Dogmothers, Barefoot Bay, the Guardian Angelinos, and the Bullet Catchers.

In addition to being a ten-time nominee and one-time winner of the prestigious RITA™ Award for the best in romance writing, Roxanne's novels have won the National Readers' Choice Award for best romantic suspense four times. Her books have been published in dozens of languages and optioned for film.

A mother of two but recent empty-nester, Roxanne lives in Florida with her husband and her two dogs, Ginger and Rosie.

www.roxannestclaire.com
www.twitter.com/roxannestclaire
www.facebook.com/roxannestclaire
www.roxannestclaire.com/newsletter/

Made in the USA
Las Vegas, NV
07 September 2022